I0629163

THE
KING'S
ASCENT

THE RUINOUS CURSE SERIES

Mark K. McClain

ISBN (paperback): 978-0-9897092-9-3
ISBN (eBook): 979-8-9892944-1-1

Acknowledgments

For Rochelle

To honor the small cast of incredible folks who helped bring this book to fruition, I proudly present my superheroes:

Amazing author & friend, Laura Engelhardt
Brilliantly talented artist, Elissa Weaver
Charismatic beta reader and editor, Lisa Wong
Dazzling cover artist & design expert, Jess LaGreca
Extraordinary advice guru, Aubrey Green: Blue Clover Editing

Thank you all for helping to bring Barrett's story to an amazing conclusion . . . or is it, really?

Books by Mark K. McClain

The Ruinous Curse Series
The Hunt for Alesta (Book 1)
Apadora Rising (Book 2)
The King's Ascent (Book 3)

Horror Collection (Short Stories)
Passages of Peculiarity

1

Zanora

The air turned cool as night embraced the desolate spot. Barrett felt tired as he sat upon a withered tree husk to warm himself by the fire. Earlier, he sent his raven in search of Elimar and Trishar. He desperately needed their help.

Though the bird argued over leaving his side, he knew she could play no part in defeating Apadora. Further, he was unwilling to risk her safety once the Outerworld gate opened. The wicked realm was no place for a raven, especially since the bird was his mother.

Barrett muddled through his thoughts concerning Zanora, but she was only one of his current problems. Deciding her fate while planning their impending quest paled in comparison to unraveling the gate spell. Had the ancient magic been inadvertently weakened once Zanora began her chant? If so, and if Apadora discovered the error, would she soon free herself from her eternal prison to renew her reign of death and terror upon the lands?

The most troubling thought was their dwindling time, but his friends did not seem to share his concern. Even now, they argued over Zanora's fate, none of which she heard. She remained unconscious beneath a blanket he had draped over her. The redhead had not stirred since being struck down by an *Impendior* spell while attempting to unseal the Outerworld. Gaia's magic had saved the world from Apadora's wave of evil. At least for now.

Yet, even after stopping Zanora, danger remained. The companions still needed to enter the vile underbelly of the evil realm. Alesta awaited freedom on the opposite side of the gate. Crossing the threshold into what lay beyond was the only solution for her escape.

Barrett, frustrated over the arguing, turned his mind to Gaia's beauty. He studied her face with growing affection. She looked lovely, bathed in the orange firelight as the debate raged. He caught her attention and gave a wink. The witch smiled and returned his gesture.

"She's a burden," said Unger, his voice rising as he inclined his head toward Zanora's motionless form. "I'll never trust her again."

"No good will come of her being here," added Graile. "We should give her a rucksack, some food, and water, then send her on her way. She's lucky to still be alive." He pulled a bread loaf from his pack, took a bite, and chewed slowly.

"Lars and I never knew her before she turned wicked so we rely on your judgment as to her sentence," said Nell, exchanging nervous glances with her brother. "I think Graile has the right idea. Set her free, unharmed."

Lars nodded approval. "The girl is a major distraction, which is one more thing we don't need right now. Set her loose."

Barrett wished to be somewhere else, yet he listened closely as the conversation leaned towards abandoning their captive. Here or elsewhere, they would decide later. Instincts told him his friends were correct; her presence was disruptive. Months ago, after his crown had been stripped away and his kingdom seized, any authority he had to sentence someone to death had ended. He could not take her life. Besides, he thought, he was not a god and had no right to make that choice.

Guilt made him heave a long sigh. *I should have slain her during our combat.* He twitched at his coldhearted thought. *I had several opportunities to finish her. If I had, none of these decisions would be needed now.* Another twitch over the notion.

Romantic feelings for Zanora had faded weeks ago. Especially after he and Gaia shared affections. But now he would be expected to decide the fate of a girl he once loved. It was a burden he did not want.

The bickering grew. Wanting to hear none if it, he turned his gaze toward the twinkling stars and waning crescent moon, thinking they may provide some peace. But he could not suppress his innermost questions for long.

How did it come to this? My next decision could decide the fate of all lands. He studied the sky as though his thoughts would summon Elimar simply by wishing it. *Where is that blasted wizard? I can't do this without him! My magic is not strong enough.*

Somewhere in his mind, Gaia called his name. Still, he remained oblivious until she came to snuggle against him. She rested a hand on his thigh and her head against his shoulder.

"You haven't said much," she said softly. "What's your plan? Or don't you have one yet?"

Barrett covered her warm hand with his own. "I was not ignoring you. I just needed time to think." As the witch straightened, a final decision came to him. Facing the company, he raised a firm voice. "This debate is pointless until her part is fulfilled. Zanora is vital. We need her to open the gate. She is the only one among us who knows the spell. This arguing must stop. I cannot listen to it any longer."

Silence fell thick, except for the crackling fire sounds. But the quiet did not last.

"Right," blurted Unger. "Just so you know, I think we all finally agree. She should be sent on her way if she lives through opening the gate. If she doesn't survive, that would end the discussion."

"That's very cold coming from you," said Gaia, pulling her blanket tighter and pressing into Barrett.

Unger shrugged. "Maybe. But I'm not fond of being betrayed. Not to mention, she nearly got us all killed on several occasions. She brings misery wherever she goes."

"You have a point, but we've known her for ten years," countered Barrett. "She was our best friend. Besides, it has not all been bad."

Graile flicked his braid off his shoulder. "I've not known her as long as some, but you're right in saying she *was* your friend. The woman you knew has been lost to wicked ways."

"I have a question," asked Nell, raising her hand as if waiting to be called on. "Is she going through the gate with us?"

"No," snapped Barrett. "There is no reason to bring her along." He quickly reconsidered his hasty choice. "Then again, we could use an extra sword." He pointed the dead twig he toyed with toward the cavern's entrance. "Who knows what we'll face in there."

"I would rather not have her behind me with a sharp blade," said Graile, making a stabbing motion.

Barrett forced a grim smile but longed to massage his temples to soothe his growing headache. "We will decide her fortune later. There is no need to make a choice this minute. Especially since I'm too tired to think."

"We're all worn out. Let's get some sleep. I'll take the first watch," said Lars. "I'll bet the new day will bring danger—and plenty of it. We need to be sharp."

"Will we not wait for help to arrive? Samaren has already left to find the wizard and sorceress, no?" asked Nell.

"Yes, she searches even now. Though, I am worried about her." Barrett studied the empty sky for a long while and hoped to see a raven's silhouette winging toward him in the shimmering moonlight. "We can't wait forever for help to arrive, but I will delay a bit longer. Good night, all." He rose and led Gaia to a hollow spot beneath an overhanging boulder pile. "This place is as good as any."

Wrapping themselves in blankets, they snuggled together as the others searched for their sleep spots. Minutes later, the companions settled in as best they could while Lars examined the deepening blackness from atop a sloping incline.

During the small hours of the morning, Barrett grew restless. Gently moving from beneath the witch's arm, he trudged up the hill to take his turn at watch. His thoughts turned to their unenvious task, now only hours away.

If Elimar or Trishar did not arrive soon or did not come at all, the companions would face the vilest sorceress of legend alone. In their favor were two Shifters, a Fader, a witch, an archer, and his own magical prowess. Zanora would be a valiant warrior, though her willing participation was in doubt, as was the friends' faith in her.

Getting her to stand against Apadora while rescuing Alesta, a woman who once nearly destroyed them all, was a lot to ask. There was also the matter of her needing to pay a penalty for her under-handed actions. What would it be? As he wondered what advice would Trishar give, movement drew his attention to the right.

Unger approached to ease beside him. "I'm too nervous to sleep." The archer pulled his cloak and blanket tighter against the chilled night.

"We are a powerful group. I pray we have the advantage in numbers. Apadora cannot fight us all at once. Can she?" Insecurity made Barrett doubt his abilities as he watched a shooting star blaze past as the cloud opened. He hoped it was a sign of good fortune, even if he did not believe in such things.

Unger raised a shoulder. "I hope not. But I doubt she will be alone." Shivering, he rose to place more wood on the fire, then returned. "You know I trust your choices, right? I mean, we've seen a lot of danger together and we're all still alive. I would love to keep it that way." He bumped the young wizard with his shoulder. "The gods will protect us."

"You have always been honest. I value your judgment, my friend. What do *you* think I should do with her?" Barrett jerked a thumb toward Zanora.

The archer peered at the sleeping redhead. "First, let's examine something no one has mentioned. Despite Jarn being a worthless bully, his death will cause a stir. When Carick learns Zanora killed his son he will have Grimes hunt her forever. Of course, they may never discover the truth since her entire group is now dead. She is the only one left to tell the tale, so there is no way to prove what really happened."

Barrett stiffened at his friend's logic. "Excellent point. Carick may never know the truth but questions will certainly be raised about Jarn vanishing. Everything will point to her, no matter what."

Unger rubbed his chin. "By the way, I'm sorry for overreacting earlier. I was wrong. Concerning Zanora, we don't know if she truly hates magic or is under some spell. Why she turned against it is anyone's guess. Maybe she had no choice. We need to consider all possibilities before deciding her fate. I'm just saying the girl you loved may be wholly innocent and have no idea of her own wicked ways."

"Another true point. I think—"

Their talk halted as the redhead moaned and stirred. They sprinted to her side as she struggled into a sitting position to rest her head on her knees. She breathed deeply. Her feet were secured with a binding spell.

"What happened? Why am I tied up like a criminal?" She struggled against the magic only to end up frustrated.

"You have been unconscious nearly an entire day. How do you feel?" asked Barrett.

At seeing his face, she dragged herself backward. "Are you going to kill me?"

"Don't be absurd. Of course not," replied Unger. "If we wanted that, you wouldn't be talking. You would already be with the gods." His brows furrowed. "Probably not the ones you were hoping for, I imagine."

"True," agreed Barrett. "What kind of idiots would we be to wait until you were awake just to kill you?"

Their explanations seemed to pacify her. She took a calming breath and relaxed. "That sounds logical, I suppose. What do you want of me?"

"My dear Zanora, you are the most valuable member of our group," said Barrett as a sliver of the moon shone over his shoulder, shrouding him in white light to give him a ghostly glow. "You alone know the words needed to open the gate. We want that knowledge . . . or else."

"To begin with, I am not your *dear* anymore. You had your chance," she snapped before shaking her head to clear the cobwebs. Then, his final words struck her. "Or else what?"

"Or else we will extract it by any means necessary," added Unger, narrowing his eyes as he leaned closer. "There is no need for this to be unpleasant."

"Open the gate and we will have no further need for you. Leave if it suits you. But only *after* the gate is open," said Barrett.

Zanora patted the neckline of her tunic, then each pocket. She scowled, then cursed. "My necklace. It's gone, which means no key. You can't get in without it. No one can open it now."

Barrett produced his wand to summon his vortex. "Tinith O'Votus." The key floated from the swirling portal to hang suspended between them. Making certain Zanora recognized it before flicking his wand again, he returned the trinket to the depths as the void closed, then faded away. "Like I said, the spell is all we need. Give it to us, and your part will be done."

"I see. And if I refuse, you'll torture me. Is that it?" She squirmed uncomfortably. "I understand now." Pulling both knees tighter to her chest, she glared at them. "I'll never give it to you."

Annoyed she called his bluff, the prince softened his tactics. Despite his bold words, his heart did not lay in torture. Even the idea was sickening. "Please, we need your help. You were part of us once and can be again. Although no one holds faith in your word, it would be easy to prove them wrong. Had you succeeded in opening the gate, the world's greatest evil would have been set free. As it is, our friend, Alesta, is trapped inside that awful place. We want to help her escape. I owe Elimar that much."

"Oh, I see. You mean the same *friend* that tried to kill us all? And nearly succeeded, I might add," she said, her voice rising. "Yes, you definitely need more friends like her. And do not mention that feeble old man to me again. He's the cause of all this."

Unger forced air from his lips and shook his head. "That's absurd. Besides, Elimar showed us the true events. Apadora kidnapped her daughter to use her as a channel for hatred. She has controlled Alesta since childhood. We all saw it."

Zanora's head tilted back in laughter. "Sure. So everything the wizard shows you is a fact, right? There is *clearly* no deceit on his part." Her face tightened. "How in the name of the gods have you two survived this long?" She did not wait for an answer but stabbed a stiff finger forward. "Listen, I won't associate with losers. So keep your offer of joining this band of misfits."

"Apparently, you don't remember events very clearly. Not only did you betray us, but *you* tried to kill us, too," snapped the archer. "Even though these misfits could have easily murdered you, you're still alive." He shook his head and huffed. "Ungrateful little girl."

Zanora snorted. "Oh, Unger, still the childish fool, I see. Nothing has changed. When will you realize none of this would be happening if you had never met that wizard or his family? Magic is to blame. It should be eradicated."

The prince had heard enough. He wished he could wave his wand and make the entire situation vanish. He was weary of her word games and constant defiance. *Why does she thrive on spite and anger? This nonsense is just one reason why we broke up.*

Worrisome thoughts flooded his mind as he pondered his situation. Knowing he could not open the gate without her, he decided if she did not willingly reveal the spell he would extract it by magical means, no matter how painful or deadly. It had to be done.

"Both of you be quiet!" snapped the prince as he ran a hand over his face in frustration. His voice took a gentle tone as he eased beside her. "The past is just that . . . the past. We cannot change it, and I will not debate my decisions with you." He let that sink in. "What is your answer? Will you help or not?"

Zanora met his eyes. "What do I get out of it? What is my reward?" She shrugged her indifference, but her body revealed deep fear as she squirmed impatiently. Again, she tested her bonds but to no avail. "Not that I trust a single word from your mouth, but I want you to say you need my help."

Barrett ignored her.

"You get to *live*," blurted Unger, his words dripping with vehemence. "That is your reward. Nothing more shall we give you."

"My, what a bold statement from someone whose words never matter." She leaned forward as a thin smile spread her lips. "Your role is that of a jester. No one takes you seriously. You are a buffoon. Nothing more."

The words bit at Unger with cruelty, but he showed no signs of his pain. Instead, he mocked her with a smile. "That means nothing coming from you, being the treacherous swine you are. You sided with the enemy, gave away all our secrets, murdered Jarn because he got in your way, and—"

Barrett waved him off. "Stop. This does no good. She is trying to drive us apart, and I won't allow it."

"*You* won't allow it." She spat at his feet. "Who are *you*? An orphan. A throneless king. A pitiful, homeless little boy who knows a few magic tricks. You are a sideshow freak who follows a worn-out old man and his sister to no end. You deserve whatever happens. Apadora will make you beg for death."

The prince set his teeth. With a flick of his hand, he stole her air. Zanora tipped over to clutch her throat while gurgling sounds spewed from her lips. She kicked and fought against the magic, her eyes fluttering as consciousness faded. Her world was going dark.

Another quick gesture from Barrett ended her agony. Coughing and gasping, she turned an angry face to him, but fear shone in her expression.

"Take care how far your insults go," he warned. "If you cannot be agreeable you will make Unger's idea more attractive. Consider your position before opening your mouth again." He stormed toward the fire with the archer in tow.

"Where did that come from?" asked Unger, squatting to rub his hands near the flames for warmth.

Barrett parroted his actions after adding more wood. "There is enough hateful talk in the world. I can't tolerate hers, too. However, I was wrong to let her get to me, even if her words were true. I *am* everything she said—orphaned, homeless, throneless, and pathetic at magic. But she was lying about your worth, my friend. Not to mention, you would make an awful jester. You would look foolish in one of those funny hats."

"You're an ass," replied Unger, reaching over to shove his friend off balance. His gaze returned to the redhead. "I pity her in many ways. It's sad she only knows discontent and malice. Why does she always need to irritate everyone?"

Dead leaves stirred as the breeze rose. Barrett shriveled his nose at the foul odor it carried. He did not want to know where the smell came from or what it was. He thought it smelled of dead things.

"Why else? To pit us against each other, of course. We can't be a team if we always question one another's decisions. Honestly, I think she is terrified of us," replied the prince.

"Exactly," said Graile, emerging from the darkness like a living shadow. "I was awake. I heard everything. I'm rather shocked you used magic. It's not like you to harm an innocent. Especially since you two were . . . well, you know."

"She is as far from being innocent as I am from a jester," said Unger.

"I think she may have a point." Graile smiled thinly. "In the next town, we will find you a cap and bell hat for your new role. Then, you can be a proper jester. I'll even teach you how to add face paint." He pointed to his own darkly ringed eyes that contrasted the pale makeup covering his face.

Barrett assumed the Fader had applied his full mask to enter the Outerworld as a ritual before facing possible death.

"I *really* hate you," grumbled Unger. "I take back all the nice things I ever said about you."

"Not again," complained the prince as the sky began to lighten around them. "Let's get some sleep while we can. Sunrise is approaching. As Lars said, being tired today could prove fatal." He moved toward his bedroll.

"Well, Sir Fader just woke up, so it's his turn to keep watch. I need more sleep." Unger paused to mimic a juggler. "Unless you wish to see my routine before I settle in."

"That would be wonderful," replied Graile, leaning back

against a splintered tree trunk. He extended both legs, then placed his hands behind his head. "Proceed."

Unger stormed off with curses streaming from his lips. "Why do I even bother being nice to you?"

Again, Zanora squirmed to test her restraints, then laughed as she watched the exchange. "Tell me, Graile, why do you stay by their sides? They're pathetic. But from what I've seen, you're smarter than all of them together."

"Do not waste your breath," said Graile, staring straight ahead. Turning his hand to vapor, he moved it before him to watch the heavy black mist trail behind. "No one listens to your treacherous words. The only thing we want is the spell. Give it to us, then there is no need for you to speak at all." His hand solidified to give a dismissive wave. "Go back to sleep."

The redhead growled an animalistic sound. She stretched beneath her blanket and closed her eyes.

Greying dawn faded in the distance. Barrett peered into the yellowing sky, longing to feel the sun on his face. But it was not to be. Their surroundings remained cold and gloomy, as if daylight refused to touch them.

Nell noticed, too. "It's like the sun is afraid of this place. This land is truly cursed."

"At least others get to feel the warmth and enjoy the day," noted Gaia. "And we're alive. So that's something."

Graile placed an arm around the witch's shoulder. "Typical Gaia. Always thinking positive thoughts and seeing the bright side, aren't you?"

"Is there any other way?" she replied. "I refuse to live my life in misery. I control my own emotions. No one else. And I choose happiness."

"Then what is the bright side of being here?" asked Lars with sarcasm.

The witch smiled. "We may rescue someone in need of help, keep terrible evil from breaking free, and come out alive with the help of our gods." She tore a chunk from her bread loaf and began to eat.

Zanora cleared her throat to protest. "Excuse me. I'm not some disease you can catch, so freeing me won't hurt. I need food, water, and warmth. Besides, I can't kill you all." She lowered her voice. "Even though I would like to."

Barrett turned grim before he waved a hand to make her bonds vanish. "There. Happy now?" While there was no pleasure in his voice, he knew releasing her was the right thing to do. Yet, gut instinct told him to watch her every move.

Zanora's face lightened as she rubbed her ankles, stood to stretch her legs, then moved beside him. "I suppose I should say thank you." She grimaced at her soreness. "But don't hold your breath for that part."

He ignored her, knowing she was trying to goad him into another verbal war. He refused to fall into her trap. "Have you made a decision?"

She stirred the dirt with a stick as apprehension and stubbornness fought a familiar battle in her mind. "I'll do it. But understand, it's not because I'm afraid of you."

Barrett placed a gentle hand on her back. "Good choice. And honestly, I don't care about your reasons." His voice raised over the crackling fire. "Zanora will open the gate. Afterward, she is free to leave if she chooses." He turned to her. "Agreed?"

She noticed the harshness in his voice yet thought better of being testy. "You have my word," she said soothingly.

"That's perfect, except your word means nothing," retorted Graile, his dark gaze quickly covering her.

Knowing he would have the spell, unless Zanora broke her word, Barrett turned back to planning. His idea felt simple enough. After the redhead revealed the words, he would place her into a deep sleep. The action was to ensure the company's safe return. After all, what if she remained outside but held a secret spell to seal them in forever or had some other wicked plan up her sleeve? Of course, she would be furious after she woke, but in the long run, her wrath was better than being dead or trapped with Apadora forever.

Dread hitched his breath as he recalled the bloodied, battered vision of Elimar after his failed attempt to free Alesta. If Apadora defeated him so totally, the company would be no match. Survival seemed unlikely if their teamwork failed.

"Our quest is plain enough," said the prince, edging closer to the flames. "Once inside, we find Alesta and flee as quickly as able. Unfortunately, we have no idea where she is, how dangerous the search will be, or how to avoid Apadora."

"That doesn't sound too hard," mocked Unger. "You realize Alesta could be heavily guarded and Apadora's minions will be everywhere, right? She could have legions of horrible creatures and beasts. Who knows what we'll face."

"Stay together. We're strongest that way," said Graile. "Be silent. Do not draw unwanted attention." He eyed Unger. "That means no whining."

Unger made an indelicate sound. He sneered in Graile's direction as an added insult.

"Am I the only one terrified right now," asked Gaia.

"Do you still have the wand I gave you?" Barrett flicked his hand through the air. Reaching within the folds of her cloak, she produced the enchanted wood. He smiled upon seeing it. "Excellent. That will help. You're becoming an amazing sorceress and can defend yourself better than most."

"Great," said Zanora, her words dripping with disdain. "Just what we need. More magic users. And amateur ones at that. What can go wrong?"

"Those magic users could turn you into a bug and crush you beneath their boot," threatened Graile, the whites of his eyes gleaming against the darkness of his black circles. "Perhaps you should mind your manners."

Zanora scoffed as she surveyed the witch. "When this is over, we can test your theory. My sword against your stick. We could end this now, but her boyfriend would be upset if she were hurt—or worse."

"You are very obnoxious," said Nell sharply. "How did anyone here ever call you a friend? You are rude and have no concept of manners."

Zanora's face reddened as she prepared to give a snappy reply. Barrett, familiar with her angry look, cut her off.

"Though I despise waiting, we will give Elimar one more day," he said. "We'll open the gate tomorrow after sunrise. Our supplies are running low and we can wait no longer. Prepare in whatever way is best for you." He whispered to Zanora. "Give me your word you will not run. I would rather not use a binding spell on you tonight."

She snorted an insulted sound as she eyed the prince with interest. "Why free me at all? I thought you didn't trust me."

"I don't," he replied bluntly. "But we have to start somewhere."

Confusion distorted her face as she mulled over his decision, wondering if he was being friendly or trapping her somehow. "I give my oath I'll not try to escape or harm anyone who does not attack me first."

"Thank you," he replied. "I know this is already scary enough, so I'd rather waste time worrying over you double-crossing or harming someone."

Zanora inhaled sharply as an idea sprang to life. She placed a hand on his shoulder and smiled. "Take me along. I want to go inside, too."

From behind, a chorus of voices lifted in objection until Barrett silenced them with a raised hand. "Hear her out. I'm sure she has reasons." He watched her closely. "You do, right?"

"None of which are good, I bet," grumbled Lars, his voice filled with biting doubt.

Barrett cast a harsh glare over his shoulder. "Just listen, will you?"

Zanora continued. "Though I hold no love for Alesta, I'll help you free her. Consider it a peace offering. Like you said, we have to start somewhere."

More doubt wormed into Barrett's mind. His fear of the quest falling apart due to distrust and anger was real. As he listened to the complaints rising behind him, he cursed Elimar for not arriving yet. The old man's mere presence would put everyone's mind at ease, except for Zanora, of course. *Plus, if he were here, he would know what to do and how to calm everyone. Even if it took a spell.*

"I am not following her inside. Especially if she has weapons," said Unger as he produced a hunk of jerky from his pack and tore a piece free.

The friends matched his disdain, save for Gaia, who merely listened.

"Never," cried Nell. The objection bellowed from her throat as she flashed into ogre form for an instant.

Lars pounded a fist on his thigh. "I will not place my life into her hands."

"Count me out," said Graile, focusing on a bank of darkening clouds forming overhead. "Does anyone else—"

His words were ripped away as the companions' fury took physical form. Soured emotions swirled round the camp like a tornado as winds blew, thunder cracked, and the sky blackened. The companions cowered, then dove for cover as lightning split the sky, striking the earth with force and hurling dead trees and rocks through the air.

Gaia sprang to her feet to stand against the howling wind. "Everyone stop," she shouted, holding her arms high. "This evil place is feeding off of our emotions. Let go of anger and fear. We're acting like children."

"Get down!" hollered Barrett, seizing her cloak to jerk her to the ground. He covered her with his body as best he could seconds before a heavy tree branch landed where she had stood. Then, as quickly as it started, the storm ended.

Gaia took his face in her hands. "You saved me." Their lips met and lingered.

Unger rose to brush himself off, trying to ignore their display of affection. "Will you two quit? Is this really the time?"

"Our witch is right," noted Graile, removing his cloak to shake it free of dust and debris. "We need to control our emotions. Apadora will draw power from our fear or anger."

"Agreed. The sorceress will have no trouble finding us if we behave this way within her realm," said Nell, picking bits of tree bark from her tunic and hair.

"Sister makes a good point. Inside her world, Apadora will be like a spider sensing vibrations to her web," said Lars. "There will be no place to hide."

Barrett extended a hand, helping Zanora gain her feet. He brushed her off. "Are you hurt?" he asked.

"You all want me dead, so does it matter?" she snapped, slapping his arm away. Then, her demeanor softened as she hung her head. "I'm sorry. You didn't deserve that. None of you." Like Graile, she removed her cloak to shake it out before lowering onto a wilted stump. "Thanks for asking."

Barrett sat next to her while considering her earlier proposal. There was always a chance her offer could be a deadly trap. Would she raise an alarm once they crossed into the wicked world? With his companions set against her and doubt gnawing at him, he was torn to choose a path.

"Answer one thing," he said. "Why Asban? I mean, his magic was not the most powerful. Why would he know the spell? He seemed more like a fool than a wizard."

The redhead shrugged. "Do not let him fool you. That wizard is tricksy. Maybe he used magic to steal the spell, then used the information for his gain. He believes if he meets Apadora, he could grovel enough to gain her allegiance. As a reward, she would grant him significant power. He's delusional that way."

"Like you?" asked Graile softly. "You're a hypocrite. You loathe magic and everything that goes with it. Suddenly, you know spells and directions to enter the evilest place in our world. Forgive us if we carry no faith in your intentions."

Zanora wore a dreadful look as her brows scrunched downward in anger. Barrett saw a hint of remorse, too. Pondering her reaction, he watched the redhead pick at her fingernails as she fought back her anger. He wanted to say something pleasing to ease the moment, but nothing came. To his relief, Gaia intervened.

"Let's not start again, or the storm may return," said the witch, eyeing the sky.

"We need to get on with it," said Lars.

Unger nodded. "Our chances lessen each minute. Apadora could be plotting her escape as we sit here and argue. I vote to open the gate now."

"We came here to set Alesta free. The time has come," said Nell.

Barrett mindlessly adjusted his clothing as he mulled over yet another problem: time was dwindling. No one knew how long magic could keep Apadora in her prison or how close she might be to unleashing herself and all her horrible creatures upon the world. In his heart, he knew whatever time they had was slipping away far too fast.

Each decision seemed rushed and wise choices felt unlikely. Even entering the dragon's lair months ago to find the enchanted sword and bargain for the companions' lives seemed easier. Rubbing his temples as his head started to throb, he wished he had slept better.

He still did not understand many things and had no easy answers. Where was Elimar or Trishar? The companions were right. Waiting for their arrival only led to false hopes. One thing he did not wish to consider was that Alesta may have already been killed. They had not heard from her in some time. Had she escaped? *How strange would it be to enter the Outerworld only to find her gone or dead?*

But he could not dwell on any of that. Here and now, he had to choose.

2

A Friend Returns

oments before Barrett announced his decision, a collective gasp swept around the campfire. Instinctively, he spun with his wand at the ready. Shocked as a familiar form drew nearer, he sucked in a sharp breath.

"Impossible," he said. "Are you a dream?"

"Clearly not impossible. For here I stand. Nor am I considered a dream," answered the lithe woman. "I come to you in your greatest hour of need."

Like their first meeting, Barrett nearly mistook Nirith for Trishar. The young woman held a stunning resemblance to her aunt, save for the fact she dressed in happy, bright colors. At average height, with flowing black hair and eyes like orbs of swirled blue, the sorceress appeared not to have aged a day. Her smile remained as comforting as ever.

Gaia met her with a light embrace. "How is it you knew to come here?"

"Father sent a message telling me what has passed and bade me to lend aid. He and my aunt will return shortly. Both are away containing rogue Yerspins. The wicked things are slaughtering humans for fun in the city of Kolbinor. In the meantime, I have come in their stead." Her gaze covered the companions. "Your group has grown. Impressive." She studied Zanora with a tilted head. "I see your friends have shown mercy. I thought you would be dead."

Zanora scoffed openly. "Not yet, but the idea crossed their mind." She frowned heavily. "Why *are* you here? Do you mean to enter the Outerworld?"

"Of course. My sister needs me." She peered toward the cavern entrance. Her gaze lingered for an instant. "During my father's first attempt to rescue Alesta, had he told me of it, I could have helped. But he excluded me from concern over risking my life. So that brings us here. As it is, being kin, I can locate her whereabouts even within the confines of the evil realm." She inclined her head toward Barrett. "If you will have me, of course, my prince."

"Please don't call me that. And you are *most* welcome here," he replied excitedly.

"What about me?" asked Zanora, raising a shoulder in question. "If you have a new guide, how do I still fit in? Do you expect me to open the gate, then sit and wait for your return like a loyal dog?"

Barrett desperately wished to have that scenario. Since Nirith arrived, the redhead would not need to come along. Still, having an extra sword and a skilled fighter could prove wise. He answered before another argument could trigger the return of the thunderstorm.

"Zanora is a skilled fighter, and we need the extra sword," he blurted. "She will follow us into the depths of the shadows she wished to see. Besides, there is no telling what manner or number of enemies we will meet. The more weapons we have, the better."

As soon as the words left him, another thought sprung to mind. *Maybe it would be best if only Nirith and I go forward. With her magic we may succeed. Staying hidden with seven others may be impossible. Then again, if I made that choice, another argument would start and I have no time for that now.*

The archer stared at Zanora. "You can go provided you use your steel against them and not one of us," he chided with a raspy voice.

"As you command, Sir Jester." Zanora bowed low in mocking fashion and swept an arm before her. "I shall obey, my master."

Unger mumbled several curses, plopped on a dark boulder, and said no more.

Barrett gave her a disapproving stare. "Will you stop that? I can't believe your nerve. You are already unwanted. Saying foolish things does not help."

"You two can proceed with your lover's spat later?" asked Nirith. "We must go soon."

Zanora laughed as she pointed to the prince, then poked a finger against her chest. "We're not together." Her finger aimed at the witch. "*She's* with him now. They're a cozy pair, don't you think?"

The sorceress blushed. "Father did not mention that part. Forgive me." She curled her finger to Barrett, who drew close so none could hear. "Wise choice," she whispered.

Barrett chuckled lightly. "I think so, too." Regardless of his answer, a certain degree of shame bit at his innards. *Why does everyone need to know my business? Maybe I should advertise my love life in The Oracle. I can see the article now:* **Prince dumps old girlfriend for a new love!** He huffed.

"I am delighted to see you again, Lady Nirith. You are as lovely as ever," noted Graile with a respectful nod.

Oddly, Barrett noticed a hint of jealousy creep from Zanora as she hung her head to sneer at the Fader's comment. Her reaction surprised him. *Does she have feelings for Graile?* He shook his head. *It can't be. I'm just tired.*

"You are too kind, my painted Fader. The days have been kind to each of you despite all you have seen and done." Nirith spun a graceful circle with both arms out to her sides, changing from her lengthy dress to a brown tunic, black boots, and light green breeches. "This may be more appropriate for fighting wickedness."

"Yes indeed, Elimar is your father," said Unger. "Oh, where are our manners? This is Nell and Lars." He indicated each in turn. "They are Shifters."

"Dorgons. Most remarkable. I would love to chat with you both when time allows. Providing we survive."

"Now there's some positive thinking," muttered Zanora as she stared at her boots.

Nirith turned toward the entrance. "If you are willing to stand alongside me, we should proceed. Apadora is likely aware of your gate discovery. Time is of the essence. She is stirring."

"What hope do we have, then?" questioned Nell. "If she knows we are coming, our chances are slim."

"She may not yet be at full strength. She has been idle for many ages and could have grown soft and weak. Even in her faded strength, she nearly killed my father. She would quickly return to her former wickedness if she were let loose on the world. There would be no stopping her," said Nirith. "Though news still comes to her, your arrival may hold little interest. She does not view you as a threat. She merely awaits the perfect time to break free. Then, her evil will come forth in full force. We must make use of her indifference."

Barrett pushed his shoulders back and used a determined voice. "Ready yourselves. The time is nearly at hand."

"Before I take another step, I need food. I feel like I haven't eaten in a week. I'm not dying on an empty stomach," said Unger, retrieving fruit, bread, and dried meat from his rucksack.

Graile lowered his voice. "You do know the idea is *not* to die, right?"

"Why do I put up with you?" came the reply through a full mouth. Unger swallowed, then wagged the small bread loaf toward the redhead. "Why don't you go keep an eye on her? Your talents could come in handy as you watch my back. She may knife me when I'm not paying attention."

Graile closed both eyes, making them disappear in a sea of blackness. He shook his head and strode away.

"Where are my things? I need my sword and shield," announced Zanora, searching for her belongings.

Gaia ambled off to return with the familiar gear. "These were yours. It is a beautiful sword. I hope it serves you well."

Zanora jerked the blade free to swipe it through the air with speed. She spun it round in her hand, then slid its length into the scabbard in one motion. "Thank you." Gaia turned to leave, only to stop at the redhead's voice. "You can have him, you know. There are no hard feelings. You two deserve each other."

The witch displayed her usual friendly look. "Thank you for your approval. Though I doubt you are sincere. I know it hurts you here." She pointed to her own heart. "I'm sorry for that. It was not supposed to be this way."

Zanora's hand zipped toward her sword only to find Gaia's wand quickly leveled at her.

She glared at the witch. "Do it," chided the redhead, even as the threat sounded rushed and awkward to her ears. "I wouldn't blame you. At least I would die knowing none of you will ever see the sun again."

Gaia stepped back and lowered her wand. "Please do not mistake my kindness for weakness. I am no longer the same girl you grew up with. Besides, I am not like you and would never kill for jealousy. Though, I will certainly defend myself if needed." She spun and strode away.

Minutes later, the group entered the cavern's gaping outer entrance to meet the odor of rotting flesh. Barrett wrinkled his nose and made a sour face. Lighting his staff to combat the sheer darkness, he walked alongside Nirith through the long, musty corridor. The sorceress gave him unspoken confidence, yet the aura of the cavern's malevolence made his stomach bubble. It was not the first time he wondered if Zanora had fallen prey to its call. *Is that another reason she turned wicked? Had the pull of evil been too strong for her?*

Here and there, scampering creatures clung to the roughly hewn walls, giving shrill shrieks as the magical light touched them. They skittered away to hide from the blue radiance. Safely hidden in shadow while hissing and chattering their disapproval at the invaders, their reflective eyes peered from the shadows to watch the intruders pass.

Soon, the friends reached the darkened pool. The dripping water still fell from high above into the murky depths below. The dribbling sound echoed through the cavern in maddening fashion. Having been here before, with Barrett knowing the difference between a vague dream and lively sensations of reality, he wondered which this was. It all felt surreal.

"Not much farther now," he whispered, his voice swirling round as if carried by the creatures themselves to announce his presence. He winced at the soft echo.

Farther on, the enormous doors took shape in the gloom. Approaching first, Barrett, Graile, and Unger heaved their weight against them. The thick wood swung away with surprising ease, opening to the throne chamber where the magical duel with Asban had taken place. While Barrett felt a surge of confidence after defeating the wizard, he knew his powers would pale if compared to Apadora. Her strength was far beyond that of his insignificant scale.

He could not help but look upon the spot where Asban remained trapped in the Frigidus spell. His eyes rested on the disheveled, motionless wizard who stared outward, still immobilized. Gurgling and moaning sounds came from his lips as Zanora passed. She ignored him.

Whether the greasy man was warning of danger, cursing his conqueror, or asking to be set free, Barrett could not tell nor did he care.

"You need to release him," said Gaia with pity in her tone. "It is beyond mean."

The prince turned a skeptical eye to her. "He tried to kill me," he reminded her. "Have no fear. The spell will wear off soon enough and he will be alive. Hopefully, a bit wiser. What more can he ask?"

Gaia lay a hand on his forearm in a pleading fashion. "But—" Her words were cut off as Graile interrupted.

"The last thing we need is an angry wizard to contend with. Leave him where he is. Barrett's right. He will survive and we may be long gone by the time the spell wears off," said the Fader.

"Or we could all be dead," added Zanora with a raised shoulder. "Why not turn him loose." She patted her sword hilt as a smug grin spread over her lips. "I will kill him myself for being incompetent. Cursed fool!"

"Ah, Zanora, never a dull moment with you around. We can always count on you being violent till the end," quipped Unger.

She smirked in reply. "Quiet, jester. You make my head hurt."

Gaia rubbed a reassuring hand down Unger's back. "Do not listen to her. She's angry over things she cannot control and takes her misery out on everyone around her."

Walking on, they came to more empty chambers, ultimately reaching the spot of Jarn's torture and death. Zanora stared for a long moment before flashing a satisfied smile. The steam still hissed and rose steadily as they passed. Barrett shivered as he recalled the horrible image of Jarn hanging suspended in death.

Turning left, they continued through several hallways until they reached the broad, carven stone stairs. The monstrous gargoyle statues remained motionless in their stony silence, each guarding opposing sides of the landing. As during his first visit, Barrett hoped they would not come to life.

Above their stony counterparts, the bat creatures continued to dash over the walls while the hybrid gargoyle-dragon beasts scurried over the ground, wings folded, tails swishing, their orbed eyes reflecting.

Standing before the door, Barrett faced Zanora. "This is the reason you are here. Speak your words. Cast the spell."

Her hand slid up his arm tenderly, coming to a gentle rest on his neck as she pulled him close, their lips only inches apart. Tilting her head, her breath came warm against his ear. "I wanted to hurt you. Just as you did when you cast me away. I only wanted the gate open to make you suffer." She stepped back and winked.

The corners of his mouth turned down as he gave a dismissive wave. "I don't believe that at all. You have made it plain that magic is a scourge you wish to wipe away. But did you ever stop to think Apadora's type of magic would kill us all? You were going to set her free from spite just because your heart was hurt."

"Think back to all that has happened since this quest has begun. Don't you think everyone has already suffered enough?" asked Gaia.

Zanora made no attempt to hide her harsh glare at the pair. It lingered a long moment before the redhead turned to face the strange symbols circling the gate's outermost edge. The smaller inner ring held similar markings. They encircled the carved demon's face. Long, jagged cracks spread outward from the center, like awful misshapen fingers, prodding and probing for release.

"I need the key," she said, extending her hand in wait.

"No! You're not laying hands on the key," said Unger, sprinting to join them. "We may never see it again. Cast your spell, and *I* will open the gate."

"That may be best," agreed Barrett while flicking his wand to summon his vortex. "*Tinith O'votus.*" The key floated free from the portal's depths. With another graceful wand movement, he pushed the iron piece toward Unger, who seized it from the air.

"I need a wand or your staff," said Zanora, glaring at the pair. "Or are you two going to do that for me, too?"

Graile drifted across the chamber floor in vapor form to solidify next to Zanora. "Why would you ask for such a thing? Remember our trust issue?"

"I have no magic and you know it," she argued. "I only hold a spell or two that Asban taught me. I am no danger to you even with his precious stick."

"There is a simple way to fix this." Nirith extended a hand to Zanora and inclined her head toward it. "Take my hand, and I will know your words before you speak them. We will utter the spell together. Be aware. I will know if you are deceiving me."

"I'm not a child and can do this on my own," retorted the redhead, defiantly folding her arms across her chest. Shame reddened her cheeks at being disallowed from working the spell alone.

"If you are being honest, what would it matter if Nirith joined you?" asked Gaia. "With her power, you should not even need a wand. Reciting the words together is the solution."

"Why doesn't it surprise me you don't want me to have a little magic stick." Zanora exhaled heavily and took the sorceress' hand. "I just want this over with."

Atop the landing, the two women halted before the gate. Zanora drew in a breath and began the incantation as Nirith matched her words. The magic was instantaneous, spreading across the door like green lava, bending and crawling its way through the deep crevices. Sounds of grating stone filled the chamber as each crack filled with a sparkling light. The Outerworld gate was coming to life.

The creatures darted about in a frenzy before wedging deeper into their murky corners high above. When the light overwhelmed them, their squeaks and shrill whistles resounded as they fled. Barrett suppressed his desire to run, too. Though he knew this moment would arrive, uncertainty over what may lay beyond made him tremble.

"Will the gate stay open once the spell is cast?" asked Unger with nervousness edging his tone.

"I hope not," answered Graile. "The whole idea is to keep Apadora locked away. If we cannot reseal it once inside, we are making a terrible mistake. This will be the shortest adventure in history, one which no one lives to tell about."

"Oh, you're a bucket of cheer," griped Unger. "Thanks for that. I feel better now."

"We should have never come here," added Lars, his voice tense with fear. "Death is upon us."

"Easy, brother," said Nell. "We are surrounded by it. Have faith in the king and Nirith."

The title 'king' made Barrett wince. No one had used the label in a long while and he doubted if his dream of taking the crown would ever come to fruition, at least not while the Bureau remained in charge of his home. Their occupation of Westmore prickled his skin like a storm of biting insects. Hateful thoughts against Grimes flooded his mind. Revenge washed over him as he clenched his fist. *I need to calm down but this place stirs something dark in me. Like a wicked spell.*

Gaia's breath in his ear returned him to the present. "Stay close," she whispered.

After their lips met, he relaxed and smiled. "That's my plan." Yet, a new worry sprang into his mind. Caring for himself would be difficult enough, but he carried a compulsion to protect everyone, especially his love, the witch.

He owed loyalty to his friends for remaining by his side. They had followed him from one dangerous adventure to another without being asked and placed faith in his decisions. Even Lars and Nell, who were older and more experienced, trusted him and accepted him as their leader when they could have walked away. The companions' safety had become his purpose, even more than rescuing Alesta or reclaiming Westmore.

Watching the gate segments drift away to hover some ten feet overhead, Barrett secretly hoped Nirith would lead. Anxiety gripped him as the entrance opened wide. The sorceress did not stir. Swallowing his fear, he strode forward with Gaia by his side, moving headlong into the one place neither wished to see.

"Follow me," he announced before vanishing in the gloom.

"Curse him for leading me here," cried Unger as he dashed up the stairs with Graile beside him. In a blink, they faded from sight.

Nells and Lars followed, with Zanora and Nirith entering last. The opening sealed in their wake, closing them inside the most wicked place in existence.

They stood in a long stone tunnel. Barrett glanced over the coarsely hewn walls towering overhead in a massive arch. Sputtering torches were set here and there in crude iron holders, their dancing orange flames struggling to push away the inky darkness. For an instant, Barrett considered brightening his staff tip but decided against it. The act would feel more like a beacon for evil than a way to light the path, although traveling in near darkness could be their end sooner than expected, he thought.

With little light, the company traveled slowly under the heavy shadows. In places, the gloom seemed impenetrable. Before long, a loathsome aroma reached their nostrils, smelling of sulfur and dead things. Barrett gagged involuntarily. He cleared his throat, then sucked in a breath, gaining far too little air for his efforts. Holding his breath did little good except to make him lightheaded.

Maliciousness surrounded their every step. Barrett's poise slipped away as painful memories of the Trowken caves sprang into his mind. The misadventure still haunted him even during waking hours, but here, in the murkiness with despair smothering them, the memories swelled. Sweat beads lined his forehead. He wiped them away with his sleeve, but the painful incident clung to him, refusing to let go.

"Why?" grumbled Unger. "Why dark, ugly tunnels? I despise them. They stink and there is always something waiting to kill us."

Gaia held a finger to her lips. "Shhhhh! We do not know what sort of enemy may await us. Let's not wake the things in the darkness."

The archer studied the crooked passage with fear in his eyes. "Good point."

Within a hundred paces, they came to an immense opening on their right. Barrett froze as deep rumbling sounds met his ears. Whether rocks had broken loose to roll about, enemy hordes were moving in uncountable numbers, or some unnatural beast or monster shuffled by unseen, he had no idea. As the sound faded, he remained still. The hair on his neck rose up as he sensed an evil far more terrible than he ever experienced.

The void was appallingly bleak. Staring into its seemingly endless depths, he grimaced. Disgust and vileness uncoiled from within and he refused to lead his companions toward its dreadful interior.

"Come on. This should be easy walking," said Lars, heading for the murky corridor. "We should go this way."

Nirith halted him with a gentle touch and shook her head. "There is a malevolence in that place. We should avoid it."

"I'm glad you felt it, too," admitted Barrett while getting his emotions under control. "I thought I was just losing my nerve."

She continued to stare at the shadowy void. "Merely looking upon it makes me ill. Our best choice is going forward."

Moving again, the companions twisted round many corners before beginning a long, winding descent. Finally, they reached a level where the ground was mostly smooth, though small cracks, crevices, or rough spots still caught their feet in the dim light. Muffled curses were heard.

Before long, they trudged up an incline, following the path to another landing, one bathed in dull torchlight. Here, the walls fell away from both sides, and a labyrinth of misshapen caverns and chambers were below. High, jagged rocks jutted upward, some reaching thirty feet in height. Gaping chasms splintered the ground as if the mountain was in wait for an unsuspecting meal.

Barrett felt exposed and watched at every step. He hurried on until he reached a spot where uneven roads jutted off in several directions, and he was forced to halt again.

Around the irregular paths were more deep pitfalls, gaping holes, and precarious cracks. Some, as wide as a wagon bed, split the ground. The companions had no choice but to leap across the gaping crevices, as they were the only path forward.

Hot, tired, and uneasy, the company stopped for a brief rest. They quietly debated turning back but quickly abandoned the idea.

"How long have we been walking?" Zanora murmured. "It feels like we have been here for days."

Barrett agreed. All time felt lost, and no matter how he tried, his efforts to sense how long or how far they had traveled were wasted.

"We cannot sit here forever. We'll be spotted. Which way?" questioned Graile.

The sorceress closed her eyes for a moment, then extended a slender arm to the right. "This road is our path. I believe it is the safest way."

"Hold on. You *believe*?" snapped Zanora through grit teeth. "Is that the best you can do?"

Nirith furrowed her brow. "There is a tremendous amount of discord here. It is rather difficult to break through it all, even for me. Since you do not trust my judgment, you are free to stay here if you wish." The sorceress walked away to leave the redhead glowering at her back.

Unger joined Zanora with a thin grin on his face. "With all this anger around, you should feel at home," he said. "Maybe you *should* stay behind."

She shoved his shoulder. "Silence, jester boy," she countered. "One of these days—"

"Stop, you fools. Play childish games later," said Graile with force. "Keep your mouths shut."

Despite moving in the endless grey gloom, Barrett's eyes soon adjusted. Slowly, he discerned thousands of structures but struggled to see overly far through the murky layers. Focusing, he noticed these were not the irregular cave holes, cracks, and fissures from earlier. There were a staggering number of stone quarters or barracks of some sort. The housing stretched far beyond sight in every direction. He shuddered at the thought of their occupants. Fear gave way to a desolate weariness as he wandered forward.

His feet hurt and hunger bit at him. The unending shadows stole away hope and comfort, including joy from his spirit which felt smothered by their surroundings.

As the shacks were left behind, despair grew. Rapidly, all was forgotten as their path opened to a massive cavern, the size of which he had never imagined possible. He raised a hand to halt the companions. Before them stretched a dark, sprawling underground city, its enemy numbers likely far beyond their reckoning.

To the right rose a horrifying citadel, the heart of Apadora's realm. Spires jutted upward with sharp edges gleaming in the flickering light. The black stone appeared wet and freshly hewn. Roaring fires blazed throughout many open courtyards and circular depressions. The flames licked and danced, casting contorted shadows wherever their orange glow touched. Windowless openings peered back as if made for no other purpose than for the creatures or beasts to observe any who passed.

Around them lay bubbling pools of lava. Some leaked fiery streams which flowed past to merge with a river belching magma from its depths. The rancid, hot air stifled each breath. Barrett now understood the heat and origins of the odorous reek.

Before the towering fortress gates lay a smooth path leading to an immense stone bridge. Its opposite side stretched beyond sight toward the gate from whence they came. *This must be part of the opening we saw earlier. It must start here.* After silently thanking the gods for giving him the wisdom to avoid it, he joined Nirith.

"It seems you made a wise decision by not leading us there. Had we chosen the opening, we would have been easily discovered," said the sorceress, staring rearward.

The prince nodded. "That path had a more wicked feel than

our current course. Though, the walking would have been easier." He observed the citadel with distaste and tilted his staff forward. "There's a sight I never wanted to see. Several hosts could not conquer this cursed place." He pondered that. "Not that any would want to call it their own. Surely, it is defiled."

"Indeed," replied the sorceress. "Alesta is deep within the city. Therefore, we must head into the mouth of the beast."

"Wonderful," said Lars. "I was hoping you would say that."

"Hush, brother. You're whining," said Nell.

They had not traveled far when Zanora shifted to the lead. Barrett followed, eyeing her movements carefully. He concluded she would easily fit into this world if she broke away from the company. Taking his staff in both hands, he carried it waist level, prepared to strike her down if she attempted to announce their presence. Yet she walked steadily on and Barrett's grip eased as they passed beyond sight of the citadel.

The sounds of their boots gently slapping the stones as they climbed a long staircase seemed unnaturally loud. Barrett hoped it was nothing more than his imagination.

Some hundred feet later, they crossed a narrow bridge spanning a belching torrent of lava. Barrett peered over the edge and cringed. Choking down his panic, he took Gaia's hand to traverse the crossing.

Back on solid ground, the path turned toward the city. At that moment, tremendous drums began to roll and thump. The reverberations shook his body as fear took hold. Were the drums an alarm? Had the friends been spotted? Was the enemy wise to their movements? Would Apadora's forces come against them?

"Should we retreat?" asked Gaia, clutching his arm, tense with worry.

Nirith shook her head and kept moving. "No. We are close to Alesta. I feel it."

"I certainly hope you're right," said Zanora, sliding her hand toward her sword hilt.

Rounding another angular corner, they surprised two unsuspecting creatures. Their enemies were thick and tall, with yellow eyes adapted for seeing through the perpetual murk. Large, bald heads sat upon broad shoulders, which quickly narrowed to thin waists. Powerful legs supported their frames. Wide, long feet bore four toes. Crude armor covered their chests, and matching gauntlets graced both forearms. Three thick fingers and a thumb gripped jagged blades as they freed them from their belts. Their skin looked like rough green leather.

Crying out in surprise, they charged with their crooked blades wagging low. Zanora, still leading the company, had little time to react.

Barrett reacted first, thrusting his staff forward. "*Impendior*!" The magical orbs struck the attackers squarely, hurtling their howling forms over the edge to their doom. Their hideous shrieks ended abruptly as they met the boiling river with a splash. In a blink, they disappeared beneath the rolling lava waves.

The companions went still. Barrett sucked in a breath and waited, hoping the creatures' death screams had been drowned out by the relentless, booming drums. Agonizing seconds ticked by as he awaited a blaring horn or shouts of alarm. None came. He breathed again.

The redhead faced him, her expression a mixture of relief and gratitude. "I owe you."

"You owe me nothing. Defending you is not a debt to be repaid." He took her hand for a moment and smiled. "I'm pleased you are safe. Come. We must not dally."

Zanora's brow furrowed in confusion. "I see you're all broken up over saving me."

"You're still breathing, so what are you complaining about?" quipped Nell, patting the redhead's back as she passed.

Within another two hundred paces, they reached the massive stone bridge.

Unger eyed it hesitantly and ran his fingers through his hair. "It seems sturdy. Right?" Backtracking, he bumped into Zanora, who shoved him forward.

"Get moving before your body ends up down there." She pointed to the lava river, drew a finger across her throat, and stuck her tongue out to the side.

"You are twisted," said the archer.

Barrett ignored them while trying not to look down. As a child, if he would climb too high up a towering tree or high stone wall, his father would always say, 'Never look down.' To the prince's displeasure, the advice did not work this time. He felt weak and wobbly as he stepped onto the crossing. Graile joined him.

"Quick thinking back there with Zanora," he said. 'Well done, my friend." Then he lowered his voice and whispered. "Next time, maybe you could be a bit slower."

The Fader's words distracted the prince's mind from fear, making him chuckle. "That's not a nice thing to say." He gave a wink. "What's more, I bet that will not be the last we see of the enemy, especially if we stay in the open. We should hasten."

"Pick up the pace," grumbled Zanora, casting cautious glances ahead.

"For once, I agree with her," said Unger, hurrying onto the bridge. "You would think I'd be used to this stuff by now. I hate heights!" He shuddered.

"You hate everything. Bridges, heights, tunnels, and—" began Zanora.

"Shut it," grumbled the archer, cutting her off. "It's not like you don't have issues, too."

Reaching the far side, they slid into the shadow as Nirith pointed left. "This way."

Moving again, the air grew heavier and smelled of thick smoke. The sounds of the crackling fires grew as the towering flames came into view. Up close, they were larger than Barrett realized. He dreaded going farther.

They crept through the streets until a fork appeared in their path. Nirith never slowed, taking the lead as she angled right.

Barrett fought to contemplate time and distance. *How long have we been in this twisted land? Hours? Days? Is there any way to know?* One thing he did know was incredible weariness, thirst, and hunger had settled upon him. He wished to stop for another brief rest.

As if reading his mind, Nell spoke. "I can go no farther. We must rest. I need water and a bite to eat."

"Right," agreed Unger, massaging his throat. "I am parched in this cursed heat. It's like dragging a weight behind me. Plus, we'll need energy to fight if it comes to it."

Barrett shook his head. "We cannot stop here. We are exposed," he insisted.

"True enough." Gaia made a quick scan of the surroundings. She pointed to her left. "There. That cave will work."

"Perfect! What could be wrong with that idea?" muttered

Unger sarcastically. "Because dark, scary caves always are a good place to hide . . . especially here."

Graile added to the archer's anxiety. "Exactly, my friend. There could be an entire hidden army of those vile things inside. I'll take a peek." Turning to vapor, he drifted into the gloom to vanish. Mere seconds passed before clanking steel rang out, followed by a string of grunts, thuds, and muffled screams from within.

Unger found himself holding his breath until the Fader returned. "We will be safe now," said Graile.

"D . . . d . . . did you have trouble?" stammered Unger, already knowing the answer but needing to hear it aloud to calm his nerves.

Graile shook his head. "They never saw me coming. And if it makes you feel better, you were right. The enemy did occupy the cave."

Unger nodded. "Well done, friend."

The company dashed into the cavern, winding their way around several dead bodies as they neared the center. Nirith cleared the horrible creatures from their path with a swish of her wand. Barrett quickly settled on the floor to uncork his water skin, forcing himself to take slow, shallow sips.

Who knew when they would find fresh water again? One sip passed his lips. Another followed. Then, a third. He allowed himself no more. Unwrapping some dried meat pulled from the folds of his cloak, he shared it with Zanora and Gaia, then leaned back to relax.

His next memory was Unger gently shaking his shoulder. "We must go," said the archer in a cheerless tone.

The prince rubbed his face. "How I would love to feel the sun on my skin."

"You will. Soon enough, I would guess." Unger helped him stand and clapped a hand on his back to offer encouragement. "We're still alive and that's saying something."

The company loped along, keeping from sight as best they could as the drums boomed with an increased tempo.

Nirith glanced over her shoulder. "We are getting closer."

Barrett's spirit lifted at the news. *Could they escape without further conflict? Would Alesta still be alive, or would their efforts have come to nothing?* He had little time to contemplate as primal screams cut the air between drumbeats. An armed patrol, far more significant than the previous one, fell upon them with shrieks and grunts erupting from thick, beastly lips.

Nirith raised both hands to cast a spell, but arrows zipped past from behind quicker than she could utter a word. Unger's shafts of death sent the first pair tumbling down the slick rock slab to their right. The creatures landed in a roaring bonfire. Sparks flared upward in a shower of red embers while their bodies sizzled away until they were no more.

Graile drifted through two others, removing the beast's hearts before they tipped over dead. The Fader materialized on the opposite, throwing the organs away, as was his custom.

Barrett sent three more headlong into a bubbling lava pit as Lars and Nell became ogres to smash another pair against the stone walls. Gaia flicked her wand as one creature was mere inches from seizing Zanora. "*Impendior!*" cried the witch.

The beast was driven rearward to slam into the jagged rocks. A sharp fragment tore through its head, pinning it to the wall. Zanora kicked the dead body free, sending it over the edge into the shrouded gloom, then turned to face the witch with a scowl on her lips.

"Oh, come on," she complained, sliding her sword away. "I wanted some action, too. You cheated me."

"Some things never change. Like I said earlier . . . twisted." Unger winked at her. "You will always be bloodthirsty."

"Silence, clown boy," she retorted. "You're just jealous because I fight better."

"Will you two stop," snapped Barrett. "Or should I send up a signal so *all* the enemy knows we're here?"

Zanora huffed. "No need to be so dramatic, my dear." She softly ran a hand down his chest as she passed. "After your girl-friend's shouting and your handiwork, it's no wonder we're not already surrounded."

Puzzled over her words, Barrett placed a palm on his fore-head. "Are you whining about being alive? She saved your life. At least you could give her thanks." He felt Gaia's gaze on him and fidgeted, raising a shoulder as their eyes met. "What? She's being annoying on purpose. I swear it."

To his relief, Nirith changed the subject. "I have never been in a battle where I simply stood by. This group gives me hope." She smiled. "Those creatures may have been a small part of those guarding Alesta. I sense her stronger than ever. Go higher. Nearer the citadel."

"Well, that's welcomed news," griped Unger. "It's not bad enough we're in the Outerworld, but we need to go deeper toward Apadora's lair, too. Huzzah!"

"Stop complaining!" demanded Graile, his face twisting in anger. "You've been whining since we stepped foot in here." His hand turned to vapor as he waved it before his chest. "To keep your tongue, close your mouth."

The archer moved away. "By the gods, you are getting bossy

lately," he mumbled. "Zanora is rubbing off on you. If you couldn't drift through me and tear my heart out, I would take you aside and teach you a lesson."

Graile softened and hung his head a moment in thought. "Apologies, Unger. It's this place. There is a malice here that sinks into your skin and twists your mind." He squeezed the archer's shoulder. "I'll be pleased to be gone from within this nightmare."

"I have never seen you scared before, Graile," Nell said. Inwardly, she respected the Fader's strong will and found it shocking he openly admitted his apprehension.

"Every living thing knows fear at one time or another. This must be my time," he replied. "Something about this place sets me on edge."

The friends hurried past a rectangular structure on their right. The quarters had no doors or windows, only empty openings where they should have been. Candles and low-burning torches lit the interior. Like everything else in this world, even the sparse furnishings appeared unrefined and vulgar.

This is not a place Alesta would be held, thought Barrett. After all, Apadora must have some deeply suppressed love for her daughter. Surely, she would imprison her in a place suited for a sorceress. However, the location could be covered by magical safeguards.

We will find out soon enough.

3

Death Comes

Staying to the shadows, the company navigated the avenues of uneven, rudimentary rock when Barrett motioned for a stop. Advancing alone, he slipped farther into the darkness, pressed his back against the stone, then edged forward. Ahead stood a thick gate, considerably smaller than the main entrance but no less stout. Several bat vermin patrolled overhead.

He cursed himself for bringing his companions into this world. Even if they found Alesta, escape seemed dismal at best. Forward was his only option now. Turning back meant failure and he refused to give in to defeat. So after rejoining his friends, he whispered a hasty plan and nodded to the archer.

Unger sped arrows from his bow in rapid succession. Barrett struck down several bats with magic. They fell to slap the stone with a crude sound. Two more beastly guards fell dead by Nirith's magic as they charged from beneath the wall's frowning arch.

With clawed limbs still on their sword hilts, the beasts stiffened under her spell. She advanced slowly, sweeping her hand to the side, tossing their rigid bodies from the path like leaves in the wind. Several bats took flight as the drums continued to thrum.

Barrett gave another curse. "They're going to spread an alarm."

"There's nothing we can do about it now," said Nell. "Let's hurry."

"How much farther?" asked Lars.

"I feel her drawing closer," said Nirith, touching her temple. "I sense pain and confusion. She is afraid."

Barrett huffed. *Had the sorceress invented the answer to avoid confrontation, give a sense of hope, or dodge the fact she had no idea where Alesta was held?* His doubting thoughts shocked him. *Graile is right. This place breeds anger. We need to get out before we turn on each other.*

Gaia dashed to the entryway with her wand at her side. She cautiously unlatched the heavy doors to peer inside. Empty. The company filed in, resecured the opening, then quickly followed.

"This revolting realm wears on my nerves. Its wretched aura is creeping into my bones like a disease. It's difficult to think," said Barrett. Sluggish and tired, he wished for rest as images of Alesta filled his vision. When she appeared in his chamber to plead for help she seemed weary and sick. That day seemed another lifetime ago and she could easily be dead by now despite Nirith's beliefs, he thought.

Besides pleasing Elimar or other members of Alesta's family like Nirith and Trishar, he wondered if saving her was worth the risk. What's more, if Apadora still controlled her servant's actions, would Alesta try to kill the company as she had done months ago? He worried her mind may not be her own.

They sped onward, coming to a place where dim light from the roaring fires lit the stonework with sporadic flickers of orange. The dancing light probed the darkness as though trying to reveal their presence. Barrett dreaded taking a single step forward. But at Nirith's gentle urging, he carried on.

"Keep moving," he said, more to himself than the others.

Their current path led between two sizable courtyards. Around them, the drums rolled deeper and fires sprang taller, bringing the Outerworld to life. The enemy poured from caves, caverns, and each opening in waves of uncountable creatures. Their advance vibrated the stony streets and passages while their harsh, guttural speech filled the air. The throng dashed toward the citadel courtyards to form a circle. The bats and gargoyle creatures flew overhead, coming to perch high above on nearby rooftops, towers, or spires.

"What do we do now?" asked Nell. "We'll be spotted for sure."

"This is actually lucky," said Gaia excitedly.

"Have you gone daft?" retorted Lars, scratching his head. "You realize we're surrounded."

"Gaia makes a good point. The enemy is making constant noise and giving us cover. Their focus is elsewhere, not here. It's perfect," agreed Zanora.

Barrett nodded. "Exactly. Pick up the pace. Keep a sound watch." Despite his words, inner fear added to his desperation. One stray look from a beast or accidental encounter could bring their quest to a sudden, gruesome end.

Poking their heads into the light, the companions checked their surroundings. Unobserved, they scurried from one darkened spot to another, turning here and there while rushing through other areas that took them straight for long distances.

After what seemed like months rather than minutes, an unusual door came into view. Long spikes protruded from its front. Like everything in this realm, the iron handle appeared large and rough. Lars and Unger rushed to it, then slowed to avoid the skewers.

Reaching through the pointed barbs to take the iron piece into his palm, Unger tried working a small dagger blade in the keyhole. But after several turns or twists, the lock remained closed.

"Blasted rust. How do they even open this thing?" He kicked the door from frustration, nearly impaling his shin on a spike.

Barrett freed his wand, then waved the archer to back away.

"What are you doing?" cried Zanora, seizing his forearm. "No more magic. You'll bring the entire Outerworld down on us."

"Hopefully, they will be occupied with all this noise and commotion! Apadora will never know. Now hush, I'm counting!" Barrett studied the drums, which had become rhythmic in their beats—*boom, boom, tap, tap*. As the various drums fell in time with one another, the noise grew deafening. The prince stretched out his arm in wait, still counting in his head. As another round of *tap, tap* sounded he released his magic to destroy the lock, reducing it to pieces as another *boom, boom* echoed around them.

"There," said Zanora, throwing an arm around the archer's shoulders. "Your lock problem is solved."

Shrugging her arm off, he dashed inside. The towering structure held rows of blazing torches hung from wall sconces. Stout pillars upheld the thick, crooked ceiling. More crude furnishings dotted the lower level. There was no cheer here, only wavering orange light bathing several passages and a twisted set of stone stairs before them.

"Which way?" asked Barrett, shooting a pleading look to Nirith. "Where is your sister?"

"There," the sorceress answered, pushing her chin upward. "Near the top."

Unger let out a soft whistle as he peered upward. "That's a long way."

Nell pushed him forward. "Complain later. Move."

Outside, thundering roars and bizarre chanting rose and fell in waves between the pulsating drums sounds. The enemy was working itself into a frenzy. Barrett wondered if the creatures were preparing for war.

Would they soon march forth? Had his worst fear come true? Was the gate now unsealed for Apadora to walk free? Could she release her legions because the companions entered her world? Had Barrett's vanity set the stage to unleash the most wicked sorceress known? Images of her anger sweeping over the lands made him shake and sweat.

When he first considered the quest, rescuing his mentor's daughter felt heroic. He felt he had something to prove to himself, as well as Elimar and Trishar? If successful, he would have done one deed people would forever sing about in tales or legends. But in a blink, the idea felt horribly wrong and conceited. Had he doomed the rest of the world to terrible deaths all for the sake of one? The sick feeling returned with force. He fought down a wretch as he made for the stairs.

Up they went as drumbeats continued. The pulsating sound reached them in waves, yet they did not falter. One floor, then another, and another went by.

Hard and bitter was this place. The cold, ugly rock persisted in draining life and joy from any who drew near, making their steps slow and wavered. Barrett held onto Gaia's hand, but they did not speak. Growing exhaustion and grouchiness gripped him tightly.

Reaching the topmost floor, they crept down a long hall. Nirith stopped at its end, where a heavy stone door with many bolts and hinges barred the way.

"Are there no guards?" questioned Lars. "That seems odd."

"They must have headed for their mistress' rally," whispered Graile. "At least, I hope so."

"Maybe these creatures no longer fear Alesta," offered Gaia. "Her powers are likely weak. And after seeing this place, escape would be awfully difficult even without guards at your door."

"Are you sure this is it?" whispered Barrett. Nirith nodded. Turning to the door, he went to work, sliding the thick iron bolts from their holds. They squeaked in protest as he worked them open. He grimaced at the sounds.

Next, he pointed his staff at another padlock and counted the drums once more. In a flash, he cast his spell. A clank echoed through the passage as the iron unbolted itself to hang free.

The friends went still again, waiting for more angry guards to rush them with murder in their eyes and drawn swords at the ready. They never came.

Barrett's conviction wavered as he braced himself for whatever may lay within. With a deep breath, he lifted the handle and edged open the door to peek inside. Alesta was cowered in the corner as if expecting an attack or more torment from her captors. Only the gods knew what she had endured within these walls. The prince did not want to guess.

He stepped cautiously into the chamber. Even by candlelight, her haggard appearance was clear. Her flowing chestnut hair had grown longer but was matted and dull. Her sparkling blue eyes had lost their shine and her body looked pale and thin. She was an awful image of her previous self.

Hatred over her previous attempts to kill the friends vanished from his mind, leaving only pity. Alesta looked frightened, hungry, and worn as her hollow expression turned his way. A gasp escaped her cracked lips as relief flooded her gaunt face.

What would seeing a familiar face feel like here in her sweltering prison? She is likely used to twisted beasts coming to drag her away or inflict more cruelty here in her tiny room. Perhaps her own mother tortured her with acts of twisted malice.

Slowly, the gaunt sorceress stood and approached with care. Then, in a surprisingly quick move, she threw both arms around his neck and hugged him before stepping back. "Are you real?" she asked, squeezing his shoulders and arms in disbelief.

"Yes. And Nirith is with me. My friends, too," he said, attempting a comforting smile. "We have come for you."

Alesta peered over his shoulder, gasping at the sight of the others gathered round. An awkward moment passed before the sisters rushed to embrace one another. "Sister! How is it you are here? I've missed you and believed you had forgotten me."

"Never. However, I felt certain you were lost to the world of the living, or at the least, were turned evil," said Nirith. "There is a lot to discuss, but the story is long."

"Yes. There is much to talk about," said Alesta, nodding in agreement.

Graile waved them off. "We can do all that later, providing we survive. We need to get out while we can."

"Smoky is right," chimed in Unger. "This place makes my skin crawl."

"Quickly, my ladies. Time is precious," said Barrett with urgency clear in his voice.

Sneaking down the hall, they reached the stairs and tried to hurry a descent but Alesta's weakened state made for slow going.

"Drink this," said Nirith, handing her sister a vial of swirling purple liquid.

Alesta pulled the stopper and swallowed the contents. "Was that Vimlian?"

Nirith nodded several times. "I assumed you would be weak, so I made the concoction to help restore your strength. With the condition you are in, I am unsure how long its effects will last, but it should help."

Reaching the ground floor and sprinting toward the entrance, Barrett burst outside, startling two dragon-like creatures perched on a low wall. They spun toward him and hissed. His staff zipped magical blasts at each to send their shapes drifting away in clouds of smoky vapor.

To his right, the nearby fires were still burning bright. The drums continued their rhythmic sound while the creatures' harsh voices rose in their guttural, chanting speech. The enemy remained fully occupied.

Returning to the shadows, Barrett led the group over an uneven, winding path. Soon, one by one, they were forced to leap across a deep crevice but things turned terribly wrong as Zanora attempted her leap. Her footing failed on slippery stones, throwing her off balance. She teetered on the edge of a precipice for an awful moment, then vanished from sight.

Unger was there in an instant to seize her arm with surprising strength. As the bubbling lava flowed some hundred feet beneath her, their eyes met. Fear flashed over the redhead's face as her legs dangled helplessly over the abyss.

"I won't let go," declared Unger, grimacing as he tried desperately to gain a foothold. Her weight was pulling him toward the edge with no signs of slowing. The archer watched her eyes widen in terror as they gained no traction on the worn rock. The waking nightmare of approaching death seized him tightly.

Suddenly, Graile appeared to reach for Zanora's free arm. Seizing it, he held tight. "Pull together," he said.

The duo scrambled and twisted to haul her to safety before collapsing on the path. To Unger's surprise, Zanora dragged him into a tight embrace, holding him for a long moment. After several long breaths, they gathered themselves and quickly pressed on.

Rejoining their friends, they bolted over the slick slabs, running headlong while retracing their route to the gate. At least, Barrett hoped he was following the same path. To his dismay, he soon understood he was lost as the expansive bridge came into view. He cursed, realizing he had drawn the friends closer to the citadel instead of moving away from it.

From somewhere unseen, an enormous horn blared. They cowered in unison at the sound. Time had hurriedly become even more of a nemesis.

"I do not think that's part of the celebration," said Gaia.

"Our presence has been discovered," said Alesta, increasing her pace. "We have little time now."

"Run!" cried Nirith.

It was too late. A wave of twisted creatures came onward to block their path at both bridge ends. As they advanced, their misshapen feet slapped the cold rock with a horrible, discordant sound. Spinning round, Barrett saw dozens more closing on the flank.

Trapped high above the lava, the prince freed his wand and sent blazing magic into the throng. His attempts did little to turn the tide but it did anger the enemy.

Beside him, arrows flew, and swords swung against any who drew close, yet their efforts were not enough. They were being overrun. Thick fingers reached for them as furious growls filled their ears. Green blood splattered Zanora's tunic as she hewed and hacked all who reached their distorted hands for her. Several severed limbs lay at her feet, twitching and spasming in fits.

"We need to get off this stinking bridge!" cried Lars, morphing into an enormous troll. "I will clear a path. The gate is just ahead. You can make it. Keep my sister safe! Run, you fools!"

Sweeping a tremendous arm from one side to the other, his power sent scores of the enemy plummeting to their deaths. With a leap, he sprang amongst them, flattening several beneath his feet. The way now stood clear as Lars forced the creatures into a hasty retreat—one that did not last long.

From behind, his sister's screams rent the air as he seized handfuls of his attackers, swinging their broken bodies like clubs against the advancing horde. More beasts were swept over the sides.

Squealing and shrieking as Lars progressed, the enemy was filled with anger and desperation. More beasts fell beneath his giant steps while greater numbers toppled into the fiery river. Several of the nastiest beasts braved the troll's onslaught to hack and hew at their attacker's shins and feet.

Unger pierced them from afar as he fired well-placed arrows from his vantage. The wooden shafts leveled many until his quiver lay empty.

Barrett and Nirith rounded to the horde behind them. "The bridge!" he cried. "Destroy the bridge."

Hurling spells high overhead, the magic fell with speed and force to strike the ancient stonework, turning it into fragmented pieces, obliterating the citadel's path. Death shrieks resounded as the creatures tumbled and bounced from the dark stone wall to vanish into the deep chasm.

"Lars!" screamed Nell. "Come back. Hurry."

"Run!" came the slow, booming troll voice as the Dorgon fought on. Blood flowed steadily from his shins. Arrows and spears protruded from his thick, green hide, yet he pushed deeper into their ranks, pounding, stomping, and dashing.

Though scores of beasts had fled from his approach, their numbers were deceiving, for another wave swept over the stony ridge and came anew in a mindless effort to destroy their attacker.

"We have to go," shouted Unger, seizing Nell's hand to pull her toward the gate.

Nell resisted the archer's strength. "I cannot leave him. Lars!" she screamed.

Just then, from within the citadel, a tremendous flame rose, spreading across the sky in a thunderous wave, shaking the ground beneath the friends' feet. Shaping into a fireball, it streaked overhead, bringing an angry voice to ride the air as the battle continued.

"Kill them all! Leave none alive!" it proclaimed.

"Apadora knows we are here. *She* is coming," said Alesta as the ground heaved with magical fury at the sorceress' approach.

Meanwhile, weakened and overrun, Lars could fight no more. He tipped from the stony rim, his arms and legs flailing helplessly for a hold that would not come. Seconds later, after a viscous splash, he vanished beneath the boiling red liquid, sending a surge of flaming lava upward, only to resettle in seconds.

Nell screamed again while Unger continued to drag her along.

Coming to the tunnel they avoided earlier, its interior was still hideously dark, but safety was no longer a concern. Barrett lit his staff tip and never slowed as he plowed ahead.

Scratching, sniffling, and snuffling sounds met his ears, but he dared not glance at any new abominations pursuing them. Knowing if he slowed or stumbled, he would be overrun, only to die horribly within the grim depths of the Outerworld. The thought added energy to his legs which worked harder than ever.

Gaia ran to his right as the others kept good pace at his heels. Graile, silent and vigilant with his grim, painted death face, brought up the rear with Zanora by his side. Daring a peek backward Barrett knew Alesta's concoction was fading by the look on her face. She was slowing down.

Finally, after a seeming eternity, they stepped into the arched tunnel from which they originally entered, turned a quick left, then sprinted forward.

Nirith worked the gate spell as the approaching fireball illuminated the passage behind them. Apadora was drawing ever closer. Shrill cries of her boundless anger preceded her arrival. Fireballs zipped around them, their impacts flinging fragmented rocks around them. Dozens pelted Barrett. He grimaced in agony with each blow.

"Hurry! The gate is open!" cried Unger.

The stones floated outward as the companions rushed beneath them. Only Barrett remained, firing spells at the sorceress as she streaked onward in uncontained fury. Nirith spun to join the assault, firing one orb after another. Soon, Gaia was there too.

"Get ready to close the gate," shouted Barrett over his shoulder. "Focus on Apadora. Fire together, then run. One, two, three, FIRE!"

The trio's magic converged to form a single, perfect orb as it hurtled through the air. Their sorcery struck hard, knocking Apadora off course, hurtling her through the rock ceiling and far from sight. The roof shook and quivered violently before breaking loose to crush many of the minions foolish enough to follow. The tunnel was collapsing.

"Run!" cried Barrett, grabbing Gaia's hand.

Diving for safety, the trio landed on the chamber floor. Nirith scrambled to her feet to hurriedly reseal the gate. As the magic worked, the stones drifted into place and solidified, glowing an emerald green.

Barrett lay on his back panting, waiting for relief that would not come. Gentle sobbing reached his ears and sadness took him as he faced Nell. His worst fear had come to fruition: a friend was dead.

4

Partings

Nell wept into Unger's shoulder. He comforted her the best he could by stroking her hair and holding her hand. Sweaty and tired, Barrett sat up to suck in deep breaths. The chamber air still contained a rancid odor but smelled far better than the Outerworld.

Alesta knelt by his side to take his hand. She kissed it. "You saved me. I am free and forever in your debt."

"Is Apadora's hold on you broken or should we fear you again? Are you Nirith's sister or the evil's one puppet?" he asked bluntly, too exhausted to play word games. His wand lay gripped in his hand.

Her face, which had regained some of its beauty, softened. "You need not fear me. I owe you my life." She lowered her voice, glanced toward Nell, then squeezed his hand. "I am sorry for your loss. Your friend's bravery helped save us all."

"Yes, it did." He stood, helped the sorceress to her feet, then did the same for Zanora and Gaia. "Though saddened with loss, it is time for us to leave this wicked place."

Downtrodden, hungry, and weak, the company filed toward the entrance to the outside world. Passing the steaming pit, Asban was gone. Barrett was too tired to think what that might mean now that the Frigidus spell had worn away. The old wizard escaped into the scorched lands beyond and his destination or survival could forever remain an unanswered question.

"Good riddance. I hope we never cross paths again," mumbled the prince. "If we ever meet again, I may not be as nice."

After leaving the cavern to take brief rest beneath the blue sky, Barrett urged the company forward. Along with Nirith, Alesta, and Gaia, the four healed the land as best they could as they lumbered along. Signs of reemerging life on the barren wastes bolstered their spirits. Tree saplings appeared along the hillsides and path. Bushes sprouted, and flowers bloomed as the devastation of Outerworld faded. As the trail led the friends on a westerly course, Alesta's energy left her, forcing another rest.

Famished, Barrett lowered himself against a boulder, then rummaged through his pack to produce dried meat and fruit. *It will have to do until I can get a proper hot meal.*

Nirith joined him. "We will be leaving you soon. My sister must recover and needs ample rest to do so. We shall return home where I will tend to her care. To her credit, she is young and will heal quickly. However, your destiny lies in another direction. What will you do now?"

His heart skipped a beat. He had envisioned the sisters accompanying him to Westmore, but that dream vanished like smoke.

"I . . . I . . . I have not thought that far ahead," he admitted.

"My goals were to recover Alesta and stay alive. At least we did that much." He took a small rock into his hands and toyed with it. "I feel like a failure. Lars is dead and it's my fault." His gaze remained firmly on the ground. "Still, I must head for Westmore. The city is my birthright and I wish to take it back."

She patted his knee. "My dear, young king, at what cost? One companion has already met his doom. How many more will you sacrifice for a new quest?" Nirith swept an arm toward the friends. "Would you see them all die in battle simply to regain your throne? Your honor? What becomes of your dreams if you fall?" She paused to straighten her sleeves. "If you do this, do so with little violence."

Barrett snickered softly. "It seems to me we just performed a bit of violence back there," he answered, jerking a thumb over his shoulder. "We killed the enemy by the score. How is that different?"

"Killing a twisted force bred only for death and destruction is far different than wiping away your kind simply because they have different views or have done you wrong. You know the purpose of the Bureau was to destroy magic entirely. They will do so at any price. No doubt they must be stopped, but take care how you do so."

"How do you suggest I do it? Talk nicely to them? Perhaps I could invite them to dinner for a chat. We could solve the problem over a meal." His sarcasm was clear and biting.

Nirith chuckled. "If it would work, yes. You are a brilliant young man. I am certain you can devise a way to lessen the bloodshed while working toward the throne."

The prince pondered the problem. "I may be able to come up with something. And it is not about being king. It is they robbed me of everything I hold dear." He thought on that for a moment. "Except for my friends. At least I still have them."

"What more do you need? Riches? A crown? A city? You have a trusted group of companions and my family is like your own. Is there more you desire? Can you not be happy with what you have?"

Barrett scowled. "Scores of civilians would still be under the Bureau's rule. What kind of life would they have if I abandoned them?" Nirith's words quickly took root in his mind. "To be honest, I am confused over it all. Maybe pride and hurt feelings do lead my actions. I'm unsure. All the same, I'll think on what you have said. For now, I need to ask a question." He peeked over both shoulders to ensure his words went unheard by the others. "Can you clear Zanora's mind? Is there a spell to remove her disgust of magic and continual anger?"

Another chuckle. "My, you ask interesting questions." The sorceress paused as Alesta joined them, then spoke on. "So you wish me to change her thinking to align with yours. Or would it be better to have her forget all her life experiences to this point? A fresh start, if you will."

"Yes!" Barrett's face lit with joy for an instant before changing to a frown. "I suppose it sounds awful when you put it like that, right?"

Alesta nodded in agreement. "Yes, it does. Tell me, why would you wish this upon a woman who loves you?"

The prince jumped at the comment, then snorted. "What? She only loves being angry! Nothing or no one else occupies her life. Our time together is over."

"Silly young man, I am weakened, not blind. Zanora carries strong feelings for you, no matter how she tries to hide them. She feels slighted by those around her. Her dislike of magic is merely a way to lash out against the true love she feels abandoned her." She gauged Barrett's baffled expression. "Of course, I speak of you."

"Agreed," chimed Nirith. "Her aura betrays her when she draws near you."

"B . . . b . . . but she tried to kill me," he stammered.

"Yet, here you are," noted Alesta.

Barrett mulled over when Zanora spared his life in an alley-way weeks ago. Then, he recalled images of her hateful eyes glaring at him during their gate room battle days ago.

She seemed different then, just as Graile had transformed with anger within the Outerworld. Was it merely a coincidence? Did she battle for her life in the gate room because a foul spell or dark magic made her do so, like when Alesta was forced to do Apadora's bidding?

"This is completely absurd. Besides, I am with Gaia. She makes me happy and is a better person. She is kind, intelligent, and warm," he replied firmly. His words were meant to comfort his inner self, but instead, they sounded hollow.

"While your observations are true, they do not lessen Zanora's feelings," noted Alesta. "However, I will add that she changes around your Fader friend, as well."

Barrett laughed. "That match is even more unlikely than if she and I got back together. And why has Gaia said nothing? She is wonderful at reading auras, too. She would know if Zanora was lying or hiding something. Explain that bit."

Nirith held up her two fingers. "Two reasons. One, since Zanora previously departed your group in anger, Gaia has not wished to touch upon the sore subject. Two—"

Alesta interrupted to finish her sister's thought as if their minds were linked. "She may be as confused as you are over her sudden change. In any case, Gaia is your love, meaning facing new facts may prove difficult for everyone involved. In truth, a past love maintains feelings, and your current love is unsure what to do with that emotion. How you resolve this issue could define your character."

The prince studied Gaia, then Zanora. "So you can't wipe her mind clean?"

Nirith gave an uncharacteristic huff. "No, we will not. One should not use magic to interfere with such things simply because it would solve your problem. It would open the way for many other issues."

Straightening herself as best she could, Alesta smiled thinly. "Here is where we must leave you. I am weary and have little strength for a long journey."

"We depart with a final warning. There are people known as Trackers spread throughout the lands. They follow magical trails," said Nirith. "They report to the Bureau and can be found in the most obscure places. Use your powers sparingly, if at all. Warn your friends, as well."

"Do you mean we must *walk* to Westmore? No fairy rings or telelocating?" asked Barrett.

"Unfortunately, yes. Until the Bureau is stopped, magic is unsafe in public," confirmed Nirith. "Even now, Trackers are headed this way since I used magical means to arrive here and from our restoration of these lands. The surge of power will bring them this way. This was an error on my part. One which I should have spoken of earlier. But my plan involves making them follow us, not you."

"Why did you do that? That was a huge mistake," said Barrett, raising his voice. "We cannot be caught." Thoughts of being captured and brought before Grimes only to be hung, tortured, or put to death in a variety of horrible ways bit at him. He shuddered, remembering his imprisonment within the horrid Trowken caves. No doubt Grimes would make that ordeal seem fun.

"Once we depart, they will follow *our* magic trail, which is another reason we must leave quickly," said Nirith. "We mean to keep you safe. Of course, our trail will lead to a dead end, but it will divert them long enough for you to be far away from here. We can keep them busy chasing us for some time."

"I wish we could stay together," said Barrett as a tear ran from his eye. Exhaustion was taking its toll on his emotions, lowering them to the point of openly weeping. He hurriedly wiped the water away, hoping no one noticed, then rose to exchange embraces. Alesta held the prince long enough to whisper in his ear.

"I have done many wicked things against my will, yet you believed in me when few would. For your kindness and wisdom I will ensure your name is part of wizard and sorceress lore forevermore," she said, releasing him to smile.

Barrett blushed. "I should not be mentioned with the great wizards. However, I thank you all the same."

Gaia came to take the prince's hand. "What is happening? Sadness surrounds you," asked the witch as the friends gathered round.

Barrett perked up. "See just like I said. She is very observant," he said with a hint of pride.

He explained the sisters' departure plans and the news of the Trackers, leaving out all parts concerning Zanora, her feelings, and possible reasons for her anger. He was bewildered by what to believe. *This is a mess. Nothing is going like I wanted.*

"Can't you stay longer?" pleaded Nell. "We feel safer with you two here."

Unger bit his lip. "There is much news I wish to hear. I have so many questions."

Graile gasped in mock surprise. The whites of his eyes highlighted against the blackened circles. "Imagine that. You, with a lot of questions."

"Oh, shut up. Go paint your eyes or something while the adults talk," snapped the archer.

Zanora made a grunting noise. "Fools! I am surrounded by fools. I thought I had rid myself of them once I ditched Jarn and his bunch."

"There is a way to fix that," said Graile. "If we bother you, why don't you leave?" He inclined his head sharply to the right. "There's the road. You have done your part, you have your pack and weapons, so . . . farewell and good luck."

Zanora made a crude gesture, then turned to Barrett while ignoring the Fader's scrutinizing gaze. "Do you have a plan or should I take charge?"

Unger snickered in the background. "Sure. Let's follow you. There's a plan I would vote for."

Barrett smirked at their bickering. "We head for Westmore. I know several places outside the city we can stay, for I won't willingly endanger anyone else with our presence. We can discuss a plan to oust Grimes and his bunch as we go."

"The time has come for us to aid your cause. We will ensure the Trackers turn north to follow our magic," said Alesta, taking her sister's hand. "Make good your escape during their search. Farewell, friends. We will meet again before the end."

Amidst a chorus of waves and tears, the sorceresses cast their spell and vanished.

"I detest when people say, 'before the end.' It sounds so final," grumbled Unger. "Those are my least favorite words."

The bottom fell from Barrett's heart. He was deflated. Empty. Days ago, though he never spoke of it, he envisioned sweeping into Westmore with Elimar, Trishar, and even Alesta to reclaim the throne. Those images were satisfying, even happy. They helped drive him forward.

But that daydream suddenly felt impossible. Although their views on his problems stung his pride, the sisters were right to question his reasoning, he thought. *How far will I go to regain the throne? What if another friend dies? What if I am killed?*

Focusing on Nell as remorse took him, he stared at her cheeks—still reddened from crying. Had his choices led to her brother's death? While no one forced the twins to step into the Outerworld, no one would have thought less of them if they declined.

Still, Lars was gone. Only a painful memory remained now. Barrett felt even worse as his mind filled with endless questions.

Gaia's warm lips pressing against his cheek distracted him. "We should go," she noted. "With these Trackers roaming around, I wish to find shelter before nightfall."

Unger overheard and moved closer. "Why does it feel like we are always being hunted?"

Graile raised his hood, putting the usual deep shadows over his face. "Because we are. Especially since Grimes and the Bureau banned magic."

"I will explain what I know about the Trackers as we go. But my pressing thought is to remove Grimes from my city. The more I think on it, the more I would not mind knowing where Asban made off too, either," said Barrett. "Curse them both for entering our lives." He waved a hand toward the road. "Like Gaia said, it'll be dark soon and I wish to be safe for the night." Placing a hand on Unger's back, he guided him aside. "Can Nell travel? Will walking take her mind from her brother for a bit?"

Unger shrugged. "Maybe. Either way, I'll stay with her. You mind Zanora for me."

"You saved her life. I doubt she will wish you harm after that bit." Barrett's voice went soft. "Tell me the truth. Did you consider letting her fall? I know you two are not best friends."

Shaking his head, Unger chuckled. "Only for a moment. Then, when I saw true fear on her face I thought she deserved another chance, no matter what's happened in our past. And for the record, I do not hate her. I just don't care to be around her." He leaned in. "You know, you saved her, too. Why did you do it? Did you consider letting her die?"

The prince's face blanked. "You know me well enough to understand I would never let a friend die, no matter how much they irritate me." He threw his arm round the archer's shoulder. "Saving her like that was a big decision for you. Well done."

"I just hope she doesn't prove my choice wrong," replied the archer tentatively.

5

Trackers

Light grew as they went. The veil of Apadora's evil was falling away at last. Overhead, the sky spread blue and bright, yet Barrett could not help but think of the sorceress and many dark, recurring questions. Making matters even worse, he felt no cheer in his heart. He tried desperately to maintain the false appearance for his friends' sake to keep their hopes high.

Cresting a tall hill, they came to a sweeping, treed valley. Evil had not scarred this place. Beauty abounded. The path dipped into a low, green dale, which spread wide, leading to towering mountains climbing high before them. Taking a long inhale, the prince's cares seemed to vanish as he reveled in nature's beauty.

Zanora distanced herself some twenty paces in the lead. She walked alone. Barrett followed. Behind him came Unger and Nell.

Farther back were Gaia and Graile. The prince focused on the redhead's back and suppressed a sigh as the sorceress' words ran through his mind.

Though he held every intention of avoiding his former girlfriend he knew they ought to chat. Or he should at least try. He sprinted to catch up. They did not speak at first, but Barrett wished to move his thoughts away from trouble.

"I'm surprised you haven't told me to go away. I will leave you alone if you wish."

The redhead studied him, then made a soured face. "Is there a point to this?"

"Actually, yes. I need to say something," he said, scanning ahead for movement. "I'm sorry for everything, including what happened between us. I never meant to hurt you."

Zanora shrugged and turned away, seeming unaffected by his confession. "First, it's too late for apologies. Your words are empty. Second, you and I were only a dream. It would have never worked. Third, it's too bad since I was adjusting to the idea of becoming queen." She chuckled softly while fiddling with her necklace as if gathering thoughts. "Do you love her?" she blurted.

The subject had to come up sooner or later. Whether she was using it to gain information or set a bizarre trap remained to be seen. "Yes, I do. She's a brilliant person and I have strong feelings for her."

The redhead remained stoic. She raised a questioning shoulder. "More than you felt for me?"

"No," he replied quickly. "The same, but for different reasons. She and I have a lot in common. And she loves magic as much as I do. She's fascinating." He shrugged, trying to act casual while hoping he had not said the wrong thing. "Sorry."

"No need to be sorry as long as you are happy. Besides, you're not my style anymore. I want a warrior by my side."

Barrett pretended not to be offended, but her words wounded his ego. "That's not fair! We have faced dragons, Trowkens, and death together. What more do you want?" Frustration slapped him like a physical blow, and he inclined his head rearward without realizing it. "Graile is available. Ask him out. You two are perfect for one another."

"Right," she snipped. "Everyone here wants me to disappear or fall dead. Now you say I should date the Fader. You're more mental than I thought."

Back at the group, Gaia edged closer to Graile. "What do you think they are talking about?" she asked.

Graile eyed the pair closely. "Who knows. Hopefully, is about her leaving the company."

"You have no faith in her, do you?" she questioned. "Do you hate her?"

The Fader shook his head. "No, I do not, on either count. Besides, I never hate anyone. It is a wasted emotion. Aside from her being constantly irritating and angry, I cannot shake the feeling she is hiding something. She acts differently around me, but I cannot say why."

"I have noticed a change in her aura lately but have no idea what is causing it. Until now, I have kept it to myself. I will watch her a little closer."

"Maybe it has something to do with the Bureau," he offered. "Perhaps I make her uncomfortable. It's odd." He peered ahead. "I bet she learned some disturbing tidbits while working with Grimes and Jarn. Everyone has secrets and she probably knows a lot of them. Sadly, keeping secrets weighs you down."

Wispy clouds rolled by to hide the sun, giving a sudden rush of cool air to chill Barrett. To his delight, an unexpected raven's call broke the air. The prince dashed off into a grassy field to start shouting while waving his arms wildly. "Samaren! We are here! Here, Mother!"

"There you are," came the voice in his head. Her voice grew as she swooped lower. "Stop that blasted shouting. I am more than capable of seeing you. There are men coming. You should hide. They do not look friendly."

Barrett spun around to face the company. "Quickly, find cover. Men approach," he announced.

"So what," said Unger, scanning the tree line. "They could live here. Likely farmers or woodsmen, I would guess. Why the panic?"

"Or Trackers. I'm betting they know our faces, too. I'm certain Grimes still has a price on our heads. Our pictures are on wanted posters," said Nell. "Hide, now."

The companions bolted toward thick tree shadow, spoiling Samaren's return as Barrett's thoughts ran rampant. *Why didn't Elimar accompany Mother? Nirith mentioned he was far away, but he should be done by now. Perhaps Trackers found him, or worse, captured him.* Thoughts of performing another rescue forced a heavy sigh from his lips.

To their luck, suitable shelter soon came into view. They hastened inside the spacious opening, which was wider and deeper than Barrett expected. He ran his hands over the smooth, polished walls, thinking it would serve nicely as a home if it held windows or doors.

His face crunched as he recalled a frightening story he read during his youth where weary travelers took rest in a cave only to have the floor open to drop them into a horrible lair of twisted beasts. To ease his mind, he stomped here and there for hidden cracks and crevices. His friends watched his antics in shock and, in Zanora's case, disgust.

"I knew all along magic was rotting your brain. Have you finally gone insane? *What* are you doing?" asked the redhead, continuing to watch the prince tramp on the stone floor.

"Nothing." He scowled at being caught. "Just making sure the floor is solid."

"Of course, it is solid! It is rock, you fool," she retorted.

Throwing a finger to his lips to silence her, he rushed forward to squat and peek from the entrance. There, between the towering trees lining the roadway, several men slowly rode past. Their matching garb bore the Bureau's symbol.

"Trackers?" questioned Gaia in a whisper, squinting for a better view.

"I think so, yes. In fact, I would bet Zanora's life on it," said Unger, glancing sideways at the redhead.

"You are such an ass," she replied, punching his arm with force.

Unger's mouth opened to shout in pain, but her hand quickly covered it.

"Not one sound, jester. Not one," she warned. "If you draw their attention, you'll be dead before they reach us. Understand?"

Unger nodded in compliance, then let his eyes wander downward. She followed his gaze to a knife blade poised inches from her heart. She removed her hand, her lips parting.

"Before you think of threatening me again, remember I have tricks of my own," he said.

Zanora grinned broadly and slapped a hand on his back. "Smart move. I'll give you that one. You are full of surprises. Keep it up and you may grow on me."

"Why must you two talk constantly?" grumbled Graile. Turning to vapor, he floated forward to solidify next to the prince. "I will return. Keep watch, in case." Changing again, he drifted to the tree line, darting between the trunks and boulders like a sentient thundercloud. He solidified near the road to catch the travelers' words.

The friends spent several agonizing minutes awaiting his return.

Graile floated into the cave and reformed by the prince.

"That was risky!" he grumbled.

"I thought it was magnificent," admitted the redhead. "You certainly come in handy at times. I never get tired of you doing that."

The prince huffed, wondering why her pleasant comments irritated him. "Were the Trackers searching for us or simply local men riding to town?"

Graile blinked slowly—his eyes going black as they closed. "They were clearly Trackers. Unfortunately, they barely spoke. Though I did hear something about a wizard in Westmore."

Barrett's stomach sank. Had Graile heard the conversation wrong? "A wizard? That must be nonsense. Magic isn't allowed there any longer."

"Too bad you didn't catch more," said Nell. "It would have been helpful."

"Maybe it's Elimar," suggested Gaia, clapping lightly and sounding hopeful. "Perhaps he's been spotted in the city."

"We certainly could use him." Barrett's mind danced with suspicion. Had the wizard ignored the friends' monumental cause, choosing to enter the city first while shunning them altogether? Where exactly did the companions sit on the old man's priority list? "Maybe he's finally here to help." His doubting tone revealed his search for answers.

"Either way, the Trackers have no idea we are here. I bet they will focus on the nearest villages and towns in their search. If we can avoid them, we may reach the city unnoticed," said Nell.

Unger peered outside, then slunk into the forest to return with an armload of dry wood and kindling. "I'm starving. Some warm food would be amazing." He began stacking the wood in a triangular shape before placing dry pine needles at its base, then struck flint and steel together to start a hearty blaze.

Samaren swooped into the cave to land on Barrett's shoulder. "Greetings, my son. Those men are gone. I watched closely until they moved on. I saw Graile watching, as well."

"Love to you, Mother. It is good to see you again. What news? Where is Elimar?" he asked. "Or Trishar, for that matter?"

"Elimar is still delayed. Trishar sends blessings and will try to arrive soon," she replied. "Did you succeed in freeing Alesta? What of Apadora?"

"Thankfully, Nirith arrived to lend aid, but the sisters have already left us. We are on our own during our return to Westmore," he answered. "Who is this wizard the Trackers spoke of? Any ideas?"

Samaren tilted her head to one side and cawed. "I cannot say. I have seen no proof of a magic man within the city, only silly rumors."

Barrett settled against the floor near the fire, recounting their events since her departure. The raven listened intently. Their talk went late into the night until the moon rode high above.

The night proved awful. Dreams haunted Barrett at every turn. Images of Grimes torturing or killing magic users seemed real. The skinny man peered at the prince and laughed his awful, shrill sound.

Town criers moved through the city shouting the Bureau's latest proclamations. Lengthy parchments and fliers, all containing a list of punishable offenses, were pasted on every street corner. There was to be no magic, secret meetings, disruptions against the Bureau, or hiding magical users. All violations were considered crimes with imprisonment or death as the sentence.

To further their most recent campaign of fear, Agents and Trackers rounded up Mundanes to extract information concerning their families, acquaintances, or magical neighbors. Those suspected of being collaborators were locked in dungeons or hung in the courtyards, their bodies left to rot, swaying in the breeze as gruesome warnings to those unwilling to betray the magic users.

Morning came and Barrett was huddled beneath a small blanket resting his head on his rucksack. The stone floor had been his mattress. With a grimace, he stretched, his bones sore from sleeping on the cold rock. He sat in a sweat, relieved to see the friends still asleep, save for Zanora. Even Samaren snoozed atop a boulder.

Chilled and exhausted, he slipped his boots on and ran to fetch more firewood. After stoking the fire, he rubbed his palms together before turning them toward the flames. The redhead came to his side to mimic his actions.

"Rough night?" she asked as the orange glow flickered in her eyes. "You were mumbling and tossing in your sleep."

Barrett hesitated. An inner debate raged as to what degree of honesty he should admit. Should he confess his genuine fears? Were the visions premonitions of what would come should he not retake the throne? Or was he seeing present-day images? Had Westmore become a pit of depravity and death? Surely, if that were the case, Samaren would have announced it. She had not, so he held hope.

"I saw . . ." The sentence trailed away, lost in fleeting thoughts before he decided to shoulder the weight of his fears alone no longer. "I'm not sure what I saw. Grimes was mocking me as the Bureau fools made a mess of things. They were hurting innocent people. I have to stop them. Even Mundanes are being abused so the Bureau can get at those with magic."

After rubbing her eyes, Gaia came to sit by his side. She snuggled against him. Self-consciousness washed over the prince as the redhead watched their every move. To his surprise, the witch greeted Zanora happily. They were pleasant to one another.

"How can you stop them? You have no army. Together, we are not strong enough to make a change." Zanora's face hardened. "I do want to see Grimes again, though."

For once, her tone was not patronizing or harsh. There seemed to be genuine concern in her voice. Oddly, the single word that struck Barrett was 'we.' It gave rise to a spark of hope, which grew into a flame.

Like in the Outerworld, having an extra sword on their side could help greatly, but would the tradeoff be worth it? Aside from the bad attitude and constant friction she brought, was it wise to tolerate someone who tried to kill them all mere months ago? "Does that mean you are coming with us?" he asked. "Will you help?"

"Yes. Please help us. Your insight into the Bureau could be valuable," said Gaia. "You may know things we would only guess at. I thought of asking Nell since she once worked there, but your time with them is more recent."

"So you know, if you mean to kill Grimes, it may be harder than you think." Zanora edged closer to the dancing flames and placed more wood in its center. "Getting close will be difficult. The little worm never goes anywhere without a bodyguard or two."

Barrett waved her off. "I can use the tunnels to get into the castle. No one knows them better than I do." He tapped his temple. "I thought on this exact subject last night. But I wish to avoid bloodshed, if possible. I told Nirith and Alesta I would consider a nonviolent approach. And after what I saw in my dream I want to uphold the concept. So Grimes is safe for now."

Zanora laughed and pointed a stiff finger at him. "I knew it. You *are* turning soft. The next village we come to, we'll buy some parchment and supplies so you can write Grimes a nasty letter. That should do the trick. Harsh words will make him pack up and leave straightaway."

"You're not funny," he retorted, dejected at having his admission battered so easily. *So much for her niceness.*

"Do you know anything of this wizard Graile mentioned? Any ideas?" questioned Gaia, retrieving a brush from her pack to run it through her long hair.

Zanora knit her brows in thought and tapped a finger against her chin. "Hummm. Nothing. Whoever they spoke of must have come along recently. Maybe it's that goof, Elimar."

"I considered that, but it can't be him. He would find us first, I think," said the prince, hoping his idea was true.

Unger and Graile moved to the fire to cook what little breakfast they could. Samaren cawed to greet the greying morning, then flew to Barrett's knee. Gaia stroked her feathers and wished her a good morning. Nell remained asleep.

"Zanora, you mentioned killing Grimes. Why do you assume

violence is an answer to everything? It's one point we will never agree on," said Gaia. "But in this case you may be right. I see no way of removing Grimes or Carick without being mean."

"Hold on. There must be other ways but what could we do against them?" said Unger, yawning and stretching his arms toward the high ceiling.

"Blackmail works, but we have nothing of value to hold against him. It would be a simple way to keep your word to Nirith. There would be no bloodshed," said Samaren.

The prince perked up as his heart pounded. "Yes!"

"I loathe when he does that," said Zanora, slapping her knee with her palm. "You're always talking to that blasted bird. Care to share?"

Barrett conveyed the raven's words, then continued. "Think of it! No death or destruction, and we could give them a choice to leave or be exposed."

Bleary-eyed, Nell shuffled to Unger's side, rubbing her sleepy face before settling against his warmth. "Who are we exposing?" The archer wrapped his arm around her shoulders and pulled her close.

"Grimes and the Bureau," said Graile. "Forget that for now. How are you feeling?"

At first the Shifter appeared impassive, but seconds later a lone tear rolled down her cheek. Her bottom lip quivered. "I want my brother back," she choked out as Unger tenderly patted her back.

"We are *so* sorry for your loss," said Gaia. "I know nothing we can say will make it better. Just know we liked Lars and will miss him, too."

Moods turned uncomfortable as the friends chimed in their sympathies. Barrett offered his own, then fell silent, wrapped in memories. After losing his father, he understood mere words would not ease the girl's grief. Only time and understanding would help. Though her pain would never go away entirely, it would lessen to where she could function again without constantly verging on tears. He knew that part too well.

Trishar had given him that same advice and only now did he understand how right she had been. Though the king's death remained fresh in his mind it was not as painful as before. Still, if he thought on it long enough and lowered his emotional guard, he would have a hearty cry. For now, he no longer wished to talk about death. He had already seen enough in both dreams and real life.

"Zanora, you must know something we can use to hurt Grimes or the Bureau itself," he said, turning back to the redhead. "You worked for them."

"Yes, I did, but I have nothing to offer." She mindlessly picked a bit of mud from her boots.

"Excuse me, but that was a lie," blurted the witch.

The redhead snapped her head up. "Are you calling me a liar?" Her glaring eyes met Gaia.

The witch smiled. "I'm saying your aura fluttered when you answered. Your colors changed. There is something you're not telling us, or you're not being totally honest."

"I love this girl," added Samaren. "She is a perfect fit for you. She will make a glorious queen."

"Not now, Mother," whispered Barrett. Edging closer to Zanora, he took her hand, again surprised she did not pull away. "I beg you. Help us stop this madness."

Zanora slid away to braid her hair. "I will tell a story Jarn shared one night." She paused as Graile handed her hot food. After thanking him with a smile and a wink, she took a quick bite and continued. "Did you ever wonder how Grimes came to power so quickly? It's because he murdered his predecessor."

"Why the greasy little fool," said Graile. "I didn't think he had it in him."

"How did he do it? Poison? Ambush? Assassin?" inquired Unger, perking up as the conversation turned more interesting.

Zanora met his stare to raise an open palm in the air. "I'm not sure, but there's more. Rumors say he forced the villagers of Mordoria out of their homes. He wanted their land to build his ego-sized castle and claim lordship over all around him."

"That sounds cruel. How did he force them out? What happened?" questioned Gaia, her guileless ways showing through her words.

"What do you *think* happened?" The redhead's sarcasm was sharp. "He gave them a chance to clear out. Any who refused were slaughtered."

Gaia covered her mouth to try and trap in a gasp. She failed. "Absolutely awful!"

"Oh, great job!" said Unger. "You killed the only one who could tell us more—Jarn."

"Shut it! I told you the little vermin tried to kill me. I defended myself but left him alive. Whatever his men did as I searched for the gate room was their doings, not mine," the redhead countered. "I had nothing to do with it. Besides, he was an idiot. He knew nothing of value."

"Defended yourself by stringing him over a steaming pit to die a slow, painful death," added Graile. "I'm convinced you're innocent."

Zanora's face turned to a hurt look as her voice softened. "For the last time, I did not hurt him. You, of all people, should believe me. I counted on your support."

The Fader looked puzzled by the exchange and fell silent. However, Barrett understood. The redhead had performed the same behavior when they dated. Normally, she would shrug off the doubting words of others or blurt out some smart comment to hide behind. But if someone she held affection for chastised her it had profound results. *Maybe Nirith and Alesta are right.* His heart tightened with a painful thump. If that was the case, were they right about the redhead still harboring feelings for him?

"She makes a valid point," said Gaia, coming to Zanora's defense. "We were not there and should not judge."

"Come on," said Nell with dripping scorn as she recalled Jarn's body with its peeling skin as it hung over the steaming pit. "It's not as if Jarn jumped on that rack by himself. Are you saying you didn't order the deed done or know what would happen?"

Zanora spun the Shifter's way. "That's funny coming from you, Nell. After all, both you and Lars worked with Jarn, right? Or have the rest of you forgotten that part?"

The Shifter drew a quick breath. "Everyone knows my brother and I worked there for a time. But we were spying for a good cause. And Jarn didn't die while we were around."

"Enough," said Barrett, his voice deepening. "What happened is over. True enough, we were not there, and no one here can point a finger without proof. Concentrate on bringing the Bureau down, not squabbling over what cannot be changed."

"So, what is your plan?" asked Unger, chewing on a thick piece of jerky. He tossed some to Barrett.

The prince nodded thanks, then parroted the archer's actions. "We need more information," he said, pausing his chewing to speak. "I'm unsure who to trust, which makes news even more difficult to discover."

"Oooo, news! That gives me an idea," said the witch, excitement spreading over her face.

"Do tell," said Graile.

6

Radiant Randolph Rollie

Gaia presented her solid plan. "Who better to discover news than a reporter? We should contact Randolph Rollie. Unless things have changed, he has no love for the Bureau. And he has resources we do not. Surely, he could discover some useful information."

"What? You mean Radiant Randy, the reporter! *That's* your plan?" questioned Unger, knocking his palm against his temple. "He's a fool. *The Oracle* is a ridiculous paper. Besides, it's not like he is Barrett's biggest supporter."

"Revealing Grimes' alleged crimes and those of the Bureau may be the only hope of having Westmore return to its rightful owner: me. This is actually a marvelous idea. Who knows what he may be able to dig up," said Barrett.

"Or he may refuse to speak to us at all," said Graile, carving loose a piece of apple with a dagger. "He didn't treat you kindly when you were preparing to take the throne. What if he is on their side and turns you in?"

"I can handle him," said the prince. "I'll give him the same as I gave Asban. That will hold him for a bit until I decide what to do with him."

Samaren squawked and flapped her wings. "Your girlfriend is wiser than all of you. Before the Bureau took full control, Rollie wrote several articles condemning their takeover of Westmore. You would be smart to use him as a resource. Plus, there are things about him you do not know. Secrets."

Barrett lifted a questioning eyebrow, then repeated his mother's words. "Though I value mother's opinion, I'm not a fan of him or his newspaper. It's true he has criticized me from the beginning. Still, Gaia and mother make sense. He seems to find ways to learn the truth about current events."

"Maybe Gaia wants to use Radiant Randy because she has a crush on him," said Zanora with a gratified smirk. She puckered her lips to make a kissing motion, then gave a noisy swoon.

"Ridiculous! *And* untrue," replied the witch. "I admit he's rather handsome in images, but he could be uglier than a mud fence in person. By the way, stop calling him Radiant. It's childish."

"Whatever we call him, if he is willing to help, we should use him. Our options are limited. It's not like we have a long list of allies." Graile held a finger up as another thought took him. "And for the record, Gaia's feelings have nothing to do with it."

"Agreed," said Nell. "I'm all for the idea."

Unger's nostrils flared. "I still think he's strange." His jaw squared from aggravation. "And I will never forgive the article he wrote bashing Barrett about taking the throne at a young age."

"Does anyone have parchment?" asked Barrett, rummaging through his rucksack. "I have an idea."

Nell grabbed her pack and searched the contents. "I have a diary. You can use a blank page." She tore one free and handed it over. "But I have no ink or quill."

"And you can't use magic," reminded Unger, waving his hand round like casting a spell.

Barrett scowled. "We have no choice. Besides, Nirith said to use it sparingly. It should only take a few seconds." He pulled his wand from the depths of his cloak, aiming at the blank sheet. "Scribious Verba." The small sheet glowed orange for an instant as the prince cleared his throat.

As he spoke, the words emblazoned themselves upon the page. The note asked Randolph to meet the friends at dusk in four days' time at the Ashton festival grounds. Barrett thought the secluded spot would be perfect concealment. Finished, he tore a small piece of cloth from the frayed edge of his tunic to tie the note to Samaren's leg.

"I know you have flown a long way and are weary, but can you do this task since I dare not use more magic to make contact?" he asked.

"If it will help keep you safe and regain your rightful place on the throne, I will do whatever it takes," she answered. "We shall meet again soon." After several loving strokes from his hand, she winged from the cave to disappear into the cloudless sky.

"The road awaits," said Unger, hoisting his pack onto his shoulders. "I have to admit it will be tough being so close to home and unable to see my family. We haven't spoken in a long time."

Gaia displayed an uncharacteristic frown. "I miss my folks, too. I hope they have already left the city or the Bureau has left them alone if they stayed behind."

"You know we can't just waltz into Westmore and visit people . . . including your parents. The Bureau would find us," said Zanora. "It's too dangerous."

Her words came as a cold blow of truth. Inwardly, the friends knew their wishes would never come to pass while they remained fugitives. Still, the reality was painful to hear. Her candor suffocated their dreams in seconds.

Grimly, they placed cloaks round their shoulders, then hoisted packs up high to cinch them tight. Barrett snuffed out the fire, then took Gaia's hand.

"On the bright side, I have no powers, so Trackers won't care about me. I may be able to slip into the city and deliver messages to your folks. But I advise against sending notes. If your folks are caught communicating with you, they will be killed." Zanora swished her arm around with an extended finger like a wand. "Nirith did warn you about using magic."

"Excuse me," retorted Barrett with a mocking tone. "I am well aware of what Nirith said. However, certain times need drastic measures. I did what needed doing."

"In your opinion!" she argued as they stepped into the open field. "Before you waved your wand around, you didn't even bother to ask if we minded having danger drawn to us. Are you purposely trying to bring Trackers here? What am I supposed to think?"

"Maybe you should let it rest," said Graile. "Your presence is still tense enough. Let's not make it worse. On the bright side, we haven't killed you yet, right?"

"Just so you know, I never wanted you dead," said the prince. "I just wanted the old Zanora back again. Not this angry version."

Nell glanced around as the path dipped into the trees. "Forget all that and focus. These woods are known to hold goblins. I hate those crooked, nasty little beasts. They will attack simply because we look tasty."

Unger took her hand and laughed. "There hasn't been a goblin sighting in an age. They moved from here long ago. Or so the stories go. Who really knows? Whatever made you think of them?"

"This is the type of forest they enjoy. Thick, dark, and seldom traveled. It makes me nervous, to be honest. They're ugly little pieces of work." She squeezed his hand. "I'm sorry for bringing it up. I guess I'm occupying my mind and trying not to think of Lars."

Walking was easy. Morning mist had lifted and the sky hung blue and clear. Birds sang cheery songs and wildlife grazed openly, though they cast cautious glances as the friends passed. Barrett kept his senses alert for goblins while silently cursing Nell for putting the thought in his head. *As if I didn't have enough to worry about.*

After a long distance passed behind them, the road slowly climbed to a green hilltop where the trees thickened. Barrett's spirit remained high. Going on, they walked until reaching the shoulder of another hill. To their right, a small stream trickled down from high above.

The soothing sound relaxed him as he wholly forgot about scary goblins, killing Grimes, or where Asban had gone. Despite trying not to care about the greasy wizard, his mind refocused on him. *If he is the wizard in Westmore, then at least I'll have a chance to stop him for good.* His fists clenched before he remembered Nirith's words.

On the second day, the companions hid as several groups of goblins appeared. Barrett peeked from behind the leafy cover to see their twisted, ugly shapes meander past. Their dark green skin blended perfectly with the forest colors. They lumbered along with a surprising stealth to their steps. He shuddered at their likeness to Trowkens.

Raspy voices croaked from their throats as they uttered their gruff language. Bulging eyes were set close together on their large, hairless heads. On their hips were dark, short swords with curved blades. Several carried shields on their backs or arms. Two pairs carried bows with many arrows. Misshapen noses made odd snorting sounds as they sniffed the air.

Barrett wondered if they had trouble breathing or were communicating in some strange fashion. Thankfully, like the Trackers had done, the creatures passed by unaware of their observers, but not before several left the trail to sniff and inspect the bushes and shrubs as if smelling food or finding some strange new scent.

Despite Barrett's hand tingling with a spell, he patiently waited, knowing he could not fight them all. The friends were heavily outnumbered. To his relief, the tense moments passed quickly as the hideous beasts rejoined the others and then vanished down the long trail.

"I was wrong. I guess the tales were true," admitted Unger. "I thought goblins were gone from these lands. Now I can say I have seen them. They are gnarled little beasties, aren't they?"

"Indeed they are. Also, do not worry yourself. You're a man, so I expect you to be closed-minded." Nell laughed, then kissed his cheek. "I still think you're wonderful, though."

"Hey!" cried Barrett. "That's unfair. Not all men are like him."

"Right. You're even worse," said Gaia, bumping him with her shoulder. "And he's polite enough to apologize when he's wrong."

Barrett made a disgusting sound in reply.

The next few days passed quickly, but not without more tense occasions and stealthy hiding. Again, the friends hid from strangers and more meandering bands of Goblins. Oddly, during these moments, Barrett began to worry about food. They were running low and had to find a meal or they would be in more trouble than evading goblins.

Trackers were seen as well, making the friends' journey even slower. They stood out from ordinary travelers since the Bureau symbol was upon their tunics or cloaks as they patrolled the land searching for residual magic. The insignia brought fear to those who resisted and comfort those who followed their twisted beliefs. The design was a red rectangular banner holding a white circle in its center, inside which lay a long black sword. Though it did not strike dread into the hearts of those who saw it, its meaning was clear—Trackers were merely robed bullies in positions of authority.

One small band stopped to dismount and study the ground. Their methods were like Goblins, though Barrett doubted their noses could detect scent as well as the ambling green creatures.

On the third day, a ragtag band of greedy bounty hunters pursued them. To their stalkers' misfortune, they would never be seen again as they foolishly attempted an ambush. Not one hunter survived to tell the tale. The friends dragged the dead bodies into the woods and left them.

"Scavengers have to eat too," said Zanora as they struck the road again.

"I agree this time." Barrett held heavy disdain for their kind, though he resigned himself to evading or fighting more of the Bureau's mercenaries as the companions neared the city. After all, a high price still rested on their heads.

By early afternoon on the fourth day, they struck the well-traveled, tree-lined road to Ashton. Barrett sensed the friends' tension swell. Like him, they were homesick—not to mention hungry and tired.

Unger could barely keep himself from bypassing the meeting and heading straight for Westmore. Beside him, Gaia fidgeted nervously with her wand as she stared northward toward home.

Even the prince longed for the comfort of his city. However, their group kept to the seclusion of the woods, following deer trails, knowing the closer they drew to home, the better their chances of being recognized.

Walking steadily, the trees soon receded on either side of the road as the land opened. Vast green meadows spread before them. Barrett halted on the forest's edge to scan for the reporter.

Like answering an unheard summons, a rider reined his horse from the road toward the field's edge. Barrett studied him closely, shocked at his appearance. Randolph Rollie was nothing like he had envisioned. He pictured a bitter, worn old man who enjoyed humiliating people through printed words. In reality, Rollie cut a dashing figure. He bore broad shoulders, thick, wavy brown hair, and dressed fashionably. A squared jaw gave him a rugged appearance. His persona was like one Elimar would choose when performing his magical transformations.

Jealousy edged into the prince's heart, knowing Gaia would be drawn to the newcomer. He could not help it.

"Are you feeling well?" came the witch's whisper in his ear. "Your aura—"

"I know! I know! It's dark, right?" interrupted Barrett, his voice snappy and blaring firmer than intended.

"Yes, it is. Is there something wrong?" she asked, lightly running her fingers down his back.

"No. Everything is fine," he bristled before his conscience gnawed at him. The truth spilled out. "Alright! I'm jealous. I see why you think he's attractive and I guess it bothers me. It's childish, I know. Especially since I have never seen him before."

Gaia giggled. "He's twice my age. Plus, there's no need to worry. I already have the man I want to share life with."

"Awww, isn't that special," quipped Zanora as she pushed past to stride into the open. "Now, if you're done playing cutesy, can we go meet the man?" She gave a shrill whistle and waved an arm to signal the rider.

"By the gods, I could choke her sometimes!" cried Unger after running a hand over his face.

"You don't have a mean bone in your body," said Nell, kissing the archer's lips. "Stop that silly talk."

"Unger's right. Her impulsiveness puts us in danger too often," said Graile. "She's going to get us captured or killed."

Randolph waved and loped his sleek black mare toward them, smiling as he drew nearer. After reigning to a halt, he swung from the saddle with a quick motion, then turned her loose to graze on the lush forest grass.

After bowing to Barrett, he extended a hand. "Sire, it is a pleasure to meet you finally."

Barrett ignored it as frustration surfaced. "Pleasure, you say? Nonsense! You have printed countless articles questioning whether I should be king and now you want to be friends. Are you daft?"

"Apparently, he has forgotten the plan of using Rollie to help us," mumbled Unger.

The others nodded agreement, but Randolph never lost his smile as he withdrew his hand.

"Right you are," he responded. "For the record, I have always been on your side. *The Oracle* forced me to write those articles. If I had refused, they would have fired me long ago. Since I am a bit of a celebrity, they use my name on many things to sell copies. Also, if I had not written them, someone else would have. I meant no disrespect, Sire." His eyes were keen and bright with no deception in them. Barrett hesitated, unsure of himself. Feelings of distrust were softened by the reporter's honest demeanor.

Unger whispered in Barrett's ear. "I admit he does make sense."

"His aura is pure. What he says is the truth. Or at least his version of it," said Gaia. Despite her voice coming light and clear, her face was thoughtful, as if reminding the prince of the seriousness of their situation.

Barrett huffed, then extended a hand. Rollie smiled and took it happily, shaking firmly.

"Excellent. Now, let's get to it. There is a lot to discuss," said Graile, sweeping his arm to the side. "Come join us and hear the real story."

Randolph perked up at hearing the friends' difficulties and triumphs. Retrieving a silver, oval-shaped object from his saddlebags, he settled onto the forest floor, placed the gadget before him, and nodded. "I am ready whenever you are."

"What is that thing?" asked Nell, craning her neck for a better view.

"Have you never seen a Commenteria before? You will love it. The principle is like a Chatterer, only in a portable version. It takes down voices and images. Very ingenious, if I say so. That is only one small reason I support magical folks. Their inventions are top-notch," said Randolph, waving a hand over top the device. "Obceptium," he said, bringing the sphere to life to emit a radiant orange glow.

"Wait a blasted minute! Hold it right there!" cried Barrett, stiffening. "You have magic?"

Randolph shrugged as his face flushed. "Correct!" He placed a finger to his lips. "I do not make it known. It is yet another reason I wish for the rightful king to recover his throne and bring magic back into the open. My job would be easier." He straightened his clothes and smiled on. "Since your note did not say much, how may I help?"

Settled in comfortable spots on the forest floor, the companions relayed their troubles, joys, failures, successes, and more as the day's remainder passed slowly. The tale began on the day of the annual Festival of Witches, in which their lives changed forever. Once the afternoon faded to evening, the story reached the present.

"Can you help us?" asked Gaia. "The information we need is vital to our cause."

Randolph tapped his chin in thought. "I have heard the story you speak of and have already investigated the rumors of Grimes being involved in murder. Unfortunately, I returned with little proof. However, once I dug deeper, I discovered more. Soon after, I wrote a piece about the horrendous event, but the Bureau squashed its printing and then threatened my life. As you would expect, it was all swept under the rug. So, to your question, yes, I will help."

"Thank you," said Nell. "It means a lot."

"Finistio," said Randolph with another wave of his hand. The color drained from the Commenteria, returning it to a cold, silver state. He packed his belongings away. "The death of Jarn may cause a stir. The Bureau will double its efforts to find you. Even without proof, they will label you as killers. Besides, the lad has been missing for weeks and his father is upset. Once they discover the news, things will worsen."

Zanora sucked in a quick breath. "Then you mean to keep it secret? Or will this bit wind up in the headlines, too?"

"Young lady, I have no intention of printing anything of the sort. Can you imagine the questions it would bring? How did I know of his death before anyone else? Was I there? Who was my source? Can I confirm it? And so on. It would put you all in a difficult position, no?" asked Randolph, placing a foot in the stirrup before swinging into his saddle with a practiced, graceful movement.

"It would indeed." Barrett extended a hand, which Randolph accepted for another handshake. The prince felt a rush of embarrassment. "I was wrong about you. I'm truly sorry for my part. Perhaps when this is over, we'll meet again in a place where we do not need to hide our true selves."

Randolph slowly bowed his head. "I am excited for that day, my King. Oh, and it was a brilliant touch to send your raven. The bloody bird pestered me relentlessly at my home until I realized she had a message tied to her leg. Well done!"

Barrett chuckled. "She is good at that sort of thing."

"Before you go, have you heard anything about a wizard in the city? And what is the state of Barrett's soldiers? Are there any left?" asked Gaia.

"Yes, to both questions," nodded the reporter. "I have heard no name but know some magician or wizard is doing things they should not. I will dig deeper for you. Concerning the soldiers, those loyal to Barrett have taken to hiding in safehouses or several outlying villages until his return." He sat tall and raised a hand like a victorious knight. "Farewell, friends. Stay alert and trust no one. I will contact you soon." With that, he reined his mount toward the road and loped away.

Barrett leaned against a tree looking surprised. "Who would have ever guessed Randolph Rollie is a magic user."

"Right?" said Unger with wonder in his voice. "I take back all the nasty things I thought and said about him. He's the next best thing to a spy."

"Can we not get ahead of ourselves," grumbled Zanora. Her forehead crunched tight in displeasure. "He could be heading straight to Carick or Grimes right now. Even he said to trust no one."

Graile scowled in return. "I don't think his statement included him. How stupid would that have been?" His words came out smooth but forceful.

"There is a certain genius to this plan, my liege," said Nell.

"We are not going back to that again, are we?" complained Barrett. "I am not king and may never be. I'm not even a prince any longer. Please do not address me as one."

"She is practicing for the day when you are crowned," added Unger with a wink. "Westmore is yours by birthright. You *are* the prince. Like it or not."

Wishing to stop the squabbling, Gaia rubbed her growling stomach. "It's been a long day. I'm tired and hungry. Has anyone wondered where we'll eat and sleep tonight?"

"Trishar's house is close but too dangerous to reach," said Graile, placing his hands behind his back as he paced. "I bet the Bureau is watching it closely. Fairy rings are needed to reach Nirith's house, so she is beyond us." He halted. "Where is that dratted wizard when you need him?"

"Who cares? We're better off without him," said Zanora.

7

Unexpected Aid

Keeping to the edges of the darkening forest, the companions journeyed toward Westmore, hoping to find shelter. Barrett watched the sun meet the horizon knowing deep night would soon prevail.

Meandering through with long grass under their feet, they paralleled the road far to their left. Ashton faded from sight as the company rounded a hard shoulder to steer them farther away from the road.

Navigating another curve brought them to a woman sitting patiently atop a boulder by the path's edge. Barrett instinctively drew his wand, but Gaia appeared at his side to gently lower his arm. "Relax. She is not threatening us. And I think she's alone," said the witch.

Barrett frowned at his hasty reaction. "You're right. I overreacted. I'm edgier than I thought." Randolph's warning resounded in his ears as his jumpy nerves attempted to calm themselves.

"I recognize her. She was going to roast us and make snacks of us all," said Graile, his low voice steady.

Like the prince, Unger shrieked as the twisted adventure within the Trowken caves replayed in his mind. "By the gods, it's Mearis."

"You're correct." Gaia waved enthusiastically. "Hullo! Welcome!"

Mearis was smartly dressed in a maroon tunic and breeches. Her wavy blond hair had grown to her waist. Her hazel eyes, which had darkened to brown on the edges, were even brighter than Barrett recalled.

"I have no intention of eating you. Why would I eat those who saved my life?" said Mearis, rising to bow.

"How can you be here? And why?" asked Gaia, moving to embrace their friend. "Once we transformed you from your Trowken body we never thought our paths would cross again."

"Life is funny that way, yes?" Mearis laughed a light sound like a glorious bird song. "Long ago, I learned never to make enemies of those you may rely on someday. We parted as friends and I am in your debt. One which I have come to repay."

"The parting advice you gave saved our lives once we faced Alesta. Without the idea you planted in my head, I would have never used thought forms to defeat her. It was brilliant. Thank you," said Barrett, still an embarrassed shade of red.

"You have a grand future ahead. So, I helped in any way I could."

"It certainly does not feel like I have anything to look forward to right now," grumbled the prince.

Zanora edged closer. Suspicion ruled her tone. "But that does not explain how you are here."

"Magical folks still share information despite our powers being banned. Plus, I have foreseen your arrival. Hence, I arrived to sit in wait," said Mearis.

"That is amazing," said Unger. "I wish I could see the future."

After flicking her hair from both shoulders, she motioned for the company to join her. They gathered round to sit as she continued. "With our hurtful past behind us, Nirith and I have reconnected. She informed me of your plight. So, while she nurses her sister to health, I have come in her stead to lend aid. It is the least I can do in exchange for the life you returned to me. I said we would meet again and here we are."

"Your timing is perfect. You are a Seer, right?" asked Unger. "What does the future hold? Does Barrett get his crown back?"

Mearis chuckled. "Viewing, as I call it, does not work that way. Currently, there are too many factors to consider and many players on the board. We cannot know yet." She pulled a length of hair over her shoulder to casually toy with its end.

"If you can't tell the future yet, what *can* you do for us?" asked Zanora, her words still coming sharp.

"Keep you alive, providing you trust me. There is a hidden network of folks who despise the Bureau," said Mearis. "They defy them at every turn while awaiting the king's return. Until a viable plan can be made for Barrett to take the throne I will take you to a safe house where you can hide and rest. There, spells protect your magic, but do not use your powers outside its boundaries again. If caught, anyone connected to you will be put to death for lending aid. Now follow me."

"Wait," said Barrett as his heart filled with distrust. *If Eli-*

mar can change his appearance, so can others. "No disrespect, but how do we know you are who you say? Or that you will not double-cross us?"

"Excellent questions," replied Mearis, tapping her chin. She ticked off her fingers. "One, you killed Billam in the Trowken lair far away from here in the Othalan Mountains. Two, you received the soul vial in exchange for my freedom. And three, Korth became King. Does all that ring true?"

"Nirith could have told you any of that news, not knowing who you truly are," argued Zanora, placing both hands on her hips in defiance.

Mearis smiled at the redhead, then turned to Barrett. "Does she know you still fear tunnels and passageways? Billam's memory haunts you to this day, does it not?" She brought her hands together, her fingertips touching one another. "I foresaw your dread before we ever parted."

Air drained from Barrett's lungs as the wretched memory sprang to life. Even now, he held vivid recall of the Trowken's knobby hands and feet pummeling him within inches of his life. To save himself, the prince lashed out with a powerful spell, sending the creature hurtling across the prison to his death. Billam's neck had made an awful snapping sound as he impacted the stone wall. He never moved again.

Barrett shuddered where he sat, trying not to retch in front of the company. Had the circumstances been different, perhaps the killing could have been avoided. But it came down to Billam's life or his own.

"I have already told my friends that much," he stammered, struggling to regain composure. "You will have to do better."

"Then know this, my liege." Mearis pointed to Zanora. "The angry one tells the truth. She is innocent of Jarn's death. The young man died at the hands of her men."

"How could you . . . ?" asked Unger, his words trailing away as he considered her news.

"That *is* impressive," said Graile. "Even Nirith didn't know those events."

"See!" cried Zanora, looking satisfied. "I told you I had nothing to do with it. A little trust would be nice from now on." Her face scrunched into a frown. "And stop calling me 'the angry one.'"

Barrett waved her off. "Very well, Mearis. We're convinced. Lead the way."

"Hold on! Don't we get a say in this?" asked Nell. "I am not convinced I trust her."

"Trusting Mearis is a wise decision. Considering we cannot safely enter the city, our money is nearly gone, we are tired and hungry, and neither Elimar nor Trishar has arrived yet, what choice do we have?" asked Gaia. "Not to mention, having a safe place to stay sounds superb."

"True. I would love a hot bath and some good food. A lot of it, too," said Unger, rubbing his empty stomach.

Graile waved his hand before his nose. "Agreed. You definitely *do* need a bath."

Unger shoved his shoulder, then pointed a stiff finger at the Fader. "I hate to break it to you, but you don't exactly smell like a bed of roses, either."

The golden light of the fading day filtered through the high branches, making tree shadows come alive. Deepening darkness pushed away all hopes of reaching safety before thick night arrived. Frigid westerly wind wormed its way through the forest.

Barrett grabbed the edges of his cloak and pulled them tight, shivering as the breeze snuck into every opening to chill him to the core. Footsore and grumpy, he no longer cared for the luxuries of the safehouse and was prepared to call for camp.

It was then gurgling water met his ears, so the company halted to drink cool water from the creek's depths. Mearis came to him.

"Just ahead. There," she said, pointing ahead. "Stay strong, young ones."

"Are we staying with foxes? Is this house a den in the ground? There are no people out here," grumbled Zanora. "Only wildlife lives within these woods."

No sooner had the words escaped her lips than yellow light peeked between the low boughs, giving the friends hope and renewed energy. Taking to a faint path, they pressed on with speed as the gloomy night gained firmer hold.

Barrett cursed the darkness as his feet snagged tree roots or rocks. Each foot felt weighed down by heavy blocks, a problem that brought him concern. This close to Westmore, as they prepared to oust the Bureau, his plans would halt if he broke an arm or leg from a fall in the murky night.

Stepping into a small, tree-lined clearing, a cozy, solid house came into view. The creek passed to its right and a garden lay on the left. Behind was a steep mountainous rise over which dim stars hung low, growing brighter each moment. The air smelled of pine, fir, and chimney smoke.

To Barrett's delight, as the front door opened, Trishar stood on the stone threshold waving excitedly.

"Come, my dear friends! Shut out the night and join me in safety," she said, magically closing the door with a swish of her hand as Graile entered last. She hugged Barrett tightly. "I am *so* pleased you are here." Scanning the friends' faces, a terrible understanding took hold. "Wait. One is missing."

The prince hung his head and nodded dejectedly. "Lars gave his life to save us all."

Trishar's happy expression dimmed as the air left her lungs. "I am truly sorry to hear this news." She faced Nell. "My sympathy, dear one. Your brother shall never be forgotten." Then, as if bitten, the sorceress sprang up and dashed to the kitchen. "My stew!" Removing it from the heat, she turned and smiled. "Just in time to eat."

After embracing Mearis, the sorceress swished her wand to magically set the table with tall, black candles, ample dinnerware, and deep mugs. Food came next, drifting overhead from the kitchen to settle before her guests.

Unger's face brightened with a growing smile. "This is exactly what I was waiting for."

Barrett took Nell's hand and led her aside. "Are you okay? We have not discussed your brother's death. Care to talk about it? It helps. I know how it feels to lose someone you love." As he spoke, a vision of his dead father passed before his eyes. He slammed them shut for an instant to rid himself of the painful memory.

When they reopened, he saw Nell smiling half-heartedly. "I'm handling it. But if I need to talk, I will find you."

Barrett led her toward the kitchen by following the aroma. "Food, rest, and drink will help. Talking does wonders, too. I'm here for you if you need me. And so you know, you cannot handle it alone. I know, I have tried."

"Your offer is very kind and I will not forget it," she said.

Trudging around the table, the friends ate a meal of fruits, fresh bread, cheeses, hot bread, cider, and thick, steaming stew.

"This meal is a feast," said Graile. "Thank you, Trishar. You are a glorious cook, my lady."

"It is both magnificent and delicious," agreed Zanora. "Did you actually cook all this or use magic?" She eyed her food with suspicion.

Trishar smiled and leaned back in her chair. "Does it matter? Will you stop eating it if I used magic?"

The redhead pulled her plate closer. "I'm way too hungry to care how you did it. I was only curious. In this case, I suppose using magic isn't too awful."

"By the gods," said Graile. "That is a big change for you." He placed a hand on her forehead. "Do you have a fever? Are you feeling ill?"

She scowled in return and pushed his arm away. "Will you stop it and eat your food." Her gaze swept over the others. "No smart comments either. Let it drop. I am too tired for any nonsense from any of you."

Barrett elbowed Unger and lowered his voice. "That means you. Do not stir up trouble."

"I wouldn't dream of it," the archer replied with a wink.

As they had done for Randolph, details of their latest adventures spilled out between bites. Trishar listened intently until the end, asking questions only now and again. Finally, the friends' inquiries began.

"Samaren has already shared the highlights of your plan with Randolph Rollie. He is rather tenacious when it comes to discovering facts. Even though his articles announce the Bureau's view, I agree they are not done under his own will," said Trishar. "Your mother is following him now and will hopefully bring news soon."

"Where is Elimar?" questioned Barrett. "Did Samaren find you days ago? Once she flew from the Outerworld no one ever came to help, save for Nirith."

She huffed. "That foolish brother of mine would be late even if the gods demanded he arrive on time. Besides, he is a wizard. He does not work on a schedule." She poured tea in her cup and sipped. "Yes, your beautiful mother brought news, though I could do little to help. Unfortunately, if I am gone long from my home, Trackers or the Bureau will notice. They watch me with regularity and I give them no reason to think my life is anything but boring and regular. Exactly like a Mundane, I would say."

"Graile said the same thing—you are being watched," said Barrett.

"How can you be with us now? Will you not be caught?" asked Gaia.

The sorceress frowned and shook her head. "This is one sorceress who still knows a few tricks. Trackers are nothing more than tyrants in robes. They are not paid to be intelligent, so slipping past them for a time is not overly difficult. Providing I do not use magic, of course. I am always back before sunrise and they never know I left."

"How is Alesta?" asked Graile after dabbing his lips with a napkin. "Recovering well, we hope."

"She is healing nicely. Nirith is taking excellent care of her."

Trishar leaned forward to place her elbows on the table. "So let us get down to it. Share your plans. You mentioned blackmail. That may work, but what if it fails? What will you do then?"

Barrett fiddled with his bowl and spoon. "I have considered several things but have not discussed them with anyone."

"Do tell," said Zanora. "I need a good laugh."

Graile nudged her arm. "Stop it. Now is not the time."

The redhead raised a stiff finger and started to object but reconsidered after meeting the Fader's steely glare. She returned to her food.

The prince moved closer to Nell. "Since you are a Shifter and can take different shapes, would you be willing to become Jarn?"

"Whatever for!" cried Unger, stiffening. "Have we not had enough of him? And he is a bit dead, in case you have forgotten."

"What purpose would it serve for Nell to become Jarn?" asked Gaia.

Barrett's face lit up with a smile. "Here is the good part." He paused for effect, making sure all were listening. "To haunt Carick." He rose to pace as his plan unfolded, gaining steam as he spoke. "Nell and I can sneak into the castle using the tunnels. Jarn once said the king uses my old room as his study. We could walk right in and make life uncomfortable for his royal highness."

"How *stupid*!" said Zanora, emphasizing her last word. "Do you think the ghost of his dead son is going to chase him out?"

"It would scare me," mumbled Unger, bobbing his head. "Blackmailing Grimes and haunting Carick may work, but what about the Bureau? We can't get rid of them so easily."

"Perhaps easier than you think," said Mearis. "Certain things have come to me that made no sense until now. The Bureau is terrified of magic and will not rise against it unless they can intimidate any involved. Not to mention, they have no organized army at their disposal. They would be forced to back down, allowing you to regain your kingdom and restore order. Many folks, including your former soldiers still in hiding, will not raise arms against your bid for the throne."

"While that sounds nice and easy, the Bureau fools will not go away without a fight," said Graile. "How do we destroy their organization?"

"You cannot," added Trishar. "Their reach will never disappear entirely. However, they can be turned into a toothless saw. Meaning, they are good for nothing."

"Your plan is absurd," chided Zanora. "I can fix this for you. Use the tunnels to sneak inside, kill Carick and Grimes in their sleep, then the castle is yours. Problem solved. The Bureau's hold on the city will be over. Crown yourself king, and they will not stop you."

"I am *not* killing anyone while they sleep," cried Barrett as low throbbing filled his head. "How can you even suggest it?"

"Wake them up first, then kill them. Is that better?" she snapped. Seizing her fork, she made several stabbing motions in the air.

"There are so many parts of that which are hideous. Why don't you just stop talking if you have nothing to say other than killing," said Unger. "We could rally Barrett's scattered forces, but that may not be enough. Also, Elimar is not here. Not with a thousand men could you do this. Getting rid of the Bureau is impossible."

"Perhaps. But we have Trishar, Mearis, Nirith, and Alesta," countered Graile. "Those are some powerful lady allies."

"I agree to the peaceful way. There is no need to kill anyone just yet. Try Barrett's plan first. I think it's a wonderful idea," said Gaia, squirming nervously, making her chair squeak in protest.

"Of course you do. You are his *current* girlfriend and will agree with anything he says," snipped Zanora before giving a dramatic eye roll.

"Silence," said Trishar, her voice stern and booming. Her face was grave with hints of anger showing. "Gaia has a point. Subtly may be best. Driving them mad is not a bad plan. Though anger makes me consider Zanora's idea, logic says to proceed with the haunting first."

"So let's do just that," said Mearis. "Plant the seeds to regain your throne, yet be aware Grimes is sneaky and false. Be careful around him. He feels violent beneath his superior attitude. There is something about him . . ." She sat trance-like for several long, uneasy moments. Then, as if the thought was forgotten, she went on. "I see him bringing bloodshed into your lives."

Zanora tapped her sword hilt. "That is exactly what I've been saying. We need to be sure the blood is his."

"Calm down, killer," said Graile, tapping the air like patting a dog's head. "Grimes and Carick will get what they deserve. I agree with Trishar. The idea of using fear to drive them out is brilliant."

Trishar cleared her throat for attention. "It is late. Each of you is weary from travel and adventure. Take rest, for I must return home. Mearis will watch over you. I will check in tomorrow if I am able. Good night, my dear friends." She slowly waved a hand, allowing her words to flow with a calming energy that passed directly through her friends.

Tiredness swept over them as her covert spell took hold. None argued as they slogged along to their rooms. Barrett was so worn he did not care if he slept standing up, on the floor, or atop a mattress. He thanked the gods as he entered the first door he came to.

Before him was a comfortable-looking bed, which he cast himself upon to instantly fall into a deep, unbothered sleep.

Barrett groaned as he stretched. He wondered how long he had slept. It felt like days had slipped away. Moving to the window, he drew back the curtain, squinting as the brilliant sun lit his face. The yellow orb rode high above the tree line while a hovering pool of morning mist lay thick on the forest. It was akin to a god peering down from high above, waiting for the world below to wake beneath his stare.

The prince understood the feeling well. Many times as he stood upon the castle balcony surveying the city below while allowing himself the indulgence of pride and ego. Now the thought of returning to those royal responsibilities spread fear in his heart. He wondered if he could ever truly satisfy the citizen's feelings and desires if he regained the throne. The dilemma of ruling so many when he found struggles in leading a group of just six or seven made his head hurt. Nonetheless, kingship should be his. Regrettably, it was all gone.

Then a peculiar thought struck him. Did he truly want to regain a higher responsibility than what he had during his youth? So little time had gone by since his ousting, yet things had changed at a lightning pace as his conflict of seizing the throne increased. He knew fury drove him to conquer the Bureau, yet his logical mind questioned his readiness for the crown.

Fumbling to dress, he realized Samaren was perched on his dresser. A smile stretched over his face.

"I am so glad you are here and safe," he said. "What news?"

His raven pecked at the Chatterer by her feet. "Randolph has given you a gift of sorts."

Barrett retrieved the tiny letter which grew to fit his hand. He broke the seal and waited as the parchment leapt free, unfolded itself, and displayed Rollie sitting at a worn wooden desk with scrolls and books piled around him.

"Sire." He gave a polite head bow. "I have done extensive research after our previous meeting and learned some interesting things." He patted a thick, worn book, making a resounding thudding sound. "It seems Zanora was correct about everything. The death of a man named Hollim was suspicious. Apparently, he and Grimes were running for the position of Inquirer General of Mystical Affairs. But it was not to be. Hollim was mysteriously murdered but his death was ruled an accident. However, a servant witnessed the entire thing. She fled for her life and went into hiding but I tracked her down. It took several visits over many days and a promise of a romantic late-night dinner, but I unlocked the story. Considering the Bureau bribed her handsomely, getting the scoop was a stroke of luck. She is a huge fan of mine, so that helped. She was rather attached to me." He paused to smooth his hair, smile, and wink.

Lifting a scroll, he continued. "I also discovered proof the Mordoria villagers were thrown from their homes or slaughtered so Grimes could seize their lands. It seems the crime was barely investigated before being shoved deep into the archives and forgotten. The Bureau clearly had a hand in the concealment. I pray we chat soon. Be careful. Trust no one." The letter refolded, then faded into nothingness.

"Thank you, Mother," said the prince as he slipped on his boots. "As always, your help is well-timed. You have brought valuable news. Take rest while I tell the others." He stroked her head. "I could not do this without you."

"Think with your head, not your heart," said the bird. "You are facing a dangerous adversary who will stop at nothing to keep power. Some men will fight to the death to protect what is theirs, even if their reasons are misguided. Be cautious."

"I promise," he replied, opening the door. "I have not come this far to let this madman keep what is mine." *Even if I'm still unsure, I want the throne back.* The entry closed with a soft click as he exited.

8

Into Westmore

Earlier in the day, the companions raised a noise over who would accompany Barrett into the city. And though the debate raged for some time, no decision was reached. Finally, Mearis placed their names in a small iron cauldron and drew them herself. Graile and Nell were chosen. Zanora quickly grumbled about the procedure being unfair, but nonetheless, she remained behind.

Within the hour, the trio headed for the city. Graile resembled a dark, traveling monk with his usual black flowing cloak and raised hood which set his face in deep shadow. His nails and the circles round his eyes were also black. He cut an imposing figure as he stood silent, mysterious, and grim alongside his friends.

Nell had morphed into an older woman as tall as Barrett. Her long hair and sparkling eyes were green, while her skin had become a lovely shade of light brown. She covered herself in a vibrant-colored jibbah and wore blue trousers to her ankles, ending just above a plain pair of brown sandals. Her disguise was of a female spice trader from Trinopra.

Unger could not stop staring.

"You're catching flies, you idiot," whispered Zanora, noticing his gaping mouth. "Close your mouth."

Embarrassed at being caught, he made a rude gesture and turned away.

Barrett used a spell Elimar taught him. He turned his hair light blonde and eyes blue, then dressed in clothing matching that of a Durinian sailor. Loose, deeply tanned breeches and a long tunic covered his body. Round his waist was a short, double-edged sword with a leather-wrapped handle, the favorite weapon of their people. Three red, crudely drawn lines covered each cheek and forehead, representing fighting skill, status, and maturity.

Disguises alone would only give passage through the main gates. Barrett reasoned the elf gate was the easiest way to minimize exposure, though he had hesitated to lead his friends through it. Who knew what the Bureau could track within the walls of Westmore?

Thankfully, Trishar quelled his worries, assuring him the opening spell was undetectable from any, save for elves themselves. Trackers, Bureau Agents, and even wizards and sorceresses would not sense it, regardless of their skill. According to her, the secret doors were safe, just as the elves had planned. Even better, no one could ever accidentally discover the locations of the entrances through means of wicked magic.

"The doors were routinely placed around old elven kingdoms. Think of the mess it would have caused if the gate's magic or opening spell could have been felt or easily discovered," she added. "Enemies could have invaded at will."

Barrett nodded to himself as the trio neared the secret spot. Only a small handful of trusted people knew of the gate's existence and they were either loyal to him, dead, or had forgotten the entrance still remained.

"Is this a good idea?" asked Nell as he stopped. "Won't the Trackers come if you use magic to open the gate?"

"No," said Barrett, explaining Trishar's story. "The elven design was ingenious that way. Elves carry foresight, too, like Mearis. Perhaps they saw these exact events coming and designed it as such." Pressing his hand against the stone, he muttered his spell. "Aperith Notim."

The stone wavered like an illusion for several moments before the companions crossed the threshold to emerge into the open field on the opposite side. The gate solidified behind them. Within a hundred yards, after weaving through the trees and bushes, the group casually merged onto the main street.

Barrett studied his surroundings, shocked at the state of his city and its people. They looked downtrodden, even frightened. The streets were unkept and most windows were shuttered against the outside world.

Gone were the fairy streetlamps, cyclops, dwarves, and each talking door had fallen silent. Even the door knockers were still. He hoped they were all merely hibernating until the worst was over. With luck, their magic and unique personalities had not been lost or destroyed. Though he used to complain about them, he realized he had grown rather fond of the talkative doors and chatty knockers over the years.

Months ago, the fairy Taleen had called these the Dark Days. Barrett now understood why. Westmore paled in comparison to its former glory. It felt sick, joyless, and strange. The city bore little resemblance to the Westmore he was raised in.

Even as he looked on, uniformed Bureau Agents patrolled the streets, paying little heed to the newcomers. The friends watched in shock as the Agents strutted around, staring down, shoving about, or bullying anyone before them.

Sadness and anger swirled within him. He wished to give the arrogant clods something to fear—magic.

"How dare these fools openly abuse my people," he muttered, reaching into his coat to grasp his hidden wand. "I'm going to stop this."

Graile suddenly appeared in his path to rest a hand on his shoulder. "You can be angry later, but do not risk our lives right now. We are here for a reason and should move along now," said the Fader, extending an arm toward the castle. "The time to fight will come soon enough."

Knowing the Fader was right did little to end Barrett's anger.

"Right," agreed Nell. "These tyrants will get their rewards. I don't imagine it will be very pleasant either."

Barrett forced himself to take a calming breath. The air felt heavy, reminding him of the Outerworld. Another breath steadied him and a third allowed him to stow his wand. He made a silent promise to never forget this day.

They walked on until the castle came into view. The sight of his former home brought a different dread. Would it be in ruins? Had the Bureau discovered the secret tunnels and sealed them? Were the dungeons full of innocents? Dead bodies? Ones falsely accused and awaiting trial? Entire families? Or was the new, unfair justice system swift, having suspects put to immediate death? Barrett's pace quickened with the sudden onslaught of troubling questions.

Nearing the Triple Moon Inn, he turned into the alleyway. Ducking behind a row of stacked wooden barrels, he checked around him for prying eyes. Satisfied they were unobserved, he opened the hidden entrance, hurried the others inside, then shut the door with a soft clank.

Pulling his wand, he prepared to cast his flame spell to light the torches. Graile stopped him again.

"No magic. We are unprotected here," he said softly. "If they catch us, there is little chance of escape."

Barrett frowned and stroked his smooth chin. "Spells are a reflex for me. Wise choice, my friend." He turned away for a moment, then faced Graile again. "Earlier, I wanted to make those Agents pay. But I appreciate you stopping me. I was going to do something rather foolish."

"Yes you were," agreed Nell. "Do not dwell on it. That moment is past and cannot be changed, so there is no use of letting it bother you. Mistakes do not define who we are. Everyone makes them. The key is to learn from them and become a better person from each one."

Barrett chuckled. "Perhaps you should run the kingdom. You are smarter than I am concerning many things."

"No royalty for me," replied Nell with a thin smile. "I love my freedom too much."

Rummaging within the depths of his cloak, Barrett produced flint and steel, then set to work. Moments later, the torch sprang to life. Holding it low, he went forward, letting the orange glow light the passage.

This time the memory of Billam did not haunt him. Instead, Nell's words replayed with each step. He enjoyed his freedom, too. No matter the benefits of being king, having power held just as many drawbacks. His main fear was his friends would drift away or leave him entirely, save for Gaia.

With his friends trailing silently behind and as his inner struggles faded, anticipation grew as they neared his old room. His hands shook as he wondered if Carick would be on the other side of the wall. Dabbing the sweat from his forehead, he tightened his grip on the torch, readying himself for whatever lay in wait. Flattening his hand against the door, he concentrated, pushing his senses outward. After a moment, relief hit him.

"The room is empty," he said. "I can't say for how long, though."

Slowly, he worked the lever, then eased his head around the bookshelf as it popped ajar. His sensations were correct, the study was indeed vacant. As he entered, an overwhelming urge to weep gripped him, but he fought the feeling.

Standing within these four walls again was a bittersweet moment. This was the room he had spent his entire life in, at least until he had been evicted like a common beggar. Thankfully, Carick had not destroyed it.

But as Barrett looked closer, anger boiled within him. Save the bookshelves and their contents, all his former belongings were gone. The family portraits, his comfortable bed, desk, Samaren's perch, sitting chairs, and more, had vanished. In their place sat bland, tasteless furniture unbefitting a royal castle.

The prince ran his fingers over the unfamiliar table and

frowned. He choked down the lump in his throat, not wanting to allow his friends to see him cry. *Why not cry? It doesn't mean I'm weak. I simply cannot let emotions rule me right now. Just being here hurts.*

"We're here. What should we do now?" asked Nell.

Her voice brought him clarity. "Change everything we can. Move books around, relocate furniture, pull clothes from the dressers, and anything else you think of." Barrett jerked back the curtains, opened the balcony doors, and stepped outside to view his city as he had done many times before.

Before the takeover, his fairy friend, Taleen, lived there in her fairy lamp and would often visit, especially following his mother's death. He longed to see the little fairy again. She had provided wise counsel and taught him the world could be a positive place. Now her home was destroyed, ripped away once the Bureau took over. He hoped she was still alive and safe.

Re-entering the room, his heart pounded as fury rose. He wanted to make Grimes and Carick pay for their misdeeds. "Let's begin."

It took mere minutes to lay the foundation of their plan. Books were reversed, the desk relocated with loose parchment spread haphazardly over its top, pictures hung upside down, chairs turned to face the corners, couch cushions thrown about, and more.

Just as Barrett smiled at their handiwork, things went horribly wrong as a hapless guard entered the chamber to stop in his tracks. Shocked beyond words at the sight of a Durinian sailor in the king's study, he stood with a gaping mouth. Thankfully, Graile and Nell were hidden from his view.

As the burly fellow reached for his sword hilt, he flew through the air to smash into the wall with a thud, collapsing in a heap.

From behind, Nell had morphed into a cave troll. She swung her fist to strike the side of his head, sending him soaring like a discarded child's toy. Dazed, the guard lay moaning before rising to his hands and knees. Barrett rushed to his side, grabbed a handful of hair, pulled back with force, then whispered in his ear.

"Tell Grimes we know what he has done. He is a murderer and must leave Westmore forever or his past deeds will come to light. And the idiot Carick must go with him," he hissed. The prince raised a fist high in the air, then brought it down with force. The guard's face bounced from the floor as he collapsed unconscious. Barrett cursed as he stood. "None of this was supposed to happen."

Graile folded his hands behind his back. "Well, it did. The moment he walked in our plan was ruined. We should leave. Now."

Nell scurried to open the chamber door a bit wider. "That should do it."

"What are you doing?" asked the Fader. "What purpose does that serve?"

"I wanted to make them assume the intruders escaped through the open door. Otherwise, the guards will start searching inside and possibly find the tunnel," she replied.

"Great thinking," said Barrett, hurrying them into the passage before resealing the entrance. He fumbled with lighting the torch as his hands shook. "How did I ever come up with this stupid plan? Haunting! How ridiculous."

Nell gave him a sympathetic look, then took the flint and steel and lit the fire. Dancing orange flames cast a wavering glow as the smoke spiraled upward to vanish in the thick darkness. Now they rushed headlong down the passage and emerged in the alley whence they came.

"We all try and fail, Barrett. We will think of something new and go forward. Don't be hard on yourself," said Nell.

"Unger is lucky to have you," admitted the prince. For the second time, her words settled in his heart. "You are remarkable."

Shortly after exiting the tunnel, the friends stepped onto the main thoroughfare and headed for the gate. Hide in plain sight, the prince thought. Elimar had told him that on more than one occasion. A sudden frown pulled down the corners of his mouth. He missed the old man more than he wished to admit. The wizard was the only father figure he had in his life, save for Yaris, whose whereabouts remained unknown. The lack of a stable male figure was disheartening in many ways. *Then again, Elimar is not exactly a stable example.* He chuckled at his silent joke.

Along the way, anxiety grew in his chest. Something felt wrong. He led the others into thickly shadowed corners and halted. A commotion rose from his right as a group of drunken men stumbled past, singing incoherently. Inquisitive heads popped out of windows or from behind open doors to yell their complaints.

As the drunkards stumbled along, the friends moved past with a sense of urgency. Their efforts to appear casual was failing. With the city entrance sitting open some hundred yards ahead, it took every ounce of courage Barrett could muster to stop and lower on one knee. Graile and Nell hovered nearby, casting cautious looks about them. After pretending to lace up his boot, a trick to ensure they were not followed, the prince rose and headed on.

Reaching the city's main gate, they passed through uneventfully after nodding politely to the guards. No more than forty paces passed beneath their feet when an alarm sounded behind them. Bells rang, horns blew, and the gates were slammed shut.

The sounds of heavy timber being lowered into place to bar them filled the air.

Fading from the main road into the tree line, the trio disappeared into the thick night.

Mearis had arranged a display of food. Barrett popped a piece of cheese in his mouth, chewed slowly, then swallowed as he waited for Trishar's obvious discontent to reach him.

She looked unhappier than he had ever seen her. Sitting at the table's head, she tapped her finger against the table in quick rhythm. "I leave you alone and now the entire city is in upheaval. The king has increased security everywhere, especially the castle."

"But . . . but . . . but it wasn't our fault," stammered Barrett, disbelieving his words as they faltered from his lips. He knew the plan had plenty of pitfalls even though it sounded wise at the time.

The sorceress stopped tapping as her mood lightened. Her face relaxed. "I am not placing blame. I am simply stating facts."

"I knew I should've gone along," said Zanora with irritation. "I could have helped."

"How? The events would have turned out no differently. You may have even made things worse," said Graile, raising a shoulder. "At least we don't have a dead body on our hands."

The redhead displayed a rude gesture but the Fader ignored her.

"They were disguised. So no harm was done, right?" questioned Unger. "This can't be traced back to anyone here. Those Bureau fools can only guess who invaded the castle."

"Right. The guard only saw a Durinian. Agents will be hunting someone who doesn't exist," said Gaia, turning away after giving the prince a hard look.

Barrett wondered what he had done wrong. Or had Zanora said something to her in his absence? Influencing Gaia at her first opportunity would not be beyond her. *Perfect! One more thing to worry over.*

"It is upsetting I did not see this event prior to your leaving," said Mearis. "It is as if my visions were blocked by magical means."

"It is not your fault," said Trishar. "I believe there is more here than we are seeing."

Zanora stopped fiddling with her long braid. "Hold on. The Bureau has no magic, right? There is no way they could have a hand in keeping you from seeing, right?"

"Not unless the crooked, vile fools are being deceptive— which is entirely possible," said Trishar as she straightened to stir her tea. "I think Mearis is right. Someone is protecting the Bureau with magic."

"Agreed. Our enemy is using spells to gain their goals," said the Seer, swishing her spoon about as if casting magic.

"But they hate magic and are trying to eliminate it," said Nell. "That's awfully hypocritical."

Trishar made an indelicate sound. "Like many evil ones, they care about results, not the methods used to obtain them. They will use whatever means suits them to keep control."

Barrett silently agreed. There was no other explanation for Mearis' sudden lack of sight inside Westmore, let alone the castle. Everything she had told them until now proved accurate. Nothing less than protective spells from within the Bureau could be hindering her.

"The Bureau is expanding their underhanded ways," he offered dryly. "The days are growing darker because of them."

"Who? Who would do such a thing?" asked Gaia. "What could they gain?"

"The possibilities are endless," replied Mearis. "The Bureau could be torturing a magic user to do their bidding. Whoever they are using must have significant skill to fool me."

"Powerful magic is undoubtedly involved. I sense grief and loss but cannot see more since the way is too cloudy," said Trishar.

"What should we do?" asked Graile, moving closer to Zanora. Their shoulders pressed together. The redhead did not move away. Instead, she leaned in as a thin smile spread over her face.

"More like, what *can* we do?" corrected Unger. "Grimes could have set anyone against us, even a friend or someone we once trusted. We may never know."

"I have an idea," said the redhead in a subdued tone.

Trishar smiled at her. "Go on, dear, we are listening."

"We need a Tracker of our own," she said firmly, her conviction rising. "It would be a way to get a load of answers."

Unger gave a solid belly laugh before smirking in her direction. "Are you crazy? Why in the name of the gods would we want or need one of their people hunting us?"

Gaia went to Zanora's side to brush several stray hairs from the redhead's face. "I think your idea is excellent," admitted the witch. "If they track magic, they can discover who is holding us back."

Graile nodded. "Hummm, that makes sense. Why *not* use a Tracker against our enemy? Like a double-cross."

"That is bold, even for us. But how do we find one we can trust? They're all Bureau lackeys," grumbled Unger, throwing both arms in the air from frustration. "It's impossible."

"We don't need to trust them; just capture one and threaten them with death if they do not do our bidding," suggested the redhead. "The Bureau is likely doing the same thing anyway."

"Sure!" Barrett snorted his dissatisfaction. "Since threats and distrust always work really well, we should do it your way. After all, look how well my people are doing. They are thriving on hate, lies, and intimidation."

"Really, genius?" she retorted. "Then you come up with a better plan. Your haunting idea turned out perfectly, didn't it? Maybe you should do this all on your own."

Graile rested a hand on Zanora's knee and shook his head. "Be nice. He's doing the best he can."

But the redhead's words froze Barrett. She was right. A Tracker may be perfect for the job. Even better, the Bureau, would never suspect one of their own. Embarrassment flushed his cheeks as he desperately searched for an alternative, yet he found nothing but his pride. Usually, he was the first to formulate plans. But this time, his lack of preparation annoyed him.

His confidence was slowly draining away. After departing from the Outerworld he felt his decisions were scattered and unwise. Then there was Zanora. Was he being spiteful toward her on purpose? She had made a good point and the concept was sound, yet he discarded it as soon as she said it. *Why?* He was being immature and knew it.

Logically, getting to the disadvantages of her idea was easy. First and foremost, they could easily be betrayed. Success meant finding a Tracker who secretly despised the Bureau's ideals. But it was not as if they could advertise to find a traitor. Or could they?

Unger spoke up, calmer this time. "What about our friend Randolph Rollie? He could word an ad to draw out potential help. Better yet, he may know of some secret sect within the Bureau fighting their oppression. There has to be a few who do not wish to see the lands remain under Bureau control."

"Oooooh, I like that idea," said Gaia.

The prince chewed on more cheese, then took a long sip of cider as he searched for the right words. At length, he set the mug on the table and mindlessly straightened his silverware. "I agree with both of you. We need a Tracker and Randolph can help again. Brilliant ideas."

The redhead winked at him and quickly nodded to show her satisfaction. Her actions lifted his feelings. *Good. She's not angry at me for being rude.*

"True. Rollie would be a good choice," said Graile. "He did an amazing job getting information on Grimes. He is thorough and quick."

"I feel bad for being against him all this time," said Unger, showing his remorse with a frown.

"Let's not forget *The Oracle* prints garbage," added Zanora. "They constantly bash Barrett. Their articles help spread rumors and nonsense. I'm still not sure I trust him."

"He explained the articles away," added Gaia. "Besides, I would have known if he was being deceitful."

"It is of no matter. He's all we have and is doing a terrific job so far," added Barrett. "I'll ask Samaren to carry him another note. We can arrange a meeting for tomorrow if he can make it."

"Excellent choices," said Trishar. "Now I must pop home for a bit so the spies see me before making their nightly reports. I imagine seeing my thought form is keeping them satisfied for now. Farewell, one and all."

9

Shardira

With breakfast done, Mearis chose Barrett, Unger, and Gaia to attend the meeting with Randolph, saying there was no need to send all the companions since it increased the chances of being seen or captured.

Tree shadows grew thin as the sun rose higher above the horizon. Barrett wished for a horse. Walking was boring, tiresome, and left the friends exposed for too long. Turning north for a distance before swinging away to the east, he studied the trail to take his mind from his aching feet.

They came to a treed slope with a wide stream flowing across their path. To their relief, a hearty stone bridge spanned the distance. Taking pleasure in the sounds of the gurgling water, Barrett paused halfway across the stone structure to watch the blue water flow past on its journey. He took time to admire the stonework.

"I never knew this was here," he admitted, touching the ancient craftsmanship.

"Since we're not even sure where we are, it's no wonder we've never seen it. But it sure is beautiful," said Unger.

"It makes me forget the reasons we're here. There is a glorious peace surrounding this dale," said the witch. "I still wish none of this had ever happened."

"Don't we all," added Unger.

Barrett smiled after leaving the bridge behind. The place brought joy and peace, both of which they had very little of lately. He wondered if the future would hold any more delights.

After a lengthy walk they reached the familiar open field outside the city. To their right lay the fairy ring. The witch, compliments of Trishar's magic, had flowing red hair and green eyes. Unger's hair was blonde and short, while his eyes were green. Barrett bore a Marune woodcutter look. His rough, dark-colored clothing had patched knees and elbows. Thick, heavy boots covered his feet. His shoulder-length black hair was pulled into a small ponytail, and his eyes were sea blue.

Since Barrett was old enough to dress himself, he was attracted to frayed clothing. Royal dress was boring, uncomfortable, and itched. But well-used, tattered clothing made him relax. They felt natural. *Dressing how I want is another reason not to become king.* He broke the silence to keep his mind off his worries. "I told Randolph we would be in disguise. I didn't want him panicking if he saw strangers."

"Great idea," said Gaia as the wind stirred her long, ginger hair.

He guided her away from Unger, stopping under an ancient

towering pine tree. Since their mishap in the castle she seemed reluctant to talk. It was unlike her and made him uneasy. "Is there something wrong? Are you mad at me?"

She kissed him softly. "Of course not. I just have a lot on my mind and it's distracting." Gaia nervously adjusted her necklaces. "I did a reading a few days ago and it worries me."

The prince drew back. The last thing he wished to hear was more bad news. "Do tell."

"I saw death return. Even my dreams have the same theme." She put a hand to her heart as if in pain. Her face twisted. "There's more, too."

"More?" Barrett repeated. Gaia's dreams were remarkably accurate and over the years he learned never to discount them. "Mearis is a Seer. Have you talked to her yet? Maybe she could help clarify things."

Gaia shook her head. "I was hoping to work it out for myself first."

"Don't wait too long," he urged. "Time is a luxury we do not have. Things are moving too fast. If you bring it up, you may be able to save a life."

Unger spied an approaching horse. "I think our guest is coming." He pushed his chin to the witch. "What are you two talking about? Or is it private?"

Barrett searched for words, unsure if the dilemma should be discussed openly or with anyone other than himself, Mearis, or Trishar. "We may discuss it on the way back to the safe house," he replied. Secretly, he hoped Unger would forget the entire thing before then.

Randolph crested the treed hill on his sleek mare with the sun casting long, yellow rays around him as if a god approached. Minutes later, he dismounted with his usual smile, bowed politely to Gaia, then shook the boys' hands.

"Did you have any trouble leaving the city? Has the Bureau restricted travel?" the witch asked.

"A bit, yes. Thankfully, they are used to seeing me come and go. Still, Agents eye everyone closely and stay busy pestering Mundanes in their attempt to trap magic users. At this rate there will be no one left to round up or question. By the grace of the gods, the fools still trust me since they believe I do their bidding." Throwing a glance over his shoulder in worry, he continued. "Time is short, so let us continue. May I assume it was your group that broke into the castle?" He did not wait for an answer. "Since your failed venture, suspicions are high. My slipping away for this meeting was risky."

Barrett's chest swelled. "First, I didn't break into the castle. It's my home," he said defensively, jamming a thumb against his chest. "They are the intruders, not me."

"We know that, my love," said the witch as she faced the reporter. "To answer your question, yes, it was our group."

"Too bad our plan fell apart," added Unger. "After the incident with the guard, we changed strategies."

Randolph placed a small piece of parchment in Barrett's hand. "You must meet with Shardira. She will help you. Like you, my liege, she is an orphan." The reporter gave a sweeping bow. His face flushed a shade of red. "Apologies. No offense intended." He continued after taking another glance over his shoulder. "She has no love for Grimes and his fools. Her father was hung for having magic and her mother died from torture as the Bureau tried to extract names of magic users."

"That's horrible," said Gaia, scrunching her face in a sour look.

"How do we find her?" asked Unger.

"She will be along directly and you can meet her for yourselves. I told her of this meeting. She is intelligent and quick-minded. You'll like her," replied Randolph.

"You invited her here?" questioned Barrett, pointing to the ground, surprised at his sudden anger. He had spent months worrying over the companions' safety, but with a few words from someone he barely knew, his plan vanished into thin air. He wanted to shout his annoyance.

Randolph studied him. "Yes, I did. I believed it best to introduce you as quickly as possible."

"She could unknowingly bring the Bureau with her," grumbled Barrett. "Maybe we should leave before she arrives. There are other ways of getting things done without involving strangers."

"Why would she be watched? That doesn't make sense," said Unger. "She's one of them."

Barrett felt slighted. He puzzled over how Unger could forget caution so easily. Was it because they were on Westmore's doorstep, finally within reach of their families and he wanted to go home?

"Caution has kept us alive this long," he snapped. "Now we are being asked to entrust our safety to a total stranger. There are no guarantees she won't double-cross us."

"Being a Tracker likely places her above suspicion," said Gaia. "The Bureau will not suspect one of their own. At least, not yet. It is reaching that point, though. The more we delay, the sooner our window of opportunity will close."

Realizing his behavior was slipping into anger, Barrett stopped. "I'm sorry for my outburst. I guess all this sneaking around and disguising myself keeps me on edge. I meant no offense."

Randolph smiled knowingly. "The entire city feels the same, Sire. They know something is coming. Good or bad, none can tell. But they sense it. And after all you and your friends have been through, one can certainly not blame you for taking precautions."

"There's another rider coming this way," said Unger, jamming a finger straight ahead as a figure approached on a muscular, groomed, chestnut gelding.

Barrett focused on the stranger. She was slim with pale, smooth skin, full lips, and hazel eyes—a vision of loveliness. Lustrous purple hair hung down her back and pointed ears poked out between the strands.

"Oh, you did not mention she is an elf. How exciting!" said Gaia.

Randolph nodded. "True. I forget. She is half-elf. Her mother was elf kind and her father was a royal soldier. His minor magic was nothing to be put to death over."

"No wonder she is a Tracker," said Unger, confirming his thoughts with several nods. "Elves are known to be sensitive to detecting magic."

Shardira reined to a halt, then raised a hand in greeting, the same as Randolph did during his farewell. Swinging from the saddle, she came to Barrett. "Greetings, Sire." She bowed with a fluid motion.

"How do you know I'm not the king?" asked Unger, thumping his chest with his palm. "I do have a royal jawline, do I not?" He turned sideways to profile his face as he ran his hand over his smooth chin.

The elf smiled. "Though you are handsome enough to be a sovereign, I have seen the king on the street. I know his face, scent, and the way he carries himself. Your disguises do not fool me."

Unger puffed out his chest as if he had won a prize. "Can she come with us? I like her already."

Barrett's ego deflated. "I didn't know our magic could be seen through so easily. Most impressive. And please do not call my sire, liege, or any other names to give me away. I beg you both."

Randolph startled. "Apologies. I should have known." Placing a foot in his stirrup, he performed another smooth mount. "Before I go, I must give warning. The Bureau is growing nervous over the rumblings of your return. I am to run an article announcing an increase in the bounty for information leading to your capture or death. Stay vigilant. Now I must be off before I am missed at the newsroom. Farewell, friends." He departed with another knight-like wave.

The others waved goodbye and watched until he was out of sight. The prince turned to Shardira. The thought of revealing their plans to a stranger seemed wrong but there was little choice now.

"Does the Bureau know I have returned or are they feeling the people slipping from under their rule? Are Mundanes going to help fight? After all, the lines between them and magic users are no longer important. We must band together," said Barrett, watching the elf's reaction closely.

"No one enjoys suppression. Talk of revolt is rampant but not done in the open," she answered. "Also, I again offer apologies for my choice of earlier words. From here on out I will select my words more carefully."

"No harm was done." Barrett pointed toward the castle where the pointed spires and parapets rose above the tree line. "Can you discover who is casting magic over my home? Our ability to see the future has failed and we can no longer trust our visions."

"Right. We're sure magic is at work but don't know the extent of the spells," said Unger.

"That explains a lot, actually," said Shardira. "I have felt strange sensations for weeks but can never discover the source or sources. The hunt has been most frustrating."

"Excellent point. Why didn't we think of that?" asked Gaia, speaking more to herself than the others. "There could easily be more than one magic user protecting the Bureau. I'm ashamed I missed that bit."

"How false can these people be?" griped Barrett. "They abuse or kill anyone with magical powers yet use magic to shield themselves against a world they cannot comprehend. They have no understanding of what they are doing."

Shardira gave a slow nod and moved toward her mount. "Like Mr. Rollie, I must take my leave. I dare not be out of touch overly long." She paused. "He mentioned your raven. If permitted, I shall communicate with her. There shall be no passing of notes since I can speak directly to her. It is safer that way." She evaluated their disguises with a scrutinizing stare. "It is surprising you have not been captured yet. Thank the gods other Trackers do not have elf senses or your adventure would have been long over by now."

Barrett took her words like a punch in the stomach. "I thought I was pretty convincing."

Unger stood open-mouthed until Gaia elbowed him. "I wish we would have met months ago. You are certainly handy to have around," said the archer.

"Shardira, I'm so sorry about your parents. I know what it feels like to have them gone," said Barrett. "Their loyalty shall not be forgotten. Their deaths sadden me. The world is dimmer with their loss. Particularly under the circumstances from which they perished. Know that the pain becomes smaller over time but never goes away."

"You are gracious and kind, Barrett of Westmore. I appreciate your words and return the feeling. I am well aware your parents were taken from you early, as well."

"We will have our revenge," said Unger, pounding a fist into his open palm.

Gaia shivered. "I hate that word ... revenge. It feels and sounds horrible."

"I agree," said Shardira. "Perhaps say that you wish to set things right instead."

"True enough," said Barrett. "In the end, I want the Bureau held accountable for all the misery and death they have caused."

Shardira vanished over the hill, keeping to the forest and out of sight as the trio angled toward the safe house. Barrett thought her actions were odd. Why not take the road? Was she worried about being tracked? Perhaps she was being spied on. Or was there a nefarious purpose to her hiding amongst the trees? He pursed his lips, still angry over Randolph's foolish actions. It seemed he abandoned all precautions.

The meeting had put him on edge. So much rested on a stranger's word. Shardira could end the company for good if she desires. Barrett shook the thoughts away rather than let them drive him mad.

"Tell me about your readings and dreams," he said to the witch, scanning the woods for unusual movement.

Gaia's gaze remained fixed ahead, focusing on the towering trees and winding road. "Death. I keep seeing death. Not the Death tarot card meaning change and transformation, but I feel a strong impression of loss and sorrow. Perhaps it is related to Lars being gone. My heart goes out to Nell. I wish she would discuss her grief. She should not hide the pain. It is unhealthy."

"I've mentioned it to her, too," said the prince. "She needs to talk to someone to start healing."

Unger pulled his pack off his shoulders, dug through its contents to free his cloak, then swung it round his shoulders to fasten the clasp. Settling his rucksack onto his back again, his steps felt lighter without being weighed down. "She'll talk when she's ready, I hope," He adjusted the straps. "Back to your dreams . . . you're unsure about your visions, right? Could one of us die soon? Are you seeing the future like Mearis?"

"Even Mearis is being deceived somehow," countered the prince. "Gaia may be seeing exactly what someone wants her to see. Think about it. A Seer with faltering vision and a witch struggling with evil dreams and death." He took her hand in his own. "This is not your doing. There is more here than we know. Let's talk to Trishar."

10

An Enemy's Return

Barrett recounted the story of their meeting with Randolph and the addition of Shardira to the friends' circle. Though hopeful over their new ally, the helpless feelings persisted. He felt too reliant on others to gain needed news. It proved bothersome and slow. Internally, he wished to storm the castle, drive Grimes and Carick out, then dismantle the Bureau once he regained the throne. Yet, his internal voice over being king still haunted every thought.

He felt ashamed he had not spoken to anyone over his worries, especially Gaia. However, she had her own problems and he would not willingly add to her turmoil. The blunder with the guard in the king's study certainly did not boost his confidence. Now, neither the king himself, Grimes, nor the Bureau would take strange ghostly happenings seriously. He had failed in every respect and it bothered him.

"Having an elf on our side could be very helpful," said Trishar, swirling the contents of her teacup with magic. The liquid spun in small, clockwise circles, forming intricate designs as it moved. "I had no idea any of her kind were still in Westmore. I thought they fled weeks ago."

"She is a half-elf," corrected Gaia. "Her story is like Barrett's own. Following the deaths of her parents, she had no place to go. Since the Bureau is forcing her to use her skills, she might as well take advantage."

Barrett's expression soured. "Yes, I know exactly how she feels. Homeless, orphaned, and penniless." Gaia scooted closer to rest a comforting hand on his thigh as she kissed his cheek.

"As long as they are trustworthy, anyone willing to help is fine by me," said Graile, applying a fresh layer of black polish to his fingernails.

"That is my concern, too," added Zanora. She bumped the Fader with her shoulder, then winked at him. "See, you are smart. We think alike."

"You have a keen intelligence," he replied. "If you could keep your temper under control, more people would listen to your point of view."

Zanora made a stern face but remained quiet. Surprisingly, she scooted closer, pressing herself against his side. 'For you, I'll try harder."

"What's next?" asked Nell, raising both shoulders. "Are we stuck waiting again?"

"Yes, but not for long," said Trishar. "Things are moving faster since Carick realizes the castle is vulnerable. The Bureau's grip will tighten with a harshness unlike any have ever seen."

"Meaning many will slip through their grasp. The more they

try to control people, the quicker dissension rises." Though the sorceress spoke lightly, Barrett heard worry in her tone as she continued. "Folks throughout the land are fed up with being subjugated."

"Subju-what?" asked Unger, leaning his chair back on two legs as he mused over the word.

"Subjugated," repeated Graile. "It means being dominated, overpowered, or suppressed." He placed both hands on his knees and angled toward the archer "I thought you were going to start reading more. It would broaden your vocabulary."

"When have I had time?" complained Unger, dramatically tossing both arms in the air. "Do you recall having any books handy lately? It's not like I did casual reading on the way to or from the Outerworld."

"Speaking of the Outerworld, how are Alesta and Nirith?" asked Gaia, shoving yesterday's edition of *The Oracle* aside without reading a single word. She had heard enough bad news the last few days and wanted no more today. "I do hope Alesta is resting after all she has been through."

"Alesta has the resilience of youth and heals quickly. She is nearly at full strength and will visit when she can," said Trishar. "I am proud of them both. They work together beautifully."

"Has there been any word on Apadora?" asked Graile. "Has she broken free? Is the gate's magic holding?"

"Bless the gods, she is still locked away where she belongs," said Trishar before her mood turned serious. "She should hope she never escapes, for if we meet, I will make her pay for what she has done to my brother and niece."

Gaia looked shocked. "Revenge isn't like you."

The sorceress dismissively waved her words away. "Perhaps. But every action in life has an equal reaction. As a witch, you know this to be so. You cannot go about using people for your gain or nearly killing them, then expect no repercussions. I disliked her even before my brother married her. Nothing has changed."

Uneasy silence crept over the room, but Trishar paid little attention as she conjured an apple while smiling steadily. She took it and began to eat.

Unger edged next to Nell to whisper. "Do you think she was serious? Could she do it?"

Nell patted his knee like comforting a child and snickered. "She was *very* serious. And yes, I think she could. She would be like a boiling pot with a lid on it. I would not wish to be around when she erupted."

"If Apadora defeated Elimar what makes you think Trishar could do better?" asked Graile, overhearing.

"Because my sweet Fader, she is a woman," said Nell. "Fierce, powerful, and intelligent. Not to mention a firestorm of uncontrollable fury when her loved ones are threatened."

Graile's eyes found the sorceress. She winked knowingly as a thin grin spread her lips. He turned back. "Good point. Well met," he said.

Barrett debated taking time to speak to Trishar over Gaia's concerns, then decided—without asking the witch's permission—to voice the matter aloud. He reasoned the more folks who heard the issues the more answers he may get. He cleared his throat for attention.

"We need to discuss Gaia's dreams and readings." Scowling at the redhead, he waited, expecting a rude comment. But to his wonder, she stayed silent.

As Gaia took the lead to delve into her her dreams, she became visibly uncomfortable. She shifted often or paused several times to consider her words, especially ones involving the darkest endings. Once finished, she waited patiently for responses. Yet, not before glaring at the prince.

"My dear girl, you have no cause for alarm," said Trishar in a comforting, motherly voice. "Those barriers are not surprising, especially after we have established dark magic is at work." She sipped more tea, placed the cup and saucer on the table, then straightened her tunic before continuing. "Trust neither your visions nor tarot readings. At least not for some time to come. There is no doubt Westmore is being protected with magic. It is interfering with our sight."

"Does anyone else die? You know, any of the friends?" questioned Zanora, nervously tapping her boot heel against the hardwood floor. "You never mentioned that part or said who was next." She cringed at her last words and gave Nell an apologetic glance.

Gaia appeared sick. "I would rather not discuss it since someone may be putting wicked visions in my mind. Like Trishar said, I cannot trust what I see."

"Maybe not, but—" began Zanora as an unreasoning fear gripped her.

"Stop, please," whispered Graile in the redhead's ear. "She is upset and this solves nothing. Anything she sees will likely prove false since someone or some *thing* is interfering, just as we have said."

"You can't know that for sure," retorted Zanora, struggling to maintain a hushed voice. "Maybe she saw something accurate but it is mixed with all the other junk. We should decide for ourselves."

"She has already said everything she knows. And even if you heard her words, what difference would it make? It could be completely false." Graile took Zanora's hand and let his warmth seep through her skin. "Please, drop it for now."

Peace came over her like a spell. She flashed a smile. "True, she isn't seeing things clearly anyway. Consider it forgotten."

Barrett watched their interaction with interest. Graile had an undeniable calming influence over Zanora. One he never had. *Is he starting to like her? She isn't pulling away or making rude comments. How interesting.*

"Thank you for sharing, Gaia," said Mearis. "It comforts me to know I am not alone in suffering and my powers are not failing. I was worried I had tapped into some wicked source and could not break free."

We must end this magical hold on Westmore before acting against Grimes and his band of fools. This waiting game is awful.

Three agonizingly slow days passed before news came. On the fourth morning, Samaren flew through the open window to land on the table where Barrett sat eating a hearty breakfast. As was their way, he set aside his plate and stroked the raven's head.

"What news, Mother?" he asked, barely suppressing his joy at her arrival. "I hope it's good for once."

"News from the city is never good any longer," the black bird answered. "However, Shardira has discovered a possible source of the spells. Though, you will not like her answer."

Barrett chuckled in reply. "How bad can it be? Another sorceress or wizard we have to face." Shrugging his indifference, he covertly hoped his cool exterior did not betray his racing heart.

Another magical battle was not his desire, though at least Trishar or Nirith would be there. He hoped, anyway.

"Asban has returned," the bird said simply. "Shardira heard the entire story from his lips. After escaping your spell, he came to take revenge by helping the Bureau bar you from the throne. He knew you would try to reclaim your crown and wishes to punish you for your stupidity, as he called it."

Barrett sprang to his feet. "Asban! That worm! I should have killed him when I had the chance. Why did I ever spare him! He needs to die!" Working into a furious froth, he paced about while mumbling over the past.

"Please sit down, son. Anger solves nothing. It merely makes matters worse," said Samaren calmly. "You cannot make good decisions with rage and frustration ruling your heart. Besides, you have defeated him before and I imagine he fears you. However, my first concern remains unanswered. Does he have aid?"

"Excellent question, my dear friend," said Trishar, entering the kitchen to pull a sturdy wooden chair beside the prince. "What can you say on that subject?" With a flick of her wrist, the food tray floated from the counter to settle on the table. She took bread and cheese.

"It is unclear if he has any others with him. Shardira says he resides on the castle's third floor near the old training room," offered the raven.

"Elimar taught me magic in that room," said Barrett as happy memories flooded his thoughts. His longing to see his friend still burned in his heart, just as it did while awaiting his arrival near the Outerworld. The old man's absence hurt the prince's feelings, but he understood wizards are always busy, even more so with wickedness running rampant over the lands.

Wizards and sorceresses could not possibly be everywhere at once. With Trishar bouncing between her house and the safe house, the main burden was on her brother to help those in need. Plus, Elimar was not at a lone teenager's beck and call.

"Well, this is inconvenient, to be sure," said Trishar. "We will need to handle him."

"I beg your pardon," squawked Samaren. "Do not turn my son into a killer."

Trishar laughed. "I was doing no such thing. I am simply implying the wizard is a problem that needs solving." She tapped her spoon against the tabletop. "You are being a bit overprotective, Samaren. You are forgetting your son, our future king, has already taken lives all on his own."

"Your point is taken. However, their duel took place with no outside interference," said Samaren. "Asban could now have several others by his side. My son would stand no chance. I forbid him from doing this foolishness." She cawed loudly. "Unless a sorceress was with him." Her dark eyes settled on Trishar and lingered.

The prince puffed his chest out. "Hold on! I can take care of myself and will make my own decisions. To be king, I must stand on my own two feet, right or wrong." His tone softened. "But I will still hear wise advice and try to follow it. Especially from two of the women I hold most precious."

"You have been exceedingly sensible to this point, so do not start acting like a fool now," said Trishar. "Your mother is certainly right. Magic or not, only a halfwit would willingly walk into a trap where they could be heavily outnumbered. *You* will be the death Gaia has foreseen. Now put your pride away and figure this out."

The raven squawked in agreement. "Exactly," she added as the others slowly gathered round the table.

Nell eased into a chair. "What's all the noise about?" She grabbed a handful of red grapes to pop them in her mouth one at a time, then grabbed a plate and loaded it full. "Um, I love breakfast."

Unger patted the prince's back as he passed. He winked. "Glad to see you're causing trouble already. Excellent work." He sat beside the Shifter, kissing her cheek as he settled into the chair. "And did I hear the name Asban? Or was that my imagination?"

"The whole house heard it," moaned Zanora, standing in wait to see where Graile would sit before choosing her seat. They smiled at one another. She slid an arm around his waist from behind and pulled him close. "Good morning."

He grinned in return. "It is a good morning." Moving a food tray closer, he slid it to her. "Hungry?"

"Starving," she answered, helping herself.

Again, Barrett watched. *I can't be the only one seeing these two, right?* He cast a look around. *Why is no one saying anything? Then again, why say anything at all? Let them be if they are happy.*

"Well, what are we going to do about the wizard?" asked Nell.

"Shardira offered to kill him," thought Samaren as Barrett spoke her words. "I told her we needed to discuss it first."

"Why? What is to discuss?" questioned Graile. "Barrett had the right idea. We should have finished him when we had the chance."

Samaren croaked another objection. "Did you really wish to kill him?" She hopped closer to her son. Her beady black eyes locked onto him as if searching his mind for an answer.

Barrett was unnerved by his mother's steady gaze. "I've said it before. I'm tired of everyone trying to kill us," he blurted as Samaren hopped closer. Her beak nearly pressed against his nose. "Besides, I didn't harm him. I only hurt his pride." He leaned back to create a distance. "Mother, you played a big part in my decision to allow him to live. Though, I didn't realize it until just now. You taught me compassion."

Zanora's mouth fell open as her cheeks flushed red. "I still think it's weird he talks to that ruddy bird and we can't hear her. It's like he's losing his mind."

Graile waved a fork before his face. "I don't even notice anymore. You'll get used to it. But truthfully, I think it's one of the most amazing things I've ever seen. I wish I could do it."

"That fool Asban is only a small part of our problem," Trishar chimed in. "Nonetheless, take a moment to think what would happen if he mysteriously wound up dead, especially after the failure in Carick's room. The Bureau may close off the city and start an inquisition. Thousands would suffer needlessly."

Barrett's reality hurriedly took shape. Trishar was right. Revenge would need to wait. If Asban suddenly wound up dead, things would be far worse and the prince was unwilling to be the source of more suffering, especially for his people.

"Wizards can be dealt with," said Mearis with a sly smile. "Many can be easily tricked at times. We should—"

"No. This is my doing and I will fix it," he interrupted. Barrett's thoughts faltered as an appealing image of Asban dead on the floor in the training room, struck down by a particularly nasty spell, brought relief. *I can do it. I can defeat him again.* "I'll find him—" he started.

"Not alone, you won't. I am going with you," blurted Gaia. Her face was stern as all eyes turned to her.

"Gaia must *really* be mad if she's snappy," muttered Unger.

Nell nodded with wide eyes.

"Whatever happens, I stress the importance of not using

magic," said Trishar. "Once we get more information we can make a solid strategy."

"Strategy to do what? We need Asban gone. How plain can it be?" asked Unger. "Going into Westmore to take notes or gather more news seems pointless. At this rate Barrett will never be king and the Bureau will surely find us. They are bound to spot us, even with our disguises. Shardira saw right through us, so maybe others can too."

"We need to split up," blurted Zanora. "Nell goes with Unger, Graile is with me, and Gaia goes alongside Barrett. We'll find Asban's source of power. I am fairly certain he can't do this on his own. Destroy his helpers or device, and, huzzah, it will be done."

Graile leaned back in his chair. "That's brilliant."

"Right you are. The old man will revert to being worthless—a minor magician and nothing more," said Nell.

"What if we're wrong?" asked the prince, unable to stop himself from poking holes in the redhead's plan. The thought of inflicting pain on possible innocents bit at him. "Suppose he has a dozen magic users as a source? I would rather not hurt a dozen people to stop him. What if they are forced to help, like Randolph or Alesta, and we end up hurting them, too? There has to be a better way."

"How would you feel if they are helping willingly?" asked Gaia, letting that sink in before going on. "I don't like to think of it, but not everyone wants the Bureau to fail. Some magical ones could be on his side. What if they are freely performing wickedness?"

"It's a chance we'll need to take," said Graile. "We could discuss plans until we are old and grey. It is time for action."

"Maybe. Just remember that planning keeps us alive," countered Barrett, wondering how reasonable he sounded after having

Asban escape to return as another adversary. *Our list of enemies is growing.* To date, there were Grimes, Trackers, Agents, Asban, and the Bureau of Mystical Affairs itself.

"This isn't living. It's captivity," said Zanora, sweeping her arm before her. "This problem needs solving. Not endless talking and debating. You have all that power . . . use it!"

Unger snorted as he sided with the prince. "Planning has saved us several times. And it's better than the alternative since I'm not keen on being dead just yet." His expression switched to anger. "Besides, you know Barrett can't use magic. We would have the entire Bureau after us in an instant."

"Stop there," said Trishar, raising a hand for quiet. "We do need action and each of you makes valid points. However," she added with a sharp glance at the prince, "give it two more days. Samaren can return to Shardira and have her discover what she can about Asban's source. We have waited this long to see the return of the king, so a few more days will not hurt."

"Remember, Shardira is a Tracker. If Asban or his followers use magic, she should know. Considerable hopes rest on her skill and willingness to help. I know you want to fight for what is yours, but patience is best. Trishar is giving excellent advice. Try and listen for once," urged Mearis.

Samaren cawed her agreement as Barrett finished his food and quickly excused himself. Once the friends cleared the table, he caught Graile's eye and slyly signaled him to follow. He led the Fader upstairs to his room, then shut them inside.

"What has gotten into you?" asked Graile. "You—"

Barrett spoke in a rush but quietly for fear of being overheard. "I'm going to Westmore tonight and hope you will come along. I know I'm supposed to wait, but we're so close to breaking the Bureau apart that I can't sit still. So you know, I will not willingly put you in danger. Refuse if you wish. There will be no hurt feelings. Zanora spoke truly, saying all this sneaking around was wearing thin. I want action, not waiting for the Bureau to mess up."

The Fader was skeptical. "And what is our purpose? You heard the others. We could ruin everything. This may be one time you should actually *listen*. It's only two days."

Barrett wrung his hands in nervousness, then inclined his head toward the window. "I'll send Samaren ahead. She can have Shardira meet us behind The Pointed Hat. I want to track Asban. It is time for answers, not talking or sitting on our backsides."

Graile's eyebrows pinched downward as he pondered the possibilities. "Trishar will be furious if anything happens like the last time. I'm not sure I want to see that." He paced the room with both hands tucked behind his back. After some time, he heaved a long sigh. "I will be ready after dinner once it gets dark."

Barrett nearly leapt from his skin with elation. "Excellent! I knew I could count on you. Meet me out the backdoor after the others go to sleep."

He flung open the door, then thundered downstairs to find his raven.

Perched on his shoulder, she squawked endlessly as they moved outside for a lengthy debate. After pleading and reasoning from her son, Samaren ultimately agreed to do as asked. By mid-morning, she had vanished into the sunlight as she winged toward the city.

Time could not pass fast enough as Barrett waited for darkness to overtake the day.

11

The Orb

Freeing his wand, Barrett turned his hair auburn, extending the length well down his back. He had to make several jagged streaks of blonde right, but otherwise, things went smoothly. He was pleased the color contrasted nicely with his dark green tunic, black breeches, and cloak. "Trishar does it better, but this will work," he said, staring into the tall mirror.

Graile wore freshly painted eye circles. This time, he added his white death face, similar to the one worn when entering the Outerworld. Irregular black streaks extended from the corners of each eye and his mouth to meet his chin.

He wore his standard attire, clothed entirely in black with a raised hood concealing his face in shadow. His intimidating presence gave the appearance of a giant, wicked bat, not unlike the creatures they had faced in Apadora's realm.

Stepping from the house, the two hurried toward the road. The Fader blended into the night so well that Barrett lost track of him several times. More than once, he looked around to ensure his friend was still with him.

"Can't you dress normal?" complained Barrett.

"I do," replied Graile. The corner of his mouth curled upward. "You are the one who dresses funny. Besides, black suits me. As a bonus, I do not need to mix and match clothing."

Barrett snickered and raised his brows in surprise. "I've noticed."

Fortunately, once they broke from the protection of the trees, a waxing gibbous moon shone brightly overhead. As they had grown accustomed to over the last months, the pair secreted themselves away from approaching riders or wagons, staying hidden in the tree line.

Their path, barely seen in the pale light, led round the foot of the nearby mountain. Tall trees swayed in the gusting wind, creaking and moaning as if talking, announcing the presence of the nighttime intruders. A pack of wolves trotted past some short distance ahead, their eyes glowing in the moonlight as they slunk from sight.

There were other eyes, too, but Barrett did not wish to know what they belonged to or whether he and Graile would become midnight snacks for some unnamed creature in the wilds outside the city.

Despite the late hour, Barrett was too energized to be tired. He kept a spry pace, partly from fear, partly from exhilaration. As they went, he could not shake the questions he knew would soon come. Trishar's angry face swam before him, then Gaia's hurtful look seeped into his heart. What would he tell his friends concerning his unexpected absence? No matter how many scenarios he concocted, none sounded believable. He suddenly regretted involving Graile in his deception.

Though the Fader would keep their adventure private, Barrett never wished to bring trouble to him. If caught, the prince decided to take full responsibility. It was his idea, after all, that led to Graile breaking the rules Trishar had set down. His friend should not have to suffer the consequences.

After great length, they reached the elf gate. From there, they quickly slipped through the city's outer wall. They hurried across the sprawling field, one filled with swaying shadows as moonlight sent pale rays between the swaying tree boughs. As the breeze moved the limbs to and fro, making the light quiver around him, Barrett imagined Agents hiding in wait to claim their reward for catching two dangerous fugitives. In his mind, every sound and shadow held the enemy.

After passing several city blocks, Barrett tugged on Graile's cloak. They angled into a darkened alleyway, vanishing unnoticed, except for a beggar huddled in a corner with a tattered blanket wrapped tightly around him. Barrett knelt by the man's side and slipped the dirty fellow a silver piece for food and clothing.

"May the gods bless you, my lord," the man kept repeating as the duo moved from his sight.

"You're always kind to those less fortunate," said the Fader, clapping the prince's back. "It's why you'll be a good king."

"I appreciate that, but I stand no chance of giving more if Asban isn't stopped," answered Barrett, patting his coin purse. "I'm nearly broke."

The inn seemed farther away than the prince recalled, but they arrived in the alleyway after several turns. Except for the smell, it was beautiful in many ways. Crickets chirped, an owl hooted high above, and mice scurried about in search of a meal. Barrett picked the freshest food from the top of a trash bin and tossed it on the ground. The mice ran to it, sniffed, and began to eat. Five others came from hiding to join in the feast.

"See. Soft heart," said Graile. "It's one reason I like you. For all your talk of killing Grimes and Asban, you don't have a mean bone in your body."

"They are creatures of this world simply trying to survive," replied Barrett. "I see no harm in helping them. Why does everyone want to kill innocents or things they do not understand? Grimes and Asban are something different."

"You *are* indeed very kind," came a voice from above.

The pair rounded to see Shardira squatting on the dingy stairs leading to the second story. She sprang over the railing to land before them with only a soft tapping sound as her feet touched the ground.

"Greetings again, my liege," she said with a graceful bow.

Barrett struggled not to stare. *She's even more beautiful than the first time I saw her.* He wished to slap his head for having the thought. *I'm glad Gaia cannot see my aura right now.*

"I have never met any elf kind. It is a pleasure and honor," said Graile, as if voicing his friend's thoughts.

Shardira gave another bow. "The pleasure is mine, my Fader friend." She reached to move his hood away as she examined his face. "Most remarkable. I see you are skilled in creation and have a vivid imagination."

Graile nodded slowly, then raised his hood. "Thank you, my lady. It is a custom of my people. Especially when facing danger."

"What did you learn of Asban? Have you discovered anything?" asked Barrett.

"Indeed," said Shardira. "With a bit of help from Randolph, I have learned during Grimes' raid on the village they discovered a Protium Lapis, known as an Orb of Protection. Years ago, it was said, the stones vanished from all knowledge, yet we were all deceived. This particular one was hidden away, so it must hold value."

"The name gives its function away, yes? If we could steal it back, a majority of the Bureau's power would disappear," said Graile, flicking dust from his cloak. "Where would you guess Asban keeps it hidden?"

"First, you are correct, my dark friend. The stones once protected entire villages and cities in ancient days. How the orb came to betray the Mordoria villagers, or why it was hidden from knowledge, we may never know. Yet, the problem is ours now. I have finally sensed it within the walls of the castle."

"The castle?" Barrett mumbled several curses under his breath. "Take us to it if you can. I wish to see this treasure for myself," he said. "From there, I will ask no more of you this night. No other Tracker will lend us aid. If you fall, our cause and the world will be poorer for it."

Shardira smiled and lay a hand over her breast. "You are my king. Your safety is far above my own. If I fall, you are still able to regain your city. Though, if you fall, hope is lost. I will protect you with my life and will not leave your side, Sire."

The prince went speechless. *How should I reply?* The elf did have a point, but the reality sounded cold and selfish when said aloud. The willingness of another to sacrifice their life for him was humbling.

"Let's not think about that right now. I would prefer if no one died tonight," he finally said. "Especially with you offering to sacrifice yourself." An awkward smile turned up the corners of his mouth.

"Lead on," said Graile, casting wary eyes around them to ensure solitude.

Shardira's footfalls were so light Barrett felt like he was beating a drum with his steps. *She makes less noise than a family of mice. Yet another quality I admire about her kind.*

Keeping to the shadows, they passed houses with manicured bushes lining their yards. Chimney smoke caught in the wind circled them like grey crowns. Barrett inhaled, loving the smell of burning wood as it filled the streets with a layer of fragrant aromas.

They soon turned down a quiet alley. Stopping once to hide as a pair of Trackers ambled by, complaining to one another about night patrol, Barrett grasped his wand, praying he would not need it.

"If those Trackers spot us, hunting down magic users will be the least of their worries," he whispered.

Shardira pressed a slender finger to her lips and tapped her knife hilt. "I shall handle them if needed. Magic will merely draw more to us."

Barrett felt foolish. *Things will only get worse if I use my wand. The she-elf is right.*

To his relief, no defense was needed. Once the Trackers disappeared, he took the lead, steering the trio toward the hidden entrance. He remained uncertain if he should divulge the secret of the tunnel system's existence to their guide. Halting beyond moonlight's reach, he stared at the elf awkwardly for an instant. Her inquisitive look was even more piercing than Gaia's gaze and he found it difficult to hold.

"Is something wrong, my lord?" she asked, stepping closer. Her sweet fragrance filled his nostrils, making his concentration weaken.

Barrett cleared his throat. "We wish to show you something very few have seen. Under pain of death, tell no one. Ever." He waited for her nod, then worked the secret stone to pop the entrance open. Urging them inside, he lit the torch as Graile sealed the door.

Shardira touched the prince's shoulder as the orange flame sprang to life. "On my word as an elf, I will not betray your trust." She inspected the passage with keen eyes. "I never knew these were here. They are beautiful in their own way. And very handy, I imagine."

Off they went through the dank tunnels leading deeper into the castle bowels. Barrett never slowed save for emerging from one passage to another. This required crossing hallways, rooms, or chambers since not all corridors were directly connected. He took caution and care with each one.

Still, even with the ever-present dangers, memories of boyhood adventures within the castle walls returned as they ventured on. Here, his parents lived and loved, his mentor Yaris trained him to fight like a soldier, and Elimar taught him magic. His first kiss with Zanora happened there, too.

He had also studied horseback riding, archery, courtly manners, and, most of all, never giving up no matter how awful things appeared. That was what he was doing, he told himself. Another pang of grief shook his heart as his father's voice replayed in his head. "Stay the course,' he used to say. Barrett was trying to do just that, but uncertainty nagged him.

Finally, they reached the back of a tall bookcase. "Asban's chamber is on the other side of this wall. At least, I think it is," he said softly.

He pressed his palm against the wall, reminding himself it was safe to use his senses. *No Tracker—not even Shardira—can detect this probing. It's not magic, just intuition.* Pushing his power outward, he sensed the room sat empty. Satisfied, he flicked a small lever to unseal the panel, then raised his hood, just in case.

The friends slunk inside before Graile quietly resealed the wall. Meanwhile, Barrett frowned while he inspected the chamber, noticing all his old furnishings were gone, just like in his private chambers.

To his left, the fireplace held a low-burning fire. The furnishings looked well-worn and drab. Four oil lamps hung from the high ceiling beams. No pictures graced the walls, though several tapestries and banners hung there, undulating as a breeze stirred them from an open window.

The friends crossed the marble floor, which held a woven rug. An image of a bear's face was in its center. It felt dingy and ugly, exactly like Barrett thought of the greasy wizard.

In short order, they rummaged through several cabinets, shelves, boxes, and drawers. Barrett cursed. "There's nothing here. Head for the training room."

Back inside the tunnel, they climbed the winding stone stairs as the prince had often done when Elimar was teaching him magic in the training room. Advancing with caution, they reached the hidden entrance—the panel beside the fireplace.

"We're here," whispered Barrett.

Graile turned to vapor to drift beneath the door's floor gap. Seconds later, a clanking sound filled the tunnel as the heavy wooden entry was unlocked. Solid again, he opened the passage from the room's interior. "We are alone."

"That was wondrous," said Shardira. "I admire Faders in many ways. Long ago, my people gave your kind shelter when you were hunted for sport. Humans can be cruel to beings beyond their comprehension, even elves. We have often debated how men survive as such a violent race."

"You are very kind," replied Graile, pushing the panel shut with a soft clank. "And you are right. Even now, my kind is still hunted in other lands."

Barrett shuffled next to the she-elf. "Here is the part I need you for the most. Can you find the orb?"

Shardira paused. "I am unsure. Usually, I detect the use of magic. Of course, I must be nearby to sense it. But I feel nothing now. The orb may be protected by a spell, but with luck, if Asban is using it to shield his doings, it will give itself away. Allow me to try."

She drew a deep breath, stood motionless for a long moment, then exhaled slowly. Moving around the room, she placed a hand here and there, waiting for a feeling or vibration. In some places, she sniffed the air. Others, she tapped on a wall or desktop. After several attempts, she halted.

"The object you seek is not in this room," she whispered.

Panic spun the prince's mind, forcing words out faster than intended. "It was a mistake coming here. We need to go. I should have listened to Trishar. I thought finding the magic source would have been easier," he confessed.

"Patience, my friend," said Graile. "Where else would it be? Think. We must find it. If we fail, who knows when we will be able to try again."

"It could be anywhere. There are a million places to hide the thing." Barrett rubbed his face as he considered several ideas. "Maybe the top of a tower. The orb could cast its magic far and wide from there." His voice wavered as the painful notion of failure smacked him like a physical blow. "I felt positive he would keep it in his room. From here out, I am only guessing where it could be."

"Let us make for the western spire first. It is the closest," said Shardira. "This orb must be powerful to hide itself from our searches. Perhaps it is the most potent of all the old stones. It would explain why it was hidden away so it would not fall into evil hands. Or someone wished to keep it for their own."

Barrett moved to the hearth, using his torch to reveal an intricately carved leaf pattern below the mantle. He pressed the end piece to watch the door swing open. "Come. Up, up we go." He led the trio in silence, save for the annoying clack of his and Graile's boots against the stone. Again, the elf's footfalls made little noise.

"I would favor a straight-on fight more than all this sneaking through walls and passages like a crafty spider," said Barrett.

"Safety lies in concealment," said Shardira softly.

Barrett thought of the safe house, hoping no one there had noticed their absence yet. *Slim chance of that. They will find us missing soon enough.* The notion of returning to an angry sorceress, especially empty-handed, brought another wave of dread. She would be livid he disregarded her instructions. Yet, with luck from the gods, all things would be set right if he could only find the orb. His rashness and disobedience may be forgiven if this misadventure could restore Mearis' powers and help Gaia's readings.

His legs ached and breathing grew labored as the stairs wound ever upward. An unnatural chill gripped him the higher they went, driving home the harsh reality before him. The cold did not come from cool night temperatures but from a presence staining the walls with evil, as if his home had been sullied by the Bureau's vileness. He was certain Asban's energy was the source since, according to Shardira, the orb itself was not said to be evil. *The wizard, on the other hand, is a greedy little worm whose mere presence could taint my home.* Cursing both him and Bureau for their deceitful ways and foul magic, the prince's resolve hardened.

Just then, they reached an arched framework. Again, Barrett pushed his senses outward. The rock seemed to speak to him. Empty, it said.

Patting the stone, he thanked it for its word and pressed the foot pedal to open the door. They went inside, but brandishing the orange torchlight in the thick gloom did little to splinter the wavering darkness.

Then, as if the clouds were swept away by a god's hand to aid their cause, pale moonlight shone through a tall window to illuminate an intricate altar. The low, thick stonework stood squarely in the chamber's center.

"The Orb," Barrett whispered as he hurried forward. "It's smaller than I imagined." The fist-sized stone made his breath catch. Awed by the amber-colored sphere, he extended a shaking hand to touch its smoothness. The surface felt like expensive crystal, yet hard and impenetrable. Inside was a swirling red mist he fascinated over as it twisted about like a sentient being trying to escape or waiting to be heard.

"It's magnificent. It feels ancient," said Graile, taking his turn at feeling the magical piece.

"It *is* remarkable," said Shardira, extending a hand to hover over the orb. "It surges with power. It is very strong."

Barrett regained his wits and seized the trophy, wrapping it in a woolen cloth before placing it in his pack.

"Time to go," he whispered. Sliding the rucksack onto his back, he headed for the stairs and lifted his hood.

Suddenly, heavy boots and voices wafted from outside on the connecting parapet, the stone walkways linking the lookout towers. Barrett cursed. He had forgotten about the guards that surveyed the city from high above.

As the sounds and voices grew, Barrett hurriedly unsealed the passage and herded Shardira and Graile inside. Outside the chamber, keys jangled as the guards unlocked the door and swung it open. At the same instant, the prince resealed the tunnel.

Hidden within the walls, the trio went still, barely breathing. Barrett's heart leapt as he listened to the guard's torch sputter just inches away on the opposite side of the door. Sounds of the flame being waved about made the friends exchange concerned glances.

"Do you smell smoke?" said one. "Like a lamp or somethin' was burnin."

"Of course, I smell it, you idiot. I'm carryin' a torch," said the other, waving the flame on purpose. "What do you expect? Now do your job and check the city. Are we being invaded?"

The other laughed. "Don't be a dolt! We're safe, as usual. With magic on the run, things are peaceful. There's no more of that wand-waving nonsense to stir up trouble."

"You really are a total fool," said the second one. "Magic was the reason we stayed safe all these years. With it gone, these Bureau buffoons are going to get us all killed. Our enemies know full well we are nearly defenseless. The city is leaderless and the army is in disarray. Carick is senseless. Honestly, I'm surprised we ain't been raided yet."

"But we're not defenseless. That peculiar little wizard . . . Asban, I think his name is . . . says this little ball will keep us . . . By the gods! It's gone!" cried the first. His hurried footsteps echoed as he rushed to the altar. "Where is the wretched thing!"

"Sound the alarm! Blow the horn!" cried the other. "Thieves! Intruders!"

Precious moments ticked away as Barrett remained still, unnerved, and unsure of what to do. He could not reveal himself without exposing the tunnels, nor was magic an option without setting Trackers on their trail. Standing helplessly on the opposite side of the wall with panicked guards mere feet away, he fought to control his breathing.

Their silence would carry a high price—death, but he had no intention of slaying two innocent men for doing their jobs. *What should I do? We may never escape if they sound the alarm.*

Graile acted, fading to vapor to glide beneath the door. Drifting into the chamber like a writhing shadow, he solidified, seized the guards' heads and crashed them together. Their helms and weapons clattered noisily against the floor as they crumbled in unconscious heaps. Vaporous again, the Fader re-entered the passage to reappear at Shardira's side.

"Hurry," he said. "We must go."

Down and around to the third floor they went, moving from one hidden entrance to another, pausing only when entering a hallway or room. Time felt stilled. Barrett wondered how long they had been dashing through the maze of passageways.

Finally, breathless and nearly free of the castle, they halted at the final door to listen before making a push toward the city streets.

"That was quick thinking," noted the prince between deep inhales. "You saved us."

"Did you kill them?" asked Shardira, breathing easily.

Graile lowered his hood and shook his head as pale strands of moonlight touched upon his death face. "No. They had nothing to do with our plight. There was no reason for them to die. But they will have headaches once they wake up."

"For reasons I do not fully understand, I am drawn to your little company." The elf gently touched the prince's hand. "Perhaps your bravery and wisdom, like that of elves, draws me in. You are not like most, and your actions are quite impressive."

Barrett smiled as his eyes met the she-elf. "Thank you, but I'm unsure how wise any of this was."

In truth, he felt anything but brave and wise. Thanks to his impatience, he and Graile would likely be caught once they returned to the safe house. That bothered him more than he thought possible. Nearly getting caught stealing the orb did not bolster his confidence, either. He had already made a mess of things and the night was far from over. Worst of all, he would need to lie about his actions to avoid being in hot water. If Gaia read his aura, she would know and that bothered him. He hated lying to her.

Touching the elf's shoulder, his expression changed to sadness. "Regrettably, we must part ways for now. We will contact you again soon. Please have Samaren return today. Meanwhile, we will decide what to do with the stone."

"Agreed," said Graile. "I have a feeling that decision may not be ours. Trishar will have something to say about it."

Barrett flinched at the thought of the sorceress. "I bet she will have a lot to say about it. She's either going to ground me or change me into something unnatural," he said with a shaky voice.

"I meant what she will say about the orb," replied the Fader.

Barrett flushed. "I knew that," he lied. "I was only kidding."

"I will send your raven by morning's light." Shardira pushed her chin toward the main gate. "Will you leave the city by the elf gate?"

Barrett stiffened. "You know of it? How? That's supposed to be secret."

Shardira chuckled for the first time. "I *am* part elf. The gates are called *Limardil* in my tongue, meaning 'hidden to most.' Like the orb you hold, there are but few remaining. Once, Westmore maintained a strong alliance with the elves. The entries were built for special people or places. Your city is honored to have one."

"How interesting. I never knew. I wonder why no one ever mentioned its history?" said the prince.

"Discuss this later. We need to go," reminded Graile.

Slipping into the alleyway, they made for the street, pausing as three well-dressed men appeared. They halted in the dim light to converse. *They sound like businessmen finishing a late-night meeting*, Barrett thought. Squinting through the gloom of night, he studied them as they spoke. They looked familiar.

Finally, he remembered. On occasion, these same men had paid him respect as they crossed his path within the city, though he could not recall their names. Soon, the men faded from sight, vanishing round a corner.

"I don't think they saw us," said Graile.

"Good. Let's move," said Barrett.

So it was the trio merged onto the street with only moonlight showing the way through the clear, cold night. After brief farewells, Graile and Barrett headed for the elf gate as Shardira faded into the shadows.

12

Decisions

Mearis sat snuggled in her plush chair, flipping pages of a book. Her mind was not on the words. Instead, it was fixed on the disappearance of two young men under her care. Sipping her tea, she peered over the cup's edge and huffed as Graile and Barrett slunk into the house. They attempted to sneak upstairs, but their game ended once the front door closed.

"Where have you two been?" the Seer asked with remarkable calm. "I've been worried sick. Trishar will be most displeased. Not to mention, I have lost substantial sleep waiting for your return."

The prince jumped at her voice. "Please don't tell her!" Pulling off his pack, he rummaged inside to produce the stone. "We went to steal this little beauty." Uncovering the orb from beneath the soft cloth, he extended it for inspection.

Mearis sat bolt upright and shot from her chair with a gasp. "How did you come by this?"

Graile removed his cloak, then lowered onto the sofa to wipe away his makeup with a napkin. "From a high watchtower within the castle."

"How did you learn of it?" she asked.

Barrett was thrilled Mearis had already forgotten her threat of telling Trishar. He hoped it stayed that way. "Shardira and Randy were very helpful with their information. Without them, we may have never found it. Oh, and the she-elf went with us."

Mearis turned the corners of her mouth down in a frown. "You mean to say the three of you snuck into Westmore, entered the castle, stole the orb, then returned here even after Trishar said to stay put?" She pointed to the floor.

Barrett turned his humiliated gaze downward as he shrugged. "More or less, yes." Awaiting a scolding, he was surprised when the woman wrapped him in a hug instead.

"Such a spirit you have!" She kissed his cheek, then turned to Graile. "All of you remind me of myself in my younger days. My heart sings when I hear your stories. I once lived for adventure, too. At least, until Nirith turned me into a Trowken."

"Hold on. You're saying we're not in trouble?" questioned Graile.

"Of course not." She paused to weigh her words. "Not with me, anyway." She wagged a scolding finger at them. "But your actions were foolish and could have brought the end to us all. Lucky for you, it worked out for the best, yes?"

Barrett could only nod while wanting to cement his victory of sorts. "We were trying to get your vision back." He set the orb on the table, still captivated by the swirling mist. Its hypnotizing motion drew him in, like pulling him from the room toward a darker place he had never been. But just as he moved toward it again, longing to immerse himself in its gloom, Mearis hugged him a second time.

"I am amazed at you two," she said.

"Well . . . there was a problem," added Graile. "Two guards got in the way."

The Seer backed away. "Tell me you did not kill anyone. You know the stir another incident would cause. After your ransacking failure, the Bureau will go on a relentless hunt to find the culprits."

The Fader shook his head. "They are alive and well but decided to nap for a little while."

His words did not seem to appease Mearis. "Things are going to change quickly now. And not for the better," she insisted, souring the prince's brief ego boost. "We will discuss the details in the morning. Get some rest." She waved them toward the stairs. "And stay in your rooms this time before Trishar discovers your antics and turns you both into trolls."

"I thought it would be slugs or a Malnorvian Yeti," muttered Barrett as he trudged upstairs with Graile in the lead.

The sun rode high in the sky on a cloudless day while light breezes swayed the curtains through the open pane. Long, yellow rays slanted through the window to shine on the prince's bed as his eyes fluttered open. He stretched and yawned.

"It is about time, young man," came a voice.

"Good morning, my dear mother," he said, facing the raven perched on the hearth's thick wooden mantle. She glided to the end of the bed, then hopped closer so he could stroke her feathers.

"You took a risk," she said, sounding displeased. "Your father and I taught you to think your actions through beforehand. It seems you have forgotten that lesson?"

"I . . . I . . . oh, let me wake up before having this conversation." Barrett pointed to the floor and circled his index finger. "Can you turn around, please? I wish to dress."

Samaren tilted her head. "Feel free. I am not stopping you."

The prince exhaled heavily. "I'm naked, Mother. Will you please turn around?"

"Children!" She glided to a small table in the room's center, folded her wings, and cawed as she turned away.

Barrett rushed to the dresser to grab his only spare tunic. After giving it a quick sniff, he slipped it on, followed hurriedly by his breeches, socks, and boots. Lastly, he ran his fingers through his hair. *Good enough.* "I'm starving. I hope I didn't miss breakfast."

Samaren chuckled. "Breakfast was hours ago. But do not worry, there is still plenty of food to your liking. So you know, Shardira confided in me and I relayed the news to Trishar.." She flew closer again. "I am sure she has already told your friends what you have done. They had a right to know."

"Mother!" cried Barrett. "Thank you! Now, I will need to endure a million questions. And Trishar will probably lock me away. Please tell me you didn't tell her."

Samaren purposely ignored his last question. "Then perhaps you should not keep secrets or disobey when you are told something for your own good. Not to mention the good of others." She tilted her head and changed the subject. "What will you do with the stone?"

"Great question," he replied, heading for the door. "I was hoping Elimar would be here by now. I could use his guidance. Where is that blasted wizard?" He straightened his hair again. "No matter, a plan will come to me."

The raven flew to land on his shoulder. She pressed her head against his cheek. "I am pleased you are safe."

Barrett entered the hall, turning left to take the creaking stairs down to the sitting room. He headed for the kitchen where Gaia greeted him with a hug and kiss. *I could get used to waking up this way every day.* He opened the back door to let his mother outside.

She flapped her wings and glided past. "Stay out of trouble, young man. I will return soon."

Barrett grunted, hoping his mother did not hear. "Yes, Mother." He lowered next to the witch and smiled.

Gaia slapped his knee with her palm. "I am *so* upset with you for not telling me you were sneaking out. I would have come along," she said, folding her arms over her chest. "It was rude not to ask. You took Graile, but not me."

"But . . . but . . . I—" he stammered.

Zanora cut him off. "You always stutter when you get caught doing something wrong. Stop it. It's bizarre." She wagged a finger at him. "Your girlfriend is right. We should've all gone along."

Hearing her mention 'girlfriend' so casually confused him. Was she jealous and meant the word sarcastically or had she finally accepted that he and Gaia were together? He said nothing, fearing a stuttering fit would come. *Why do I even care what she thinks?*

"Our number would have been too many," said Graile. "We would have been caught or killed if the whole company would have been found fumbling around. It was not worth the risk. Only Shardira joined us."

When a chill ran over Barrett, he looked instinctively at the redhead as if she was the cause. She sat sulking with a dour expression. She took clear offense to the Fader leaving her behind.

"Oh, you'll take the she-elf, but not me," she said.

"Stop whining. You hurt my head," said Unger, rubbing his temples with his palms. "Can't you just say you're happy they didn't die?"

"I *am* going to hurt your head, you—"

"Is there any news?" interrupted Nell, waving away the sound of their banter. "I mean, stealing the orb had to cause a commotion. Right?"

"The Bureau will never admit what happened," said Barrett. "It would give away their secret. They would have to confess to suppressing magic with magic of their own."

Mearis grabbed the morning paper from the counter and tossed it on the table. "Trishar has been delayed this morning, so I took on her normal daily duties. Earlier, I picked this up in the city. I have not read it yet."

"Then let's find out," said Graile, grabbing the latest edition of *The Oracle*. He scanned the front page, then read aloud.

Manhunt Underway

"Wily thieves unlawfully entered the castle last night, stealing numerous belongings, many of which were precious to King Carick. In the age-long history of Westmore, no such offense has ever taken place within the castle walls. Even as this article is being written, the culprits are being pursued. Risnor J. Grimes, Inquirer General for the Bureau of Mystical Affairs, assured this reporter the burglars would be caught, tried, and punished for violating numerous laws against the throne. There are multiple leads to the suspects.

Agents and Trackers are currently following the trail. Stay tuned for all Bureau updates. Yours truly, Randolph Rollie."

Frowning, Graile folded the paper and tossed it back onto the table. "Ridiculous. The only thing those fools could catch is a cold."

"Does that mean Agents or Trackers are coming here?" asked Nell, toying with her fork. "Can they find us? "

"Except for opening the elf gate, which cannot be tracked, we never used spells," replied the prince, hoping to comfort the churning doubts. "There is nothing to find."

"Utter rubbish," said Unger, sneering at the newspaper as if it had personally offended him. "I feel bad for Randolph having to write this garbage."

"You can be sure of that fact," said Gaia. "He said more misinformation would be printed to frighten or stir people up. This must be it."

Graile held up his index finger. "One thing in particular is a lie. Yes, we took the orb, but nothing more. They're blowing the entire event out of proportion."

Mearis, after excusing herself to make tea, shuffled in from the kitchen. "I almost forgot this one." She pulled a different newspaper from beneath her arm and waved it about. "Here is a special edition Randolph sent over. It was printed within the last hour. For the bad news, the Bureau hung three men for your crime just this morning." She tossed the updated edition of *The Oracle* on the table and frowned.

Barrett could not turn away from the ghastly, moving image of three men dangling from long ropes. Their lifeless bodies, necks bent at odd angles, swayed before the castle gates. He choked back the bile edging up his throat. Shaken and ignoring his previous hunger, he slumped into his chair as Graile seized the latest paper.

"We saw those fellows," said the prince, slapping the table with his palm. "Curse the Bureau for their cruelty."

"Hold on. Where do you know them from?" asked Nell.

The Fader tilted his head as if doubting what he saw. He brought the paper closer to study the image more intently. "Those are the businessmen from last night. Aside from us, they were the only ones on the street. I bet someone complained about them being out past curfew, so Agents started asking questions and found them. They are scapegoats for our actions."

"While you slept, Trishar informed us the city now has a curfew. The Bureau is on edge after the break-in," said Unger. "No one is allowed on the street after ten o'clock."

"This is awful. Those men died because you stole the orb," said Gaia. "It's unfair."

"Our sweet, innocent Gaia." Zanora snorted at the witch's goodness. "This may come as a shock, but life isn't fair. Don't forget—innocent people have been put to death for ages. This is nothing new, terrible as it is. And what does it even matter? They were going to die someday anyway. We all do."

"That's the dumbest thing I've ever heard," snapped Unger. "Yes, we're all going to die. But being executed for something you had no part in is wrong. They were murdered because of what Barrett did." He gave an apologetic look to the prince. "But it is not his fault."

"He wasn't alone," added Graile. "I'm to blame, as well. This will be on my conscience from here out."

"Don't take it too hard," Zanora patted the Fader's knee with a softened look. "It was simply bad luck for them. They were in the wrong place at the wrong time. Mystical Affairs needed someone to blame and these fellows were convenient."

"True," said Nell. "The Bureau would come across as fools if they could not solve the crime quickly. They needed pawns to take the fall. Like Zanora said, wrong place, wrong time. Still, it's horrible they had to pay the ultimate price." Her eyes fell on Barrett as the last words came out.

Guilt struck the prince hard. He kept his gaze low to avoid their angry, blaming stares. The burden of the men's death weighed heavy in his heart. He cursed his impulsive decision to sneak out and wished he could take it all back—erase it entirely. *Why can't I listen? Trishar said to stay put and now this is the weight I must carry for being willful. It will haunt me forever.*

Struggling to hold back his anguish, his eyes sought the witch's, hoping to gain some unspoken comfort. But her face was stern. A frown perched on her lips and her arms remained folded, rejecting his touch. Barrett replayed her comment in his head. Though she did not accuse him directly, she blamed him for his thievery. The worst part was knowing she was right.

"I never wanted to upset you, but this needed to be done, so I took action," he said.

"No matter how you try to justify this, words will never be enough," said Gaia. "If you didn't steal the orb, those men would be alive."

An imaginary cloud of guilt formed over the prince, quickly turning into a raging thunderstorm. His energy for defending himself was draining away.

"All of you, please be quiet," said Mearis. The Seer's calming gaze touched on each friend in turn. "I know this is upsetting. Still, we cannot change what has been done. Even the gods cannot undo this tragedy. Right or wrong, stealing the orb stripped away a good bit of the Bureau's power. Someday, these men's sacrifice shall be honored."

"That's easy to say," said Zanora, eyeing Barrett with an annoyed look. "You have messed everything up. The city will be flooded with Agents and Trackers now. Three people died because of your selfish antics."

"A minute ago, you said they died because of bad luck. Now you're blaming us. Make up your mind," said Graile. "Or do you simply enjoy arguing?"

Zanora's expression changed to anger before she turned away from the Fader.

"I have another idea," said the prince.

The redhead sprang at the chance to chime in again. "Your last one sure turned out to be a gem. If it works, maybe this one can get more people killed."

"Will you please shut up?" snapped Unger, his voice rising an octave. "Now, do you see why no one wants you around? We don't need your nasty attitude. Why don't you go back to Grimes and let us handle this? You're not really helping anyway."

Zanora froze in her chair. Her usual sharp comments did not come. Instead, her face paled and her mouth fell open. She gazed at her friends with a horrified look, then rose to back into the hallway. There, she turned and rushed to her room.

Gaia slapped the table. "That was the meanest thing you have ever done. You were an ass. Go apologize!" She jammed an arm through the air to point her fork down the hall.

Unger mumbled under his breath, then leaned back. "I will not."

Mearis rose. "I will talk to her." She placed both hands on the table and leaned in. "Have an apology ready when we return. You were disrespectful and mean. Maybe it is you that should have gone to your room."

Graile rose slowly. "Mearis, would you mind if I went instead? She may be more comfortable speaking to me."

"Good idea," said the Seer. "Thank you. At least one of you has manners."

Nell nudged the archer with her elbow. "This entire thing has us all on edge. You need to tell her you're sorry. It's the right thing to do. You were cruel and that is unattractive. Treat me like that and a horned ogre will bite your head from your shoulders and gnaw your skinny bones for a snack."

Unger gulped down a breath. "Is there anything you cannot morph into?" He exhaled heavily and wiped his slick palms on his breeches. "Fine!" Dejected, he trudged toward Zanora's room, knocked, then waited for a conversation he was not keen to have.

13

Love Arrives

Two days passed before Samaren flew to her perch. "I have seen both Randolph and Shardira today," she said as Barrett relayed her words. "They delivered grave news. Asban has come forth with several Trackers. They seized members of the dead men's families and are torturing them to reveal the orb's location. Those Bureau idiots believe the men they murdered actually committed the theft."

A collective gasp swept the room as Barrett continued. "They have even taken the children. Some are as young as six summers. They are being held in the dungeons. We must stop this."

Trishar nodded in agreement. "True. But it is too risky for all of us to attempt this quest. Zanora had a wonderful idea of splitting into pairs. Each of you will need specific tasks. We cannot wander about aimlessly and hope not to be spotted."

"What do you see, Mearis?" asked Gaia. "What comes next? Now that the orb is ours, your sight should have returned." The witch perked up. "I know my dreams have changed for the better."

The Seer nodded. "Agreed. Things are sharper now. However, Seeing does not show me unchangeable events. The visions are merely images of what can happen should the present course not be altered."

"Then altered they shall be," came a baritone voice from the kitchen.

A tall, handsome man stood leaning lightly on an ornate walking stick. Roving blue eyes scanned the room. An emerald green cloak hung from his broad shoulders. Brown boots graced his feet. His breeches and tunic were the shades of a fern. Long brown hair, flecked with grey, fell past his shoulders. As he spoke, his deep voice rumbled round the room.

"Have I been gone so long that I cannot even receive a proper hullo?" he asked. "Or have you all forgotten me already?"

Barrett rushed to throw his arms around the wizard. "Elimar! I was beginning to think you would never arrive. It is great to see you."

The old man gave a resounding laugh that shook his frame. "My boy, have you become a man overnight? Certainly, I have not been away that long. You have sprouted a few inches, yes?" He measured his student's head to his own. Their height was nearly equal.

The prince's euphoria was broken as the others swarmed in, save for Mearis and Zanora. After proper greetings, the wizard settled into a chair and conjured a steaming drink, saucer, and smoking pipe. He lit it, took a long drag, and smiled.

"Zanora is here, too. What a delight you chose not to kill her.

An interesting decision," he noted, winking as he took another long puff.

"I've missed you too, you old piece of—" she started.

Graile whispered in her ear, quieting her. "Please do not ruin this moment. We need him whether you like it or not. And I'll admit, I've missed him the same as Barrett has. He grows on you."

"Right. Like fungus," she replied.

"Have you learned nothing about your attitude yet or do you purposely make it hard for anyone to be your friend? Do you like anyone at all?" asked Graile.

She leaned closer and rested a warm hand on his thigh. "I *like* you. That's someone, right?"

So it was, for the fourth time, the companions spent their next hours retelling their adventures to the present day. Several times, Elimar's eyebrows raised in surprise while other news caused them to furrow in dissatisfaction. Yet, he said little as each told their version of tales. Even Zanora and Mearis shared. But it was the redhead's tales that the old wizard seemed particularly interested in. Barrett could not fault him for that.

"So, Sister," the wizard said to Trishar when all was told, "it seems I have come just in time."

She forced air through her pursed lips. "Do not return believing our hope was lost due to your absence. You do not get to play the hero who saves the day, you old coot."

Elimar gave another laugh. "Right you are. I see some things never change. You were always an onery, opinionated woman. It is why I love you."

"Truthfully, you should thank me for not turning the future king into a troll for what he has done. I am perturbed with him right now. He disobeyed my rules, has gotten three innocent men put to death, and there is plenty more I could name." She eyed the prince with a stern gaze.

Elimar wore a serious look for a moment, then brightened. "But on the good side, he saved my daughter, retrieved a stolen Orb of Protection, faced Asban alone, and his magic is growing every day." He winked at the prince. "Well done, young man."

"No wonder he pushes boundaries," griped the sorceress. "He has you as a teacher. You are a bad influence, you buffoon."

"Look, you two, all this family argument is fine, but what about our problem? Can we focus on that bit?" urged Unger. "What are we going to do?"

"An excellent question for my dear brother," said Trishar, inclining her head toward the pipe smoking wizard. "What schemes are brewing in that thick head of yours?"

Still reeling after the sorceress' harsh comments, Barrett sought the same answer. Every recent plan he had come up with failed. It was difficult to look past that part. In his moments of wavering doubt he formulated another plan.

Turning the companions over to Elimar would be a good idea. He would be a better leader. He considered the idea for an instant. Unfortunately, the wizard was not always there when needed, which created another problem altogether. *How can I get things back on track? I really messed things up and people died because of my latest scheme. I can't make another mistake.* He eyed the wizard, who seemed to look through him as if knowing his struggles and understanding them.

"The innocents must be saved first," said Elimar after exhaling several colored smoke rings. One was fashioned as a roaring dragon, another a raven, and another was a large sailing ship. "Afterward, it is time to put Grimes and the Bureau in their place."

"And how will we do that?" asked Graile.

"Well, since I have just heard the latest news, give me a bit to ponder it. I will figure something out," said the old man.

"Take all the time you need," snorted Trishar. "It's not as if anyone is in danger."

Elimar exhaled heavily. "No wonder mother liked me best."

"I have a plan," said Gaia softly. The room fell silent as she took Barrett's hand. "Zanora, Unger, Graile, and Nell should make the rescue while—"

"Stop right there!" cried the redhead. "The place will be crawling with those Bureau freaks. We'll never get in. There's no—"

Graile calmed her once more. Zanora resisted, mumbling curses under her breath before going quiet.

"Continue, please," said the Fader.

The witch flashed a smile and went on. "Elimar, me, and Barrett can make a sizeable distraction to draw out every guard, Agent, and Tracker within the castle. You four retrieve the families and get them to safety. Hopefully, without being noticed."

"Saying 'hopefully' is really not encouraging." Unger slicked back his hair and puffed out his cheeks, slowly letting air leak from his lips.

"No, she's right. Follow the witch's words," chimed in Mearis. "Just this morning I saw this exact scenario within the orb. At the time, I was trying to understand the images before seeing the newspapers, which is why I made no mention of things. However, now it all make perfect sense. Gaia speaks destiny. Listen to her."

"It always sounds easy when we plan it," added Zanora. "It rarely works out that way, though."

"I'll be by your side," said Graile. "What could go wrong?"

The redhead laughed. "Seriously!" She tapped the side of her chin in a mocking fashion. "Where should I start?" She jammed a finger in the air. "Oh yes, I remember. Your last adventure got three men killed and now we need to save their families. Who knows how many others are there. Sound familiar?"

"It wasn't supposed to be that way," grumbled Barrett, his anger rising again. "Being angry over it solves nothing. What's done is done. So stop rehashing the past. I already feel terrible about it." He smacked his palm against the table in frustration. "I'm with Gaia. Especially since Mearis' visions back up her idea."

"We'll leave tonight," said Graile, bumping the redhead's shoulder with his own. She lay her hand atop his and squeezed.

"Right," said Elimar. "I am certain we can cause enough stir to give you a fighting chance." Again, he winked knowingly at Barrett and smiled.

The prince moved next to Gaia. "He has that look again."

"What look?"

"The tricksy, troublemaking look. We may get more than we bargained for tonight." He forced a smile, aware the old man had a way of causing a stir wherever he went. Barrett dreaded to think what would happen if they caused a ruckus on purpose.

"It is settled," said Trishar with finality. "Now, I must return home before being missed. May the gods watch you all." She turned to her brother. "Keep them safe or face me when you return."

Elimar appeared stunned. Long seconds passed before he flashed a toothy grin. "I don't suppose giving my word would comfort you."

His sister waved his comment away. "Not in the least."

Evening came cloudy and wet. Steady drizzle fell and low fog lay draped over the land. The air was chilled and unmoving. Barrett pulled his cloak tighter and cursed under his breath.

"This stinks," he moaned. "We should be in front of a warm fire, in my castle, in my bedroom, in—"

Gaia took his hand. "You're complaining and putting negative energy in the universe. Nothing good will come of it. Focus. Think about saving innocent lives tonight."

"She's right . . . again." Elimar tenderly patted the witch's shoulder and whispered. "You're going to make an excellent queen." His voice raised. "Thinking about your past problems only leads to more problems. Stop being grouchy, focus on staying alive, and let's move." The wizard counted heads. "I can get us close to the city without being discovered by Trackers. We'll walk from there."

"Can you fix the weather, too?" asked Zanora.

"I could, but that sort of magic would draw attention no matter where we are." The wizard spun to change his appearance. Now he stood average height with short brown hair. Green eyes stared out from beneath thin brows. Plum-colored breeches and tunic graced his frame. He wore a closely groomed beard, matching grey boots, and a flowing cloak.

"I love when he does that. It always amazes me," said Gaia.

"Maybe so, but there's something weird about it," said Zanora as her face soured.

"I wish I could do it," said Graile.

Unger laughed. "Why? Turning to vapor isn't enough for you?"

The Fader turned vaporous, drifted next to Unger, then solidified. "You're right. It is enough."

"Focus, everyone. Join hands. The time has come to do some good." Elimar's face hardened. "Remember, this is serious business. Avoid people when possible. Do not cause trouble or draw attention. We want to get in and out. Meet by the fairy ring in the field above Westmore. You recall it, yes?" The friends nodded in unison. The wizard raised his voice. "Evonis Visu."

In a blink, they stood at the edge of the familiar grass field, staring down at the sprawling city. The rain had increased.

Barrett's emotions clashed at the sight. Another painful spasm of homesickness made him gasp. He missed the city, his home, and his room. If acting on impulse, he wished to charge down the hill, storm the castle, and oust Grimes, the Trackers, and all the Bureau lackeys. He wanted Asban dead for his treachery and misdeeds. Several nasty spells filled his mind. He wished them against Grimes, too. He clenched his fists.

Gaia wiped water from her face. "I sense your anger and pain. Your aura betrays you again. Trust in the gods to help. Things will work out as they should."

"Well, they haven't so far," he retorted. Then, he softened as anger drained away. "You have a habit of being right, don't you?"

"Most of the time, yes." She patted his backside, then kissed him.

"Excellent!" said Nell, lowering her cloak hood to peer skyward. "Look, the rain has stopped just in time. That makes things a little less miserable."

Barrett eyed the wizard suspiciously. "Did you do that?"

"Perhaps," replied the wizard with a sly grin. "That, along with our arrival, may have alerted the Trackers. We do not have long before they find us."

"I thought Trackers could not follow wizards or sorceresses," said Barrett, rubbing his chin in thought.

"The stronger the magic, the harder it is to conceal. I can easily move myself around without ever being discovered, but to move an entire group makes it difficult to remain hidden." His bright eyes covered the friends. "Everyone knows what to do, right?"

Zanora smiled and adjusted her sword. "We know exactly what to do. If anyone stands in the way, kill them all." She freed her blade and spun it in a quick circle to her side. The steel blade whistled through the air. She sheathed it with a practiced move.

"You need help. There is something seriously wrong with you," said Unger.

"I was only joking, fool!" she snapped. "I wouldn't kill them *all*. I'd leave some alive to torture them for answers."

"Zanora! Ewwww," said Gaia, shriveling her nose in disgust.

"Gaia! You are the girl who nearly killed me with magic at the gate, so your objections don't mean much after that bit," replied the redhead.

"Enough," said Elimar, heaving a sigh as he looked skyward to speak with the gods. "Why must I work with teenagers? How have I wronged any of you?" He faced the city and strode away, then halted. "Oh, one more thing. Graile is in charge. Follow his directions to the letter. Unger is next in line should anything happen to our Fader."

Graile, with his usual painted eyes and death face, lifted his hood. "I'll do my best."

Elimar placed a hand on his shoulder and smiled. "I know. It's why I picked you."

"How will we know when to begin our part?" asked Nell.

"You will know. There will be no mistake. Use the passages to get inside the castle, head for the dungeons, free the prisoners, and await the signal." The wizard swished his staff forward like a broom. "Go on now. Trackers are coming. I sense them." He turned to Barrett and Gaia. "You two will be easily spotted." He changed their appearance with another swish of his staff.

Barrett wore blonde hair with green eyes. He was heavier and shorter. He complained about that part. Conversely, Gaia took his breath away, dressed as a traditional witch. Like Graile, she was clothed in all black. Raven-colored hair hung to her waist. Intense blue eyes stared outward. Her long cloak stirred in the rising breeze. Her nose had widened a bit, but if anything, it only made her lovelier, thought the prince. His mouth hung open.

Elimar nudged him with his staff. "You're embarrassing yourself. Stop it."

"Y...y...you look...amazing," stammered the prince.

"Aw, that's sweet. Maybe I will dress like this more often," said the witch.

"Come on. I have an idea," said Unger, sprinting toward the road. Racing over the grass field, he reached the road's edge to leap in the path of an approaching wagon. The driver reined his team to a halt—the horses stopping mere inches from the archer's face.

"He's gone mad," said Zanora. "What is he doing?"

"With him, who knows," said Nell. "He's a little unpredictable but has a good heart and splendid mind. Let's not forget he and Graile saved your life."

Zanora nodded. "True enough, he did. I owe him for his efforts." Her gaze covered the Fader. "I owe you, too. I'll gladly pay up." She batted her eyes coyly.

"You owe me nothing," said the Fader, pushing his chin to Unger, who was chatting with the wagon driver. "I'm sure he has a plan. We'll follow him whatever it is." He took the redhead's hand.

Zanora grumbled but didn't pull away. "You're supposed to be in charge, so why did you let him dash away like that?" she asked spitefully.

"Because I trust his quick mind." Graile guided her along as they dashed down the hill. Nell followed closely at an easy sprint.

Unger waved them on. "Come on. We have a ride."

Seconds later, the winded trio arrived at the archer's side. "You have problems, my friend," Zanora said, tapping the side of her head. "We have no idea who these people are. They could be Bureau spies."

"Untrue. But we have no time to argue. And this is not the place." Unger helped the others climb inside the covered wagon, then closed the heavy canvas flap. "I would recognize the Frieberg's wagon anywhere. The old couple driving have been our neighbors since I was little. I trust them. Plus, I gave them my last piece of silver for passage and asked them to take a message to my folks to let them know I'm alive. I hate purposely avoiding my parents to keep them safe. But I have no choice."

Nell hugged him. "Very smart. And well done, I might add."

"Nice work," said Graile, nodding approval. "They will be thrilled to hear from you."

The friends settled onto padded benches inside the close, cozy space. Around them were a variety of oddities. Colorful scarves, boots, and dishes sat about in an orderly fashion. Herbs of various kinds dangled from an arched, muraled ceiling, swaying to the wagon's rhythm. Dozens of contraptions, most of which the friends could only guess their use, lay on shelves or sat stacked in bins. The air smelled of calming lavender.

"This is amazing," said Zanora with awe as she touched everything within arm's reach. "I could live in here. Who would've thought such a tiny space could be so bright and happy?"

"I'm surprised you noticed," said Nell. "This doesn't exactly feel like someplace you would enjoy. If there were swords, shields, severed heads, or torture devices hanging here, I could see it."

"I've discovered she's full of surprises," noted Graile as he examined a hanging cloak by his side. "This is great craftsmanship. I would buy this in a second."

As the wagon rolled on, its wheels found a rut, rattling the frame and throwing Zanora off balance. She tumbled from her seat, only to have Graile catch her in his arms. They lingered for a long moment before she pressed her lips to his. As they separated, he helped her straighten. Zanora had trouble finding a place to put her eyes. Her gaze kept gravitating back to the Fader but wound up aiming toward the floor whenever he looked her way.

"I was hoping you would do that sooner than later," he said.

Zanora gasped, then slugged his arm. "All this time, I wasn't sure if you were interested. You could have told me earlier or made the first move." She made an indelicate sound.

The Fader nodded several times. "You're right. I could have."

Her fist lashed out again, but this time passed through his arm. She cursed him.

"You had your one free chance." He winked.

She snorted, then glared at Unger, her face flushed with embarrassment. "Say a word, and I'll—"

"I know, I know, you'll kill me," said the archer, turning away and waving a dismissive hand. "It's all you think about."

"I was going to say tear your tongue out, but your idea works, too," she added with cheer.

The wagon rattled to a stop. Its swaying halted before two solid thumps came from the front.

"That's our signal." Unger cautiously peeked outside, then eased himself onto the sparsely populated street. After checking his surroundings, he signaled the others to follow. Once Nell stepped down he knocked the wagon's side twice before the friends slid into an alleyway.

As the Frieberg's wagon rounded a corner and disappeared from sight Graile slapped the archer's back. "Brilliant, Unger," he said. "Well done, my friend."

"Honestly, I'm shocked. It *was* a surprisingly intelligent move. We wanted to avoid the gate guards and this worked perfectly," said Zanora while mock clapping. "Now, to find a tunnel."

Nell took the archer's face in her hands and tenderly kissed his lips. "I've wanted to do that for a long while. This seemed like the perfect time."

Unger pushed out his chest as a grin grew on his face. "I was thinking the same thing." He furrowed his brow. "Does this mean we're a couple? You know, going together?"

Her head bobbed. "Yes, it does." She tenderly ran a hand over his chest. "Lucky you."

14

Saving the Innocents

The alleyway was unclean and smelled musty. Crows, rats, and other scavengers picked through the garbage, paying little heed to the intruders.

Unger led the trio to an entrance, one forgotten by anyone other than Barrett and himself. He picked the lock. "This has not been opened in some time. Be patient." To his surprise, even Zanora had nothing to say about waiting. Soon, the heavy iron piece loosened.

They stepped inside and bolted the door shut. Zanora grabbed two torches from their holders and lit them. She gave one to Nell and kept the other. The orange glow flickered on the walls in a display of shifting shadows.

Unger took the lead, moving through the narrow passage until reaching a set of dark stairs. Here, there was neither light nor comfort. Chilled air met their faces as they descended the slick steps. There were no sounds save for their soft footfalls and the steady drip of water leaking from the weathered rock.

Down and around they went, often angling left, right, or turning sharp corners until all sense of direction was lost.

Unger stopped suddenly. Nell collided with him, nearly pushing him into an intersecting tunnel. The archer cursed softly. "I have no idea which way to go. I feel like we're back in the Trowken caves. And *what* is that smell?"

"It is death and decay," she replied, taking the archer's face in her hands to kiss his lips. "Wait here." Handing him her torch, she transformed into a bat, then winged into the darkness to vanish.

Another curse. "Why did she do that?" he asked.

"Shhhh! Will you be quiet?" Zanora cringed as her whispered voice bounced off the tall, arching stone.

Aside from the sounds of the fluttering torches, which seemed drowned out by a suffocating heaviness, the trio crouched in the penetrating silence. There were no scurrying mice with tiny claws clicking over the stone, no men tormenting the prisoners, only deep quiet. Even the dipping water had been left behind. Unger sorely missed the sound.

Time stilled as long, uneasy minutes passed until Graile tapped his ear and pointed right. "Listen."

Faint wingbeats rose above the torch sounds. Zanora held the flame low and peered into the gloom as Nell winged into view, transforming into a human as she neared.

"There were guards farther down, but they will not be waking up for some time," the Dorgon said in a hushed voice. "Follow me."

"What did you do?" asked Zanora with excitement. "Are there dead bodies to hide?"

Nell shook her head. "They accidentally fell down. I placed them in a side passage that reeked of foul odor. It may be hours before they are discovered or awaken."

"Accidentally?" asked Graile, his sarcasm clear as he raised a questioning eyebrow.

She made a clicking sound with her tongue before a pleased smile spread over her face. "It was a shame. The clumsy oafs tripped and wound up unconscious." Nell rested a hand on his arm. "You would have been proud of me."

"The more time we spend together, the more I like you," said the redhead, staring with admiration. "You're a woman after my own heart."

Nell studied the redhead with narrowed eyes. "Not entirely, but we do have things in common," she replied.

It came to be, in the near impenetrable darkness, that the companions arrived at a sizable chamber. Many iron rings were set in the walls at waist level. Thick leg manacles lay scattered on the floor. Shackles were set overhead, some ten feet off the ground. One pair held a partial skeleton, which had many bones loosened over time and fell away in a pile.

Passing through, they came to thirteen roughly hewn stairs leading downward to an iron door with thick bars set in it. Above it were two small windows, equally barred and secured. Sparse rays of torchlight came from high above but gave no comfort or warmth.

Graile peeked through the bars. His breath hitched. "I hope I find who did this."

Inside lay four young children dressed in filthy clothing. Like the others around them, they were unkept. Three adults were securely chained to the walls, clanking and jingling their restraints as they shifted about. Four teenagers, despite being messy and bruised, hung next to them. Their movements were more vigorous but just as futile. Considering the conditions, they seemed to have fared the best.

"Free them, then head for the surface and wait for Barrett's signal before reentering the city," said Graile.

"I hope those three know what they're doing," said Zanora. "Elimar better not mess this up."

"They'll do a good job. Barrett's confidence always rises when Elimar is near," said Nell. "They won't let us down."

"How are we supposed to open that lock? It's huge," grumbled Unger, laying the stout padlock in his palm to examine it. He pulled and tugged on the thick iron. It did not open. "This one is too rusted to lockpick."

Zanora placed her face against the bars. "We're here to help. No harm will come to you. No matter what you see, do not be frightened." She turned to Nell and inclined her head toward the door. "Can you—"

"Absolutely." Nell morphed into a large blue ogre, grabbed the padlock, and jerked it free as if made of paper. Swinging the creaking door wide, she squatted in the entrance and slowly advanced toward the children who were paralyzed with fear. They shrank back and covered their faces with both hands.

Nell halted. "No, no, no," she said in a soothing voice, holding up her hands. "Look, your parents aren't scared. It's okay." She leaned toward the nearest woman and slowly extended her thick arm, seized the chain binding her to the wall, then gave it a quick yank. It broke free with a grating sound as the stone released its grip. Everyone cringed at the sound.

Next came the lock holding her ankle manacle. Nell crushed

the iron into fragments, making the manacle drop away. She turned back to the children. "I will set you free and carry you, yes? It will be fun. And you can tell your friends a Ralitorn Ogre carried you." She nodded several times until the children parroted her actions. "Good, good. Let me free the others first. Your family can help, too."

Graile worried over the noises as the smooth walls sent each sound bouncing down the passage's length. He expected to see a squad of angry guards stepping into the light to come for them any moment.

To his relief, the families were quickly released from their bonds. Nell carried one child in each arm while the healthiest teenagers carried the remaining two.

Unger extended a hand to a thin, gaunt man, then helped him to his feet. "What's your name? How long have you been here?"

"I am Deidrick, the shoemaker," he replied, poking a thick finger against his chest. "Teris was my brother. They murdered him for no reason, then dragged us here to interrogate us." He coughed a hacking, raspy sound. "Many of the others have been here for days. We have been beaten and starved."

The archer looked at the man's broken wrist. "Where's a wizard when you need one?" he cursed under his breath so Deidrick could not hear. "Elimar could fix this."

"We're taking you out of this nasty place," said Zanora with hope in her voice.

Graile took the lead. Nell followed close with the children held firmly in her arms. The prisoners came next with Zanora and Unger trailing to the rear. Twisting and turning here and there, they retraced their steps, meeting no resistance along the way.

The Fader pondered that part as he scanned ahead. The escape almost seemed too easy. *Could this be a trap? Did Grimes know we would come for the prisoners?* Shaking the thought away, he decided the Bureau would never suspect the prisoners being set free. Likely, they had forgotten about them. They held no information of value and were left to die.

Weakened by a lack of food and water, the captors moved slowly and noisily. Their grunts and groans filled the air. The Fader slowed against his will.

Unger noticed the longer they stayed beneath ground, the more his senses dulled from the lack of light, sounds, and proper air. Soon, all things began to look the same. Passages and tunnels intermingled until direction was lost. Then, in a moment of clarity, he recognized the tunnel he stumbled into earlier and was relieved when the Fader turned toward it.

"Not much farther now," said Graile, seemingly unaffected by his surroundings. His tone was encouraging, yet he lied, knowing in his heart there was a long distance to go. "The air smells different here. We are drawing close to the streets."

Zanora scowled toward the archer, then whispered to him. "What is he doing? We're not even halfway there . . . I think. I'm sort of turned around. I hope our fearless leader was paying attention."

Unger pushed his chin forward toward the families. "Some can barely walk. I think he's only trying to give them hope." Glancing over his shoulder to ensure they were not being followed, he added, "One thing I admire about Graile is his sense of direction, even in spaces like this. He knows exactly where we're going. Besides, back there was where Nell turned into a bat. I recognized the spot."

"Good point," admitted the redhead. "By the way, don't tell anyone about the kiss in the wagon."

"That's what is on your mind right now? I can barely breathe or think and you're worried over a kiss." He groaned in disbelief. "We can discuss this later. And I will not say a word."

Zanora smiled at him. "You know, you're not so bad after all."

Unger scowled. "Thanks, I . . ."

A clatter of weapons and voices ahead interrupted their talk. Graile held up a hand to halt the procession, then went vaporous to drift ahead, leaving the others quaking in fear.

In the darkness, he paused here and there to hover like a blackened storm cloud. He listened intently while watching several torches grow larger as they approached. Taking shape, he hid in a small crevice to count six men ambling toward him like a flaming snake.

"Fetch the women first," said one. "They'll break the easiest. The kids don't know anything and the men will be harder to weasel out information. Start with the ladies."

One chuckled. "Especially since they ain't ate nary a thing for days now," said his mousy voice. "They'll be ripe to talk."

"They're all cursed traitors," said a higher pitched one. "They deserve what's coming to them. Rob the castle, will they! Let 'em pay for what's been done."

"They know nothing of worth. And they certainly didn't do anything wrong," said a younger-sounding fellow. "We should have fed them."

"Just do what you're told," grumbled a deep voice. "You don't get to question the Bureau. Unless, of course, you want to take a prisoner's place on the rack."

"N . . . n . . . no, there's no need for that," stammered the young one, his former courage suddenly gone.

Graile gritted his teeth. So, the Bureau had not forgotten the prisoners after all. Anger jolted his stomach. *Making people, especially children, go hungry for days is horrid.*

The guard's shuffling steps grew louder. Graile considered his options. Hide, flee, or fight. He opted for the last, knowing hiding or fleeing would bring the same result: if these men passed by, they would surely find the others. He needed to be their silent defender.

Turning to mist, he moved to the highest point in the passage and drifted along, quickly closing the distance like a nightmarish wraith. Stopping directly overhead, he dropped among them.

Shocked by an enemy only visible in quick glances, the men drew their swords to hack, hew, and swing wildly around them. But neither steely blades nor limbs had an effect as they passed through the Fader's vaporous body.

During the melee, shouts and death screams echoed from the stone as three guards died at one another's hands. The remaining men now lay unconscious once the Fader drove their helmeted heads against the stone walls.

He quickly set to clean the bodies from the path, not wanting the children to see the bloody death scene. To his disappointment, there was no way to clean the blood and mess away. Hurriedly drifting back to the company, he solidified. Zanora ran to his arms. Concern was etched on her face.

"Are you wounded? How many are there? Are they coming for us? Will they—"

He kissed her lips to stop her. "Do not let the children see the blood."

Zanora's breath caught as she ran her hands over his torso and arms to check for wounds. "Bless the gods, you're unharmed. I was so worried."

Gathering the friends, he explained their dilemma, then turned back to the tunnel. Underway, the column formed a single-file line. Graile instructed them to stay against the right wall for the next fifty yards. No one questioned him.

From there, they climbed until the air felt thinner and smells of cooking food drifted through the sparse air vents. The blind darkness and stifling space lay behind them. How long they had been traveling, none knew, but the streets of Westmore were not far away.

Finally, Graile halted the weary group in wait of a signal, hoping Elimar and friends would soon come through.

15

Distractions

Barrett adjusted his cloak as the trio merged onto the main street. For the second time in as many days, he longed for the past. In truth, he wanted to head for The Pointed Hat with his friends and pretend none of this ever happened. He also wanted his father back, to see Yaris, and have the city as it once was. But mostly, he wanted the return of magic. Hatred spread through him like the disease the Bureau and Grimes represented.

"Things will never be the same again," he muttered.

"Of course not," said Elimar plainly. "Nothing ever stays the same. Dreaming about 'what could have been' is a waste of time. You can never go back. Concentrate on moving forward. Always show your best self, help others, be respectful, and accept differences in people. It is the best way to live."

"But how can I learn all that?" he asked.

"Practice. Loads of practice," said the wizard. "You will make thousands of mistakes in life. Learn from them and do not hold past failures in your mind. Release those feelings or they haunt you forever."

Barrett nodded and went silent as the old man's words swirled in his head. He was well aware of everything Elimar said. His parents taught him the same ideals during his youth, but living by them seemed harder than simply knowing the ethics or reciting them.

"Do we have a plan?" asked Gaia, kneeling to pretend to retie her bootlaces. Covertly, she eyed the passersby while keeping a lookout for Trackers or Agents. Barrett had taught her that skill.

"Of course, dear child. Wizards are always prepared." Elimar gave a fake cough into his hand. "I know exactly what to do."

"Care to let us in on it?" asked Barrett, swiping strands of hair from his eyes.

"We're going to start a roaring fire by burning down a building," said the wizard as calmly as ordering breakfast. "And we're using powerful magic to do it."

"You have finally gone crazy!" shouted Barrett, cringing as his words drew strange stares from the townsfolk. His tone lowered as they hurried past. "Trackers will follow us for sure," he added. He turned to the witch, expecting her to back him up. She merely shrugged her confusion.

Elimar calmly adjusted his cloak and sleeves. "That is the idea, young man. We want Graile and his bunch to get away without being seen. And what better way than to have everyone chase *us* instead? Chaos works wonders for that sort of thing. And, my friends, I excel at chaos. Just ask my sister." He chuckled. "I suppose I am like Zanora in that respect."

"No wonder your ideas are always strange," chided the prince.

"I should've asked Trishar to lead us instead." Since she was being watched, he knew she could not take the wizard's place, yet he wished to jab the old fellow's pride.

It worked. Elimar looked offended. "Well, now! After all I've done for you." Pushing his nose upward, he blew air from his pursed lips. "Some king you'll be."

"Stop it, you two idiots. Are you five years old!" snapped Gaia. "I should have gone with Graile. I would rather talk to Zanora than the two of you."

Barrett looked insulted. "B . . . B . . . but . . . he started it." He pointed an accusing finger at Elimar.

The witch pushed past, huffing her dissatisfaction as she went.

"See what you've done!" griped the prince. With a quick turn, he hurried after her.

Elimar followed, complaining to the gods once again about teenagers. He asked why he was forced to tolerate them.

Dipping into a dark alley, the wizard took the lead. "There is an old abandoned blacksmith shop in the northern corner of the city. Rumors say it will be torn down to make room for the Bureau's new headquarters."

"Wonderful choice. Anything to keep the Bureau from expanding its hold within our city," said the witch.

Barrett felt more confused than ever. Never did he imagine Gaia agreeing to such a drastic action. "There's no danger of the fire spreading to any homes, is there? I want no innocents to be harmed," he said.

"It will be fine," said the wizard with little conviction. "Relax, young man. If the flames spread, we will snuff them out."

Barrett wanted to trust the old man's words, but watching someone's house burn—especially if he was powerless to stop it—

held little appeal. The townsfolk had already been through enough and he did not wish to deepen their misery by setting fire to their homes. As long as the Bureau did not mistake it for some evil plot against them and toss more families in the dungeons, the prince would burn down every empty building he could find.

"That did not sound reassuring. Will we wait until five or six homes go up in flames before lending aid?" Barrett asked with a sarcastic, low voice. His brows pulled downward. "This makes me rather nervous, but it is my city and if it will help take it back, count me in."

The wizard stopped to shake his student's hand. "Excellent. I'm proud of you."

Barrett's pride swelled at the compliment. Not counting Mearis showing him affection over the opportunity to relive her youth through his orb story, it was the best thing anyone had said to him in a long while. His love for Elimar's presence and guidance returned.

Turning down Gryphon Street, Barrett noticed the street sign had been torn from its post and cast aside near the road's edge. A new marker naming the road 'Bureau Avenue' hung in its place. Anger swelled in him. His shoulders hunched at the thought of the Bureau pushing all magic-related things aside.

Pausing to kick the signpost, he hurt his toes but said nothing. "It's like advertising they have won. We'll see about that."

Several more strides brought them near the two-story, dilapidated structure with its broken windows, holey roof, and rotting doors. Barrett had forgotten this place existed. In years past, his father spoke of rebuilding here. Though, he had planned a center for the arts and magic, not the atrocity Grimes and his fools would soon erect in its place. His face soured, picturing a building towering high overhead like a beacon of opulence and power, one declaring the Bureau's hypocritical superiority for all to see.

He crossed the field to cup his hands and peek inside a dirty window. Broken chairs and upended tables were strewn about. The walls had been vandalized with bizarre markings he had never seen before. One caught his eye. On the far wall was a freshly painted Bureau symbol. His jaw clenched.

As he backed away, grasping for his wand, it struck him the work his father had been unable to accomplish would burn to the ground in a magical firestorm. What would he think? Would he tell his son he was proud of him for fighting the oppressors? Or would he say the possible future king was making an awful decision?

Standing with his wand aimed ahead, Barrett paused as guilt swept through him. For a fading instant, he swore a ghostly image of his father's face appeared on the building's front, smiling as if giving his permission to begin. That stiffened his resolve.

"I hope I don't regret this," Barrett muttered softly.

"Many lives depend on us, especially those of our friends," said Gaia, aiming her wand forward, too. "You want our help, right?"

"I'd like that," he replied. He met the wizard's gaze and inclined his head sharply. "Join in. You've known this city since long before I was born. You are as much a part of it as I am. It is basically your home away from home."

Elimar's garb glistened in the pale moonlight. "I would be honored, son." With two hands, the wizard leveled his staff and nodded. "Ready."

"By my command," said Barrett, his voice akin to a king giving an order. "One . . . two . . . three . . . fire!"

"Flaminious," they cried in crisp, clear voices as their magic sprang to life. Spheres of sparkling red flames arched high into the night to descend through the darkness like fiery meteors, gaining speed as they plummeted downward. The spell struck with force to engulf the old building in a crimson blaze. The forceful impact swept back the trio's hair with its fury. Barrett raised an arm to shield himself from the debris and heat.

The wizard leaned his staff against his chest and extended both arms, lifting his voice above the roar of flames. "Touch my sleeves quickly now."

As smoke billowed upward and fire raged through the dried wood, horns sounded, bells rang, and distant shouts filled the air.

"Hurry!" shouted Elimar as Barrett and Gaia dashed to him. "Evonis Visu," cried the wizard. They vanished in a swirl of motion, reappearing in the field above Westmore. "Quickly! To the ring."

"B . . . b . . . but we can't use it," stammered Barrett.

"Do as I say," ordered Elimar.

Grabbing Gaia's hand, Barrett hurtled toward the fairy ring as the sound of pounding hooves reached their ears. The wizard glanced over his shoulder as a Tracker patrol crested the ridge, riding toward them with speed.

"They arrived far quicker than anticipated. They must have been close by." He shoved the teens along. "Faster."

Arrows thumped the ground as they ran. One whistled by, its blade slicing Barrett's ear. Blood spilled onto his shoulder as he cried out in pain. Steel rang as blades cleared their sheaths.

Barrett skidded to a stop. He rounded to blast the nearest rider from his saddle. The spell struck the Tracker firmly. His dead body tumbled from his mount to pinwheel across the ground, ending in an ugly, twisted pile.

Suddenly, Elimar's strong hand gripped Barrett's collar to

drag him along. The young man was still off balance as the wizard shoved him into the ring.

Long weeks had passed since the prince had last stepped inside a fairy ring, but he had not forgotten the experience.

For the moment, this trip seemed no different than his first as utter silence engulfed him, save for his heartbeat and steady breathing. Gaia drifted into view on his left as he tumbled through the darkness. She looked far more at ease than him. He tried to speak her name but no words came. As panic built, he twisted round in search of the wizard. Had the old man escaped? Had Trackers captured or killed him? There was no sign of Elimar.

Meanwhile, Gaia drifted from sight as the familiar pulling sensation tugged at his belly, drawing him deeper into the blackness. Westmore and the grass field were left behind. He was alone.

To his relief, as if the gods aided him, a small light rapidly grew ahead. Only the size of a pebble, it rushed toward him with blinding intensity. With a suddenness and a swooshing sound, he was free as the ring closed behind him. Wobbling on shaky legs, he shook his head clear and steadied himself.

Before him, partially hidden in a small grove of lofty elm and oak trees, sat a two-story rectangular house. Pale light emanated from the many square windows, which were flung open, their purple curtains swaying in the breeze. Curling smoke drifted skyward from a tall, stone chimney, filling the draw with a thin layer of grey haze.

Both the house and land were clean. Neatly trimmed shrubs grew round the outer edges of the tree-filled property. It looked like a garden gnome's work. To the rear lay a sizeable, tended vegetable garden.

The structure itself appeared solid. On the left was a babbling brook flowing by in a steady fashion. Squirrels chattered noisily overhead to announce the prince's sudden presence. Several birds and a lone red fox took notice before resuming their activities.

Barrett smiled. Had he entered another world? *This is like visiting Nirith's home.* The tranquility drew him in, making him forget all else, even his still-bleeding ear. He ambled toward the door and gasped with delight as the door came to life.

"Well, bust my buttons!" said a Hydra as its three heads protruded from the wood. "Guests are such a rare thing!" said the first. "Welcome!" said the second. The door popped ajar. "I love visitors," added the third.

"Where am I?" asked the prince after giving a polite nod, hiding his excitement over seeing a magical door again.

A clawed limb reached forward to point at the porch. "You are here, of course," said the first. "Or we wouldn't be able to see you," said the middle one. "And you are a rather handsome sight," said the third.

Barrett blushed and could not help but chuckle. "But where is here?"

"Why . . . here is wherever you are," said the first before snorting. "We will forgive your silly questions since it is well known your race is not overly intelligent," said the second. "I still think he's handsome. Considerably cuter than the old wizard," said the third, giving a slow wink.

"May I enter?" the prince asked as embarrassment made him turn away to nudge a stray leaf with his boot.

"Indeed. Step inside! Step inside," they said in unison.

The prince stroked their heads in turn as he passed. "Thank you." His breath hitched once he closed the door.

Many open books lay sprawled about on a sizable wooden table. Potion bottles, herbs, lamps, and jars of all sizes and shapes were displayed. Several bookcases filled with thick, worn books lined the walls of the second floor, visible through the thick iron railing running the length overhead.

Two robes, one white and the other black, hung from claw-shaped hooks. Magic candles hovered overhead. Worn cabinets and dressers stood in various corners. Excluding the table, the place was clean and orderly and smelled of cooking food, peppermint, and springtime.

Three large rats scurried here and there as they cleaned and cooked. A fourth mended a pair of torn breeches. They stopped to bow to Barrett, then resumed their duties. The creatures reminded him of Trishar's talking cats. He wondered if they could speak, as well.

"Good afternoon," said the brown one suddenly. "I am Up." He pointed to the grey one beside him. "This is Down." Pointing again, he indicated the remaining two, one beige and the other brown with black spots. "They are Left and Right."

Gaia slipped beside the prince and bowed in return. "It is a pleasure to know you. Thank you for having us here . . . wherever we are."

Barrett was befuddled. "Did he just say their names were—"

The witch placed a hand over his mouth and shook her head. "Don't ask. It would be impolite. They announced themselves plainly enough." She moved toward the center of the room. "How was your trip?"

He raised a shoulder. "It felt weird since we haven't used a ring in weeks. But I liked it. What about you?"

"It was refreshing. I loved it. I want to do it again." She clapped lightly in her usual fashion.

"Once magic returns, you can take as many trips as you like." Barrett smiled at his new surroundings. "Any idea where we are?"

Gaia shook her head. "Maybe another safe house? Elimar will know."

Just then, the door opened and the wizard entered. Barrett thought the old man had either changed his appearance again or aged considerably in a brief instant. Either way, he found it part of the wizard's charm.

Thick brown hair with broad streaks of grey extended down his back. His robes were grey, held round his waist by a thin, elven belt, secured by a piece of dull steel. Both boots were black but scuffed from wear. Wisdom lines, as the old man called them, etched his face like deep crevices of broken earth. Still, his step was light, and his eyes sparkled with knowledge and vigor. A matching pointed grey hat topped his head. Its tip was flopped over, aiming at the floor.

Barrett twinged with jealousy. Elimar held hundreds, if not thousands, of years of knowledge within his head, and the prince wanted to see different things, places, creatures, and beauty the world had to offer, too. Yet if he regained his crown would he ever get the chance?

"Ahhhh, forgive my late arrival," announced the wizard as he propped his staff in the corner and removed his hat. "I see you have already met my most trusted friends. And likely flirted with my Hydra, no?" He pointed to Up. "Did you know rats are a brilliant species? Not only are they smart, but they are fast learners and make excellent companions. Better yet, they are astonishingly clean, despite what others may tell you. They are glorious little creatures."

"They're so cute," said Gaia, waving at the foursome staring on from the nearby potion table.

"Exactly where are we? You whisked us away and never said a word. And what happened to the Trackers?" asked Barrett, easing into a thick wooden chair. Resting his elbows on the table, he rubbed his face, then his temples. His ear stung. Elimar noticed, pulled a wand from his tunic, then swished it to the right. Barrett's ear healed instantly.

"Thank you," said the prince, feeling the healed wound.

Elimar nodded politely, then gave his news. "Those Trackers are most unhappy. After you killed the first one, they became aggravated. The fools charged me. I was forced to . . . well, never mind. Let's just say it's over."

Barrett recognized the old man's devious look. He was hiding something. What, the prince could not say. *I bet he slayed them all but won't tell me.*

"To your first question, you are in a place I never thought you would see. It is protected by more magic than any location I know, even Nirith's or Trishar's house." Elimar pulled out a seat for Gaia, watched her ease onto the hardwood, then moved to the head of the table. "This is my home."

Barrett sucked in a quick breath. "Really?" The excitement in his voice rang through. "It's remarkable."

"I thought Nirith's place was brilliant," said Gaia. "I will say this is cleaner than I would have thought." She grinned at the old man, then chuckled. "Sorry. That came out wrong."

Elimar laughed deeply. "I know what you meant. Thank you for the compliment, but my friends get the credit. If not for them, it may be untidy. Busy minds have no time for cleaning."

Gaia laughed. "Tell that to my parents."

"We shouldn't be here," said Barrett, fidgeting with a small, corked beaker sitting on the table. "I need to know what happened to—"

"Your friends," interrupted the wizard. "Hence, my delay. After encountering those foolish Trackers, I checked in with Trishar to hear what news I could. Happily, she reported all are safe. Our distraction worked perfectly." He frowned and toyed with his shirt cuff. "Unfortunately, the Bureau alleged it was an attack on the city and has closed the gates. Westmore is sealed."

The witch gasped. "How long will that last? It's so wrong."

"So true. But Zanora was right. Life is unfair," replied Barrett. "Knowing the Bureau, it may be weeks before they allow free travel."

Nearby, the studious rats busied themselves by placing cups and saucers on the table. Up and Down worked in unison to pour steaming drinks. They bowed once again, then darted off. Meanwhile, Left and Right placed a heaping fruit bowl on a thick placemat near the table's center. Finally, the helpers handed out clean, folded napkins, then scurried away to sit and watch like happy dogs waiting for crumbs to fall onto the floor.

"Why did we take the fairy ring to come here?" questioned the prince. "And even though you already know it, I'll say it again: I really miss our friends."

Elimar shook his head. "Patience, my boy. Your friends are safe, as are the rescued families. Even now, the survivors are being moved by a hidden network of those loyal to you, Sire. Their hideout lies far from the city. They will have new lives in a matter of hours. Perhaps then they can heal from the pain of losing their loved ones."

Gaia made a relieved sound. "Thank the gods. Their safety is glorious news. But my heart still hurts for them."

"Indeed. In the end, it turned out well, if I do say so," said the wizard while the rats made another round to disperse plates of food.

"Why don't you take us to see them?" asked the prince.

"Because for now, the fewer people that know about your presence or deem it a rumor, the better," answered the old man.

Barrett wanted to argue but found it difficult as he petted the furry creatures. He smiled genuinely for the first time in a long while, feeling at ease within these walls. The place felt like a home. No politics, no hate, no wanton death, and more peace than he had felt in months. He longed to stay here—perhaps forever, he thought.

Soon, joy fled as worries over claiming the kingship resumed to the darkened corners of his mind. Did he truly want the throne with all its troubles and pressures? He looked about him. He wanted *this*, not responsibilities and power. They were the furthest thing from his desires at the moment.

If he did choose to walk away and let destiny take its course, how would he tell his friends the danger and sacrifices they made were all for naught? How could he tell them he wished to be average, just like everyone else? Could they ever understand?

Worse, hurting his mother by admitting he had lost interest in the crown scared him beyond measure. Would she be angry or sad? Perhaps she would never speak to him again. He feared her disappointment would be irreparable. Their family had ruled Westmore for hundreds of years. Now he sat considering tossing the legacy away like it never mattered.

Naturally, the friends would argue, saying he had gone insane.

What of Trishar? Mearis? Alesta? Or even Nirith, since it was her words that instilled the idea? Of them all, he hoped Trishar would understand his choice, wherever it may lead.

The rats took particular interest in the prince as they now scurried overhead on a network of ropes suspended some feet above the table. The grid system extended to every corner, with several longer pieces dangling down for entry and exit. The furry creatures scampered closer, sitting in a semi-circle to watch his every move.

"You are troubled," said Left, pointing a small digit at him.

"How could you . . ." Barrett was exasperated by how everyone could read him so easily. He'd thought it was only Gaia at first, but now he was unsure. Was he really that transparent?

"Excellent observation. They're right, you know. I see it, too," said Gaia. "Your aura has changed."

The wizard silently nodded agreement as he sliced a piece of cheese from the small wheel and took a bite. "Yes, indeed, it is."

"Oh, come on! This is ridiculous!" complained the prince. "Am I an open book to everyone?"

Elimar waved him off. "Forget that. You have something serious to say, no?" Another bite. "It has been gnawing at your innards for some time, yet you have said nothing. I was letting you work it out." He waved his sharp knife around. "No one here is going to betray you. Speak what you will. Perhaps we can help. Your friends will never know unless you tell them."

Barrett suppressed a sudden urge to dash outside and vomit as bile edged up his throat. This was one conversation he did not expect nor wish to have without time to think it through, yet suddenly he was forced to reveal his true feelings. If he did not or tried to lie, they would know. *Blasted aura gives me away every time.*

"I . . . I . . . I'm not sure I want to be king." He gasped, then slapped a hand over his mouth as both ears reddened from embarrassment.

Elimar stiffened, pausing his current cheese piece before his mouth. He placed it back on the plate and studied his student. "Well, I did not expect that one."

"Why?" asked Gaia, her voice rising an octave. "You've lost so much at the hands of the Bureau and it's all you've talked about for weeks—no, months. How can you give up now?"

"Because I'm not sure we can reclaim the city, Gaia. And my confidence is not exactly at an all-time high." The prince swept an arm toward the bookcases and shelves. "This place is peaceful, magical, and filled with wonder." He jammed a finger against his chest. "*I* want this. I want to be a wizard. Besides, tell me why I need fancy events, expensive clothing, the troubles of running a kingdom, dealing with snobby bureaucrats, and all the junk that goes with it. Just because my family did?" He pointed his fork at Elimar. "I want to be like him! Carefree. Coming and going as I please, and—"

"Alone," interjected Elimar. Deep sadness registered on his face. "Do you think it's by chance that Trishar, Nirith, and I live in solitude?" He let that thought sink in, watching Barrett's brows crunch low in thought. "I love my life and all it brings, but being a wizard is dangerous, lonely work. Do not lose sight that you are a mortal boy with tremendous powers, not a wizard. You will not live for ages as my kind does."

"Then I will enjoy my powers while I can," retorted the prince, his feelings hurt and spiraling downward.

"Your powers are in your birthright—being king. A magical king, yes, but a king first and foremost. Countless people are awaiting your return. They wait for you to save them. Now, you want to run away because it's too hard? Because you're not confident?" Gaia's face was etched with worry. "If you do not take the throne, who will? Do you expect someone like Randolph to become king? Think about that."

Barrett tried desperately to think of a snappy response but could not. They had both made valid points and he knew it. After voicing everything, his reasonings seemed to border cowardly. *Can I really shirk the duties I was born into?*

"It feels overwhelming," he added, reaching to pet Down's body, letting the creature's long tail gently slide between his fingers. Suddenly, he wished to cry from frustration. *Why does no one understand? And if Elimar and Gaia think it's a bad idea, maybe it is.* He wished Trishar or Samaren were here. They would know what to say. They always did.

Tears collected behind his eyes, waiting for the right moment to spill out. When they could be held back no longer, Barrett excused himself and rushed outside, weeping tears of confusion once he was out of sight.

16

Falling Apart

Graile sat on the porch watching the unlikely pair of a baby fox and large cat playing in the front yard. The animals ran in erratic patterns as they tumbled and nipped one another in spirited fun, stopping only to wrestle for a moment before popping up to repeat the process.

Zanora lowered beside the Fader to wrap an arm round his waist. She rested her head against his shoulder.

"Aren't you afraid someone will see us?" asked Graile, kissing her head.

"Not any longer. That fool Unger has already blabbed the news to everyone, just as I knew he would. They all know now. Meaning Barrett probably knows somehow," said the redhead. She stomped a foot on the step. "I'm going to hurt that archer."

The Fader snorted. "He's just being Unger. Besides, it's not as if we would not have been discovered soon. Trishar sees everything. She has sharp eyes, that one."

"I'm glad she told us about Barrett and the others. I'm happy they're safe."

The Fader startled. "That's the first time I've heard you say you were happy. I was beginning to think you didn't know how to pronounce the word. Repeat after me . . . Hap-py. Happy. You should use it more often."

"Fun-ny. Very funny. Like you're a vision of joy. Do you even smile? Ever?" She scowled. "I just want to experience happiness while I can. Bad things are just days away again. I feel it, and honestly, I'm scared."

Unger and Nell came to sit on the bottom step. "We're not interrupting, are we?" asked the archer.

"No, big mouth, we were just leaving," said Zanora, beginning to rise. She stopped herself, then slowly lowered back down. "I'm sorry. Just edgy, I guess."

"When are you not?" retorted Unger. He flashed an exaggerated smile at her. "And did you just apologize? That's new."

Nell bumped her knee against his and hurriedly changed the subject. "I hope the others return soon. It's strange not having Barrett and Gaia here," she noted, staring into the trees to watch birds flitter through the leafy branches. "And I like the wizard. He makes me laugh."

"Agreed," said Graile. "I admit to missing them, as well. "I wonder where they went. Some place safe, I hope."

"They're with Elimar. Even though it's difficult to admit, they're as safe as they can be," said Zanora, tracing the veins on the back of Graile's hand. "The old man's magic can keep them unharmed better than anyone."

"Those three can take care of themselves," said Unger before holding up a hand. "Hold on. Why are you not complaining about magic? You always jump at the chance to put it down."

Zanora smiled. "I've done some deep thinking and agree magic has a place. It can be helpful but also causes a lot of trouble. At least I'm on the fence for now."

"This is a big step for you," said Nell, holding her hands shoulder-width apart.

"I'm not sold that magic is not dangerous. Though, like anything else in life, it can be helpful if used correctly," replied the redhead.

Graile placed an arm round her shoulder. "I'm proud of you for opening your mind." He leaned in to kiss her lips.

"So what's next?" asked Nell, toying with her raven's head necklace.

"Fine question." Graile raised a shoulder. "We can't answer that yet. We shall wait and see once we are together again."

"What do we do in the meantime?" Unger plucked a small weed from the ground, mindlessly picking at its tiny leaves. "We should be planning or something."

"There's no sense in planning since it may all change once Barrett returns," said Nell, drawing her knees close. She watched several small perching birds flutter down from nearby trees to land in the bushes.

"With all that has been happening we have yet to ask Mearis what she can see," said Graile. "Now that we have the orb and Westmore has lost its protection, we may get a clearer picture of what will come. I snuck into the library this morning while everyone slept and did some research. The Orb's powers seem to date back to when the gods walked here. It can do remarkable things. No wonder everyone wanted to hoard the things for themselves."

"I knew there was a reason I liked you," said Zanora, kissing his cheek. "I love the way your brain works."

Unger laughed nervously and covered his eyes. "I've seen enough. I'm going to find our Seer."

Inside, sipping tea in their overstuffed, high-backed chairs, Trishar and Mearis spoke in low conversation. They watched the companions shuffle down the hallway.

"It is good to see you all again," said the sorceress. "I have brought more news." She pushed her chin toward the table where the latest edition of *The Oracle* lay face up. "It seems the Bureau is still not above using magic if it helps promote their cause. Hypocrites."

"Right!" cried Unger. "They print the newspaper with magical pictures—the exact things they try to be rid of."

Zanora focused on the moving image of unarmed Agents being struck down by magic users. Their lifeless bodies were left lying in the street by the abandoned warehouse as the attackers fled. She grabbed the paper and read the front page.

Trackers Attacked by Magic Users

"Several dedicated Agents lost their lives in an unwarranted attack on what was to become the site of the Bureau's new headquarters. After slaying the innocent workers of our worthy cause, magic users started a fire that razed the building to the ground. Though still at large, the culprits have several Tracker teams in close pursuit.

In another awful turn of events, several dangerous prisoners used this act of violence as cover to escape. They are currently roaming free after performing an alarming magical killing spree as they fled the city.

Risnor J. Grimes promised to keep all citizens safe by vowing a quick capture and public punishment of all involved in these horrendous crimes. If our dedicated readers have any information that could lead to the apprehension of these felons, contact your nearest Bureau representative today.

Any citizen loyal to the Bureau of Mystical Affairs shall be amply rewarded if their efforts help bring these culprits to justice. Magic must be stopped at all costs. Join our ranks today to help fight the scourge that is magic.

Stay tuned for the latest Bureau updates. Yours truly, Randolph Rollie."

Zanora slapped the paper on the table, staring helplessly at the repeating image of the defenseless Agents being slaughtered. "Complete garbage! The fools even had the guts to say, 'at all costs.'"

"It's propaganda, except for the building being burned down. And I'm certain no one was killed as they claim," said Nell, kicking the table leg out of anger. "And those helpless people we rescued were no more magical than this chair." She pointed to the empty seat beside her.

"No one died during the attack on the warehouse, right?" asked Unger, sounding uncertain. "Maybe Barrett, Gaia, and Elimar had to fight their way out."

Trishar shook her head. "No one was killed. Elimar assured me the place was abandoned. There was most certainly no magical attack or dead bodies lying about as those fools would have folks believe." She pointed a slender finger toward the newspaper.

"The image reeks of being altered," said Mearis. "I smell Asban's stench on this scheme."

"This is a recruiting tactic to expand their forces. They tell lies to gain sympathy," noted Graile as discord crept into his heart. He had disliked the Bureau before, but as their actions now went beyond reason, his thoughts turned to revulsion—even hate. He wondered if Barrett felt the same. How was he handling it? The emotion was overwhelming, as was his drive to expose the Bureau for fraud.

"You are not wrong," agreed Trishar. "To make things worse, neighbors are turning against one another. Many have betrayed anyone they dislike by accusing them of being witches, wizards, magic users, or some other invented indiscretion. Most labels are foul. The race of Men repeats this behavior quite often."

"The dungeons will once more be filled with more innocents in no time," said Nell, throwing her arms in the air.

"We can't just sit here and ignore this," said Zanora before taking a deep breath. Graile watched her struggle to remain composed, becoming proud of her calmness. Nevertheless, he felt her tension, as well as his own. "What are we going to do?" she added.

"Times are desperate. We should retaliate with magic," offered Nell.

Zanora slid closer to the table's edge. "Right. If it will drive this vermin from the western lands, then yes, use it. I would rather see the return of magic users than be subjugated by deceitful dolts."

Graile gave an uncharacteristic thin smile as he turned to the archer. "Do you remember what subjugated meant?"

Unger scowled in return. "Oh, shut up. This is serious. Things are falling apart and you want to make jokes."

"Will you two stop," scolded Trishar. "Zanora makes a valid point. Even the Mundanes are tired of being crushed beneath the Bureau's bootheel. Perhaps they will support an uprising." She resumed sipping her tea.

"Are you suggesting war?" asked Unger, his eyes widening. "How would we fight the Bureau? They are too strong."

Trishar smiled. "If it comes to that . . . yes."

"What does your Seeing say, Mearis?" asked the redhead. "Is either war or the downfall of the Bureau coming soon? Or is there some other ending your crystal balls show?"

"I shall try a new reading," replied Mearis, retrieving her clear sphere from a locked cabinet. She placed a small wooden pedestal on the table, set the orb atop its concaved shape, and then waved the friends round the table. "There are a few preparations. Bear with me."

Graile had never seen a Seer gaze into the future. He watched with interest as Mearis lit several candles, then lay a black cloth edged with embedded golden fillagree before her. She opened a drawstring bag and dumped a dozen small bone pieces onto the fabric's center. The Fader wondered if they were from animals or humans, perhaps leftover from her days as a flesh-eating Trowken. They appeared like human finger bones, though he kept that thought to himself.

The curtains swayed in the windows. Mearis rose to shut them, then retook her seat. After a mumbling chant, she went still as the room turned grave and quiet. She tapped her finger on the table with the rhythm of three. Tap, tap, tap, a brief pause, then repeat. The amber sphere came to life with a swirling white mist forming inside. Churning slowly at first, it quickly gained speed until changing to yellow, green, blue, and then a dazzling purple. Its radiant light swirled and danced over the room as if searching for a home.

Graile shivered as a chill ran down his arms. His gaze alternated between the bones, the orb, and the Seer.

Mearis' face blanked as she uttered the ancient incantation from a time far beyond the memory of any alive, save for the gods themselves.

"Bless my eyes
With future sight
Of what is to come
Through day and night."

The candles flickered, threatening to extinguish themselves, but not from a wind any could feel. The bones rattled, moving under their own power to form letters and words.

Graile felt a force pressing upon him from what he could not say. Yet, the room's energy was almost sentient.

Is this how life works? Is our entire future already written and lying hidden within our heads, like a map we cannot see? Do all living things hold a predetermined plan to follow until their last days? One which can only be revealed by magical means?

Suddenly, the concept of having free will throughout life escaped him. The idea of living with no control over his existence terrified him. He focused to expel the disturbing notion. The only comfort he could muster came from knowing the Seer's predictions were not a sure thing.

Then, his concentration was yanked to the present as Mearis spoke, entranced as she read the bones.

"Though he does not understand yet, his final decision has already been made. All will be right in the end." She fell quiet again, her eyes glazed over and turned dull as the ball's illumination faded.

Zanora could take no more. "But what does it mean? This is like trying to reach the dead instead of seeing the future. I'm waiting to see grandmother's ghost floating by."

"Young lady, stop mocking things you do not understand. It is rude. If you have nothing good to say, then be silent," said Trishar, her voice carrying irritation. "After all you have witnessed, and as many times as magic has aided you, it is childish to continue to ridicule it."

Zanora sank back, sullen over being admonished again. Though hard to admit, she knew the sorceress was justified. Her comments were calloused. "I'm sorry. I know there are good uses for magic, but if used in the wrong way, it can carry evil, too."

"Such is true with any aspect of life," replied the sorceress. "There are kind, decent people wherever you go. Yet there are also vile, reprehensible ones, too. Thieves, abusers, murderers, and more. You have seen this for yourself."

"You mean like Grimes and the Bureau?" asked Nell.

Trishar nodded. "Exactly like Grimes and the Bureau."

"Tell us what you saw, Mearis," pried Graile, still focusing on the sphere as the last hints of color vanished from its core. "Can we free Westmore of the obnoxious ones?"

"There is always a delicate balance between present and future. Every decision you make throughout life changes your course in some respect. Remember, these visions may or may not come to pass," said Mearis as she stowed the orb in the cabinet and locked its doors. She dropped the key in her tunic pocket.

"It shouldn't be a secret. Please tell us," said Zanora.

Mearis moved to the den to ease into her overstuffed chair. Trishar heated their teacups and lowered into the opposing seat.

"I know what you saw," said Unger excitedly. "Barrett was king, magic had returned, the people were happy, and all was as it should be. I mean, you did say, 'All will be right.' So in the end, everything will return to normal."

"Not exactly," said Mearis.

The room returned to a hush. Only the friends' breathing was heard. Mearis took a long sip from her cup, then rubbed her hands together as if warming them. Her gaze went to Unger.

"I saw Barrett sitting on the throne. The crown was in his hands, yet a weight was upon his shoulders. I cannot say if it was sadness or exhaustion. I saw bloodshed and a large struggle beforehand. It could have been months, weeks, or days earlier. Either way, it was important."

"Does that mean Barrett will become king?" asked Zanora, subconsciously gripping Graile's hand tighter.

"There is conflict within the young man. I sense it," added Trishar. "No one here can help him decide his fate. It is already written."

"You're saying the gods already have a plan for him and we are pawns in the game," said Nell.

"In many ways, yes," said Trishar. "No matter what happens, things will be as they are supposed to be. Whether Barrett reclaims the throne or not is not in our hands. It never was. We are simply following the path the deities have laid before us. All things will have led to this ending."

"Why does everyone have to say, 'ending'? I hate that. It sounds terrible," complained Unger.

"Everything has an end. Including life," said Graile. "Elves may be immortal, but we are not. I agree with Trishar. We are following a path the gods set out. But," he added, glancing at the sorceress, "even they cannot see the final act. We continually alter our futures with every action, word, and decision. It is why life is so exciting. You never know where it will lead."

"Do you have a point?" asked Zanora, flipping her hair over her shoulder.

"My point is, we should change nothing. Yes, we have made mistakes and had failures, even death. But that does not stop us. We can either sit and whine about how unfair life is or try until we succeed." He swept an arm through the air. "I have had a terrible life in my younger days but never gave up. And now, here I am with friends for whom I would sacrifice my life. Your situation does not define you. Your mindset does."

"That is deep thinking," said Unger, running his hands through his hair.

Graile nodded. "It's because I read. You would be surprised how clear life becomes if you open your mind . . . and a few books." A thin smile appeared on his lips. "I know that may be difficult for you."

"I knew you would have a smart comment, you—" said Unger.

Zanora stepped on his words. "Enough profound thinking for now. Can we get to what's coming next? Are the others coming back or not? I don't want to wait forever."

"Leave it to Zanora to break things up. Especially things she doesn't want to hear," said the archer.

"My brother is generally very good at communication. I'm sure we will hear from him soon," said Trishar. "Then, we may hear more from Barrett."

"I wonder why Barrett has not spoken to us about his problems?" pondered Graile.

"I know Trishar has her feelings, but we aren't sure he *has* a problem. We are guessing and nothing more." Zanora nodded toward the Fader and archer. "You two are the closest to him. Ask him when he returns. He may need your help working it out."

17

The Time Comes

Gaia stepped from the porch to move to Barrett's side. He was sitting by the stream watching chipmunks play. She lowered on the ground and snuggled into his shoulder. She took his hand and waited quietly.

"I made a fool of myself," he said softly.

"Why? Because you let your emotions out? Why do men believe crying means they're weak?" she asked. "What a stupid concept. Holding in grief and frustration is unhealthy. I admire you for showing your true self. It takes bravery and confidence to be who you really are."

"Everything is weighing on me. Regaining the crown, the death of three innocent men, facing Asban, the Bureau, revenge on Grimes, and Lars' death. Plus, I have no idea what to do next. It has all fallen apart. I should walk away before another companion dies."

"Barrett, you are putting yourself in a pit of despair because things have not gone your way. Stop it." Gaia stressed the last part. "Lars made his own choice to sacrifice himself for all of us. It was not your doing. Neither was the Bureau murdering those men. And, yes, we have failed. We have discussed this. Life is full of failure. Yet here we are." She rubbed his back, then paused. "Unless, of course, you don't want the throne back."

The prince's ear grew warm. Unable to meet her gaze, he rested a hand on her knee, feeling her warmth rise up to his fingers.

"I really don't know what I want. But I do know the thought of my people being abused, living in a decaying city, and waiting for me to save them, is repulsive." He scratched his head in thought. "What if I fail at that, too? Thousands of folks will be enslaved or miserable for the rest of their lives. That is a lot of pressure, my love."

"Then *be* a king, Sire," replied Gaia. "You are royalty, coming from hundreds of years of kind, fair rulers. It is in your blood to lead. Now the time has come to rescue the innocent. You are the only one who can do this task."

"Let Elimar, Trishar, and the rest of his family save Westmore," replied Barrett. "We can move to another city or land. Just the two of us. We can start a new life." Even as he spoke he knew he would never abandon his home in time of need. The thought of leaving his people to their twisted fate bit at him. That would not change, no matter how far away he was. Anger for the Bureau made his skin crawl.

"Wizards and sorceresses do not interfere in our lives. You know this. They may lend a hand when we are in trouble, but they will not solve our problems for us. It is up to us to figure this out." She kissed his cheek. "I have every faith in you, my King."

The prince observed the passing water for a long while, imagining the witch by his side helping him make important royal decisions. The idea calmed him, knowing he would not be alone. "Then I suppose we should start freeing our city, my Queen."

They kissed and headed to find Elimar.

The wizard was sharing a meal with his faithful rats. It was one of the few times Barrett had heard the old man laugh heartily. The sound was pleasant, rising like a light, airy bird song drifting about with true joy in its notes. The prince could not help but smile.

"Ah, there you are, my boy," said Elimar as the teens sat on either side of him. "Good morning to you both." He patted Gaia's hand, then eyed the prince. "Have you worked things out in your head? Or do you need advice from a wise, old man who has seen a few things in his lifetime?"

"I would love that," said Barrett. "Who did you have in mind? Do you know anyone who can help?"

Elimar's face crunched tight, filled with exasperation. "See if I teach you more magic."

"Will we be rejoining the others soon?" blurted Gaia, hoping to intercede before the two would start trading verbal stings and insults.

Barrett heard the longing in her voice. His heart went out to her. Like Unger, Gaia purposely shunned her parents for months to keep them safe lest they be accused of collaborating with a magic user. She missed them terribly yet never revealed her pain. All the same, Barrett sensed it—just like her viewing his aura. After all, he understood the hurtful emotions that came when one's family was taken away.

"I think not," said the wizard. "I have a scheme that may take a bit."

"What are you saying? I don't want to wait. We need to re-join the others," said Barrett. "We have nothing left to do from the shadows of our homes. I want to face Asban again. I owe him for this trouble."

"Revenge does not become you," said Gaia, crinkling her nose. "Why not just march into the city and start killing Trackers, Agents, Grimes, and anyone in your way? Would you feel better then?"

The wizard's attention went from one to the other as he listened in silence.

"Yes!" snapped Barrett on impulse. His chin dropped toward his chest as he hung his head. "No. I suppose not. But I want to make them all pay. And pay dearly for the pain and misery they are causing."

"Making angry choices does not become you, Sire. It does not make for a kingly figure. Rather, it feels immature and rash." Elimar stared at him for a long moment, then spoke on. "I will send a Chatterer to Trishar. We can all be working toward the good of Westmore even though we are apart. To that end, I may have an idea." He cleared his throat and smirked at the prince. "Providing you will listen to the old man trying to help you."

Barrett frowned. "What is on your mind?"

Elimar began to count on his fingers. "We delayed this moment until our forces were at full strength and we stand unified. The time has finally arrived to include others in our plans. We must send word to all magic users about the uprising."

"How would we do that?" questioned Gaia.

"You are a resourceful, brilliant girl. I am certain you can find a way," said the wizard. "Can we make it your duty?"

Gaia shrugged. "Yes. I can handle it. Consider it done."

"Wonderful," said Elimar. "Next, our future king is going to accompany me. We will root out Asban's hiding place and face him together. I am coming along in case he has magic users protecting him."

Barrett sulked. "I'm ready to face him." He puffed his chest out. "I can take care of myself."

The old man smiled again. "We know you can. But remember what happened when I faced Apadora alone? Pride and ego nearly got me killed." He shifted and lit his pipe, taking his usual long draw before exhaling his usual smokey shapes. "I will not let that happen to you. I am going along or I will bind you here and do the deed myself."

The prince mumbled under his breath, then nodded. "Fair enough. I'll do it your way."

"Well played, young man," said the wizard. "I will dash off to send word to Trishar. She can assign tasks to your friends. We begin in seven days' time. That should give everyone enough time to do what they must." His eyes roved over the young couple. "All will go smoothly," he assured.

"Both of you had better be careful," said Gaia.

Barrett went to her for a long hug. "I will not take chances. I'll return unharmed. Besides, Elimar will be with me. What could go wrong?"

Her eyes narrowed. "Don't even ask that question." She touched his cheek. "If you die, I will kill you."

Elimar shooed her from the table. "It is settled. Go on now. Time is short. Get the word out so we can make this work."

Gaia rose and headed outside. The rats followed, excited to be near her.

"I will start making Chatterers presently," said the wizard as he motioned the prince to remain seated. "First, I want to tell you how proud I am of what you have done. At your age, even I would have struggled to do some of the things you have accomplished. I was an arrogant fool early in life and it nearly killed me several times. You are a planner and a thinker and have a great mind in that head of yours. No matter what happens, I will always think of you as the son I never had."

Barrett was dumbfounded. He fought back tears of pride and joy. He wanted to spring up and hug the wizard but remained still to let the feeling sink in.

"I . . . I . . . thank you for all you have done. There is so much I still want to learn. I hope after all this is over you stay around and become my teacher."

"Let's make sure we survive first," said Elimar. "Then, I will be happy to make you a proper magic user. One even a wizard would think twice about crossing." He glanced out the window to study the sun. "I better get to work on the news for my sister."

"What should I do?" questioned the prince. "I feel a bit useless."

Elimar inclined his head toward the bookshelves. "There are hundreds of spell books at your fingertips. You want more powerful magic . . . start reading."

Of course! Barrett sprang up, rushed to the closest shelf to pull down several books, then placed them on the table. Flipping open a cover, he found spells on levitation, binding, shielding, creating fire, and more. Excitement and determination swelled with every turn of the page, and he pushed away the rest of the world for a long while. He took comfort in the rats being by his side and never noticed Elimar's departure.

Trishar had the friends gather round the dinner table. She pulled a Chatterer from her pocket and lay it on the table. "I have news from my brother. I thought it only fitting we open it together."

"I bet it's going to say when they are coming back," said Unger, his voice edging with anticipation. He scooted to the end of his chair and gripped the table's edge.

Graile inclined his chin toward the letter. "You might as well open it."

Trishar broke the seal as the letter sprang to life. The parchment leapt up and unfolded to show Elimar, dressed in pajamas with stars and the moon on them, sitting in his study. He smiled and waved.

"Greetings one and all. I will get straight to it. We have decided to take Westmore back in one week's time. Even now, Gaia is sending word to magic users, telling them to prepare for an assault on the city. We will show the Bureau the strength of those they are trying to destroy. Barrett and I will face Asban and his followers. Tonight, it would be wise if my lovely sister assigns each of you tasks. Do them well, for the entire western lands are counting on you."

"That's not a lot of pressure, is it?" grumbled Zanora.

"Shhhhh," retorted Unger, placing a finger over his lips.

Elimar continued. "There is no turning back once the attack begins. We cannot falter. We will push the Bureau from these lands forever. Send a Chatterer with your job assignments. Best of luck to you all. Farewell until the next word."

The envelope crunched into a ball and ignited, drifting onto the table in a ball of ash which Nell swept away with her hand.

"I admit this is happening quicker than I imagined," said the sorceress. "It appears we are back to planning. We must also take quick action. One week is not very long."

For the day's remainder, the friends sat round the table debating ways they could best be put to use. By nightfall, they had landed on suitable tasks for each.

It was decided that Zanora would cause more dissent amongst the townsfolk toward the Bureau. Graile and Unger were to plan attack points throughout the city. Their goal was to keep the Agents busy and spread out during battle so they could not join forces against the invasion. Nell and Shardira were to infiltrate the castle and patrol the city to judge the enemy's strength, reporting on the size and numbers of the Bureau's hired killers.

"We need to know what we are facing. To that end, I will call on Nirith and Alesta to join the fight. They have no love of tyrants and will certainly aid our cause. And saving the best news for last, I have heard from Yaris, who is still in hiding. He will be arriving by the time the invasion begins," said Trishar.

"That is splendid news," said Unger. "Barrett will be thrilled. Have you told him yet?"

Trishar shook her head. "Not yet. Though, I will tell him in the reply."

The friends parroted the archer's enthusiasm. For a long while, they each shared stories of their encounters with the Warder. Finally, after their exhilaration waned and their planned objectives came back around, the conversation turned to the tasks at hand.

"Are you going to fight, my lady?" asked Graile.

Trishar smiled, her eyes darkening as she spoke. "Try and keep me away."

Mearis placed her elbows on the table. "I may only be a Seer but handle a sword well. I will stand by your sides, come what may."

"It is decided then," added Trishar. "I will send Elimar a reply soon. Graile and Unger have a little time to plan. The rest of you will begin at first light. I will summon Samaren and ask her to take messages to Shardira and Randolph. Randolph can use his many connections to help spread the word. The man could be our ally. Questions?"

"I have one," said Zanora, sheepishly raising a hand. "I need help."

"You got the last part right," quipped Unger.

Nell elbowed him in the ribs and scowled. "This is serious. Stop that childish behavior."

"Go on, dear, speak your mind," said the sorceress, giving the archer a scolding glance.

"I would rather not be seen as I am. Especially after what happened to Jarn." The redhead fiddled with her tunic cuff as she gathered courage. "I never thought I would ask, but will you change my appearance?"

"Oh, dear, I would love to," announced Trishar. "We will make the transformation in the morning. For now, we all need rest. Tomorrow brings closer the return of the king and the salvation of Westmore."

18

Countdown

Morning dawned to find Barrett fast asleep in a high-backed chair. His chin rested against his chest as he snored lightly. A thick volume of *Protection Spells for the Advanced Wizard* lay in his lap. Several more worn spellbooks were stacked at his feet.

He stirred to swat at the insect crawling on his neck. Irritated the thing would not go away, he sat upright only to find Gaia tickling him.

"Good morning, love. Did you sleep here?" She took the book from his lap and set it on the table. "It doesn't look very comfortable."

Barrett rubbed his eyes and groaned, still stiff from sleeping. "I was reading spells and must have nodded off." He tilted his head toward the books. "There is some amazing stuff on those pages. Everything from speaking to animals to defending yourself against wicked fairies. There was even a bit about changing your enemies into crickets." He smoothed his clothing. "Did you have any luck contacting magic users?"

"Yes. Things are going as well as we can hope," said the witch. "And I have great news. As I was walking in the woods this morning, I came across several fairies. One was Taleen's niece. She agreed to help and is already spreading the word."

Rising to stretch his frame, Barrett reached for her. They kissed softly as he went on. "That is excellent, but fairies are magical. Won't Trackers find them easily?" He missed Taleen and silently asked the gods to protect her and her kind.

"Wizards are magical too, but cannot be detected unless they use their powers. The fairies are safe."

The prince touched her cheek with a gentle hand. "The gods are smiling on us. I'm learning new magic and you're organizing users all around the land. Excellent work."

"It most certainly is! You should be proud," came Elimar's voice. "Come to the table. The food is nearly ready. By the way, we received Trishar's Chatterer earlier. I was going to open it, but the young king slept longer than expected."

Barrett's cheeks reddened. "I never knew you could cook. And I'm sorry for oversleeping, but these books hold tremendous knowledge. I got carried away reading." As he settled at the table, a black cat jumped into his lap to purr. He stroked its back. "I'm sorry about last night," he whispered to the feline.

"What did you do?" asked Gaia.

The prince made a sour face. "I accidentally turned Whiskers into a hawk and panicked when I could not change her back. I changed her into several animals before returning her to a feline."

"Leave my animals alone," said Elimar grumpily. "Or you will find out what life is like as a mosquito. And they only live two weeks." The wizard served breakfast, then settled into his seat to open the Chatterer.

Once the letter sprang to life, Trishar appeared at her kitchen table dressed in comfortable clothing. She began by giving a detailed description of her plans and the friends' jobs. After the letter vanished into a cloud of smoke, Elimar spoke.

"Trishar has given your friends worthy and difficult jobs. Unger and Graile are planning attack points for the big day. Zanora is in charge of dissent. Nell and Shardira are judging enemy strength, and Randolph Rollie is, like Gaia, helping spread the word about the big day."

"Will you stop calling it the 'big day!' I already have knots in my stomach and that name doesn't help. It sounds like we are children waiting for our birthday party to begin," complained Barrett. "This is serious. We are finally done planning and talking."

"My! Someone is touchy this morning," muttered the wizard.

Barrett frowned. "I know. I'm sorry. This has been months in the making and feels unreal in many ways." He grinned weakly. "But I trust you all the same."

"To make things even better, Yaris is returning with the outcasts. Many of which are soldiers from your army, all of whom await your return."

"Yaris!" cried Barrett, springing to his feet. "Excellent. I miss him. I cannot wait to see him. This is, above all, is the best news I could imagine."

Gaia rose to hug him closely. "I am so happy for you. I wish to see him, too."

"I knew that bit would stir you up a little," said the wizard. "I hope to see my old friend soon, as well."

"By the way, did Trishar like your plan?" asked the witch as they retook their seats.

"Naturally. She loves all my ideas. She always has." Elimar waggled his fork before him as if making a point before placing food on the table.

Barrett laughed. "Those are utter lies and you know it."

Elimar made a low growling sound. "Be quiet and eat. At least the food will keep your mouth shut for a while."

The prince scowled at the old man.

"Whatever our friends are doing, I hope they're safe," said Gaia, wanting to hear no more bickering.

Zanora did not recognize herself. Wavy black hair spilled over her shoulders. Dark-colored eyes stared out from beneath thin brows. Her garb was pure black as if Graile had chosen her outfit, though she did not mind that part. Her nose was broader and both cheekbones were more prominent. She spun to peer at her backside in the mirror, then faced the glass.

Trishar pointed to a chair. "Let me finish." Zanora sat still as the finishing touches of makeup were applied.

"There!" exclaimed the sorceress. "Sheer beauty. The two of you could be a matched pair." She inclined her head toward Graile. "You go well together, but you should tone yourself down, dear. No one wants to tolerate a caustic woman."

Zanora paused to consider her answer. "I will keep that in mind." She rose to give another turn in the mirror. "This is magnificent. This style is the best. I never imagined liking something so different from my usual look." She hugged the sorceress, then headed for the kitchen. "Thank you, but I must head for the city now. I have work to do."

"Huzzah!" Unger drew out the word as Zanora entered. His fork slipped from his hand to clang on the floor. "By the gods! I would never recognize you. You look . . . f . . . f . . . fabulous," he stammered.

"I agree," said Graile, displaying a thin smile. "But I am happy with you whatever you wear."

Zanora hugged and kissed him. "You are so sweet." She turned to the archer. "Thank you. I'm glad you like it, too."

Trishar eased into her favorite seat. "As you all slept last night, Samaren visited again. Earlier, she had carried notes to Shardira and Randolph. They replied this morning and have already started their parts. Unfortunately, she brought one piece of bad news. It seems since we have stolen the orb the Bureau realizes they are defenseless. They have called for human protection. Even as we sit here, enemy forces filter into Westmore and grow in size. Unfortunately, those awful Morim barbarians are arriving daily."

A hush fell over the room.

"Do be careful, all of you," said Mearis as she lowered in a creaking wooden chair to join the conversation. "I have foreseen pain, confusion, and despair for the prince. Though, the vision is still cloudy."

Zanora grew impatient to begin. Rising, she strapped a dagger round her waist and swung her cloak over both shoulders before heading for the door. "I have waited long enough. I am off to do what I do best—cause chaos." She winked at the Fader, then blew him a kiss. "I will return by nightfall."

Nell hurried to her side. "I'll go along. I need to find Shardira anyway." She rushed back to kiss Unger's lips, grabbed her cloak, and scurried to the door.

They waved as they crossed the threshold and closed the door behind them.

"I hate being left behind," grumbled Unger. "It doesn't feel right to have the company split apart. First Barrett and Gaia, now them. I don't like it."

"It is only for a short while," said Graile, hoping to ease his friend's troubled mind. "Besides, we have our work to do. I am sure you can survive for a few hours without Nell."

"I really do hate you," said Unger, tossing a piece of celery at the Fader's head. It passed through with no effect, making the archer curse.

"Now I know why I never had children," griped Trishar.

Zanora filled an empty seat at the Triple Moon to study the crowd. She listened intently to the conversations around her. Some complained about this year's harvest. Others whined about their wives, husbands, or partners. More fussed over money or their children.

Then, there were those who moaned about the Bureau's control and the lengthy list of new laws. They objected to being controlled, robbed of their wealth and dignity, and being imprisoned within the city. That, she could work with.

Zanora moved to pull up a chair at their table. "May I join you? I couldn't help but overhear your issues." She eased into the seat without waiting for permission. "I hear many folks are unhappy with the Bureau. I am, too. How dare those knaves steal your hard-earned money. I bet you're tired of being bullied by Agents, too."

The patrons nodded and mumbled under their breath. Zanora continued, raising her voice as she went. Soon, many patrons gathered round as the conversation grew and spread throughout the room.

Before long, she had the attention of everyone at the inn. They peered over the railings to listen from the floors above, shouting agreement as she berated Mystical Affairs. A ruckus arose as some started pounding their fists on the tables. More stamped on the wooden flooring beneath their boots. As she planned, tempers grew hot, and rumblings quickly reached a boiling point. She paused for breath. *Now, the tipping point.*

The insurrection, as she put it, was coming soon. "Be prepared," she voiced over the growing dissent. Her statements garnered enough applause to rattle the hanging pictures.

Once her speech was concluded, Zanora shook many hands before making for the door. Little did she know, a few did not agree with her or the others. During her speech, they had slipped out the backdoor unnoticed as the crowd whipped themselves into a frenzy.

Zanora left amidst their anger and shouting to move on to The Pointed Hat. From there, she spoke to anyone who would listen on the streets or in merchant shops. So far, she considered her strategy a success.

Meanwhile, Nell met Shardira, veiled in shadow in a dingy alley. They exchanged pleasantries and discussed their parts of the plan.

"I move about unnoticed since I work in both the Bureau and

castle," said the elf. "Gauging the enemy's strength may be difficult since waves of wicked Men arrive daily. Malathians, Pagorians, and the Morim are here. Our count will need to be revised each day."

"I have rarely been seen on these streets so that I can move about unnoticed, too," replied the Shifter. "We should meet here again at dusk to trade information. Agreed?"

Shardira bowed her head. "Splendid idea. One other point of interest is your raven, Samaren. She is watching from high above and could prove to be the most helpful of all. She has a view far superior to ours, lest we sneak into the towers once more."

Nell chuckled. "That didn't turn out so well the last time. We should forget that idea."

"Well met. However, I may risk it since it would be of no concern to anyone if I appeared on the parapets. It is part of my duties."

Turning to leave, Nell halted. "I forgot to mention what a privilege it is to meet you. Elves fascinate me. I would love to hear more about them. Maybe I could meet your kin when this is over?"

"It would be brilliant to have a Mundane walk amongst us."

"I'm not really Mundane. I am Dorgon." Nell morphed into a grey alley cat. She meowed lightly as she turned a circle before changing back.

"That is most impressive. I had no idea," said Shardira. "Your company is full of surprises."

"We hear that a lot," chuckled Nell. She pointed to the ground. "Meet here at dusk."

Shardira nodded. "I will arrive with the latest news."

Shardira was true to her word. She met Nell to trade information, most of which was not encouraging. The elf reported another wave of mercenaries had just arrived outside the city's southern walls.

"That's not good," said the Dorgon. "Trishar will be interested in hearing this. Though I doubt she'll like it."

After their parting, Nell dipped into shadow as the main gates loomed near, then sprinted to a spot where none could witness her transformation. Changing to a sparrow, she flew up and over the patrolled walls, passing by sentries who paid her no mind. Landing a safe distance away, she changed to human form, pausing to ensure she had not been followed. Satisfied, she moved toward the safe house.

Within an hour or so, she had slunk through the woods to stop and wait close to her destination. Changing to a ferocious cat, she searched the darkening night. She was alone as she padded down the path in feline form, changing to herself once again after reaching the porch. Inside, she headed for the dining room.

"There you are!" cried Trishar. "We have been worried sick."

"Apologies. I was going slow to ensure I was not followed. At least we're all safe," she answered.

"Hold on. Isn't Zanora with you?" asked Unger, watching the door intently.

"No. I was with Shardira, remember? Is Zanora not here?" asked Nell.

"No one panic," said Trishar. "That girl can take care of herself. I am sure she will be along directly." The sorceress caught Mearis' eye and jerked a thumb toward the kitchen. The Seer followed. "Find her quickly," said Trishar.

Mearis nodded and headed to retrieve the orb.

Barrett cursed. "This spell is a lot harder than I thought!" He plopped onto a tree stump. "Why do I need to learn it anyway? It's stupid."

"You complained about learning thought forms, too. But they saved your life, didn't they?" asked Gaia. The witch sat nearby, brushing her hair. She blew him a kiss, but he frowned in return.

Elimar wrapped an arm round her shoulder. "Well put, Queen Gaia." He turned his attention to his apprentice. "You are learning this because levitation comes in handy for many situations. It has saved my hide more than once." He shrugged his indifference. "But I am not forcing you to practice. It is your choice." With a quick spin, he headed for the house. For an instant, his hair became roaring flames as he strode away. "Do not ruin my books or you will discover how well that spell can be used."

"He has a habit of guilting me into learning things," said Barrett. "Well, it's not going to work this time. I'm done."

"You are whiny today," noted the witch. "He is only trying to help, but you are too busy feeling sorry for yourself to notice. Do you need to talk about whatever is bothering you? Besides, Elimar said I am to be queen, so you need to listen since I will be in charge."

Barrett's foul mood broke into a laugh. "I suppose that *is* true enough. I do not stand a chance against the two of you. You both wear me down." He readied his wand, unwilling to further discuss the turmoil over his decision to retake the throne. "I will give it another try." Aiming at the small boulder, he braced himself, flicked his wand, and cast his spell. "Levatota!"

The boulder rose in the air, hanging there for a moment before shaking violently. Panic rose in Barrett's mind. His wand grew unsteady. His concentration was failing.

"You're doing great. Now set it down," said Gaia calmly.

"I am losing control," cried Barrett as the boulder shook, cracking into pieces. "I swear I'm not doing that. It . . .".

The rock exploded, sending fragments flying in all directions. The teenagers dove onto the ground and covered their heads. Barrett was pelted by a wave of small chunks, yelping as each one smacked his body. Two pieces crashed through Elimar's windows. The prince cursed at that bit. Sore, embarrassed, and tired, he rose and helped Gaia to her feet.

"Remind me again how I am going to defend the city, face Asban, and drive Grimes out? I bet even that worm of a wizard can do this ridiculous spell."

"In your early training, Elimar taught you to telelocate smaller objects. So if you can do that, you most certainly can pick something up and move it," said the witch. "I think you're making this tougher than it is. You are too nervous and trying too hard. Relax."

He swept an arm toward another boulder. Stinging pride prevented him from trying again. "That is delightful insight! I would love to see you do it."

Gaia shrugged. "Promise not to be ashamed or carry on when I do?"

Barrett nodded sharply. "You have my—".

The witch jerked her wand free of her cloak and aimed it squarely. "Levatota."

The stone lifted away to hang motionless. Swishing her wand, Gaia moved the rock about in all four directions. Satisfied, she placed it back in its starting point and stowed her wand without a word. Barrett eyed her, believing she would gloat over her victory, but her face remained expressionless. He suddenly wished he had her ability to read auras.

"Like I said . . . relax." She spun and headed for the house.

"B . . . b . . . but . . . I didn't—".

Gaia never heard his words as she closed the door.

Barrett palmed his forehead until it hurt. "Why is this so complicated? If I can't even do this, I will never take back my city. What if Elimar gets hurt because of my weak magic?" He lowered onto the grass as Left scurried from behind a tree to climb on his lap.

"Do not feel bad," said the rodent. "Elimar used to do the same thing. He broke more windows than we had glass. Thankfully, he learned a repair spell rather quickly."

"I'm just fooling myself. I thought I was more powerful than this." The prince waved his wand at the rock. "I can't even move a stupid stone."

"Your mind is clouded with thoughts. Something is bothering you." She raised on her hind legs to place her tiny paws on Barrett's hand. "I am an excellent listener. Tell me your troubles and the rock will be as light as a feather when you are done. Trust me."

Barrett sat to lean back against a thick tree trunk. He remained silent for minutes on end as Left waited patiently by his side. Finally, he spoke.

"I'm so undecided about being king," he said quietly. "Everyone encourages me, but I'm not sure my heart is in it. I only want the throne to see Grimes and his dolts get kicked out of Westmore forever."

"Are you certain that is the only reason?" asked Left, tilting her tiny head to one side.

Like an open floodgate, words poured from the prince in

steady fashion. Every feeling, emotion, and thought rolled from his lips. Regardless of whether Left offered a solution or not, just speaking about his pain and confusion gave him a wondrous feeling. It felt even better to speak to the rat than to anyone else—even Elimar or Gaia. He could not explain why.

In the end, he went silent before Left patted his hand. "You mainly spoke about what everyone else wants or expects you to do." She gripped his finger. "What do *you* want? Not once did you mention your desires, only those of others."

"That is true," admitted Barrett. "All I have done is whine and complain. I never really thought about what *I* wanted. I only considered everyone else's expectations. I can hardly think of anything other than kingly duties, responsibilities, my people and friends staying safe, and more." He scooped Left up, allowing her to perch on his shoulder as he stood to pace. "Still, I think I could be a good king, like my father. I can do it."

"Negative thoughts bring negative outcomes," said Left. "Be positive and good things will come to you. It may not happen overnight, but the gods will help with your desires."

The prince nodded. "Gaia tells me that a lot. I guess I am inflexible at times. It comes from my mother. But in the end, it does nothing but slow me down if I always do things my way." He stroked Left's fur. "Thank you. I needed to talk things through out loud." In a quick move, he spun, pointed his wand, and shouted. "Levatota!"

The boulder rose in smooth fashion, moving about as if hollow on the inside. Barrett had complete control. He returned it to the starting spot, then headed for the house.

"There will be more practice tomorrow," he said with confidence as Left settled comfortably on his shoulder.

19

Problems

L ike before, Mearis cast her spell and focused on the swirling mists in the sphere's center. Staring into the orb's depths, her face twisted in disbelief, then horror as her hands gripped the table's edges. Her mouth fell open in a soundless scream. Agonizing seconds passed before she slumped motionless in her chair.

Around her, the friends could only stare in silent shock.

"Zanora is captive," Mearis finally uttered. "I saw it all. Agents grabbed her as she was going about her mission. They tortured her for information, then cast her into the dungeon. She is frightened, in pain, and alone. The Bureau will try to pry knowledge from her. She has little hope if we do not help her."

Graile turned vaporous for an instant. "I'm going after her." Solid again, he rose quickly, tipping his chair onto the floor. "We freed others from the same place and we can do it again."

Unger's voice came calm and steady. "Graile, my friend, there were fewer guards then. Nor were there hired killers, bounty hunters, and every other kind of riffraff imaginable. You cannot do this. Let's talk it through and find the best way to help her without getting anyone else captured or killed."

The Fader reset his chair and lowered onto the seat. "Forgive me. Emotions got the best of me. It will not happen again. But we need to do something, all the same."

"Right. So how do we set her free?" asked Unger with a genuine look of concern. "And how long will your configuration spell last?"

"To this first part, I cannot say yet," answered the sorceress. "I will ponder the problem tonight. As to the spell, it will remain for days. With luck, she should be safely home by then. Besides, she is part of this company. Despite her flaws, she is one of us." Her gaze traveled over the others. "Get some rest and I will have a solution tomorrow. Do not do anything foolish. Rescuing one shall be difficult enough. Let's not make this more complicated than what it already is. Good night."

Zanora rolled atop the thin layer of straw and moaned. Her body ached and her head felt no better. She was bruised and bloodied from the beating and questioning she received from the Agents—first for speaking out against the Bureau and second for refusing to divulge the names of those suspected of helping her spread lies.

She snorted her disgust, confident nothing she had spoken was a lie. Yet, the Bureau rarely sees their own errors. They will see soon enough, she thought as she wiped dried blood from the corner of her mouth. Several fingers on her left hand felt broken.

"This was not the way my plan was supposed to turn out," she said, speaking to herself for no other reason than to keep her mind from the horrible situation and her agony.

Around her, the jarring sound of rattling chains filled the air. Wails and whimpers echoed from nearby. She was not alone.

How long have I been here? I hope everyone else made it back safely.

Angry over the fact she only killed two of the men trying to seize her, she cursed herself for not bringing more than a dagger.

"I could have slain them all if I had my sword and shield." She scanned her cell, noting her prison was rectangular with strange niches and disfigured walls. To her right, noises from clicking claws drew her attention. In the gloomy grey, she only saw darting shadows as the things hid in cracks and crevices. She hoped they were merely rats or mice. Nonetheless, whatever shared her confines made her heart race. The noises and glowing eyes watching from the darkness reminded her of the Outerworld. She shifted, only to wince at the pain tearing through her body. "No. That's real. This is not a dream," she groaned. "What am I going to do?"

Rising on wobbly legs, she stretched, grimacing at the simple movement. In that moment, she realized a thick manacle was fastened round her ankle, securing her to the thick stone wall. She jerked and tugged with her good hand, yet cursed when her efforts changed nothing.

"I wish Graile was here. He could get me out."

To occupy her mind and hopefully hasten her escape, she beat her chains with a stone to break a sliver free. She steadily fashioned the stony piece into a blade, then tucked it into her belt. *Whoever touches me next will be sorry.*

Morning came cloudy and windy with an unusual chill in the air. Graile shivered from the cold as he stood on the porch wondering if he should be more impulsive like Barrett. If he went against Trishar's warning, he would have already been on his way to free Zanora. He might have even succeeded by now.

But he knew stubbornness often led to disaster. And placing Zanora in more danger was the opposite of his intentions. Yet he could not stop pacing the porch's length. He warmed himself by crossing both arms across his chest to keep his hands from stiffening up.

Is this what it's like to love someone? The thought momentarily stopped him. *It must be. Why else would it be so painful?* Waiting to rescue someone he cared for proved more difficult than he imagined. All the same, he awaited the sorceress' arrival and hoped she would bring a solid plan to save his girlfriend.

The door opened behind him. Unger was there. "Trishar just arrived. Hurry up," he said, waving for the Fader to follow. Graile dashed inside to gather round the table, rubbing his hands together as he went.

The sorceress looked tired, nearly dashing the Fader's hopes as his eyes covered her. Were the strains of all the adventures taking their toll? He did not want to think so but knew it was a possible reality.

Trishar cleared her throat. "Listen carefully, for I have had very little sleep and do not wish to repeat myself. So do not get on my bad side this morning," she warned. "I spent the night speaking with Samaren, who herself worked tirelessly to obtain more news."

"Well, what did that bloody raven say?" asked Unger, unable to contain himself.

"She said teenagers should learn patience when they are instructed to listen." Trishar gave him an irritated glance. "As I was saying, Samaren has taken word to Randolph since he is best suited to find some unsavory sorts to free Zanora." She paused for questions. Graile went first.

"And what did he come up with? More importantly, is she alive?"

Trishar nodded. "Excellent questions. Yes, dear boy, she is alive. In fact, Yaris has come forward and volunteered to save her. After all, he knows every inch of the dungeons since it was part of his job. As we speak, he is on the way."

"Wait. We barely got in and out without being seen. Not to mention, that was before the Bureau tightened security. Your friend may be captured or killed," said Nell.

"I have seen events differently," said Mearis, patting the crystal ball in her lap. "There could be more death, but Zanora survives."

"I'm sorry, but your visions show past, present, and future *possibilities*. You admitted as much. There is no way you can see for sure if she lives or not," said Graile.

"Right!" cried Unger. "We need to do something, not wait on other people. Even if it is Yaris."

"I have sent a Chatterer to Elimar telling him the latest news and begging him to stay clear before he fouls things up. If anyone were going to do something rash or stupid it would be my brother," said Trishar. "The gods know all too well Barrett does not listen either. Gaia is the only levelheaded one amongst the three of them. So trust me, even if my plan fails, that trio may have your friend home by dinnertime."

"I still don't feel right about not rejoining our friends," said Barrett sullenly. "I want to go back to the safe house." He peered at the books and rats. "I love it here, but my heart is with the others."

Elimar raised an eyebrow. "I understand, but—"

Gaia cut him off. "I agree. Take us back, please."

The wizard rubbed his bearded chin. "Well, in light of all that is happening, you two have a solid idea."

"What does that mean? What *is* happening?" asked Gaia.

The wizard took a long breath and slowly exhaled. "You will find out soon enough, so you might as well hear it all from me." Elimar recited the contents of the earlier Chatterer, including the planned rescue by the Warder. "However, be calm since she has likely already been freed."

"Likely!" cried the prince. "Take us back right now!"

"I will do no such thing." Elimar paced round the room. "Once you calm yourself and we have a good lunch, we will leave. I do not want you making a mess of things already in motion. You have a way of interfering in things and making them worse. Like stealing the blasted orb, for example."

"But how can you think of lunch?" questioned Gaia.

The wizard chuckled. "How can you *not*?" He rubbed his belly. "I am always hungry. Besides, what good would you do there? You would only be sitting around waiting, just as you are now. My sister has handled the problem. She is capable."

"I don't care about who is capable," cried Barrett, springing to his feet. "I want—"

Elimar's voice boomed like a thunderclap. "Enough! Young man, you cannot always have what you want. I said we will wait and wait we shall. Another hour will make no difference. Now sit down and be quiet while I make lunch." He softened after a slow exhale. "Someday, you will learn rash decisions turn out to be the worst ones. Think before you speak or act and your life will be better for it."

Struck by the wizard's seriousness, Barrett reluctantly lowered into a chair. Though the harsh words stung his pride, he knew the old man was right. Nothing good ever came from impulsive choices. He only had to think of the three men who lost their lives the night the orb was stolen to know that fact. Nonetheless, he wanted to shout from frustration, then run out the door and escape somehow. His emotions swirled in a jumbled mess.

After facing the facts, he knew he could do nothing for his friend. It was too late. Zanora's fate was in someone else's hands, whether he liked it or not.

The downward blow struck clean. The guard never knew what or who hit him as he crumpled in the corner. Before moving past the unconscious form, Yaris stole the prison keys, slipped into shadows, and strode cautiously down the gloomy stone passage. Repeating a similar assault three more times, he added to the line of injured jailors with ease.

Going from one cell to another, peering into each as he passed, he soon reached his objective. With surprising stealth, the Warder unlocked the cell, slid inside, and moved toward the sleeping prisoner.

The woman waited until he was in striking distance. In a blink, she sprang from the straw to stab forward. The blade came low and fast, yet the stout Black man seized her wrist, pulled her close, and clamped a firm hand over her mouth.

"If you want to live, mind your manners and do as I say," he whispered, though his deep voice was hard to conceal. "Nod if you understand."

Zanora nodded and released her roughly hewn blade. Setting her free, the big fellow pulled a spare blade from his belt and handed it to her.

"Use this instead." He looked her over. "Samaren's note said you would appear differently, but I had no idea how much. I barely recognize you," he said, setting to work picking the manacle lock. Seconds later, she was free.

"Bless the gods! Warder Yaris, is that you?" she stammered. "I am pleased you made it past the Bureau fools to get here."

"It will take more than a few of these buffoons to stop me." He chuckled. "There is a lot to tell and even more I wish to know. But first, we must stay alive."

Moans and voices resonated the corridor's length, filling her cell.

Zanora gripped his tunic in desperation. "We can't leave them here." She clasped her hands together in pleading fashion, ignoring the pain stemming from her broken fingers. "Turn them loose, too. They do not deserve this."

Yaris shook his head. "There are too many. They will be free soon enough. In fact, this is likely the safest place they can be once the fighting begins." He glanced her over for injuries, then reached for her unoccupied hand. The redhead sucked in a painful breath, making the Warder wince. "We will fix that soon enough. You can walk, yes?"

Zanora grimaced with each unsteady step forward but nodded. "I'll survive."

"No wonder you pair with Barrett so well. The two of you are willful to the end." Poking his head from the doorway, he checked the passage. "We can go."

"We're not together anymore," she admitted.

Yaris turned with a frown. "I really *am* out of touch. I am sorry to hear that, dear one." Adjusting his eye patch, he smiled with silent reassurance before crossing the threshold into the impenetrable gloom.

Ascending from the bowels of the wicked place, they crept in single file as chilled air met their faces. Spongy, pungent slime grew dense upon the walls and ceiling, with only small walkways being clear in spots. Some sections forced the pair to hold their breath to avoid choking on the putrid smell. No air stirred and all sense of space was distorted, yet the Warder never slowed.

During her first trip to the dungeons she had entered from a different location. She now realized she was lost in the unfamiliar tunnels as they crept up the winding stairs onto the second level.

This floor was nearly identical to the first, but here, many rooms and chambers filled the passageway. Ahead, down a passage to their right, came heavy footfalls, growing steadily louder.

With little time to search for an escape route, Yaris guided Zanora into an unlit corner, slowly drew his sword, then waited as he coiled to attack.

"Right, my lovelies, it's torture time. Who wants to be first today?" announced the man as he rounded the corner, keys jangling in his hand. "It's always a good day when I get to break some bones or peel some skin."

Zanora slapped her free hand over her mouth to cover her retch. Yaris gritted his teeth and sprang from cover to swing a balled fist with power and speed. The blow connected with the unkept brute's face, bouncing him from the wall with force to land on the cold floor with a sickening thud. Blood oozed from his mouth and broken nose.

Together, they grabbed the man's feet and dragged him into a darkened corner. They stole his keys in hopes of delaying further harm to the prisoners. Beyond anger, the redhead kicked him several times for good measure. Breathing deeply, she viewed the crumpled body with hate.

"I owed him that." She kicked him twice more. "He's the one that broke my fingers and gave me these." She pointed to her bruised mouth and eye, then spat on him before leaving.

Moving cautiously, they slunk down the hallway. The echoing rock only allowed a certain degree of quiet. To Zanora, they may as well have been ringing a bell.

To her relief, they soon reached a stout, wooden door. The big man grasped the handle firmly and eased the exit open. Dusk's grey light flooded in, bringing stabbing pain behind Zanora's already aching head. She squinted and raised an arm as if to push away the gloom.

"Oh, that hurts. It's so bright. How long was I down there?"

Yaris gently patted her back. "Only overnight. You were lucky. Others have it far worse. But we will fix that soon. Come, let's hurry. There is a wagon waiting to take us to safety."

"That sounds risky. We're going to be caught. Isn't the city closed?"

"It is, mostly. But the sentries do not search their own supply wagons as they come and go. It is easy enough to have secret compartments they will not look for. Also, several guards still loyal to Barrett are working for the Bureau. We will be safe," said Yaris. "And if we are caught, a small sack of silver will settle the guards' greedy souls."

Within minutes, after traversing a few dim backstreets and dismal allies, Yaris threw back the canvas flap and climbed inside the sizeable wagon. He extended a hand, then quickly pulled the young woman inside to vanish into the hidden compartment. Once ready, the Warder gave a convincing birdcall. The wagon lurched toward the gate.

"Thankfully, it will be a short ride," he said as he settled back next to the redhead. "Trishar is waiting and will meet us soon enough."

20

Partings & Reunions

Zanora eased from the wagon and shuffled into Trishar's open arms. They embraced tenderly, like mother and daughter. The sorceress held her at arm's length.

"You look awful," she said, looking over the girl's condition.

"Thanks. I feel the same way, too," said Zanora, smirking.

"You had us scared to death, young lady." They hugged again, making the redhead cry out in pain. "Apologies. I did not mean to hurt you, but we are so thankful you are home I got carried away," said the sorceress. She mouthed a silent 'thank you' to the Warder. "Be aware, Yaris took a huge risk by showing himself. I hope you at least acknowledged his efforts."

Yaris bowed his head. "She did indeed, my lady. We spoke at length during the ride. It seems I missed a lot of the recent happenings."

Trishar chuckled. "Even I have trouble keeping up with current events. Teenagers move rather fast at times. Unfortunately, they do not always get their desired results." She eased an arm around Zanora's shoulder and headed into the forest's depths. Yaris followed close behind after watching the wagon disappear in the distance.

Trishar led them to a fairy ring and jerked a thumb at it. She took Zanora's hand. "Let's stay together since Warder Yaris has never done this before, and you, dear, are in no shape for a rough landing. Hang on to me and the journey will be pleasant enough."

"No! We can't do this. The Trackers will follow us to the safe house!" said Zanora with panic rising in her voice. "I won't put anyone else in danger because of me."

"Do not fret. I have planned for that, too. Shardira will ensure the Trackers will not pursue us. She is aware of this plan and knows what to do," said the sorceress. She gazed at the Warder. "Are you ready? I know this can be scary at first, but it is not that bad."

"Don't let her fool you. It isn't very good! It feels like an ogre has your head and feet and is trying to rip you in half. Your head spins and your stomach goes into your eyes. I nearly threw up for the first few times," said Zanora. She tried to laugh but excruciating pain prevented it.

"Would you stop that nonsense!" Trishar exhaled forcefully. "This is yet another time I wonder why people have children at all."

Yaris stood tall. "This type of magic scares me a bit, but if the young ones can do it, so can I." He eased his hand into Trishar's and nodded.

They stepped forward in unison and vanished in a swirl of motion.

Minutes later, a band of Trackers raced their mounts over the hill toward the fairy ring to find nothing more than a tree-lined grass field with a large mushroom ring at its northern edge.

"Do you see them, Mr. Haskins?" asked Shardira.

"No, Captain." Haskins leapt from his saddle to inspect the ground and sniff the air. "They're not here." He scratched his head. "How do they escape so easily? Maybe they're hiding nearby. Start the search."

The Captain raised her hand to halt the others. "Hold where you are." She dismounted and scanned the tree line. With her back to the others, she smiled briefly, then turned to face them. "There is nothing here. Keep moving," she said, swinging atop her mare.

"But Captain, we just got here. Shouldn't we try a little harder?" said a young man, fidgeting nervously as he spoke.

The half-elf shook her head and inclined it to the forest. "Mr. Haskins, do you see or smell any signs of magic users?" she asked again.

"No, Captain, none at all," came Haskins' low, graveled answer. "It seems we are in the wrong spot."

"Then I see no good reason to search any longer. Each second we delay the culprits move farther away. We must move."

The men nodded in unison.

"Let's trail the outlaws while the scent is fresh." Shardira reined her horse to the east, took the lead, and moved off at a trot.

"Give her a promotion and she thinks she knows everything. Blasted elf!" said the young one as he rode from behind.

"You realize I hear you, right?" asked Shardira over her shoulder. She touched the tip of her ear with an index finger. "Elf ears."

The sorceress scurried to the kitchen to brew a healing potion. After setting out her bottles, knives, herbs, and other ingredients, she carefully measured each one, then tossed them in her boiling cauldron. She hummed a tune as the concoction fizzled and smoked a bright orange color.

Down the hall, Yaris entered. Unger ran to pull the big man into a rough embrace. "It is fantastic to see you, Warder!" cried the archer. "You're even larger than I remember."

Yaris laughed a rumbling sound. "And you have grown as well, my favorite archer."

Unger moved on to Zanora but stopped short. His face soured. "You look awful," he said.

She punched his arm with her good hand. "I know. I've already heard that, you fool." She snatched his tunic with one hand and dragged him into a shaky hug. "But it's good to see you. I doubt I would've survived that filthy hole if left there too long."

Unger slid his arm round her waist to help her shuffle toward a seat. Graile arrived to help steady her. She kissed the Fader softly. They ambled to the living room, easing her into a comfortable chair.

Unger attended her every need, fetching food and drink first. When Graile attempted to help the archer shooed him away. "Go be with your girlfriend. I'll take care of this." The Fader flashed a quick smile of thanks.

The friends gathered round to hear the escape tale while Yaris moved to the kitchen, joining Mearis and Trishar in low conversation.

Unger slid the food tray closer, then prepared drinks, fruit, cheese, bread, and meat. Zanora barely took a bite before the friends started with their questions.

"For crying out loud, leave her alone for a bit. She needs food and rest. Let her eat, you dolts," cried the archer.

"Good point," agreed Trishar, coming to place a steaming mug by the redhead's side. "This poor girl needs to recover. Time grows short, and if she is going to help free Westmore she will need strength." The sorceress clasped her hands together, then quickly separated them. The chairs slid backwards with the friends still in them. "There. Now let her be, please. Why not eat this glorious meal Unger prepared, then go about your business? And drink your medicine," she added.

Zanora sniffed the steaming brew and turned up her nose. "I hope that's tea."

"Do you wish to heal your broken fingers or not?" asked the sorceress. "Perhaps you enjoy feeling the way you do now. Or would you rather help heal yourself and help your friends conquer Westmore?" She slid the mug closer and waited.

When Zanora remained unmoving, Trishar smiled and inched closer. "This can be as simple or difficult as you wish."

"If it will speed your recovery why not just get it over with?" asked Graile.

"You're right, but I'm still struggling with accepting magical things." Zanora crinkled her nose as she sniffed the air, then reached a shaky hand outward and took the mug. "If this tastes awful, you'll be sorry when I heal."

"Oh, shut up and drink it," snapped Unger. "Besides, we're already sorry."

Zanora eased the rim past her lips and took a long drink. "That actually tastes good." She emptied the contents, then handed the mug to the sorceress.

Trishar turned and walked away. "You'll need three of those a day until you can use you hand again."

"B . . . b . . . but I'm better already," stammered Zanora.

"You are starting to sound like B . . . B . . . Barrett," mocked Unger.

Barrett bid farewell to the rats. "I'm going to miss each of you. Thank you for your kindness and advice."

Left scurried forward to shake the prince's hand. Her tiny paws gripped his finger again. "You will make an excellent wizard and great king, Sire. We shall await your return with anticipation." The rats bowed together.

"You have my word we will meet again," said Gaia, taking time to pet each one. "Once Barrett is crowned, you can visit whenever you wish." Her voice lowered to a whisper. "I'll make certain Elimar brings you along. You need a break."

"Did I hear my name?" asked the wizard, entering in his fitted green robes. His beard and hair were raven black and long. Tall blue boots matched the color of his eyes. He bore a staff in one hand and patted his robe with the other. "I brought a wand, too, just in case."

Barrett extended a hand to the wizard. "I'm sorry for my behavior yesterday. I was wrong to shout and meant no disrespect."

Elimar smiled and shook his hand. "You are forgiven. Now you must forgive me, as well. I should not have raised my voice as I did." He chuckled. "I was worse than you when I was your age.

I understand how difficult your early years can be. Nonetheless, if you go around demanding things, saying untrue or hurtful things, you will continue that habit as an adult. And we certainly do not want that, do we?"

Barrett and the witch shook their heads.

The wizard clasped his hands together. "Perfect!" He strode toward the front door. "We should be off. Let's not dawdle all day. Oh, be sure to say farewell to the Hydra or I will never have peace again."

The teens grabbed their belongings and rushed to follow. Before stepping from the porch, they did as instructed and spent several moments ensuring the Hydra was in good spirits.

As Elimar went deeper into the woods the pair hurried along behind, breathing heavily in their attempt to catch up.

"He has to be ten thousand years old! How can he move so fast!"

"Stop being ridiculous. He's not a day over seven hundred," said Gaia. "Relax. It's not as if he will leave without us."

As they crested a rise, they stopped to gulp air while Elimar stood quietly resting against a boulder. He frowned at them. "You two need more exercise." Before either could respond, he headed off again, waving for them to follow.

Within another hundred paces the old man halted to point at the fairy ring at his feet. "Here we are. This is my favorite ring. Mainly because I know every fairy living within my woods. They are caring stewards of the forest. Best of all, this is all under my protection," he said, sweeping an arm before him. "No Tracker could ever detect us here."

"Are we going to Trishar's house?" asked Gaia with hope. "I would love to see her again."

Elimar shook his head. "Do not forget she is under constant watch. We would stir up trouble going there." He pointed to the west. "Last year, when I was on the run from some nasty little creatures called Poggins, I discovered a cave not far from your current safe house. After some exploration deep inside, I came across an incredibly beautiful cavern with moss-covered rocks, pools of the bluest water, and living creatures I had never seen before. While there, I came to understand the thick rock walls interfere with the Tracker's ability to detect magic. So we will telelocate there, then walk the remainder of the way."

"Do we get to see inside the cave?" asked Barrett excitedly.

"Perhaps after all this is over, yes. Right now, we have no time for such luxuries," said the wizard. "Returning here will be a small reward for taking back Westmore."

"I simply want to face Asban. And I have not forgotten Grimes, either." Barrett's tone held unmistakable vehemence. He found himself clenching his jaws until they hurt.

"The time to face your enemies is nearly here. However, some happy times are in order first, if only for a brief while. Seeing your friends may help you forget about revenge." Elimar extended his arms and held them there. "Come along."

Some hours later, as the sky turned to a velvet darkness, the trio arrived at the safe house. They were footsore, thirsty, and hungry. Barrett entered to find Zanora limping toward him. Her body was bent with pain and still covered in nasty bruises. She wore a sling to support her injured hand.

Behind her came Unger, rubbing his arm with a wince. He just received a nasty punch for mentioning how the redhead looked as though she'd fought a goblin and lost.

Zanora's hair was its lovely ginger color while her broadened nose had shrunken to normal—thin and perfectly shaped. One thing that had not changed were the cuts and scrapes. Red, painful abrasions circled her wrists and ankles. The wounds were turning deep purple as they healed. One eye was still nearly swollen shut. But to the good, her fingers were healing nicely.

Barrett hugged her as tightly as able. "You look—" he began.

"If you say 'awful' I'm going to kick you with all my might," she interrupted.

"I was going to say 'gorgeous.' Tired and a little beat up . . . but still gorgeous," he confessed, gently touching her face. "I am so happy you are not dead."

She laughed, clutching at her ribs as she did. "I'm pretty pleased about that, too. I look like Yaris." She pointed to her bruised eye. "Only, his is missing. At least mine will open again."

"There are still many more waiting to be freed, Sire," said Yaris as he stepped from behind Trishar.

As the companions gathered round one another, Barrett sprinted to hug his Warder. The young man wept openly, uncaring who saw. It was the first time he felt truly safe in a long while. Yaris always had that effect on him. Until the Bureau took over, the big man had been a constant presence in his life. The days Barrett spent not knowing if his friend was dead or alive had been torturous. Barrett cursed Grimes for breaking them apart.

"Accurate news is tricky to come by and for the longest while I thought you were dead. I was wrong to despair and think the worse." Shame gripped the prince. "Others said you had escaped. I had no idea who to listen to."

Yaris bowed his head. "I'm sorry you worried about me. However, my King, if you will have me, I will be by your side for years to come. Besides, I am too obstinate to die yet." He gripped the boy's shoulders. "You look older, but well. And I see you have grown, too. You will make a splendid figure of a king, my liege."

Unger acted mortally offended by the words. "You have to cut out all the royal talk," he said softly. "It makes him rather grouchy if you call him king, sire, or anything, really."

Yaris laughed. "Some things never change, I see."

The remainder of that night brought long tales, a feast of food, and laughter louder than any had been part of in several months. Talk went far into the morning hours with stories of death, battles, triumphs, plans, hopes, and dreams.

Yet as time ticked away, one by one the friends found their bedrooms. Only Yaris and Barrett remained. For the first time in a long while, the prince did not want to sleep, nor did he want the night to end.

Near the wee hours of the morning, Samaren flew through the open window to join them, but even she soon fell fast asleep on her perch.

21

Doubts

Barrett woke late to the wafting aroma of cooking food. Dressing in sluggish fashion, he washed himself as best he could from the water basin by his dresser. Slipping on a clean tunic, breeches, and socks, he jammed his feet into a worn pair of boots and headed downstairs. He was the last to arrive.

Elimar held everyone's attention as he went on about his adventures. He smiled while shooting colorful orbs overhead, making forks and knives dance on the table, and imitating sounds of unknown beasts and creatures that once chased him with foul intentions.

Barrett lowered next to Trishar while the friends sat enthralled by the old man's stories. Yet, the prince was uncertain if anything Elimar said was true or pure entertainment. *The wizard certainly enjoys being the center of attention at times.*

Unger was wide-eyed, Nell was gripping his arm, Gaia appeared to be holding her breath, while Graile remained as stoic as ever. Even Zanora, Mearis, and Yaris appeared caught up in the lively stories. Trishar rolled her eyes frequently, but said nothing. Barrett noticed that part straightaway.

"My brother may not always speak the truth, but he tells a captivating story," whispered the sorceress, leaning into the prince's shoulder.

"It is one of my favorites things about him. But I often doubt what he's saying. You never know which stories are true or which are entertainment," he whispered in return as a flutter of butterflies winged by in their erratic patterns. One landed on his nose, stayed a moment, then rejoined its family.

"At times like these, I understand why some folks think highly of hearing his account of things." She laughed as she slid from her chair to move toward the kitchen. "I have a dinner to prepare."

"I can help." Barrett followed, eyeing the friends over his shoulder to ensure they remained behind. "My lady, may we speak?"

"Of course, my boy. What weighs heavy on your mind?" She busied herself retrieving pots and pans from the cabinets as if they were speaking about the weather instead of a nagging issue.

The prince fidgeted with a plate sitting on the counter, then nervously adjusted his sleeves, trying to find the courage to open up. "Do you think we can succeed? I mean, have you seen the future? I need to know."

Trishar stopped to take a seat. She wore a warm smile. "Not even Mearis can see the future with certainty." She conjured a saucer and cup of steaming tea, then took a long sip. "Think how boring life would be if we could see what was going to happen before each day dawned. Even the gods cannot see what you ask."

He pondered that for a moment. "I suppose it is a strange notion. Yet, I feel my life is somehow incomplete without knowing if Westmore will be ours again. It's like an unfinished story."

"*That* is what makes life an adventure, is it not? Treat each day as if it special . . . because they are gifts." Trishar rested a hand atop his for a moment, her calmness transferring to him as if she had cast a spell. "It seems to me, before Elimar came along, you were doing just fine without knowing what tomorrow would hold. Besides, what you said is correct. Life *is* an unfinished story until the day we are no more. Then, it begins again."

"What do you mean? That makes no sense."

"This is only one of your many lifetimes. You will have others, though completely unlike this one, I would imagine. Samaren is a perfect example. Once, she was mother—flesh and blood, now she is a wise raven. The most intelligent of birds, I might add."

Barrett considered the sorceress' point. "Hold on. Have you lived before?"

"Wizards and sorceresses live by different rules. Elimar and I have taught you as much. We live for many of your lifetimes before fading away. However, the race of Men do not have that luxury. Still, once you leave this world, you will simply wait to begin your new life."

"So if I die in battle I will come back again?" he questioned.

"I cannot answer that since I do not know what the gods hold in store for you. But I have every faith you will return. You have a young soul. I feel it. Of all of you, Graile is the one I believe has lived before." She tapped the table with her stirring spoon. "His soul feels older than the others."

Barrett gave a lingering glance over his shoulder to see the Fader chatting with Zanora. They were holding hands.

"No wonder he's so smart. I bet he has all that knowledge from a previous life," said the prince. "I bet he was a great warrior or leader of Men."

"First, being a warrior does not make you great. Conquering others or handing out death for a living is not impressive. Second, he could have been a twisted ogre or an ancient tree watching the world pass beneath his boughs." She swished a finger to reheat her tea.

The prince started. "I could be a tree?" His voice held a child-like innocence and sound of wonder.

"Probably not. You would make an awful one," replied Trishar. "You would not have the patience for it." She laughed. "Barrett, tell me what is the real issue here."

The prince toyed with a mug as if thinking or possibly avoiding the question altogether. "Promise you will not tell anyone, but I'm scared for this whole fight to begin. There are so many people counting on us—me, more than the others. It's nerve-wracking. What if I fail?"

Trishar shrugged. "Then you will fail. We all do at one time or another." Her explanation sounded simplistic, but Barrett knew it was anything but easy. She spoke further. "Keep in mind, fear means you are alive. Everyone fears *something*. You have been taught to hide your *true* emotions, thoughts, and doubts. It is part of being a king. But I say . . . hogwash!" Another sip of tea. "You are free to look however you wish or cry and laugh whenever the mood strikes you. Being in touch with your feelings does not make you weak. It makes you a better person." She rose to make ready the dinner ingredients. Barrett remained in his seat, thinking through her words.

If honest with himself, he felt haunted by Asban. Grimes remained a close second. He thought back to the days spent in Elimar's house.

Even there, Asban had invaded the prince's peace. Appearing during the day, sneering outward from a dimly lit corner of a room, the wizard's mouth would move as if speaking an unheard spell. Barrett would scramble to grab his wand and point it ahead, ready for combat. But the greasy fellow always vanished first.

The prince wondered if they were daydreams or was Asban somehow invading his mind in an attempt to terrorize him. He dreaded to think the wizard was actually there and they would duel sooner than anticipated.

"Mostly, I fret over meeting Asban again," he offered bluntly. "I mean, what if I only got lucky the first time and when we meet this time he kills me?"

"There is no such thing as luck," replied the sorceress. "Another absurd idea you have been taught. As if carrying around a piece of clover, rock, or some other charm is somehow going to grant success or happiness. Nonsense."

Trishar moved to the fireplace and gave a flip of her hand. The wood ignited in a flash. She pulled a long, straight knife from the drawer to dice celery, various fruits, and cheeses.

"Barrett, you are a young wizard who has skill beyond many more experienced magic users I have met. Asban is one example. His talent is minimal, yet his mouth and bragging ability far surpasses it. However, even the most useless fool can win magical combat if their opponent is unfocused and does not take battle seriously."

"Oh, I take him seriously," answered Barrett. "In fact, I can't stop thinking about it." He hung his head. "I rarely sleep anymore and there's only three days left until we attack."

Trishar gave him a simple, understanding look. "You have a famous teacher. Though my brother is strange, even loathsome at times, he is skilled." She threw the celery in the cauldron, then grabbed an onion to repeat the process. "You are learning from one of the best wizards I know. And do not let his antics fool you. Elimar could wipe away a small army should he choose it and has done so before."

Barrett gasped, then turned to stare at the wizard with a look of admiration. Trishar was wiping away onion tears as he turned back. "He said he was coming with me to face Asban and his followers."

"Excellent. You will have good company," she replied. "Now, I must get dinner ready. There is plenty to do before time is upon us to begin the battle for your home."

Gaia entered to lend a hand, but only after sharing a kiss with Barrett. Yaris trailed her, taking a seat and falling into immediate conversation with the prince.

So went the day. Despite approaching danger, the friends were able to rejoice in one another and forget their troubles, even if only overnight.

Barrett woke with Asban on his mind, as he had every day since realizing the horrid little man was back in their lives. Grimes pestered his thoughts, too. "Not exactly the way I wanted to start my morning—thinking of an evil wizard and a tyrant," he complained as he dressed.

"Your time to handle the problem is coming soon," said Samaren, perched on the arm of a plush chair.

"Mother!" shouted Barrett, starting at her voice. "Will you *please* stop doing that! I need some privacy or I will start shutting the windows at night!"

The raven let loose a long caw, then tilted her head to one side. "I suppose you are right . . . this time. Very well. I will try to stop."

"Well, try hard, because it's annoying," he snapped as he slid a tunic over his head.

"Take care of your words or I will peck your eyes out as you sleep . . . Sire."

Barrett grimaced. "Ewwww. That is so strange. Why would you say that? It sounds rather cracked."

Samaren made a croaking sound, snapped her bill closed, then launched through the open window.

Heading down the hall, the prince knocked on Gaia's door and listened. When no answer came he proceeded to the living room. There, Trishar seemed a bit frazzled.

"According to this morning's Chatterer from Shardira, several more Malathians arrived last night. Dozens of Pagorians are already here. At least the Morim have not come in force yet. Still, the odds are not in our favor."

"But the magical folks will arrive soon. They will break from hiding to aid the cause," said Gaia, clapping her hands. "That should help even the odds."

"Kill the leadership and the soldiers' resolve to fight will crumble. Most of them will be lost without someone telling them what to do," said Yaris. "I have seen it several times before in battle."

"That means Barrett's job is the most vital. If he kills Grimes and Asban the others will turn tail and run," said Graile.

"Must we speak of killing this early in the morning? Why can't we just chase them away from Westmore?" asked Gaia.

Mearis frowned. "It would do no good. New visions have shown Asban taking advantage of others. He sets himself up as ruler in a village where people are forced to pay tribute to maintain their safety. The man is cruel to them for spite."

"I feel confident Asban will soon meet whatever fate the gods have in store for him." Elimar winked at Barrett. "We are simply going to be their messengers."

The witch seemed disturbed by his comments. She knew exactly what he meant, but once the prince took her hand, her objections faded away.

Heads turned as Zanora ambled down the stairs one at time. She seemed livelier, her color was returning, and the groaning with each movement had decreased. Still, Nell was close by, just in case.

"You are looking better. You're already getting around by yourself. Well done," said Graile in an encouraging tone. "How do you feel?"

"Like I was beaten and tortured," answered Zanora as she took a seat.

"She *is* feeling better," noted Trishar. "It is good to hear your scorn and anger again."

The redhead managed a smile. "I admit those potions you're making me swallow are helping. I am recovering faster than imagined."

"Perfect," said the sorceress. "And I am not *making* you do anything. It is your choice—a wise one, I might add. Remember, there are only two days left before we take the city. You will need your strength."

"Maybe you should remain here and recover," suggested the prince.

Zanora's cheeks reddened, annoyed with the idea he could leave her behind. "Are you crazy! I have no intention of staying here while there is to be a battle. Give me my sword, I'll prove it." Raising up quickly, she grimaced and grabbed her ribs.

Barrett raised a single eyebrow at her. "*Now* do you see what I mean? I am trying to keep you alive. Being wounded before the fighting even begins is not good."

The prince had been through enough combat training with Yaris to know facing a foe when injured was utterly foolish. Being hurt, tired, or having a clouded mind would get one killed quickly. Blaming himself for the death of Lars was enough of a burden. He did not wish to add his former love to the list of the fallen.

"You should think about it," said Graile. "Combat is no place to be slowed down. It could be your end."

The redhead scoffed in return. "I have plenty of time to heal. And with that glop Trishar is forcing on me I'll soon be as good as new."

"Stubbornness will be your end, young lady," added Yaris. "Your friends are only showing their concern and trying to help. You would do well to heed them."

"Everyone stopping treating like a child," she snapped.

"It is your life to throw away if you wish," said Trishar, baffled over the girl's determination to rush toward war. "We will speak no more of it."

Unger switched topics. "Our plan is solid." He indicated himself and Graile. "When we take the city, things will go smoothly."

"Nothing *ever* goes smoothly during war," said Elimar. "You can plan for months, but once first blood is spilt things often fall apart quickly."

Yaris nodded agreement. "Many of you were there when the beasts invaded the castle months ago. You must certainly remember the fear and panic of battle. We had a solid plan then, too. Defeating Alesta seemed easy. But it nearly cost me my life." He pointed to his patched eye. "It did cost me something I value—clear sight."

The archer shifted uncomfortably. "I remember. I could barely think. It was chaos. All I could do was hold back my panic and hope for the best."

"So why plan at all," asked Nell. "What's the point?"

"We plan in case things *do* go right, dear," said Trishar.

In that instant, Samaren appeared on the windowsill. She pecked at the glass. Barrett rushed forward to throw the window open. The raven shivered, then flew inside to perch near the low burning fire.

"Autumn has brought chilled air," she said after another shiver. She perked up as her dark eyes met his. "Oh, I almost forgot." She extended her leg as Barrett freed a parchment tied to her shin. "Randolph sent this. He had a lot to say but wrote the quick version."

"Thank you, Mother," said the prince before raising the note to read aloud. "Grimes and Carick have increased patrols. Townsfolk know something is wrong. Asban is frantic. I stand ready with two dozen magic users. We will await your word or signal in two days' time. Farewell."

"There is little room left within the city for the army Grimes is building," said Samaren. "Many are camped along the main gate road. It is a sea of tents and small shacks. The scene looks like the annual Order of Witches."

Barrett recalled the springtime event. It was the day his entire world changed. During the festival, he met Trishar, discovered his magical powers, killed his first human being, and learned fairy rings were real and not just legends. How he survived the deadly encounter with Gray-Eye and his men still baffled him. The battle seemed another lifetime ago, almost as if he had dreamt it.

Those were the days he believed his destiny was to become the powerful, magical Helserian. Elimar helped inflate the prince's ego by filling his head with the ridiculous notion in the first place. Thankfully, Trishar finally revealed the truth. The Helserian legend was just that—a myth invented to give people hope in times of despair or war.

"I have an idea how to take care of them," said Barrett. "I will ensure they are of no threat to our cause. Or at least, very minimal."

"He's doing it again," said Zanora. "Either tell us what you're planning or don't bother bringing it up."

"She does make a good point," added Gaia. "What are you up to now, sneaky?"

"Nothing yet," replied the prince. "Let me think it through before saying anything else. And I am *not* being sneaky."

Barrett proceeded down the hall, grabbed his cloak, flung it round his shoulders, and stepped through the front door. On the porch, he shivered as strong winds pushed the thick clouds across the sky. He raised his left hand to touch the topside. "I hope this works. Laelynn, please help." Beneath his skin, the image of a roaring dragon's face took shape, then quickly faded away.

"What are you doing out here?" asked Graile, closing the door behind him.

Barrett started. "I thought I was alone. How long have you been there?"

"Long enough," said the Fader, watching the chunky clouds swirl in the grey sky. "I won't say a word. Besides, I think I can guess your plan. It's brilliant."

"Magic or not, we cannot withstand the enemy numbers. There are too many. We cannot win." Barrett pointed toward Westmore. "Dragons have a way of leveling the odds. My concern is that Laelynn has paid her debt to us for freeing her. She may never arrive."

"Agreed. Still, she is a wise choice and could turn the tide in our favor." Graile pulled his cloak tighter, too.

"Elimar lent me some old books from his personal library so I could be better prepared for what lay ahead," said Barrett. "I've been reading them each night in case the magic comes in handy when we take the city. And since I'm not in the mood for a bunch of talk today, it works out well."

The Fader squeezed Barrett's shoulder. "I'm here if you need me. If you want to talk things through or need a break."

The prince smiled. "You're a great friend, Graile. I'm happy the gods brought us together. I would have never gotten this far without you. I trust you with my life, and that is saying a lot."

22

So It Begins

Two days hurried past while Barrett practiced the ancient spells. As when he was first learning magic, he destroyed vases, a wash basin, set a painting on fire, and shattered things he hoped no one at the safehouse would miss. Each time he hollered an apology through the closed door in fear the sorceress would be waiting there to stop him if he opened it. Thankfully, magic also helped him repair the damage, but not the frustration of having his powers go awry.

During this time, he barely saw the others, except at meals or when taking a brief break. Once, Gaia managed to steal him away for a walk outside in the cool autumn air. They held hands and kissed often, which lifted his spirits.

Finally, the day of the assault arrived. Barrett had barely slept the previous night and struggled to keep a clear head once he woke.

Apprehension of facing Asban and Grimes faded into the background, replaced with the worry of keeping his friends safe. The welfare of his people, magic users, and his own survival, came next. Though in his heart he realized he could not be everywhere at once. He hated the powerless feeling of being unable to protect them all.

After rubbing his face, Barrett slid from bed to dress slowly, never noticing Samaren sleeping on her perch. She stirred at the noise and cawed as she woke.

"Good morning, son," she said. "The time has come to regain what is yours." She flapped her wings and cawed again. "I understand if you wish to walk away. Today's uprising is about stopping the horrible rule of the Bureau. Nothing more. Kingship can be decided later."

"Mother, are you telling me not to be king?"

"I am saying Gaia is not the only one who can sense things about you. I have known for some time you are struggling with taking the throne. Trishar and I have discussed it."

"But how could you!" asked the prince. "Is there anyone who doesn't already know? Have you told everyone?"

"Only the three of us know for certain but the others have already guessed. Besides, I'm your mother and will always know when my boy is conflicted or unhappy. Trishar also has a knack for knowing these things."

Lowering into a soft chair, Barrett huffed. "Can we discuss this later . . . if I am still alive?"

His mother cawed her agreement. "I flew over the city last night, stopping several times to watch and listen, as I like to do. I learned a bit of information that may help."

Barrett perked up after sliding his breeches and boots on. He ran a brush through his hair. "Do tell."

"Asban and his followers will be in the great hall at midmorning. Apparently he has some ridiculous weekly ritual he performs to keep his subjects in line. It is really nothing more than a magic show. But it is enough to scare them into submission."

"How does that help us?"

"Confront him when he least expects it. It will allow his foolish followers to see exactly how cowardly he can be. However, the battle would be in close quarters and dangerous. His followers may not help him if you attack him directly."

Barrett considered the idea. "Why Mother, I never have never guessed you would send me to a fight. You usually tell me to avoid conflict."

Samaren's feathers ruffled as she let out another squawk. "I am still against you facing him. After all, he tried to kill you the first time. He is nothing more than a bully who preys on the weak. Bullies serve no purpose but to frighten innocents in order to make themselves feel important. I assure you, they are not important in any way."

After lacing up his boots, Barrett inspected himself in a tall mirror. "Good enough," he said, smoothing his tunic. "After all, I doubt Asban will notice what I'm wearing. He will be too busy trying to stop me." He held his arm out to his side and inclined his head. "Come along, dear mother. We should get started."

Samaren hopped upon his forearm, then worked her way to his shoulder where she perched. "I will be leaving soon. I can fly ahead and see if things have changed overnight. If I do not return, proceed as planned."

"Be careful." Barrett stroked her tiny head. "Stay away from the battle. I do not want to lose you."

The two headed for the kitchen, listening to the voices drifting up the stairs. As usual, the prince was last to join the gathering. All talk and movement stopped once they entered. Samaren hopped onto her perch as Barrett took the empty seat next to Gaia. They kissed without a word.

He grew self-conscious as deep stillness set in. The surrounding silence felt even more oppressive with everyone's eyes fixed upon him. Uncomfortable, he squirmed beneath their gaze as he filled his breakfast plate. They seemed to be waiting for something. What it was, he had no idea.

Was this what it was going to be like if he retook the throne? People staring at him day after day, waiting for something, wanting for something, even if he could not give it to them?

When he could take no more, he slapped the table with his palm. His voice raised an octave. "Why is everyone staring at me? It's bizarre. Stop it!"

Unger chuckled. "Apparently, you didn't get enough sleep."

Mearis agreed. "You're not even king yet and you're already grumpy. You will be superb on the throne," she said, pushing her plate away.

"We were discussing the state of affairs in Westmore. According to this morning's Chatterer from Randolph, many Morim arrived near dusk last night. Things have become more difficult," said Trishar.

Barrett flinched at the news before shaking his jumbled thoughts into any sort of order. He had previously faced the Morim, the one encounter burning bright in his anxiety-ridden head.

He recalled the thick, ugly men carried short swords, axes, long knives, or clubs. Their clothing was made from rough material and fastened with coarse rope or long strips of leather. Uniquely painted designs decorated the sides of their shaven skulls and around their eyes. Leather bracers encompassed their forearms and crude boots covered their feet. Some went barefoot.

Several long weeks ago he had killed two of their kind while Graile dispatched another. Luckily, Elimar cleaned up the unsightly mess of three dead bodies, yet Barrett never forgot the images. They were ingrained in his mind.

Panic rose in his throat, nearly choking off his air. *Morim may not be the brightest, but they are deadly in combat. At least that is what I remember. They will make the battle even more dangerous.*

"Elimar and I will be leaving shortly," he blurted out. His seat scraped the floor as he pushed it back, leaving his plate untouched. "I know where Asban will be. I mean to take him by surprise and put an end to his stay in my city."

"And how would you know where he is? It's not like he has a schedule," said Zanora, looking close to her usual self. She was moving better and had color in her cheeks.

Barrett was determined not to be drawn into a verbal fight. Ignoring her, he made a nearly imperceptible nod to his raven. "A little birdie told me differently."

"Perfect! Once again you're risking your life on the word of a talking bird," she retorted with a cynical tone.

"Well, if you think about it, this will not be the first time," said Graile, placing his ware on the table. "Samaren's help was invaluable."

"I can't stand anymore of this waiting. Let's take back the city," said Unger, eyeing his bow and full quiver leaning in the corner.

"I agree," said Nell. "The magic users will be in place by now and everyone is waiting on us."

Trishar eyed her brother, who smiled in return. "Very well," she said. "The time has come to remove the tyrants from our lands. You all know what to do."

"If any of you are caught, the Bureau will show no mercy. Stay alert and return safely," added Elimar.

"My reading this morning was encouraging. Still, be watchful. If it is safe, we will meet in the castle's courtyard when this is over. If not, return here," said Mearis.

The companions nodded understanding as they exchanged nervous glances.

"May the gods smile on you all," said Elimar, moving to Barrett's side. "It is time to put a certain wizard in his place." He tapped his staff on the floor making the pair vanish in a swirl of violet light and a swishing sound.

"I believe that means we are ready whether we wish it or not," said Trishar.

Arriving near the outer wall, the old wizard hurried them into shadow, heading toward the elf gate. This trip, he appeared as a well-dressed, handsome man with long ginger hair tied back in a ponytail, green eyes, wearing dark brown boots and tan-colored clothing. The prince was tall, with short black hair and high boots. His clothing and eyes were brown. With a prominent nose and more muscular features, he looked nothing like himself.

Slipping through the wavering door, they headed for the main road as several Trackers rounded the corner on horseback, galloping toward them with speed.

"Are they coming for us?" said Barrett.

"No, it is only by chance they are here now. They must be chasing someone else. Play along or things may go poorly," Elimar whispered.

With cloaks flapping in the wind as they sped closer, the men were nearly upon the frantic duo before they reined to a halt.

"We saw them! They took all our money!" cried the wizard, hopping from one foot to the other. "A brute of a fellow and three shorter ones were using magic. They threatened to harm my servant if we did not give them our gold." He pointed to Barrett for good measure.

The prince bit his tongue, fuming at the old man's choice of words for him before nodding his agreement. His feet shuffled nervously against the ground as his hand edged closer to his wand, hoping none would notice his actions.

"Silence, old man! We don't care about your troubles. Which way did the vermin go!" shouted the leader as his chestnut horse fidgeted beneath him. "Answer, you fool!"

The wizard, still acting convincingly frightened, shakily pointed his walking stick to the right. "They went that way. Hurry and you may catch them. They were dreadfully ugly and vicious."

"Move aside, you dolts," shouted another as he thumped his horse's sides to propel the animal forward. The riders raced past in a flurry of movement and thudding hooves, vanishing in seconds as they raced round a corner of the nearest building.

"That should keep them busy." Elimar chuckled as he moved toward the main street. "Idiots."

"Servant? That was the best you could do?" questioned Barrett. "You could have said I was your son, a librarian, blacksmith, or something else. You chose servant."

"Do stop whining! Besides, no one would have believed any of that had I said it. I could have said the 'future king.' Would that have been better?"

The prince scowled. "You're a complete pain in my—"

"There!" interrupted the wizard, pushing his chin forward. He gasped a mixture of surprise and delight. "Asban!"

Barrett was as surprised as the old man. "Here, in the open?"

"Of course. What has he got to fear? No one here will stand against him."

Townsfolk hurriedly moved from the short wizard's path as he strode the street with several of his minions trailing his footsteps. Their wands were in full display as they brandished them about theatrically while pushing past anyone not quick enough to move. They were heading in the castle's direction.

Barrett noticed Elimar smiling. "Why in the names of the gods are you happy?" he asked.

The old man turned a knowing expression to him. "Because, my boy, their little game is up. The time has come for someone to reveal this fraud for who he really is—a minor, worthless wizard. It pleases me to know we will be the ones who end his reign of terror against your people."

The prince's brow furrowed. He stopped walking to study his mentor, opening his mind to try and read the old man's thoughts. "Are you ever afraid? I mean, what if we're killed? There are more of them than us."

"Only a fool or liar has no fear of facing death. But fear cannot rule your emotions, nor actions. You must control it. To this point, you have done wonderfully. Facing dragons, Alesta, Trowkens, and more, took remarkable courage. Yet here you are." Elimar walked on. "By the way, trying to read my mind is pointless. You will never be able to penetrate my thoughts. But I applaud your effort." He tucked the walking stick under his arm to clap lightly.

Barrett cursed at being caught and changed the subject. "Hurry, they're turning the corner."

"Relax. We know where they are going. Samaren told you so. After she told Trishar and me, of course."

"My blasted mother!" grumbled Barrett. "Why does everyone have to blab things I thought were secret? I will speak to her about that bit if I survive today." *Actually, I was going to sneak away to face Asban alone. Now that idea is ruined.*

"You are whining again. Besides, she did it to keep you safe, knowing I would be alongside and could lend aid in a tight spot." Elimar looked frustrated. "Why must teenagers complain about everything or think they know best?" He leaned closer. "Trust me, you do not. Try listening more and keeping an open mind for once instead of getting defensive over every small thing. It is very annoying."

Zanora walked at a steady pace, her cloak flowing in her wake. Her raised hood obscured her face, as Graile's did for him. They were a matched pair.

Their faces were brushed a brilliant white. They wore black clothing, had circled eyes, and both their lips and nails were painted black. Dark lines descended from the corners of their eyes like morbid tear stains, ending in the middle of their cheeks.

Some people stepped aside to mutter and point, shocked at

the sight of the duo. Others tried ignoring them, believing they were Trackers or some other ruffians coming to harass them. Many hid or ran away in terror. Even Agents stopped to quickly reverse direction or conceal themselves in a crowd until the pair passed.

"Grimes is mine for what he has put me through," the redhead said as they went.

"Barrett would not complain if you drove the weasel out of the castle," noted Graile.

Zanora paused with a soured face, struggling with her muddled thoughts as she took his hand. Finally, a light lit in her eyes as her words took shape. "Grimes made me believe I was doing the right things by getting rid of magic and he'll pay for it. I was wrong. There is a plenty of good in magic and I am no longer afraid of it."

Graile brushed the hair back from her face. "Make sure you tell that to our future king when this is all over. He'll be pleased to hear it."

Pausing here and there to ensure they were unwatched, the pair headed for the nearest tunnel. Reaching it, Graile stepped inside the hidden entrance, waited for Zanora to join him, then lit the torch and headed for the castle.

Gaia, Randolph, and Yaris stood amongst dozens of magic users, secreting themselves in the shadows of the tall trees just beyond the city walls. All held wands or staffs. Some paced nervously. Others lounged about on boulders or the soft ground, unmoving except for the rise and fall of their chests. It had been months since they escaped the city. Now, the same folks dared to step into the open without worry of recognition, being hauled away to be hung, or spending their remaining days in the dungeons.

The witch stood upon a tree stump and cleared her throat. "Excuse me, everyone. We must stay alert for any sign to begin. Elimar promised we would know when the time had arrived. Do not lose hope. Keep your eyes sharp."

"I hope our future king has a better plan than using kids to free Westmore," said a tall, lanky man with a crooked front tooth. He waved his wand around in annoyance. "I am not following a child into battle."

There was a rush of murmuring and head shaking as the crowd grumbled. Their circle tightened around Gaia.

"You will do as she says or deal with me," came a deep voice as Yaris pushed his way into the throng going nose-to-nose with the crooked-toothed man. "Magic or not, I will drag you behind a tree for a long talk if you say another word, Jacob. This woman," he pointed to the witch," has seen and done more than most of you will in a lifetime. She has faced beasts, creatures, and evil many of you would cower and run from. Now be silent . . . all of you."

A hush fell over the crowd as their attention darted from Yaris to Jacob. Finally, Jacob bowed and backed away, fading into the wall of flesh.

Randolph slicked back his hair and stepped beside the large man. "I have worked with Gaia and her friends. Yaris is correct. The young ones are wise beyond their years. You would do well to heed their words," he said.

"Leave if you must," said Gaia. "No one is keeping you here. But in the end, if Westmore remains in Bureau hands, you can only blame yourselves."

Slowly, the mob dispersed and returned to milling around in the growing light. The witch turned to the reporter and the Warder. "Thank you both, but I was going to handle him," she said, stowing her wand into the folds of her cloak. "I thought he would look splendid as a ferret."

Yaris laughed. "I meant every word. Your group is braver than some of my soldiers. Still, I will be by your side every step of the way." He smiled kindly, then tapped his sword hilt. "It may not be magic, but it has an effect on flesh and bone."

"These people are just scared. Do not listen to the ones who wish to do nothing but stir up anger." Randolph offered politely. "You are doing an excellent job."

23

Asban

Shardira and Nell wound their way through the castle, heading for the second floor common room where those disloyal to the Bureau waited. The Dorgon, who had morphed into an elf in Tracker clothing, could have passed for the Shardira's sister, a thought she did not mind.

Entering and bolting the thick doors behind them, they found two dozen ready for action. Former soldiers had cast aside their Bureau garb and once again wore uniforms of Westmore. The citizens wore everyday clothing but held anger in their eyes over their suppression. Nell could feel the excited, nervous energy of the crowd.

Shardira smiled. "Thank you for meeting us here." She placed a hand over her breast and bowed.

"Now we wait," said Nell. "This will be the hardest part." Her gaze went to the city. "I hope Barrett is safe."

Barrett fought to remain calm despite Elimar appearing as if he was on a pleasant walk in the woods instead of heading for a deadly confrontation. Annoyingly, he took the time to tip his hat to the ladies and nod politely to men.

"Will you stop that," grumbled Barrett.

"If we hide in the darkness as we go, we will draw unwanted attention," his mentor replied without missing a beat. "Now calm down or go back to the safehouse and I will face Asban alone."

The prince considered objecting but thought it better to keep silent. He hurriedly analyzed the situation. No matter how powerful Elimar was, his chance of victory against ten or more magic users was not good. Nonetheless, Trishar said he was powerful enough to wipe away an army, and that inspired hope and confidence. The sorceress rarely exaggerated as often as her brother.

Barrett was mentally trapped. If he returned to the safehouse alone he would consider himself a coward. One who missed the chance to drive Asban away forever and allow an old man to face danger on his own. More so, his friends and those citizens putting their lives on the line today, would never forgive him.

Certainly, he could not exclude Elimar and handle the bunch alone. That would be suicide and this was no time for heroics or reckless deeds, he thought. He needed the old man, not to mention the wizard was simply trying to keep them both alive. With that final thought, Barrett let panic slip away, determined to handle whatever came his way.

"You're right," he admitted. "I'm sorry I was so frantic. I have waited a long while for this day and it's making me jumpy."

"I understand," said the wizard softly. "As I said earlier, it may always feel you know what is best, but over time you will learn you are not as intelligent as you believe. You should consider advice from those of us who have seen many more years than you. Just because I am old does not mean I am not wise."

It seemed time had come to a standstill as they passed through the city, but finally the castle lay close at hand. Asban never stopped as he passed the guards without uttering a word. His minions shuffled along behind him. The guards paid them no mind.

Barrett lightly gripped Elimar's sleeve to guide him behind a row of tall bushes. "Now what?" asked the prince. "I suppose we could circle around and take the tunnels. That would get us inside."

"We have no time for that now." Elimar aimed his walking stick to the left and uttered a quick spell.

From beyond the cobbled walkway rose a woman's wavering voice. "Help me, please." The sound grew weaker but no less frantic. "Help! I need help."

Startled, the guards shared a confused look, drew their swords, then dashed to investigate, leaving the door unguarded.

Elimar pointed at the vacant courtyard. "Move, before they return. Hurry."

The pair sprinted for the opening, dashing inside in seconds. Again, Barrett was shocked at how light on his feet the wizard proved to be. The old man never ceased to amaze him.

Sprinting the hall's length, they skidded to a stop after realizing Asban and his band of thugs had vanished. In a terrible stroke of luck, voices echoed from ahead, coming from several directions.

Barrett seized the nearest door handle, gave it a turn, then rushed Elimar inside. As the chamber door shut, the prince sensed they were not alone. Whirling as he freed his wand from his tunic, he found two unsuspecting guards frozen in amazement as they sat enjoying a meal. Shocked, the uniformed men sprang to their feet to reach for their swords, but the prince's magic silenced them before they could defend themselves.

"Impendior," he cried, hurling the men out the balcony doors and over the railing with force. Their screams lasted but a few seconds before they met the cold ground in a dirty alleyway far below.

Recognizing his mistake as the voices on the other side of the wall suddenly grew in volume and hurried footsteps rushed toward them, Barrett panicked. The prince waved for the wizard to follow as he worked a lever, then ducked inside the darkened tunnel. The passage door barely closed before a terrible commotion rose from inside the chamber.

Trackers blasted the chamber door from its heavy iron hinges, sending splinters and chunks airborne. "The magic came from here," said a feminine voice. Sounds of sniffing followed. "They were just here. I smell their stench. Spread out and find them. Do not rest until they are found and destroyed."

"Yes, ma'am," said a deep, graveled voice. "Well, you buffoons, you heard your orders. Get moving!"

"Where did these fools disappear too?" asked a younger male voice.

"We'll find them soon enough. And when I do, they'll not be thanking the gods I caught up with them," said the gruff, graveled voice again. "Let's get moving."

Barrett held his breath until the room went quiet once more. Slowly, he let the air seep from his lungs as dread drained away for the moment. He shrugged sheepishly. "Sorry. I didn't know what else to do."

"Quick thinking on your part. Well done," said Elimar. "If the two you blasted would have called for help, those Trackers could have arrived while we were still in the room. It would have been a mess."

"Come on. We're in a bad spot now," said the prince.

Midmorning was rapidly approaching. There would only be one chance to face Asban. Everyone and everything counted on the outcome of this duel to set the wheels of revolt into motion. If his quest of stopping the twisted wizard proved unsuccessful, Westmore would remain under the Bureau's harsh control.

Scurrying through the tunnels with Elimar close at his heels, Barrett turned now and again, climbed here and there, and went straight for some distance before reaching the entrance.

Working the lever with stealth, the prince pressed an eye to the small crack as the door popped ajar. Remarkably, it seemed Grimes had done little to change the room from its former glory. The training hall remained lavish and impressive in its magnificence.

Its thick rock walls rose far overhead to meet the solid, polished wood of the arched ceiling. Tall stone statues graced low pedestals, lovely paintings and tapestries hung from each wall, and long wooden tables held unique sculptures. Lengthy purple drapes hung open, allowing radiant sunlight to flood the room. Yet despite the natural light, two dozen flickering torches burned steadily in iron holders, bringing warmth to the darkened corners which refused the kiss of the comforting sun.

Barrett's longing to regain his home grew. He missed the place with a ferocity he could not put into words. Having no more time to admire his surroundings, his eyes went the rear of the room where a soft chorus of rhythmic chanting rode the air.

There, in the center of a painted circle, stood Asban. He held a hand up for quiet, ending his minions' chanting, then paced as he spoke. Both his voice and fervor increased as he droned on. His knee-length cloak flowed and moved about him as if possessing a mind of its own.

Asban looked taller, healthier, and cleaner than before, and his movements had become fluid and graceful. Yet, his eyes still held a wild, sinister look. He seemed far more intimidating than the last time Barrett saw him.

The prince drew back as he watched. "Working for Grimes must have its benefits," he whispered, noting Asban's new maroon colored breeches, tunic, and polished black boots. "He looks stronger than last I saw him. Even his hair is clean."

"Step aside and give an old man a chance," grumbled Elimar as they traded places. The wizard pushed his face against the stone until his nose bent downward. He gripped his walking stick tighter. "That man disgusts me."

Spinning a quick circle, Elimar came to a stop, his look identical to the day the prince first saw him. He wore a deep green cloak with red boots, was well-groomed, and fashionably dressed. High cheekbones emphasized his neatly trimmed blue beard, and matching brown brows sat atop hazel eyes. His nose was perfectly shaped and his smile was flawless. Dark blue hair flowed down his back and strong hands lightly held a wooden staff. Various rings graced his fingers.

"Asban will know who he faces now. He has seen this look before," said Elimar. Tapping his staff on the ground, he transformed Barrett to his real self. "This will let him see who sends him to his doom before he falls."

"So we're really going to kill him?" the prince asked. His stomach suddenly felt queasy as he palmed the tunnel wall to keep himself upright.

Elimar shrugged indifference. "That is what you have wanted

for weeks, yes?" His head tilted and both brows pulled down in thought. "Have you changed your mind? Often, you have mentioned this day Well, here is your chance to set things right."

"True, I hate him. I want to make him suffer for what he has done. I want . . ." Barrett paused to rub his chin. "I want to *not* feel sorry for him."

Stunned into silence, Elimar rubbed his hands together as he pondered the dilemma. "I will admit, feeling pity for the worm is most unexpected."

Barrett nodded, each word spilling out faster than his thoughts. "In many ways, yes. No one is born evil. So he must have become that way. Maybe it's not his fault. What if he is under a spell, like Alesta was? She was a slave to Apadora, so why couldn't Asban be trapped by someone, too?"

The wizard leaned against the wall and smiled warmly. "Dear boy, you are right. Most people are not born wicked. But some are. They are different than you and I. Killing holds no meaning to them. They feel nothing as they grow up torturing defenseless animals and people in search of some twisted sense of who they are. They find joy in making others suffer."

Barrett sneered in disgust. "Which one is Asban?"

The wizard shrugged. "We may never know. But I would bet my beard he suffered during his childhood and now seeks revenge against the world for his pain. He wants others to experience the agony trapped inside him. Bullying is the only ways he knows how."

"It's rather sad, isn't it?" Barrett stared at his feet as if the answer was written on the stone floor in some mystical form only he could see. "Maybe I can talk some sense into him. Give him a chance to be good."

Elimar waved a hand. "Make no mistake, any good in him

died years ago. He will kill you if you lower your guard. Do not allow pity to sway you to kindness while facing a dangerous man."

Easing forward for another peek, Barrett watched Asban use simple magic to fascinate his onlookers. He conjured life-like illusions, ignited flames from his fingertips, and grew in size and stature, all while filling their heads with his teachings—every bit of which the prince thought to be rubbish. *The man is trying to set himself up as a god.*

Asban's desperate resort to tricks and simple magic to entice his followers furthered Barrett's pity. It was a blatant attempt to keep his weak-minded minions fascinated. *How sad he must be to need constant attention and praise for his wizardry.*

"I have a great plan," admitted the wizard. "Touch my sleeve. I will tele-locate us to the room's center. We will be surrounded, but his circle of fools will likely do nothing since they will look to their leader for protection. It will all turn out for the best."

Barrett's legs wobbled as Elimar's plan reached his ears. Was the old man was purposely trying to get them killed? "Are you insane! There is nothing great about that plan. Nothing at all! We can't use magic. Trackers will come again. And what if his followers *do* attack? We'll be dead or captured."

"First, if the Trackers sense magic, they will assume Asban is showing off again." Elimar pointed to the door. "Think about it. If what you say is true, Trackers would be here by now, right?"

The prince pondered the point, then nodded. "I suppose you're right."

Elimar chuckled. "Of course I am right. Don't be ridiculous." He extended an arm and inclined his head to it. "Now get your wand out and have it at the ready. Just in case." His other hand touched his chest. "I will do the talking to begin with."

With another nod, Barrett lay a hand atop the old man's forearm. They vanished in a blur, reappearing in the center of the minions to several gasps, startled cries, and one who fainted from fright. The onlookers stumbled over one another in a disorganized attempt to back away. Before any could recover from the disruption, Elimar spoke.

"Fools!" he cried, pointing his finger around the broken circle before aiming it at Asban. The action froze them all. "This man has stolen your will. He has baffled your small minds with childish magic tricks." He paused for effect as Asban stepped forward to open his mouth but Barrett blocked the way, leveling his wand at the short, bewildered wizard.

Asban struggled to break his own confusion and terror. Still, he knew better than to challenge a glowing wand tip—especially one aimed at him from a young man who had already defeated him. Wisely, he backed away and fell silent. His hatred was clear as he glared between Barrett and Elimar.

Turning a slow circle, Elimar spoke on. "Your hearts have been poisoned with empty words. What has he promised you? A claim to valuable positions if he were king? Perhaps you would be his magical army against any who came to dethrone him." Another pause to chuckle a disgusted sound. "Was the dolt planning to kill Carick himself?" He spun to face Asban. "You witless worm. There is no place for you here. Even my servant could force you out."

Barrett shot his mentor an ireful look over 'servant' again, but only for an instant. He was unwilling to move his stare from Asban, who trembled with fear or anger.

"They are insane!" cried a smaller, attractive woman with raven hair and dark eyes. "Cast them out, master! Rid us of their lies and deceit."

Others quickly joined in as a murmur swept round the disciples. "Out! Get them out!" cried some. "Save us, my lord," shouted many.

"Indeed!" shouted Barrett, silencing them all. "Yes, cast us out . . . if you can, you spineless maggot." He inched closer, his wand tip still glowing. "This time I will do more than deflect your spell and freeze you. Your fate will be worse if you find the courage to face me again." Inside, the prince's heart was racing and he did all he could to keep from visibly shaking. Outwardly, he displayed a calm, confident young wizard.

"Slay them both," yelled an older man with a patched eye and scarred cheek.

Asban withered under his group's bewildered stares and prodding.

Barrett knew he had struck a nerve with his challenge. "Go on, slay us!" Whether cocky or foolish, the prince dimmed his wand and lowered it. "I will make this a fair fight, if you wish."

Before Elimar could correct his apprentice, one skinny follower gained bravery and stepped forward with his wand at the ready. As he prepared to hurl magic at Barrett's back, Elimar reacted with remarkable speed.

The old man leveled his wand and fired, hitting the follower in the chest, hurling him upward, out of sight. Moments later, the sickening sound of him impacting the wooden ceiling echoed within the chamber, followed by his broken body crashing to the floor at Asban's feet. The heap of man resembled a broken, discarded child's doll.

As others in the hall found their nerve and reached for their wands, Elimar swung his staff in a circle overhead. With a wave of sparkling green magic, he swept them away like dust on a floor.

Their bodies were tossed this way and that, only to land unconscious in scattered piles. One poor soul was pierced many times, impaled upon a fallen sword display. Another was hurled through the open window, falling several stories to her death.

Asban used to the distraction to toss a small ball onto the floor. It exploded in a cloud of greyish smoke, obscuring him from view, but Barrett, expecting the trickery, was ready. He ducked low and moved left before a powerful blast landed where he stood moments before.

The prince tried to follow the wizard's movements but could see nothing. He ran ahead blindly while returning fire, cursing as he stumbled over an unconscious body. At impact, his wand was sent skittering across the floor. With a cry of dread, he scrambled to his feet, then dove for the magical wood which vanished beneath a plush wooden chair. Tossing the furniture aside, he snatched his wand, then pointed it ahead.

"Clearomous." The mist vanished in an instant but Asban had escaped again.

Suddenly, Elimar was grabbing the prince's forearm. "Hang on," he said before whisking them away in a flash of light. Reappearing atop the highest watchtower, Elimar raised his wand and tilted his chin forward, urging Barrett to do the same.

"That did not go as planned," said the wizard. "We must signal the others to attack or we will lose the battle before it begins. Remember —make your magic yellow."

Shooting bright orbs into the air, the pair signaled the assault on Westmore. Within seconds, chaos erupted as horns blared and cries of panic rose from the streets. The sounds of combat rang throughout the city. Shouts, screams, and clashing steel echoed from far below, with bursts of magic rising through it all. Even from Barrett's high vantage point, he could hear the frantic footsteps of people scurrying for their lives or engaging in deadly conflict.

"My sleeve! Take it!" ordered Elimar. As Barrett's fingers found his garb, the wizard whisked them toward the front gate. They flew over the city in a swirling cloud of grey mist to reappear by the entrance.

The prince hesitated, lost in the flurry of Elimar's quick decisions. His confidence wavered as chaos ensued below them, overwhelming his mind to a standstill. To his horror, seemingly out of nowhere, a guardsman charged onward with a raised sword to hew Elimar. An instant before the blade fell, Barrett sprang before the wizard to release a spell he had learned days earlier.

"Incendarous!" he shouted as a flaming red sphere erupted from his wand tip. The magic struck the guardsman squarely, engulfing him in red light, reducing him to a pile of smoldering ashes.

Elimar, temporarily off balance, regained his footing and smiled at his student's handiwork. "Excellent work, lad. I see you have been studying." His face returned to its grim state. "Find Trishar. Her power is hard to miss. Just go toward the place where everyone else is running from. She will be there."

Flustered, Barrett resisted. His only thought was revenge. "No! I need to find Asban, blast it all! You find your sister. I have other things to do."

The old man shook his head, frustration flitting over his face before he grew calm and fatherly. "That little wizard is the least of your city's concerns right now. Think, dear boy. Should you go after him? If you do, Westmore could fall. Which one is more important to you?"

Barrett kicked a stone near his feet from frustration. "Where are you going?"

"To help the others before they get themselves killed."

Fear jolted the prince. "Be careful. I want to see you when this is over."

24

To the Castle

After the wizard vanished, Barrett sprinted headlong into the stream of fleeing Agents and Trackers, striking down several as they tried to assail him. Weaving and dodging, he ran onward, but fleeing enemies or townsfolk made it difficult to keep on a straight path. Hurrying along, he scowled at the numerous bodies littering the streets. Most of the dead belonged to the Bureau. Yet, his heart skipped a beat as his eyes found familiar folks lying amongst them.

Kindly old Mr. Marlik, who had baked fresh bread for him since the prince was a child, had met his end. In a morbid way, it seemed the old fellow no longer had a care in the world as he lay on his back watching the sun rise on a lovely autumn's day with both eyes open.

To his right was Mrs. Warton, the seamstress who had tailored Barrett's royal clothing. She died with a wand in her hand and several arrows piercing her body.

The pity felt earlier for Asban vanished. Barrett blamed the underhanded, lying magic man for all the death and destruction. True or not, the prince did not care. Revenge sprang back into his thoughts as his legs pumped steadily onward.

Rounding a corner with speed, he came to a hurried stop. Trishar was there. At least, the woman he believed to be the sorceress. She looked far different than her usual self. Dressed in black, like Graile, her face was twisted with fury as her magic swept over all before her, striking down Trackers and Agents alike.

The Bureau pawns became floating vapors, ash piles, or were transformed into unnatural beasts before scurrying from sight. Several went mad, grabbing their heads to run screaming through the streets as insanity took them.

Barrett waved his hand high as he called out to her but the bedlam drowned out his voice. With his attention on the sorceress, two Trackers charged him with their long swords gleaming in the sun.

Catching their reflections in a store window, he spun round with a graceful move, thrusting his wand forward to strike them down with force. Their bodies smashed against the cobblestones and moved no more, causing the running crowd to divert around them like a flowing stream. None paid the dead men any attention.

Amidst the chaos, agony, and horror, the prince's heart found joy as Gaia, countless fairies, and rows of magic users came into view from behind the sorceress' path of destruction. They were spread to each side like an ocean wave flowing to meet the shoreline. Dashing through the ranks, he ran to embrace her.

"I am glad you're safe," he said, stroking her hair as he stared into her eyes.

"The plan is working. Graile, Shardira, Nell, and Zanora are heading for the castle. Randolph is coming from the west and Nirith is pushing from the east, tightening the circle to force the enemy to its center. Where is Elimar?" she asked.

"He went to find the others. You know him, never in one place too long."

They watched Trishar swish her wand to halt three charging Morim brutes. One clutched at his neck as if strangled by an unseen foe. With bulging eyes, he danced about in wild fits, trying to rid himself of the force choking the life from his lungs. After a snapping sound, he fell. His head was bent at an odd angle.

His counterparts fared no better. The next, as if holding a red hot club, cast his weapon aside and blew breath over his hands as if on fire. Suddenly, he stiffened, then bolted away in blind terror. His last steps took him inside a burning building where his screams lasted mere seconds.

The third tipped backward to bounce from the ground with an arrow through his eye. The shaft came from high above where Unger scurried along the rooftops sending deadly wooden shafts upon the enemy. He caught Trishar's gaze, nodded, then scurried from sight.

Yaris, with Mearis by his side, led their small force with military precision as the big man swung his sword, hewing a bloody path forward. Those soldiers loyal to the future king of Westmore, ones who had been in hiding with the Warder, fought by their side.

Enemy forces, filled with Malathians, Pagorians, and the barbarian Morims, met them head on. Yaris' men were quickly dwindling in number against the overwhelming odds but their fortune changed as the ground shook beneath their feet.

So came Alesta, moving onward in a rage. Several who foolishly shot arrows at her paid with their lives. With primal yells bursting from their lips, a band of Morim rushed in, their blades wagging low and clubs held high.

The sorceress faced them as her eyes changed from green to fiery red. Her arms whirled through the air, twisting and writhing as if performing a graceful dance while her magic lashed outward.

A small orb which quickly grew in size hung suspended before the attackers. Its magic changed colors like a lovely prism caught in the sun. Her spell turned shades of blue, then grey, to match a dusky sunset. In a blink, the sphere went as black as a starless sky. Undulating and twisting, it hung silently, weaving thoughts of despair, malice, and death in her foes' minds.

The young sorceress pushed her arms forward. The globe obeyed, releasing it contents to sweep through the enemy ranks with ease. Flesh stripped from bone as, one by one, their skeletal remains fell where the men once stood.

Realizing too late the magic was alive, the enemy tried to dash away. Their high-pitched shrieking proved pointless as the entity washed over them, leaving nothing more than boots or scorched ground behind.

Though staring death in the face, many Morim refused to surrender and the bald warriors continued their assault. Trapped between Alesta's magic, Nirith's mighty spells, Yaris' forces, Randolph and his helpers, and Trishar, the Morim were wiped away in their entirety.

Watching in stunned dismay, the Malathians and Pagorians still alive, fled the city. Handfuls of those lucky enough to flee were cut down by Unger's deadly arrows.

Alesta recalled her spell, thanking the drifting black shadow for its help before opening a void to allow the entity to disappear inside.

Then, it was done. The city was freed, save for the castle.

Graile and Zanora left a long trail of dead bodies behind them as they strode the castle halls in search of Grimes. Tracker and Agent robes littered the passages.

"It seems Grimes' men were not as loyal as he thought," said Zanora, wedging her foot under a lifeless Agent to flip him onto his back. "They have abandoned him and the Bureau." She looked down with remorse, seeing a young man about her own age staring back. Kneeling beside him, she closed his blank eyes. "It's not fair," she said softly.

"I would bet not all of them have left," said Graile. "Let's head for Grimes' chamber." He scanned ahead. "Nell and Shardira should be here. Be certain you don't kill them, too."

She punched his arm again. "This is not the first time I've held a sword, you know."

"You're beautiful while you are slaying invaders," noted the Fader, before giving a wink.

Zanora forced air through her lips and pushed stray hairs from her eyes. "I'm beautiful all the time."

Graile snickered. "Good point. Except when you're angry and cannot control your words or actions. Then you lose a bit of your shine."

"Can we discuss this later?" she asked, rolling her eyes.

Just ahead, Nell rounded the corner into the hallway with Shardira by her side. The four ran to one another, meeting in the center by the tall open window that peered down onto the city.

Smoky plumes dotted the sky while battle continued in small skirmishes throughout the streets. Waves of those still bearing the Bureau's mark fell as dwarves, cyclops, fairies, and others, crushed the remaining resistance.

Many Trackers fell to their knees to beg for their lives. Agents stripped off their uniforms to blend in with the townsfolk in hopes of making unnoticed, hasty escapes.

"It's like watching a board game where the players are real and staying alive is the prize," said Nell. "It's hard to watch."

Graile turned his painted face to her. "That is dark. I am surprised you would think such a thing. Impressive."

Shardira turned away from the opening. "She is correct, though. Magic has won the day so far, but do not expect Grimes to go quietly."

"We cannot forget about Carick. I don't see him as being valiant but I will not lower my guard against him," said the Fader.

"They have not been seen since the siege started," offered Nell. "Let's root them out."

None opposed the foursome as they wound through the passages and halls in search of their villains. During their quest, only terrified cooks, servants, teachers, and the like, were found. They were sent to safety as the companions continued the hunt.

Finally, after opening a stout door on the second floor, King Carick was found. He looked old and worn as he sat in a comfortable chair reading a book. No longer the broad-shouldered, square jawed stranger that once ascended the steps to claim kingship over Westmore, he placed the book on an end table and rose to bow. He seemed insecure and confused.

With an angry face and a shining dagger in one hand, Zanora advanced with rapid steps. She stopped short as Graile suddenly appeared at her side.

"Wait," he said, pushing his chin forward. "Look at him. Something is not right."

"I am Carick," he announced, sounding unsure of himself as he bowed again. "Where am I? How did I arrive here? Can you help? There seems to be a commotion outside and I am afraid to leave my room."

"What game is this!" cried Zanora, leveling her blade at him. "You vermin. I will drag you before the true king and have him decide your fate."

Carick verged on terrified tears. "I have done nothing wrong, my lady. Please do not take me before the king. How have I hurt you?" He peered round with a muddled expression. "Am I in the king's house? Is he here? I will make amends, I swear it."

Graile edged closer. "I think he's telling the truth. He has no idea where he is or what is happening. Maybe the death of Jarn drove him to madness."

Zanora's face softened as she lowered her blade. Her stare turned soft, and like Barrett had felt for Asban, pity rose in her.

"The Fader speaks wisely. I sense no deception on this man's part," said the elf.

"How can that be?" asked Nell.

"Quite easy, actually," said Graile. "If madness has not taken him, then he was, or still could be, under a spell. We have always said he was used as a puppet for Grimes to control the kingdom. Like Alesta was for Apadora."

"Right!" said Zanora. "That makes perfect sense. Do you think his memory will ever return if the spell is broken?"

The Fader shrugged. "Perhaps Trishar can help him." He went to Carick's side and guided him toward Shardira. "Can you take him to her, wherever she may be? It isn't fair to hold him for what he has done, especially if he had no idea of his actions."

The elf nodded. "I feel shame at never knowing this had happened. I hope your sorceress can make it right." She pulled a long green cloak from the back of a chair and wrapped it round Carick's shoulders. "Come along, my lord. Let us seek help."

Carick grew excited. "Oh, that would be appreciated, young lady. Are your friends as nice as you?"

"Of course we are," added Zanora. "My lord, before you go, do you happen to know where your friend Grimes is at?"

The false king stopped and rubbed his chin, then shook his head. "I am sorry, but I know nothing of this Grimes fellow to which you speak. Should I? Is he important?"

"Not at all, my friend," said Graile. "I am certain we will find him soon. Thank you for your help."

Shardira stepped into the hall, guiding the befuddled man all the while. They moved down the hall toward the stairs, disappearing around a hallway corner.

"That was very strange. Whose spell was he under?" asked the redhead as she watched them go. "All this happened before Asban ever arrived so that rules him out."

"We have no way of knowing who holds magic and who does not," said Nell. "For example, who would have thought Randolph Rollie would be magical?"

"From here on out, we should not trust anyone we do not know. Stay alert and on guard," said Graile.

Moving from one room to another, they searched the entire floor. Finally, the trio reached Barrett's old bedroom. Swinging the door wide they dashed inside, then faltered. A cold chill overtook them as their eyes turned up, unable to take their gazes from the horrid sight.

From a rafter high above dangled a man's skinny body. His feet were well off the ground as he swung from the thick rope fastened round his neck. His head tilted sharply to one side. Grimes appeared dead.

"By the gods! I never expected this," said Zanora, stepping closer to inspect the corpse. She poked his foot with her sword tip. "Am I the only one who finds this strange?"

Graile studied the body. His circled eyes darkened as he covered every inch of the corpse, then, in a moment of dread, they flew open as he lunged for Zanora. He arrived too late. The spell struck before they could escape.

Cackling laughter filled the room. "You three fools have caused me nothing but grief," said Grimes, stepping from behind a long curtain. "You were so occupied with my death that you overlooked what was right before you."

Zanora cursed and struggled but remained flat on her back, struggling against the magic binding her. Her head was throbbing and blood trickled from the corner of her mouth from impacting the floor. "You have magic! All this time you have been lying."

"We should have seen it. Asban could never perform such complicated magic. He was merely a means to an end—a show piece. And Carick was little more than a puppet, just as we thought," said Graile, trying desperately to turn to vapor but the spell held him tightly.

"You have a quick mind. I admire that," said Grimes. "It's too bad you did not figure it out sooner. Now you must die."

He flicked his wand toward the dead man dangling in the room. The illusion fell away. Grimes smiled as he nudged the corpse to make it swing eerily, the rope creaking as the fleshy weight swayed back and forth. Hanging silently in death was a royal guard dressed in soldiers' attire. There was a wound over his heart where the magical strike had ended his life.

"Murderer!" cried Nell. "You killed an innocent man to fake your own death, then covered it with magic."

Grimes laughed as he drew closer to the trapped Shifter. "Stupid girl, no one is innocent. We are *all* guilty of wrongdoings. Think on that before you die." He paced a slow, deliberate circle. "Even you have killed." His wand came level with her head. "I should make you pay for your crimes right now."

"Leave her alone!" cried Zanora. "Turn me loose and face me, coward. I'll show you who is willing to kill."

Flashing a sly smile, Grimes turned a cold gaze onto her. "So the traitor now speaks bravely. How amusing." Taking immense pleasure in the trio's helplessness, he eased into a chair, made himself comfortable, and spoke on to the redhead. "*You* are the worst of all. First, you betrayed your companions by siding with the Bureau because of your hate for magic. Then, being the treacherous, disloyal Mundane you are, you abandoned me to return to them."

He paused to laugh. "You friends seem rather idiotic to take you back and show you trust. And you, sweet child, are as much a murderer as I am. Everyone in this room is one."

Reality struck Zanora hard. She felt ill knowing everything the thin, weasel-faced man spoke was the truth.

"What do you plan on doing with us?" asked Graile with his calm voice.

"I plan to replace the three innocent men we hung by the gates with your bodies." Grimes displayed a wry smile. "Of course, you'll be dead by then, so you will not need to endure the sudden stop of the hanging, but your purpose will be a warning to all who try my patience."

"But you *knew* they were innocent. Why kill them?" asked Graile, his curiosity peaked as he stalled for time, hoping a plan would come or a friend arrived to save them.

"Someone had to pay for *your* crimes. Tsk, tsk! Three men died due to your stupidity." He waved a dismissive hand. "I hope that thought haunts you the rest of your short life." He laughed a surprisingly deep sound.

"You've gone mad!" said Zanora.

Grimes flicked his wand to steal away the redhead's voice. "I tire of your disrespect. Since you cannot be polite you are not allowed to speak. Irritating girl."

"It's too late for you, Grimes. Even now your forces are being destroyed. Look out the window and tell us what you see. Your pitiful resistance is being wiped away. Your men are dead or have already fled. I watched them fall," lied Nell. Like the Fader, she hoped her harsh words would delay their deaths until she could muster an escape.

"Sad little girl, no one will defeat the Bureau. We control the western lands." Grimes pondered his words, then jammed a thumb against his chest. "*I* control the western lands and no group of snot-nosed kids will force me out."

With a deliberate stride, he went to the widow and yanked open the curtains. He jumped at the sight of a fairy hovering by the balcony doors as if listening. She darted off in a blink. Kicking the doors open, Grimes fired blasts from his wand but missed with each attempt.

Then the truth struck him like one of his own magical assaults. Dashing to the stone railing, the thin man gasped at the billowing smoke rising steadily from the burning fires. Shock and fury pummeled his frame as he took in the scene. With rage overtaking reason, Grimes grit his teeth and made an animalistic noise in his throat. He slapped the railing with his palm.

"Impossible! It cannot be!" Spinning, he leveled his wand at the friends. "You will not live to see the ending, I'm afraid." Suddenly, a swishing noise caught his attention.

With his wand at the ready, his head turned left, then right, as he scanned the room with a predator's stare. Finding nothing, he moved closer to the redhead. "Trickery will get you nowhere. Do not try to escape. I will strike you down before you reach the door."

25

D'morkar

From a shadowed corner rose a steady, familiar voice that drifted through the air like a calming spell. It wrapped around Grimes, slowly squeezing him as he squirmed like prey caught in a serpent's grip. He could not escape.

"Does that threat hold true for me as well or have you been reduced to picking on children?" asked the intruder.

Grimes turned with anger etched deep on his face as he attempted to raise his wand. Hs movements came too late as the intruder summoned the wand to his own hand, holding it tightly as it smacked into his palm.

"You!" cried Grimes as his eyes settled on his foe. "I should have known you were part of this, old man!"

Elimar smiled. "I would say it is good to see you, Grimes, but it would be a lie. I feel certain you are not who you say, so let's see who you really are, shall we?"

With another swipe of his wand, the wizard stripped away Grimes' false appearance. Before them stood a tall, stout fellow with a heavily scarred cheek. A deep, jagged line stretched from his hairline to his chin. His rounded face, shoulder length brown hair, and glint of evil in his dark eyes gave him a menacing visage.

Elimar studied his enemy. "D'morkar! I should have known your foul stench was all over this war." The wizard glanced him over. "You look weary."

To the surprise of the companions, D'morkar's posture relaxed. Again, he lowered into a chair as his voice became smooth and kind. "So the mighty Elimar finally graces my presence." Revulsion filled his eyes. "I should have killed you years ago. You and your meddling ways have always been a thorn in my side."

"It seems you are slowing in your old age. After all, I did just sneak up on you." Elimar swished his wand to free the teens. "Liberatium."

The redhead quickly drew her sword and charged D'morkar, but again Graile reached her in time to hold her back. She struggled and cursed several times. "Face me without your stick, magic man."

"Zanora," said Elimar softly. "Behave yourself or I will put you back where you were." The threat took hold in an instant as she quit her ramblings and came to a standstill. "That is better," said the wizard, turning back to D'morkar.

"So you believe you have won?" asked the evil one as a menacing light flickered over his face. "How sad you will be when I return with a boundless force to retake this city for my own. Even your pathetic magic will not stop me."

"I will not need to," replied Elimar, his voice firm and steady.

"The true king and his forces will destroy you, just as they have done on this day."

The sinister laugh returned. "A mere boy! Ha. I see you are easily confused in your advanced age, old man. No child—"

"Barrett can defend his castle perfectly well," interrupted Elimar. "He has become more powerful than you could possibly know. He would wipe you away like cleaning dog dung from his boots."

Fear lit D'morkar's face for a fleeting second before he composed himself. Yet, anger at allowing his true feelings to be revealed, if only for a blink of time, could not be missed.

Behind him, the friends exchanged baffled glances.

"Enough talk," said Elimar. "You shall now face your peers so they may decide a fitting punishment."

D'morkar's poisoned words continued. "I have no peers. I stand alone against a corrupt world that has become weak and sad. You should be ashamed for your part in this, Elimar the magnificent." His last words dripped with sarcasm.

"Throw this vile thing in the dungeon. Let him spend the rest of his life there," spat Zanora. She wagged a finger at him. "Your actions will not go unpunished."

"Is she always like this?" asked D'morkar.

Elimar frowned and raised his eyebrows. "Mostly, yes." He motioned for their captive to rise, then conjured a binding spell to hold both his wrists. "I do not wish to kill you but try anything foolish and today will be your last."

D'morkar turned to the friends. "Do you see? Everyone can be a killer at one time or another."

Zanora moved behind and poked his backside with her sword. "Say another word and I'll cut your tongue out."

Yaris posted soldiers by the castle gates and courtyards to keep looters from making a larger mess within the king's home. At the same time, the remaining companions strode across the square in an attempt to locate their friends.

Barrett took the lead with Gaia by his side. Two soldiers rushed past the pair to swing open the heavy wooden doors leading to the castle's main hallway. Coming to attention, they gave snappy salutes. The prince nodded thanks as he passed but did not slow.

Halfway down the hall, they halted as a group of five approached. Swirling gray smoke drifted through the windows to obscure Barrett's vision. Tightening the grip on his wand, he waited, only to see Elimar and the others emerge through the dark cloud with a captive stranger by their side.

Behind them, Nirith took a long gasp. "No! It cannot be," she said. "He has been dead for years."

"Apparently not," said Trishar, coming beside her. "Is that not—"

"Shhhh," retorted her niece. "Not here."

"It's too late for that," said Alesta. "The truth will come out now."

"What is happening?" demanded Barrett. "Someone tell me, now. What is all the secrecy about? What have you not told us?"

Elimar stopped the procession several feet away. D'morkar quickly perked up, looking unexpectedly delighted once Nirith came under his view. His eyes softened. Longing and regret replaced the darkness.

"Hello . . . my darling wife," he said. "You are even more lovely than the day we met."

Confused waves of murmurs and rumblings swept the hallway.

"I have *not* been your wife for ages," insisted Nirith. "Never call me that again, you cheating filth."

Barrett cursed and repeated himself. "Someone tell me what is going on. Why is this man bound and why does Zanora have him at sword point? Who is he?"

"Allow me to introduce the ancient wizard, D'morkar, who was disguised as Grimes this entire time," said Graile, stepping beside the prince.

Barrett turned ghostly white. "Ridiculous!"

D'morkar laughed. "I hear that a lot, actually." Facing Graile, he sneered. "Mind who you are calling ancient, young man."

"Is he really your husband?" asked Gaia, her head turning from husband to wife.

"Absolutely not," insisted Nirith, but after a nudge from Trishar, she relented. "At one time, yes. I admit that part. But after I caught him with Mearis and evil consumed him, I rid myself of his wicked ways."

"So *he* was the reason you turned Mearis into a Trowken! You cursed her over him?" asked Unger, scratching his head.

Another laugh. "So that's what happened to her," said D'morkar. "I always wondered why I could not find her. I searched for years. I would never have guessed you had revenge in you."

"Hold on!" the archer suddenly cried. "You're saying there never was Grimes, only this fellow pretending to be him?"

Elimar raised an eyebrow. "Exactly. And now that I think of it, we were fools for not seeing it. Not too long ago, Grimes did not exist. But once he appeared, he weaseled his way into the Bureau and quickly took control. No Mundane could move up the ranks that fast in such an organization."

"Unless he uses magic to control the minds of those around him," said Yaris.

"Precisely," said the old wizard. "His smooth words and spells helped him gain status, I am certain of it."

While the conversation continued, D'morkar listened but did not hear. Instead, he slowly inched toward the wizard, taking full advantage of his inattention. Spinning round, he rammed his shoulder into Elimar and snatched the wand from the old man's hands.

"Evonis Visu," he shouted, disappearing in a cloud of magic.

"No!" screamed Nirith. "After him, *now*."

"Stop where you are," commanded Elimar, his voice rising like a terrible thunder. "Calm yourselves. He is likely one hundred leagues from here by now. There is nothing we can do. It could take years to find him again."

"Blast that tricksy man," cried Trishar. "I should have been paying more attention. Curse him!"

"It is not your fault," said Yaris, placing a comforting arm round her shoulder. "We are all to blame."

"I told you I should have killed him when I had the chance," grumbled Zanora. "This would be over by now."

"For once I agree with her," said Unger, smacking his fist into his palm. "He should be dead."

"That is rather dark, my friend," said Gaia. "I can make a potion to help control that anger, if you wish."

Unger replied with a soured face but no words.

"Now what do we do? Our mission was a failure," said Barrett. "Asban and D'morkar both escaped and may return at any time. They just need a new army. Then all this will start over again."

"It was a triumph, Sire," said Yaris. "You have regained your city, freed your people from a tyrant's rule, and will soon be king."

"He's right," said Nell. "Besides, it will take years for those two fools to build an army strong enough to stand against Westmore again. Since we know he will return, we can be ready. We will not be caught unawares next time."

Barrett twisted his lips in disagreement. "If he was Mundane, I would agree. But wizards can be crafty folks. Their words hypnotize or give hope, yet they do whatever they deem is right." He gave Elimar a knowing look. "I will not put anything past him."

"Elimar, how did you know where we were?" asked Zanora. "This is a big place and you just suddenly popped up like you always do."

"Fairies, of course. Remarkable race, those fairies," replied the wizard. "Once D'morkar was spotted by my flying spy, she found me straightaway to tell me of your troubles. I telelocated while D'morkar was busy planning destruction on you. He likes that sort of thing. Thankfully for you, he is always long-winded which gave me time to arrive."

Outside, the sky darkened for a long, curious instant. Barrett rushed to the window to peer out, searching for the source of the cloudy sky. Poking his head from the tall window, he scanned the roads below. His heart filled with fear as sounds of magical battle reached his ears. His attention went to a commotion near the front gates.

Without another word, he whirled around and dashed the hall's length, ignoring the cries and shouts from his friends. Skidding round the corner, he ran for the gates with all the strength he could muster.

There, D'morkar and Asban came onward in crazed anger,

waving their wands to cause renewed death and destruction to all in their path.

Barrett stood his ground as his hand tingled. "Stop hurting my people and destroying my city," he cried.

Asban laughed a maniacal sound. "It is not yours any longer, foolish boy. Stand aside or die."

"No! You will need to get past me before harming anyone else," said the prince, planting his feet for battle.

"I was hoping you would stand and fight. Your death will make my victory even sweeter. Now meet your end like one of your city's peasants," shouted Asban, flicking a spell outward.

Barrett swiped the magic away, then sprinted right, heading for cover. "Now!" he shouted.

The sky blackened for the second time the as the dragon, Laelynn, passed overhead to rain fire upon the wizards. D'morkar quickly shielded himself, yet the physical strain of holding back dragon flames proved overwhelming. As his spell weakened and the blaze leaked through, he screamed an awful sound as the firestorm struck him.

Panicked, wounded, and desperate, he limped for cover moments before his defense shattered completely. Throwing an unsteady glance over his shoulder, his frightened eyes found the spot where Asban had stood. Only scorched ground and bones remained.

"I'll raze this city to the ground," yelled D'morkar, grimacing as he fought to stand. "I will destroy you all. I am king!"

Overhead, Laelynn made a graceful turn to position herself for another pass. D'morkar defiantly braced himself against a tree and raised his wand to the sky. This time the tip glowed a brilliant white.

Barrett watched the scene unfold. Then, the rage he had held in for months suddenly burst to the surface. He could no longer control it. He thought of how Grimes imprisoned and executed innocent people, how the skinny man smirked as he kicked the prince from his own home, and worst of all, how he helped cause the death of his father.

Wrath leapt into his heart. Then, his inner fury was not enough as Barrett's hands glowed a deep violet before bursting into writhing purple flames. This time, he would not hold back.

As D'morkar struggled to cast his spell on the dragon, he ignored the prince altogether. The mistake proved fatal as Barrett's spell engulfed him in a whirlwind of magical heat. Taken completely unaware, the wizard withered away, giving a final agonizing scream as the blaze consumed him. Within seconds, D'morkar was no more.

From behind came a burst of light. Barrett spun to defend himself but lowered his wand instead. Smiling broadly at the sight of Elimar, Trishar, and his friends, he breathed a sigh of relief.

The old wizard peered around, then strode to Asban's fiery, bubbling pool, then to the crater left by D'morkar's death. There, he stooped to recover the dead wizard's wand. Turning it over in his hands, he presented it to the prince. "Do you feel better now that you have been avenged?"

"They are gone and we will never see them again. That's good enough for me," said Barrett. "And to answer your question, no, I do not feel better." Again, the sky darkened.

Raising his eyes, Barrett watched Laelynn glide to a nearby field as her children rode the breeze high above to stand guard.

The prince approached her massive shape to give a low bow.

"Again, I find myself in your debt. I was worried you would not arrive."

Laelynn stretched a clawed limb forward. Barrett crawled onto her palm and was lifted high in the air to look into the dragon's eyes.

"My vow to you was to be at your beck and call. I am free because of you. I will always be at your service, King Barrett of Westmore. From this day forward two of my children will remain behind to protect your city. Vexor and Aliza are at your command."

From his high vantage, Barrett studied his burning city and sighed. "Thank you, Laelynn. Though, I am not king yet. I have a long road ahead, and truthfully, I'm not sure I can do it."

"Being a leader is never easy," replied the dragon. "But you are intelligent and surrounded by faithful friends. Your kind spirit balances justice and compassion. You will be a magnificent king, Barrett Telenar."

He stroked her muzzle as her breath blew back his hair. "If I take the throne, one of my first acts as king will be to make you and your children royal guardians of Westmore." He jammed a finger in the air. "That is, if you accept."

"It would be an honor, my king." She politely nodded her horned head, then pointed downward. "Your friends are awaiting your return. I shall not be far away, Sire. Summon me when ready to take a long ride." She winked a scaled eyelid at him. "Even kings need time away to keep their minds clear and thoughts in order."

Barrett hugged her muzzle tightly before being lowered to the ground. Then Laelynn coiled her legs and launched into the air with a tremendous roar.

"Awww," said Gaia, watching the dragon leave as she came to Barrett's side. "I never got to say hello."

They kissed. "She'll be back very soon," he said. "She is part of our city now."

26

The King

So began the mourning period. For long days, many wept over those lost in battle. Their tears stained the ground like rain. Nonetheless, hope soon returned to Westmore as the city began the long process of rebuilding that which was destroyed. The task of clearing away the dead was given to the captured Trackers and Agents as punishment.

Funeral pyres were built and set ablaze to honor the brave souls who gave their lives to defend the city so others could live free from the Bureau's tyranny.

Firstly, Nell and Elimar cleared the dungeons of the innocents. While some were relieved to be free and reunited with their kin, others emerged to grieve the death of their loved ones as wartime victims.

Elimar, Gaia, and the three sorceresses spent many days wandering amongst the wounded, healing those who yet lived, including those who stood against them in battle.

Barrett walked the streets helping as he could—clearing debris, comforting townsfolk, clearing dead bodies, or any other chore needing done. He refused to allow his people to believe he remained in the castle while they toiled with rebuilding. Plus, he thought, the city's near destruction was mostly his doing.

The fallen enemy were thrown in a pit and burned just as the beasts and creatures had been after Alesta's attack. Once more, towers of thick smoke rose skyward to blot out the sun from shining on Westmore. Remarkably, joy quickly returned to the voices of the townspeople.

Fairies began rebuilding their worlds. This time, they took to the trees, bushes, and fields instead of fairy lamps—except Taleen. She and her kin returned to Barrett's home, taking her place upon his balcony in a fairy house specially built for them.

Dwarves marched through the streets in long columns as they took back their smithy works, stone crafting, and iron creations. Firing up their forges, they set to repairing the massive gate hinges, rebuilding watchtowers, repairing walls, houses, and anything made of stone or iron.

To Barrett's delight, and with Randolph's help, the magical doors came to life once more. Unfortunately, several were lost during battle. Elimar promised to start work on replacements after the healings had been completed.

Within the New Days, as Barrett's reign would become known, Yaris and Zanora reorganized the army. Graile, with Trishar's guidance, supervised the city's reconstruction. The Fader made a favorable impression on the stout dwarves. After making fast friends with them, he showed he had not only had an ability to organize but proved knowledgeable concerning metal crafting and design. Before long, he grew to be highly thought of amongst the Hearty Folk, the name the residents bestowed upon the dwarves.

Alesta and Nirith secretly used sorcery to speed rebuilding along while trying not to offend the pride of the dwarves. Mearis happily stayed on to become the official Seer of Westmore.

During this time, Unger rarely left Barrett's side, following him everywhere but the bathroom. Shardira was charged with personally selecting new castle guards since Barrett trusted her judgement and honesty.

Carick received a fresh start. With the death of D'morkar and Asban, his spell was broken. He remained in Westmore as a citizen until the end of his life.

In the blink of an eye, ten days had passed. The smoking pits still burned, adding sorrow to the air as a daily reminder of the horrors that had taken place. Despite the happiness of rebuilding, the sight of the flaming holes weighed heavily on all, especially the prince. When it became overwhelming, he retreated to his bedroom to occupy himself by decorating the space exactly as it had been.

The stresses of repairing the city were falling away. Now, as he had done for weeks, Barrett sat struggling with the decision of becoming king.

With the crown in his hands, he sat alone upon his father's throne chair with both elbows on his knees and his head hung in misery. Tears fell from his eyes, splashing steadily around his boots. Often, he wiped them away on his sleeve.

Leaning within easy reach to his left was his wizard's staff, the gift Elimar had given him. The broken shields, arrows, and swords had been cleared away days ago, yet the feeling of despair and death hovered like an unrelenting storm.

Samaren winged into the chamber to perch upon the chair's arm. The two did not speak for some time as the prince continued to weep. Finally, the raven broke in.

"Do you wish to talk, son?"

Again, the prince wiped a sleeve across his face. He shook his head. His courage wavered, renewed itself, then fell away again as he absently toyed with the crown. Working through his future was sapping his energy. He felt worn as he searched for answers that would not come.

"So many have died for this day and so much has been sacrificed," he said softly. He met his mother's small black eyes. "I'm not sure I want to be king. I just want peace and happiness, the way things used to be." Another wipe of his tears. "And I want my father back."

Samaren hopped upon his knee and pushed her head against his chest in comforting fashion.

"Son, after all you have seen, you know there will always be evil. It is the way of the world. But," she added with a ruffle of her feathers, "there is peace within you. Only inner strength can give you what you seek. To my heartache, your father will never return. Still, know he would be proud of you and all you have done."

Before he could utter a response, the chamber doors opened. Elimar strode forward to stop near the chair. "My liege," he said with a bow before giving another to Samaren. "I come with updated news. All is well and your city is returning to a state of normalcy."

Barrett did not hear a word his friend said. His mind was elsewhere. "Bring my father back," he blurted as his cheeks reddened with embarrassment.

The wizard smiled warmly. "I cannot do as you ask, Sire. For what would return would not be your father as you remember him. Those powers are reserved for the gods and even they do not meddle with death."

The prince cursed and tossed the crown onto the chair arm. "It's not fair. I never had a chance to say goodbye."

Elimar's eyes turned sullen and distant for a long while, as if recalling a painful memory. Then, his voice rose again. "Though I would be breaking many wizarding rules, I could conjure him for a very brief time. No more than mere minutes, you understand. Then, it shall be done forevermore."

Samaren cawed. "Do not meddle in this, old friend. My son must learn handle his pain on his own. He cannot always have his way."

Barrett scowled. "I know. Everyone tells me that."

Elimar made a small bow again. "You are correct, my lady. But I ask you what you would give to see your husband once more. Can I deny the young king a fleeting moment to heal wounds and have peace of mind?"

The bird tilted her head and flapped her wings. She resettled and hopped on her son's shoulder. "For all your hard talk, wizard, you are soft inside."

The old man gave a chuckle. "Do not dare tell a soul, my lady." He reached to stroke her feathers. "I miss our talks. Perhaps someday soon we will resume them."

"You're trying to butter me up to make me see your way, you old troll," she said, flapping her wings at him again.

"Am I that obvious?" he asked with a growing grin.

"Forget all that and get on with it," grumbled Barrett. "I'll die from old age by the time you two are done."

Samaren pecked at his bare neck, making him squeal in pain. "Mind your manners, young man. I raised you better than to be rude."

"Ow! I'm sorry," he said, rubbing the red mark forming on his skin.

Elimar moved to the room's center to place both hands on his staff as if ready to stir a cauldron. He tapped the end on the floor and chanted strange words Barrett had never heard.

Suddenly, the prince felt overwhelmed with self-loathing. It gnawed at him for asking the wizard to break the rules—a wrong and selfish choice, yet one he craved with desperation. Tangled in his thoughts, he nearly told the wizard to stop, but after a moment, remained seated. The desire to see his father a final time burnt like wildfire in his heart.

The magic swirled, popped, and crackled as it took human shape. Barrett stiffened as anticipation rose in his chest. He squinted, looking for any sign of life within the churning magic. Only disappointment gripped him.

Then, things began to change. First, there was nothing but an outline, yet soon enough, a man slowly appeared, though only a shadowy figure which wavered like a banner caught in a breeze.

Barrett bit his lip and gripped the chair arms as he slid to the edge of his seat. Tension tightened his head with a painful pounding as he waited helplessly. Samaren squawked beside him.

Slowly, a figure solidified before them. Barrett gasped, on

the verge of tears again as the shadowy figure formed details. Eyes, nose, mouth, square jaw, and broad shoulders took shape. Large arms stretched outward as if the king was awakening from a long sleep.

Though the figure was ghostly in appearance, the prince cared little. Soon, whether a trick of his mind or something he could not understand, his father appeared as clear and solid as the wizard. Barrett wiped away his tears as joy found him.

Dressed in the royal attire he was placed in prior to his pyre ceremony, King Telenar stood solid in all his glory.

"F . . . f . . . father," stammered Barrett.

"My son," said the king, smiling broadly. "You are a welcomed sight. I see you have become a fine man in such a short time."

"I miss you so much," said the prince with a warbling voice as he fought back more tears. "I need your advice. I don't know what to do or where to turn."

"Son, you are surrounded by people even wiser than I. Have you spoken to them? Given them a chance to help? Elimar and your mother would provide true counsel."

With a surge of emotion, Barrett blurted out his true problem. "I can't do it. I can't be king. I would never be like you. I don't know how."

He kept his eyes on his father's form, longing to hug him one last time, but as the man moved, horror gripped the prince. Small pieces of the dead king slowly loosened and drifted away like fiery embers reaching for the sky in a final attempt to shine before fading forever.

The king did not seem to notice. Turning kind, patient eyes upon his son, he stepped closer as more pieces fluttered from his form. "True enough. You would never be like me. Because you are not me. We are all unique. Not two living things can ever truly be the same. Perhaps in appearance, yes, but never the same." Taking his son's hand as more fragments floated away, he patted it to comfort the young man. "You will be your own kind of king, just as I was different than my father. You will be a fair ruler."

"What if I don't want the responsibility?" Barrett asked, gripping his father's hand as if he could not bear to let go. "I just want to live a normal life."

Pieces of the king's leg loosened to float past his head.

"What is normal? Do what you were born to do. You have already found your mother, and with luck, perhaps I will return to your life, as well. Who knows what the gods have in store for me. Remember, I am never truly gone." He pointed to his son's heart. "I am always there." Another smile spread over his face. "Trust your mother. She was the wisest of us both. She can guide your reign. Besides, you are already a knowledgeable leader."

The king faded faster as Elimar strained to hold the magic together. He staff shook under the stress. His face reddened and sweat beaded his brow. "Only a few more seconds, Sire. I cannot hold this any longer," he said.

Barrett rose, still holding the king's deteriorating hand. "Goodbye, Father. Thank you for helping make me become who I am. I love you."

"And I will always love you, my precious son." The king's gaze went to Samaren with sadness in them. "I love you both more than you could imagine. Farewell."

With that, he was gone. Elimar swished his staff, then leaned upon it to breathe heavily. Samaren cawed as the king faded from sight. It was a mournful sound that chilled the prince's blood.

Barrett ran to the wizard and hugged him closely. "Thank you."

Elimar stroked his apprentice's hair. "I hope you found the answers you were seeking." He held him at arm's length. "Because now it is time to be the king of Westmore. Make your parents proud."

Samaren cawed again. "Indeed. And what a king you will be. You are going to take your throne, are you not?"

Barrett moved to stroke the bird's feathers. "I love you, too, Mother." His eyes came to rest upon the crown still draped over the chair arm. "As long as I have your guidance, I will wear the crown."

Elimar clapped lightly in the background. "Wise choice, Sire." With another movement of his staff, the chamber doors swung open. The friends entered as a group to bow slowly.

"Stop that," ordered the prince. "I am not king yet."

"Then we should fix that, my liege," said Yaris with his usual deep voice.

Four days later, as his pain and unease slowly passed, an official crowning ceremony was held in the city courtyard amidst cheers and celebration. Barrett Telenar began his reign as the King of Westmore.

After seeing his father and recalling his discussion with Trishar, he looked for the dead king in every animal, person, or any living thing he came in contact with. Gaia made him stop before people would whisper he was cracking under the pressure of the kingship.

As his first official act, he pardoned the wounded and captured enemy forces. Healing Westmore was his goal and staging executions or having prisoners rot in the dungeons was no way to begin his reign.

Then, after many long nights of thought, he chose to surround himself with the wisest, most trusted people he knew. Hence, he created the King's Council. No one was surprised by the company he kept.

Yaris resumed his position as Warder while Zanora became the man's assistant, bearing responsibility and control over training soldiers in battle tactics and warfare. Though, it did take a bit of talk to convince him to allow her near the training grounds.

Nell, due to her shifting ability, was made a spy for the kingdom, a talent in which she would excel.

Shardira became Commander of the Armies. Her fighting skills, ones surpassing even Zanora's talent, made her the clear choice. The king valued her calmness and logical thinking, as well.

Unger, his longest, most trusted friend, became his personal advisor. This, too, seemed a natural choice. Since childhood, Barrett had relied on the archer to speak the truth, no matter how undesirable, and to be present through the toughest times. These days would be no different.

Gaia, destined to sit beside him as queen, was charged with returning magic to the city as it was before the Bureau intervened. Her accomplishments did not go unnoticed by the people, either. They took a shine to the young woman who would help rule them. She was as popular as her future partner.

Graile, due to his rational mind, was named the King's Engineer. His position included all things logistical, from organizing new streets to placement of new buildings. Ideas for city improvements were his, as well. With his dwarf friends by his side, he accomplished more in a short time than any could have foreseen.

Samaren remained mother, councilor, messenger, and guardian rolled into one. As with the fairy, Taleen, the king had ordered a cozy space designed for the raven to be her new home within the castle walls.

Barrett kept his word to the dragons as well, officially dubbing Laelynn and her brood, Guardians of Westmore. And though many residents feared her at first she grew to be beloved amongst the people, especially once her children agreed to be occasionally ridden by the townsfolk.

Finally, there was Randolph Rollie, who found his place as the King's Reporter. His new mission was to inform the public of all important news, daily happenings, and upcoming events. This time, not only was he free to use magic, but he would never again be forced to write articles. The man never wrote another insulting word against Barrett.

Barrett saw to it the unselfish sacrifice of Lars would not be forgotten. The king dedicated the new library to their departed friend.

Then came the hardest part of all—farewells.

Fourteen days after Barrett made Trishar, Alesta, and Nirith honorary members of the King's Council, the time arrived for the sorceresses to depart. This was one of the toughest moments of his life, only outdone by the death of his parents.

Though he knew their departures were inevitable, he loathed the idea of the companions splitting apart. Despite their lives being forever linked, each of them led separate ones he no longer had cause to be in, other than by close friendship.

When the day came it was far more emotional and difficult than he cared to admit. Seeing Trishar leave, even knowing she would return frequently, left a miserable hole in his heart. He thought of her as a second mother. She had nurtured him, tutored him in many things, and was kind even when others were not. Most importantly, she always made time to talk and give advice.

Alesta and Nirith returned to their home, deciding to live together for a short while to get closer after their years of separation. Barrett promised to visit often and gave them leave to enter the castle whenever they desired. After all, they too were part of the Council, he thought.

Elimar silently stared from his room window as Barrett lowered next to him. It took a long while before the king could find his voice.

"I don't want you to go," he said, fighting back tears. "You're like a father to me. Can't you stay a little while longer?"

The wizard patted the young king's knee and smiled. "A wizard's work is never done. Besides, I will return when able. You have my word. Plus, you have Trishar, Nirith, and Alesta not far away. They will visit often." He leaned closer. "They are very fond of you." He pointed to his face. "It's those puppy dog eyes of yours." Laughing a resounding sound, he lightly clapped the king's back.

"You know, maybe it's best you're not around," retorted Barrett. "Can I help you pack?"

"Well!" exclaimed Elimar, clutching his heart with exaggerated effort. "I see some things never change."

Barrett chuckled. "To be honest, I'm not sure how I survived all this without you. Thank you, my dear friend."

Elimar winked. "I only taught you magic and a few life lessons. Everything else, all the hard parts, you did on your own. Just remember, you will make mistakes. We all do. Never let those failures stick with you. Learn from them, do not repeat them, move forward, and keep your wonderful spirit, Sire. The people are lucky to have you."

Barrett choked back the tears welling in his eyes. "Are you sure you cannot stay?"

"I'm sorry, my boy, but there is always evil to fight or things to be set right. But fear not, the people around you love you and would fight to the death to prove it. In fact, you would not be sitting here had they not already done so."

"Where will you go?"

The wizard shrugged. "Wherever I am needed." His face turned serious. "I hope you understand you defeated a very powerful wizard in D'morkar. That shows your cunning, planning, and intelligence. Well done. I am proud of you."

Sadness washed over the king in a wave. "Give me your word you will not be gone long."

"Wizard's promise," said the old man, extending a hand.

Barrett clasped it and felt warmth creep into his skin. "Did you just put a spell on me?"

Elimar merely smiled and puffed his pipe, blowing the smoke into the shape of a flying dragon.

Barrett's dreams of being surrounded by magic and races of all kinds was coming true again. Beyond that, dragons had returned to the western lands, just as it had once been in times long forgotten, save for on the pages of ancient texts.

This particular evening the companions gathered round an enormous table in the Great Hall for a final meal and farewells. As before, it was a time mixed with deep sorrow and unbounded joy.

During the evening, there was no shortage of laughter, food, or high spirits. But as with any parting, as the night drew to a close, tears flowed and hearts grew weary with sadness.

Even with Barrett taking comfort in having his friends near, his heart knew things could never return to the way they had been. Just as one can never go back to the carefree days of youth, soon, times the companions shared would become little more than memories—both good and bad.

Truth wormed its way into his mind, casting a veil of sorrow over the king. Sadly, he knew the friends would never gather together again, making this dinner even more difficult. He could not push away his despair and his heart continued to sink despite the false smile he bore.

Staring around the room, he let his gaze linger on each of his friends as his father's words came to him. *We are all unique. Not two living things can ever truly be the same. Perhaps in appearance, yes, but never the same.* He realized how true those words were and but one reason he loved his friends.

In far too short a time, as the day progressed and the sun slipped beneath the horizon, only Gaia and the king remained as the sky turned a shade of deep grey. They held hands and moved to the balcony to stare down on their city.

"I hope I can do this," said Barrett.

The witch kissed his cheek. "Don't worry, my love, we can do this together."